Secrets, Spies and 7/7

Tom Secker

Secker Publications

Dedicated to authentic truthseekers

and all victims of terrorism and injustice.

Contents

Contents

Acronyms

BTP	British Transport Police
CIA	Central Intelligence Agency
DOJ	Department of Justice
DIS	Defence Intelligence Staff
ELG	Executive Liaison Group
FBI	Federal Bureau of Investigation
FCO	Foreign and Commonwealth Office
FRU	Force Research Unit
HMTD	Hexamethylene triperoxide diamine
IRA	Irish Republican Army
ISC	Intelligence and Security Committee
ISI	Directorate for Inter-Services Intelligence
J7	The July 7th Truth Campaign
JIC	Joint Intelligence Committee
MI5	Security Service (SyS)
MI6	Secret Intelligence Service (SIS)
MPS	Metropolitan Police Service
NERIC	North East Regional Intelligence Cell
PISCES	Personal Identification Secure Comparison and Evaluation System
RUC	Royal Ulster Constabulary
TATP	Triacetone Triperoxide
TFL	Transport For London
WYP	West Yorkshire Police

Prologue

In the late 19th century the Western world fought its first 'war on terror' against the militant aspects of the Labour movement: Communism, and Anarchism. The world's first terrorist suicide bombing occurred when members of Narodnaya Volya (or *The People's Will*) assassinated Tsar Alexander II. Their demands were a series of radical social reforms including universal suffrage, communal self-government and the return of land ownership to the people.

Alexander was not an easy target – he rode in a bulletproof carriage with mounted Cossacks riding behind him. On March 13th 1881, Narodnaya Volya had several bombers positioned in the crowd as the Tsar passed through St Petersburg. Two threw their bombs and missed the Tsar but killed and wounded several of the Cossacks.

As the story goes, Alexander stopped and insisted on getting out of his carriage and examining the scene. Several other guards and members of the public formed a crowd. When asked whether he himself was injured the Tsar replied, 'Thank God, no'. After assuring himself that the injured were being tended to, the Tsar prepared to ride on but Ignaty Gryniewietsky approached and shouted 'It is too soon to thank God yet, Alexander Nikolaevich'. He threw the bomb at the Tsar's feet and the explosion killed Alexander, Gryniewietsky and several others in the nearby crowd.

This means that Gryniewietsky was the world's first terrorist suicide bomber. The notion of suicide troops is as old as military history but using a suicide bomber to strike a political target is a phenomenon of the modern era. Ironically, Narodnaya Volya had succeeded in killing perhaps the most progressive Tsar Russia ever had. Maybe it wasn't so ironic.

Beyond Russia, the Anarchist movement was spread across Europe and into Northern America. In the late Victorian period and into the early 20th century they carried out daring acts of terror and sabotage, laying the framework for the 1917 revolution. But the movement, from London to St Petersburg, was riddled with spies.

Peter Rachkovsky, a cunning and devious spymaster, ran the Russian counter-terrorism secret police, the Okhrana. In Britain there was the Special Branch, whose anti-terrorist duties were under the command of William Melville. Melville would go on to head up the Secret Service Bureau, which in turn became MI5.

One early provocation was the 1887 Jubilee Plot – a planned assassination attempt against Queen Victoria by Irish nationalists, provoked by British spy Francis Millen. The plot went all the way to then Prime Minister Lord Salisbury, and was used to help demonise Irish nationalism and portray it as dangerous. These same methods were then used against the anarchists.

On January 6th 1892 an anarchist from Walsall named Joe Deakin was arrested in London on the Tottenham Court road. He was on his way to the Autonomie Club nearby – the hub for anarchists in London in the Victorian period. The club was watched closely by Special Branch and the case against Deakin was deadly serious. Several other men - Victor Cails, Fred Charles, William Ditchfield, John Westley and Jean Battola – were also arrested. They became known as the Walsall Anarchists, accused of making bombs and running a bomb factory.

Falsely believing that Fred Charles was a police spy, Deakin made a confession, but he also implicated another man named Auguste Coulon. Coulon was never arrested, and was never called to testify at the trial. The editor of the anarchist/socialist journal the Commonweal, David Nicholl, was also arrested but was soon released. As Nicholl investigated, and raised money for the Walsall Anarchists' defence, he discovered that Coulon was a police informant.

At the trial, William Melville of the Special Branch was asked about Coulon by the defendants. He refused to answer the questions, and the judge ruled in his favour. Among the evidence against the defendants were letters from Coulon, and sketches and diagrams on bomb-making. The accused never actually made any bombs or acquired any explosives, though this did not stop the police manufacturing a bomb casing and entering it into evidence as though it belonged to them.

Four of the men were found guilty. Charles, Battola and Cails were convicted of conspiracy to cause explosions and were allowed to make a statement. They claimed it was a police plot. Deakin, who had initially confessed, was also found guilty, though he only got five years hard labour whereas the others got ten. Ditchfield and Westley were found not guilty.

David Nicholl then wrote a series of pamphlets proclaiming the innocence of the Walsall Anarchists, and accusing Coulon of being a police spy. Nicholl was then thrown in prison on more trumped up charges, and the Commonweal was taken over by another Special

Branch spy called Henry Samuels. Indeed, in this later 1890s period the Commonweal was mostly populated with informers and informants.

Samuels' brother in law was a young French tailor called Martial Bourdin, who in 1894 would become Britain's, and Western Europe's, first suicide bomber. On February 15th, Bourdin was headed up the hill towards Greenwich Observatory, carrying a bomb. Something appears to have gone wrong, and there was a loud explosion.

Bourdin was found with one of his hands blown off and a large wound in his abdomen. He pleaded to be taken home. He was carried to the nearby Seamen's Hospital, where he was admitted at 5:15 p.m. He died about 25 minutes later, unable to explain what he was doing, why, or what had happened. He only said that he was 'cold'.

The police raided the Autonomie club, with the press and sketch artists in tow. Despite 80 arrests, no one was ever held responsible for the bombing, or for Bourdin's death. Bourdin had left the Autonomie club earlier that day, apparently carrying the bomb with him at that time. This was witnessed by Special Branch officers who kept the club under surveillance. It appears that they had no inkling of what was to happen.

In the House of Commons the gruesome incident caused a political stir, with the MP Charles Darling calling on the Home Secretary to order the inquest to quickly give a ruling of felo de se, or suicide. The anarchists in London wanted a public burial, but Darling was known for being opposed to immigration, which he saw as a menace. He didn't want Bourdin's death to become a symbolic, catalysing event for the anarchists.

The Home Secretary refused the request, and also refused to delay the burial until after the inquest verdict. The funeral was a large public event with hundreds of mourners gathered to see the coffin passing. Someone in the crowd raised a red and black flag, resulting in the mounted police charging the crowd, scattering them and tearing down the 'offensive symbol'.

The coffin reached Finchley Cemetery and as it was being lowered into the ground one of the senior anarchists attempted to give an oration. He was quickly grabbed by the police and dragged out of the cemetery, where he was let loose. That was on February 23rd. Three days later, the jury in the inquest into Bourdin's death gave a verdict of felo de se. At the time, suicide was a crime and the verdict resulted in Bourdin's property being seized by the Crown, leaving his wife destitute, albeit in supportive company.

These two events, the setting up of the Walsall Anarchists and the response to Bourdin's death in London, caused tremendous resentment towards the authorities. There were some internal squabbles. A Special Branch officer named Patrick Macintyre had fallen out with Melville, his boss, and been forced out. In one of the earliest cases of secret police whistleblowing, he published a serialised memoir in Reynolds's Newspaper in 1895.

The memoir is a fascinating read, available in newspaper archives, though I was provided a copy by a private researcher. It casts light on a lot of the events of Special Branch in this period, and particularly on Coulon and Bourdin. According to McIntyre, Coulon was a police informant for the whole time he was involved with the Anarchists in London and Walsall.

McIntyre described the Autonomie club, saying, 'I have met at this rendevous the Russian Nihilist, the German Social Democrat, the Italian Irridentist, the French Communist, and, on rare occasions, one or two of the sons of Hibernia.' Ultimately, McIntyre's view was that the anarchists, 'in spite of their tenets, were a good-hearted and sympathetic class of the community.' He went on to point out that, 'Most prominent amongst the crowd was the *mouchard* or *agent-provocateur*. Had you been able to take away from the club those gentlemen who were thriving on the foolishness of other people, you would have reduced the number of habitués by a third.'[1]

McIntyre openly threatened to name the names of spies - men and women in the pay of the British or of continental governments. Indeed, he outed Auguste Coulon as a provocateur who had entrapped the Walsall Anarchists. He explained that Coulon was unemployed but was well paid by the police for his information. McIntyre wrote that 'the Walsall business appears to have enabled him to migrate to a semi-fashionable neighbourhood.' He went on to explain that, 'A clever and cunning man, having his wits about him and with plenty of money at his command, can always impose upon the unwary and make believe he is engaged on a revolutionary crusade, when his real object is to sell the liberty of his dupes at the highest possible price.'[2]

Quite amazingly, Coulon was so angry that he wrote to the newspaper to complain, disputing several 'facts' that McIntyre had written in his article. Nonetheless, Coulon's letter, which was published by the newspaper, admitted that, 'I offered my services to the "Yard" and my offer was accepted.'[3] Of course, officially the police continued to deny any use of spies and provocateurs and that there was anything wrong with the convictions of the Walsall Anarchists.

McIntyre also mentioned how during the course of his investigations he happened upon a group of socialists who were conducting regular training 'drills'. He explained that they were 'being drilled according to regular military methods by a young fellow who had evidently been a drill-instructor in the army... The drillings continued for several Sundays. Each drill lasted till one o'clock, but when the houses of cull opened they adjourned to the nearest one and partook free of "four ale".'[4] The significance of this will become clear later.

But what of Bourdin? Was his death really a suicide? He had no reason to want to die, and he was found to have a substantial amount of money in gold in his pockets, very much suggesting that he intended to live. McIntyre's memoir offered one explanation. According to his informants, Bourdin was trying to deliver the bomb to two French anarchists, who would then smuggle it over the channel for use in Paris. McIntyre says that the money found on Bourdin was from the two Frenchmen, who then disappeared out of the country on the night of the explosion.

This is not the only conspiracy theory around Bourdin's death. A decade later another former Special Branch officer named John Walsh also published a memoir. In 1907 he described how Bourdin was initially not particularly involved in radicalism in London, but became more fiery over time. It came to a head one night in the Autonomie club when Bourdin was accused of being all talk and no action, and even of being a spy. Bourdin apparently became very angry and set about proving his doubters wrong.

Walsh denies that the Greenwich Observatory itself was a target, the subject of much speculation in the years after Bourdin's death. He says that Bourdin and another man who was involved in bomb-making were simply going to leave the bomb in the park, as a test and a demonstration of commitment. According to Walsh's information, the second man fled, leaving Bourdin on his own, and then some accident happened with priming the bomb.[5]

These two highly contrasting insider accounts are not the only versions of this story. Also in 1907, Joseph Conrad published a spy thriller called *The Secret Agent*. It portrays Mr Verloc, a shopkeeper who is also a spy and agent provocateur working (it is implied) for the Russian embassy in London. Verloc is effectively Henry Samuels, the police informant brother in law of Martial Bourdin. Verloc's superiors tell him that he must carry out a bombing on the Greenwich Observatory. It is explained that this outrage will help cause a crackdown against the anarchists.

It had long been suspected that Bourdin was trying to bomb the Observatory, which could have been a target for anarchists due to it being the point from which central global time zones are measured. Playing on these popular theories, Conrad's book portrays Verloc (Samuels) tricking his mentally feeble young brother-in-law Stevie (Bourdin) into carrying the bomb, which explodes prematurely, killing the young man. When Verloc admits Stevie's involvement in the bombing to his wife, she stabs him to death to avenge her brother.

Three decades later, Conrad's take on the Bourdin story was adapted by Alfred Hitchcock for his film *Sabotage* in 1936. This time the Samuels character, still called Verloc, is directed by a mysterious foreign agency, possibly German or Russian. Again, Verloc is directed to carry out an act of sabotage – a bombing at a major tube station. However, Verloc is being watched closely by an undercover policeman, so he gives the bomb (hidden in a film canister) to his wife's gullible young brother. The boy is told to leave the film reel at the cloakroom at Piccadilly Circus underground station by 1:30 p.m. He dawdles and is distracted, and to try to get there in time he catches a bus. The clock ticks down and the bomb explodes, destroying the bus and killing everyone on it.

For a century rumours floated around about a Black Book – a set of Special Branch ledgers of payments to and contacts with police spies in this period. It was said to have been pulped after the Second World War and therefore was never made available through the public records office. Then, in 2002, a thesis by a retired former Special Branch officer named Lindsay Clutterbuck made numerous references to the ledgers.

Author Alex Butterworth instigated a freedom of information battle to try to get copies of the ledgers and associated documents. After hearing every excuse in the book, including that they had been destroyed in a bombing, the Information Commissioner ruled that they should be released. The Metropolitan Police appealed, saying that it was important to keep the identities of their spies secret, and that this applied indefinitely.

They argued that, 'If the information was withheld due to fear of identities being revealed, the public will be put in danger as informants not only provide the police but other government departments with extremely valuable intelligence. In this present climate of an unprecedented threat from extremists, the MPS relies on informants to give us an insight into motives and criminal activities that are happening in those closed worlds.'[6] Without a hint of irony, they invoked the danger of another 7/7 resulting from problems with recruiting spies as a result of releasing a century-old ledger and list of informers.

The ruling allowed the documents to be released, but the names were all redacted. However, that leaves other sources that can help us piece together large parts of the picture. For example, Coulon was certainly a police spy, as Clutterbuck's thesis details in a case study. Coulon was first recruited way back in July 1890 and worked for them until March 1904. He was given a bonus for his role in the Walsall case in early 1892, and over the years was paid hundreds of pounds – then a considerable amount of money.[7]

Bizarrely, the wife of Jean Battola – one of the convicted Walsall Anarchists – received two payments from Special Branch some ten years after the convictions, around the time her husband was released. Was she, like Coulon, providing information to the police as part of the provocation plot? There appears to be no other reason why the police would give her money some years later.

In the late 19th century there was a radical international movement that was infiltrated and provoked by spies from different agencies. There was an alleged suicide bombing in London that makes no sense as a suicide. Conspiracy theories and allegations swirled around, filling the space caused by state secrecy. There was even a Western war in Afghanistan. As the rest of this book will show, in some respects very little else has changed.

Introduction

The bombings in London on July 7th 2005 killed 56 people and wounded several hundred more. After a police investigation that cost over £100 million, inquest hearings lasting over five months, four official reports and over seven years of media reporting, the crime remains essentially unsolved. No one has ever been convicted for their role in the bombings, and repeated calls for a full, independent inquiry have been rejected by successive governments.

The official story emerged in the hours following the bombings. On the evening of the attacks the BBC reported that in the case of the bus bombing that the police were investigating the possibility of a suicide bomber. The following day at a police press conference, Sir Ian Blair said that 'we have absolutely nothing to suggest that this was a suicide bombing attack, although nothing at this stage can be ruled out'. Within a matter of days, though exactly how many days is a matter of dispute, four men were identified via CCTV footage and identifying documents and items were found at the explosion sites.

The men were Mohammad Sidique Khan, 30, Shehzad Tanweer, 22, Germaine Lindsay, 19 and Hasib Hussain, 18. Khan, Tanweer and Hussain were British-born Pakistanis from Leeds, while Lindsay was born in Jamaica but had lived in Britain since he was 2. Since that time, the mainstream media and the majority of the British public have accepted that these four men were responsible. Almost no physical evidence has been made publicly available and some crucial evidence, including the train carriages, has been destroyed. In dismissing clamours for a public inquiry as a 'ludicrous diversion', then Prime Minister Tony Blair offered in its place a narrative account, which was published in May 2006.

The narrative is only 40 pages long, contains very few references to sources of information, has very few footnotes, no index and was written by a trio of anonymous civil servants in the Home Office. It is extremely poorly written, claiming, for example, that three of the alleged bombers 'must have' split up at King's Cross underground station and caught the trains that were bombed. It does not cite any evidence for this claim, it simply says that it must have happened, because of course if it did not happen then the narrative could not be true. This is circular reasoning at its worst.

Similarly, the narrative does not state that the four men's bodies were actually found at the scenes of the explosions but instead says,

'DNA has identified the four at the four separate bombsites. The impact on their bodies suggests that they were close to the bombs.' Someone's DNA being found at a scene does not prove they were there at the specific time doing the specific thing you accuse them of doing. If the impact on their bodies only 'suggests that they were close to the bombs' rather than, say, 'confirms that they were in possession of the bombs' then this is not, as the narrative says, 'key evidence indicating that these were co-ordinated suicide attacks by these 4 men'.[1]

In fact, the statement 'the impact on their bodies suggests that they were close to the bombs' could be probably be applied to the majority of people who were killed in the explosions. As such, both of the narrative's statements could be perfectly true without it necessarily following that these were suicide bombings, or even that the four men were found at the scenes. The statements are phrased in such a way at to attempt to persuade you that the desired conclusion follows from the evidence, when logically it does not.

Despite its flaws, the narrative has stood for several years without mainstream criticism. It has, however, been amended due to its factual inaccuracy. According to the official story, three of the alleged bombers drove down from Leeds to Luton in the early hours of the 7th July 2005, and the fourth drove across to Luton from Aylesbury. They then met up at Luton train station, put on their rucksack bombs and caught the 7:40 a.m. train to King's Cross Thameslink station in London. From there they 'must have' split up and bombed their targets.

The problem was that even before the narrative was published in May 2006 it had been established that the 7:40 train that morning had been cancelled, hence the alleged bombers could not have been on that train. Crucially, this had been established due to independent investigators asking the questions that the mainstream media had not asked. For months the mainstream had been reporting that the men caught either the 7:40 or the 7:48 train. In fact, the 7:40 did not run that day and the 7:48 would have got them to London too late for them to have caught some of the tube trains that were bombed.

John Reid, then Home Secretary, apologized to the House of Commons for the error and two years later the Home Office published a two-paragraph amendment to the narrative saying that the alleged bombers in fact caught the 7:25 train. A lengthier exploration of the Luton station issues is contained in chapter 3 but if the Home Office narrative cannot even get simple things right, such as having the men travel to London on a train that actually existed, then what use is it? That it took the Home Office two years to correct a 'small' error such as the time of a train illustrates how resistant they are to accepting that their story is not what really happened, even on matters that are indisputable.

The ISC

A report by the Intelligence and Security Committee (ISC) was published alongside the narrative, which only confused matters further. It is about 50 pages long, was written by a committee of people appointed by the Prime Minister, most of whom have no experience of intelligence matters, has no index and contains many redactions. It initially says that the bombings 'are known to have been suicide attacks'[2] but goes on to say that 'The devices were almost certainly detonated manually by the bombers themselves in intentional suicide attacks.'[3] If it is almost certain then it is not known, it is only almost certain. The ISC clearly wrote their first report on 7/7 with an element of doublethink.

The first ISC report, along with their second report and much of the inquest proceedings, was concerned with the question of 'preventability'. The first report explained that Mohammad Sidique Khan, the alleged ringleader of the plot, and Shehzad Tanweer, one of the alleged bombers, had appeared on the fringes of MI5 and Special Branch investigations in the two years before the attacks. The report claims that prior to July 2005 the Security Service divided up their targets into the categories 'Essential', 'Desirable' and 'Other'. It specifically defined each of these categories:

> **Essential** – an individual who is likely to be directly involved in, or have knowledge of, plans for terrorist activity, or an individual who may have knowledge of terrorist activity;
>
> **Desirable** – an individual who is associated with individuals who are directly involved in, or have knowledge of, plans for terrorist activity or who is raising money for terrorism or who is in jail and would be an essential target if at large; and
>
> **Other** – an individual who may be associated with individuals who are directly involved in, or have knowledge of, plans for terrorist activity.

The ISC did not make clear which of these categories Khan and Tanweer were assessed as belonging to as a result of them being observed during surveillance of terrorist suspects. Nonetheless, the report is insistent that these categories were being used in 2004/5, saying, 'We note that the Security Service has also revised the titles of two of its target categories to '***' (in place of 'Essential') and '***' (in place of 'Desirable'). 'Other' remains unchanged.'[4]

A 7/7-related trial and a BBC *Panorama* programme showed that the pre-7/7 surveillance of Khan and Tanweer was far more extensive than the first report described. As a result, the ISC went back to MI5 for more information and then published a second report in May 2009. This report, titled 'Could 7/7 Have Been Prevented?' provides what it calls 'an unprecedented level of operational detail' about the security services. This claim was echoed by the BBC who said that 'the report does reveal, in unprecedented detail, the workings of the security service MI5 and how it goes about the shadowy business of uncovering plots to kill Britons.'[5]

In reality it is about 100 pages long, contains many redactions (including of information already in the public domain), is mostly irrelevant statistics, many of which are redacted, and doesn't even ask, let alone answer, the most important questions. Just as with the other reports, it has no index. It elaborates on the first ISC report's story of how Khan and Tanweer were classified as intelligence targets when were spotted during surveillance, saying, 'UDMs D and E (Shazad TANWEER and Mohammed Siddique KHAN) were of some interest to MI5 because they were seen meeting Omar KHYAM, a known attack planner, and were heard (on 23 March) talking about financial fraud and possible travel to Pakistan. This was sufficient to categorise them as "desirable" targets.'[6] The same three categories, along with the same precise definitions, were repeated in the second report, along with a claim that, 'The system now in place sets priorities which are based on the threat posed by whole networks and plots, rather than individuals, and uses different categories.'[7]

In summary, the ISC went to MI5 in 2005/6 and asked them what information they had on the alleged bombers prior to 7/7 and were told that two of the four had turned up on the periphery of other investigations. MI5 also told them that they divided their targets up into three categories – Essential, Desirable and Other, but apparently did not tell the ISC how Khan and Tanweer were categorized. They also told the ISC that the basic categories still existed at that time but had been renamed.

Once it emerged that the information MI5 had before 7/7 was considerably more detailed than they had told the ISC, the committee went back to MI5 in 2007/8. The same categories and the same definitions were described, it was specified that Khan and Tanweer were assessed to be 'desirable' targets but not 'essential' ones. It was also outlined that the system of categories had been replaced by one that focused on terrorist plots rather than on individuals.

There is one huge problem with this story, which forms the backbone of MI5's explanation for the 'intelligence failures' dealt with in chapters 6-8 of this book. The problem is that the story is nonsense, because MI5 did not use those categories and those definitions for operational purposes. As such, Khan and Tanweer were never assessed as being 'desirable' but not 'essential' targets, and so this isn't in any way an adequate explanation of what MI5 knew before 7/7 and what they did about it.

The fact that MI5 did not use these terms operationally was admitted by their corporate witness, Witness G, at the July 7 Inquests in February 2011. Nearly two years after the second ISC report, Witness G explained that MI5 did use the terms, but as the transcript shows, only in the context of making applications to the Treasury for funding:

> **Q.** The Intelligence and Security Committee reported that your position had been: it was decided not to investigate them further, other than the steps taken through West Yorkshire Police. But to say it was decided not to investigate them further doesn't quite reflect, does it, the precision with which any such decision, in fact, was taken. Is that fair?
>
> **A.** Yes, that's entirely fair.
>
> **Q.** Because the categories of who merits further investigation are much more nuanced and broader than that?
>
> **A.** They are.
>
> **Q.** In fact the terms "essential" and "desirable" aren't really used in this context at all in reality, they're used for funding bids and management aspects of the Service.
>
> **A.** Well, they are no longer used at all, but it's an accurate reflection of how they were used at the time.
>
> **Q.** Were they actually used at the time? So could you once say of any particular person: that person is essential, that's desirable, and that person is utterly irrelevant?
>
> **A.** They were used at the time in terms of collecting data for resource bidding, but it's not the kind of phraseology that an operational officer would have been using on a daily basis.[8]

The entire story that MI5 told to the ISC was untrue, based on terms that MI5 did not use in the context of choosing where to focus operational resources, and on definitions that could not have been applied to terms that weren't being used. Even the government's lawyer Hugo Keith QC commented that in the ISC's report the use of those terms in that way 'forms the heart of their analysis, G.'[9] For over five years this was MI5's story, told through the ISC, about what happened, when and why, and it was based on terms that MI5 use for funding applications, not surveillance targets. Were MI5 using the ISC inquiries as a fundraising exercise?

Conspiracy Theories Rise

The same basic questions remain, just as they did several years ago: Where is the evidence against the four men alleged to have been responsible? What did the security services know before the bombings about the four suspects? Was anyone else involved? Did the four men really do it or were they somehow set up as patsies?

The mainstream media has discussed some of these questions, and the alternative media has discussed most of them, at least to some extent. Sadly, the former has largely been mocking and diversionary and the latter is dominated by competitive conspiracy theorising. Falling into neither category are the small but dedicated July 7th Truth Campaign (J7), and also a handful of sincere independent investigators. Though I am not a member of that campaign, this book is very much based on their research and inspired by their spirit and objectives. However, their efforts have been stymied by a lack of funds and lack of legal authority. As a pure citizens' inquiry the government does not have to listen to them and the majority of their questions and Freedom of Information requests have been ignored or refused.

As such, most of these questions remain unanswered, or at best answered in a way that provokes great uncertainty. The space left by unanswered or poorly answered questions has largely been filled with conspiracy theories. There is, of course, the official conspiracy theory of four homegrown self-radicalised suicide bombers being responsible for the attacks. There are several major and dozens of minor alternative conspiracy theories, typically blaming the British and/or Israeli security services.

In June 2007, Channel 4 aired a news report on '7/7: the conspiracy theories', which is one of the few mainstream pieces to present this issue in a plausible light. A poll conducted by NOP asked 500 British Muslims what they thought about the 7/7 bombings and associated issues. The results of the poll found that a majority did not believe the official story and a large minority believed that the government were involved in the attacks. The respondents were given a series of statements and a six-point scale to determine how they felt about the statements.

Statement 1: The British government has told the public the WHOLE truth about the July 7th bombings.

Strongly Agree	Tend to agree	Neither agree nor disagree	Tend to disagree	Strongly disagree	Don't Know
9%	15%	8%	29%	29%	11%

Statement 2: The British government was involved in some way in the July 7th bombings.

Strongly Agree	Tend to agree	Neither agree nor disagree	Tend to disagree	Strongly disagree	Don't Know
11%	13%	14%	22%	26%	15%

Statement 3: The British security services were involved in some way in the July 7th bombings.

Strongly Agree	Tend to agree	Neither agree nor disagree	Tend to disagree	Strongly disagree	Don't Know
9%	15%	14%	21%	23%	18%

A wider poll that included non-Muslims was carried out for a 2007 Channel 4 programme *Conspiracy: Who Really Runs the World?*. It found that 15% of those polled believed that 'the British government planned the London bombings'. Both polls found that a substantial minority believes that the British government was complicit in carrying out this act of mass murder. To put it into perspective, it is a larger minority than all the people who voted for the minor political parties at the last British general election put together.

The Channel 4 news item was not without its flaws. In outlining the official story of 7/7 the piece made use of CCTV footage from Luton station that is actually from a different day. The timestamp showing the real date as 28/06/05 is briefly visible. It is disingenuous to not clarify that the reason for using CCTV footage from another day is that, at that time, only one still frame from Luton station on 7/7 had been made available. This is particularly disingenuous in a piece on outstanding questions and conspiracy theories about 7/7.

The alternative conspiracy theories are likewise not without their flaws. In many cases they are loose accumulations of cherry-picked mainstream media reports and eyewitness accounts, mixed with outright speculation that is presented as if it were proven fact. Rather than fill the void with speculation this book compiles evidence and information, zooming in on different aspects of the attacks and also stepping back and looking at the context in which they happened.

It shows how the official version of what happened on 7/7 is a tissue of lies, half-truths and guesswork. It documents a cover-up that may have begun years before the bombings in the form of 'intelligence failures' by the security services. It shows how the mainstream media have not only failed in their duty to discuss questions and alternative theories after 7/7 but may also have colluded with the state in conditioning the public even before the bombings took place. It also shows how the majority of the alternative media has largely failed to continue investigating 7/7 and instead subsumed the atrocity under its own agendas in an equally unscrupulous way to that of the mainstream.

State-Sponsored Terrorism

One cannot broach this issue without considering the possibility of state-sponsored terrorism. This is a very real phenomenon that takes various forms in different contexts so a brief history is necessary to outline the different possibilities. The most well known form of state-sponsored terrorism is the false flag operation, whereby agents of the state carry out an attack and manipulate or fake evidence blaming the desired culprits. This encourages the public and the authorities to blame those who are designated as the enemy and allows the real culprits to continue carrying out these sorts of operations.

One indisputable example of this tactic being used by the CIA took place during a coup d'etat in Iran that was orchestrated by the US and UK governments. The CIA's own declassified history of the operation explains how they sought to split the Tudeh (Communist) party from the religious leaders to try to destabilise the support for Prime Minister Mohammed Mossadeq:

CIA agents gave serious attention to alarming the religious leaders at Tehran by issuing black propaganda in the name of the Tudeh Party, threatening these leaders with savage punishment if they opposed Mossadeq. Threatening phone calls were also made to them, in the name of the Tudeh, and one of several planned sham bombings of the houses of these leaders was carried out.[10]

The operation was ultimately successful and saw a democratically elected leader replaced by a brutal aristocratic regime. The strategy of destabilisation worked.

Another type of operation is the provoked or proxy operation, where terrorism is carried out on behalf of a covert state organisation by members of a terrorist group. The war in Northern Ireland is a prime example of this, as members of MI5, MI6, the Royal Ulster Constabulary (RUC) and the British Army's Force Reconnaissance Unit (FRU) infiltrated and conspired with both the Loyalist and the Republican militant groups. According to a recent report in the Belfast Telegraph, as many as one in four members of the Irish Republican Army were working for the security services. When limiting the scope to only include senior members of the IRA the proportion rose to one in two.[11]

This infiltration was so successful that the IRA's own internal security officers – the molecatchers responsible for finding informers in their ranks – were themselves working for the British security services. The IRA's chief molecatcher, the 'Angel of Death' John Joe Magee, was a member of the Special Boat Service, an elite squadron of the British Special Forces. His apparent number two Freddie Scappaticci was an FRU agent codenamed Stakeknife.

One of the acts of violence that was enabled and facilitated by this collusion was the murder of Belfast lawyer Patrick Finucane. Finucane had defended numerous Republicans facing terrorism charges and in doing so had made himself an enemy of the British state. In February 1989 Finucane was sat at home in Belfast having dinner with his wife and children when two gunmen burst in and shot him fourteen times. Since then his family, in particular his wife Geraldine Finucane, have fought for a proper investigation and a public inquiry into his assassination.

Even the limited inquiries that have been achieved have concluded that there was British state collusion in Finucane's murder. The third inquiry carried out by former head of the Metropolitan Police Sir John Stevens found that the murder of Finucane and an associated murder of a student named Brian Adam Lambert 'could have been prevented'. In the brief section of his report that was made pubic in April 2003, Stevens stated explicitly that:

> I conclude there was collusion in both murders and the circumstances surrounding them. Collusion is evidenced in many ways. This ranges from the wilful failure to keep records, the absence of accountability, the withholding of intelligence and evidence, through to the extreme of agents being involved in murder.[12]

The evidence of collusion is staggering. In September 2004 one of the gunmen, Ken Barrett, pleaded guilty to Finucane's murder. Barrett was a member of the Ulster Defence Association/Ulster Freedom Fighters (UDA/UFF), the largest and bloodiest Loyalist terrorist group. He was also an RUC Special Branch informer. One of the guns used in the killing was provided by William Stobie, a UDA quartermaster and an agent of RUC Special Branch. The gun was one of a batch that had been stolen from an Ulster Defence Regiment (British Army) barracks.

Another double agent involved in the assassination was Brian Nelson, a member of the UDA and a FRU military intelligence agent. In the period running up to Finucane's murder Nelson was the man within the UDA with primary responsibility for surveillance and information gathering on targets. He regularly passed this information onto his FRU handlers, and they in turn sometimes gave him information that was useful in carrying out his task for the UDA. Judge Peter Cory conducted an extensive investigation into collusion in Northern Ireland and concluded in his 2004 report:

> The documents either in themselves or taken cumulatively can be taken to indicate that FRU committed acts of collusion. Further, there is strong if, in some instances, conflicting documentary evidence that FRU committed collusive acts. Only a public inquiry can resolve the conflict.[13]

Aside from secret or double agents being involved at every crucial stage in the plot, Cory's investigation also found that both MI5 and Special Branch received repeated warnings about a plot to kill Finucane. In every case they did nothing to attempt to investigate further or interdict the plot. The Finucane case suggests a model that will be useful in understanding the exploration of the 7/7 case in the second section of this book. The basic model is that the 'intelligence failures' by the security services are not really failures, they are a deliberate and premeditated means of protecting spies and double agents. If the

Finucane family's calls for a public inquiry, echoed in the Cory report, are ever heard we might be able to test this model more thoroughly.

What we can be certain of is that this protection extends into the public domain with the government's reaction to the findings of investigations like Stevens' and Cory's. A little over a year after the Cory report was published, and exactly a month before 7/7, the Labour government passed the Inquiries Act, which placed incredible restrictions on the scope and independence of all public inquiries. The act is a horrifying mixture of legalese and doublespeak, as in effect it provides the means for the government to control all inquiries held under this legislation.

The relevant minister can determine the selection of the chairman and panel carrying out the inquiry, its terms of reference, its budget and timetable. Public access to the proceedings and the evidence examined can be restricted at the whim of the chairman, and the Freedom of Information Act does not apply to inquiries held under the act. Shortly before the act was passed, Judge Cory told US Congressional hearings into human rights in Northern Ireland that it 'would make a meaningful inquiry impossible. The minister, the actions of whose ministry was to be reviewed by the public inquiry, would have the authority to thwart the efforts of the inquiry at every step.'[14]

In May 2006 the US House of Representatives passed a resolution calling for a public inquiry into Finucane's death, and in 2007 the Labour government announced that an inquiry would be held under the 2005 Inquiries Act. This offer was rejected by the Finucane family and this led to a stalemate. In 2011 this was broken when the Secretary of State for Northern Ireland issued a public apology in the House of Commons for the British state collusion in Finucane's murder. Prime Minister David Cameron met with the Finucane family and then announced a limited review of the case instead of an inquiry.

This decision has also been rejected by the family, who applied for a judicial review of the decision not to hold an inquiry. In their application to the court, they explained what Cameron had said to them when they met:

> The stated reasons for refusing to establish a public inquiry are not the true reasons. In the course of the meeting at 10 Downing Street on 11 October 2011 the Prime Minister stated "It is true that the previous administration could not deliver a public inquiry and neither can we. There are people in buildings all around here who won't let it happen."[15]

This model of protection whereby the security services protect their double agents, even when they are terrorists, and the government protects the security services, even when they protect terrorists, still leaves several possibilities. Deliberate, wilful violence as practiced by the CIA in Iran is one possibility, and remains a possibility for all unsolved acts of terrorism, including the 7/7 bombings. There is also the question of blowback, or the unintended consequences of the use of covert operations and double agents.

Blowback

Two such cases, one historical and one contemporary, explain this concept very well. Throughout much of the Cold War an international covert operation known as Gladio saw the security services of NATO countries infiltrate terrorist groups and provoke them into carrying out attacks. These attacks were then blamed on Communists and Anarchists, and used to disrupt the popular support for those ideas and their associated political parties. One terrorist who was successfully prosecuted for his role in this operation was Vincenzo Vinciguerra.

He was a member of the Italian neo-fascist groups Ordine Nuovo and Avanguardia Nazionale but as he explained in a documentary, 'Ordine Nuovo never had its own ideology. They called themselves National Socialists, but their boss, Pino Rauti, worked for the Armed Forces, was an SID (Italian Secret Services) expert.'[16] Vinciguerra was prosecuted in the 1980s after a lengthy investigation in the 1972 car bombing in Peteano.

Vinciguerra had left a bomb in a car on the outskirts of the town, and he scratched a five-pointed star (the symbol of the Red Brigades, a Communist militant group) into the bonnet. A phone call was made to the police saying that there was a car in the woods with bullet holes in the windscreen and three carabinieri were sent to investigate. The bomb exploded, killing the three officers.

A cover-up took place, the bombing was blamed on Anarchists and Vinciguerra was spirited out of the country. It would be twelve years before he stood trial. However, though this was a false flag attack, by a terrorist connected to the security services, and though he was protected after the attack, it was blowback. Vinciguerra explained that the Peteano bombing was 'an act of revolt against the manipulation, an act of retaliation against the state.' He had gone rogue and attacked the state, when according to the Gladio strategy the purpose of right-wing terrorism was to 'attack civilians, women, children, innocent people outside the political arena. For one simple reason, to force the Italian public to turn to the state, turn to the regime and ask for greater security.'[17]

A more recent example involves the triple agent Hammam Al Balawi. He was a member of the Islamist group the Pakistani Taliban but was arrested and turned by the Jordanian General Intelligence Directorate. He then became a triple agent, working for Jordan and the CIA while being a member of a targeted terrorist group. In December 2009 he used his double agent credentials to gain access to Forward Operating Base Chapman, a major CIA base in Afghanistan. There, he blew himself up, killing six CIA agents, two Blackwater employees, one Jordanian and the Security director at the base.

As in Northern Ireland and during the Gladio operation, Al Balawi is not an isolated example of a terrorist double agent (or even terrorist triple agent). Ali Mohamed, Al Qaeda's main terrorist trainer in the 1990s, worked for the CIA, the FBI and served in the US Special Forces. Luai Sakra, the convicted mastermind of the 2003 Istanbul bombings, was an informant for Turkish and Syrian intelligence and the CIA. Ahmed Omar Saeed Sheikh, the bagman for the alleged 9/11 hijackers, worked for the Pakistani Inter Services Intelligence (ISI) and reportedly also for MI6.

Closer to home, all the major figures in the British wing of Al Muhajiroun at the Brixton and Finsbury Park mosques have been reported to have close connections with the security services. In the late 1990s Abu Hamza ran militant training camps in the Brecon Beacons and elsewhere in the UK. These camps were run with the help of ex-soldiers, contracted through the Defence Intelligence Agency and MI6 in support of the West's dirty war in Kosovo.[18] Abu Qatada, said to be a major Al Qaeda facilitator in Europe, was reported by the Times to be an MI5 double agent. Qatada was closely monitored by another MI5 informant, an Algerian named Reda Hassaine.[19] Omar Bakri fled Britain shortly before the 7/7 bombings and has been banned from returning, ensuring he will not face investigation for his activities while in Britain. He admitted in interviews in 2005 that he had been an informant for MI5.[20]

What these ongoing relationships demonstrate is that even where the resulting violence is unintentional, i.e. blowback, that this is of little concern to the security services. The infiltration of radical, militant and terrorist organisations goes back over a century, at least as far as the Victorian Anarchists, and has always produced terrorist attacks and miscarriages of justice. Every time, the security services avoid being held responsible for the 'intelligence failures' that precipitated these events. Though the distinction is an important one the state is, or at least should be, legally and morally responsible for these instances of violence and injustice regardless of whether they are intentional, or the result of criminal negligence.

Sources and Fundamental Questions

This book cannot seek to answer or explore every facet of every question that has been asked about 7/7. However, it does seek to show the failings of official answers to all the fundamental questions, and how those answers have changed over time. The questions around what happened on the day of 7/7 are dealt with in the opening five chapters. The disputes that have raged between the mainstream and alternative media about what happened that day are also reviewed in this section.

In investigating this case over several years I have made use of a variety of sources. In making two documentary films on the 7/7 bombings I accumulated a huge collection of news clips and mainstream documentaries. Similarly, I read thousands of articles via the online versions of local, national and international newspapers. I read the official reports and watched all the CCTV as it became available, in some cases many times over. This evidence is primarily discussed in the opening chapters.

All of the images used in this book are from public domain sources, whether they are still frames of CCTV footage, diagrams of the explosion sites or surveillance photos. While considerable efforts have been made to render these images legibly within the pages of this book they are not perfect reproductions, and the original full colour high resolution versions of all the images, as well as the full CCTV video clips, can be found and downloaded for free at my website www.investigatingtheterror.com.

I have deliberately avoided interviewing the bereaved and survivors of the attacks. In many cases their accounts are on the record through the mainstream media and the inquests and I saw little to be gained by forcing them to reiterate their pain and relive their suffering. The people I have sought out for personal inquiry have mostly been those who have sought publicity on the back of the 7/7 bombings as authoritative truthtellers. Just as I have interrogated the Home Office narrative, I have interrogated the alternative narratives, and some of those putting their name to the alternative narratives. The damage caused by unfounded speculation is considerable, and is a central concern throughout this book.

I have followed for years the websites of the July 7th Truth Campaign and been fortunate to have them patiently assist me in clarifying my questions and sourcing information on the public record. During and since the July 7 Inquests I have read virtually all of the thousands of pages of transcripts and exhibits presented. This information is mostly discussed in chapters 1 to 8.

Chapters 6, 7 and 8 look in detail at the questions about what MI5 knew, when, and what they did about it. It is not just an issue of MI5 passively receiving information, they are a pro-active organisation that is meant to deter and prevent terrorist attacks. Their decision-making, or at least what they have told us about their decision-making, before 7/7 does not inspire any confidence that they are a truthful agency working to protect ordinary people.

In dealing with this topic, which is central to the book in many respects and to my mind is the most important aspect of the 7/7 case, I have been careful to avoid conjecture. In sourcing the information I relied primarily on official reports, documents and testimony. Where information has come to us through the mainstream media but is unconfirmed by other source I have attempted to make this clear in the text.

The final three chapters analyse the context in which 7/7 happened in a light that is largely ignored or misunderstood, in terms of not just how predictable the attacks were, but also how they were predicted. Many different memes that became talking points after the attacks appeared and recurred in films and TV shows in the years immediately before 7/7. In many cases I did not watch these shows or realise their significance until after the 7/7 bombings. Most are available on DVD but in a few cases they were not and so I relied on my own recollections of the programmes, and reviews.

The question of pre-conditioning the public in case of a terrorist attack is considered in some depth. 'Predictive programming' is a term coined to describe books, films, TV shows and other media that predict future events with uncanny accuracy. The word 'programming' has a double meaning, because these are not just programmes in the sense of being broadcasts, but also program or condition people's responses to events when they happen for real.

In order to fairly assess this idea I devoted many hours to learning about the history of state propaganda and in particular the portrayal of the security services in the mass media. Considerable time and money was spent on obtaining copies of government files from the National Archives and other places. I have endeavoured to provide footnotes explaining where I got the information, though it would be impractical to source every detail.

Nonetheless, all of the information I have used in compiling this book and my two films is publicly available. Unlike many writers in the mainstream on this and related topics I have not made use of anonymous witnesses, secret documents, leaks, or other sources that cannot be accessed by inquiring minds. If we are to shed light on the practices of covert organisations then we must do so without echoing or reflecting their means and methods.

Chapter 1: The Hallmarks of Al Qaeda

The morning of July 7th 2005 began ordinarily enough. The previous evening Britain had won the bid for the 2012 Olympics, and that morning's news was full of the story. This has led many commentators to describe the mood of the nation as jubilant, a bubble of positive energy that was burst by the horror of a terrorist attack. As you might expect, this rather simple story is not particularly accurate.

The callers to BBC Radio London that morning were at best ambivalent in their feelings about their city hosting the Olympics, especially when news of problems on the tube started to reach the major media. In particular, the question of paying for the huge Olympic project prayed on people's minds. One caller said, 'Maybe because I love a conspiracy, I still half think that the French premier, he's laughing.' He went on to suggest that then president Jacques Chirac deliberately failed to win his country's bid for the games so he didn't have to find a way to pay for it.

In their 9 a.m. news report Radio London proudly pronounced Britain's success in winning the Olympic bid before asking, 'So, what to do? Well, there's a lot of building - 560 million pounds worth to be precise – and with that comes security. It's a big deal, the chief of the Met is Sir Ian Blair.' The item then included a clip of Ian Blair saying, 'London *is* a terrorist target and particularly the postcard sites of London have been all along.'

This is far from the only prescient coverage of 7/7. Showing a suspicious degree of foresight, on the evening of July 6th Fox News host John Gibson said, 'By the way, just wanted to tell you people, we missed - the International Olympic Committee missed a golden opportunity today. If they had picked France, if they had picked France instead of London, to hold the Olympics, it would have been the one time we could look forward to where we didn't worry about terrorism. They'd blow up Paris, and who cares?'[1]

Gibson's apparent foresight did not stop then. The following day, once it had become clear that there had been a terrorist attack but before the investigation had really begun, Gibson said, 'The bombings in London: This is why I thought the Brits should let the French have the Olympics. Let somebody else be worried about guys with backpack bombs for a while.' In the same piece of 'journalism', both a published article and a section on the Fox News show *The Big Story With John Gibson*, he went on to say that the attacks were carried out by Al Qaeda and that, 'The terrorists managed to get a few guys to be suicide bombers.'[2]

At that point in time there is literally no possible way Gibson could have known whether or not the attacks were carried out by suicide bombers using backpack bombs. Trains and buses are what are known as 'soft targets', in that there is realistically very little that can be done to prevent someone from carrying out an attack on them. This is one of the major problems with the whole suicide bomber explanation for 7/7. The alleged bombers could have simply left bags or packages on short-delay timers in those four locations and escaped alive.

Rather, so we're told, the four men killed themselves in order to murder 52 other people completely at random. They took their own lives not because it was the only way to hit a 'hard target', or to carry out killing on a mass scale, but instead, we are to presume, purely because of ideological fanaticism. This story makes little sense as the whole point of a suicide bombing is to use someone's willingness to sacrifice their life in order to accomplish an attack that is not otherwise possible.

As detailed in the prologue, the Western world's first ever suicide bombings were carried out by 19th century Russian anarchists Narodnaya Volya. They are best known for their assassination of Tsar Alexander II in 1881. By contrast, a single bomb left in a rubbish bin in Bologna train station in August 1980 killed over 80 people. The multiple bombs left on trains on the Madrid subway in March 2004 killed nearly 200. By comparison, using suicide bombers just to blow up a London bus and some tube trains and killing 52 is an extremely ineffective and irrational form of terrorism. Four people willing to sacrifice their lives could hit a much harder target.

Nonetheless, this is the official story of 7/7, foreseen by John Gibson of Fox News, that we are presented with. Gibson's comments do provoke two deeply concerning questions. First, did he have inside knowledge? Did someone feed the idea of suicide bombers to him, despite it making no sense in terms of the history of terrorist attacks? We can only answer that question with access to inside knowledge, which we do not have. So we turn to the second question: How and why did the official version emerge faster than it should have emerged?

This question becomes ever more pertinent in the context of a close analysis of the mainstream media coverage of 7/7. What I found in the course of making two documentary films on the bombings is that we were presented with an ever-changing story of what was happening. The number of explosions, their locations and their causes were all subject to vastly contradictory reporting, in the chaos of what was the biggest emergency incident in London's recent history.

Power Surges

The first explanation of what was happening was one of a train collision causing electrical power surges in turn causing 'bangs' or explosions at as many as ten tube stations. Aldgate, Aldgate East, Liverpool Street, Moorgate, Bank, Old Street, Russell Square, King's Cross, Edgware Road and Paddington were all reported as possible explosion sites. Initial descriptions were of 'walking wounded' at Liverpool Street station, and the story spread from there.

Shortly after 9:30 a junior BBC executive named Ian Wade phoned in to Radio London with the first report that something had happened at King's Cross. He outlined that he was on a southbound train on the Piccadilly line, 'the train that it happened to,' that had been delayed throughout the journey. He joked, 'I knew I was going to be late in'. Shortly after the train left King's Cross, Wade described how there was, 'an almighty bang, lights went out, soot filled the actual carriage we were in.'

Wade said that while they were being walked out through the tunnel he asked one of the officials what had happened and was told that 'one of the overhead lights fell down and hit the front of the train.' There was no mention of an explosion, heat, flames, or anyone seriously injured. Wade reiterated that he was 'on the train it happened to' but when asked whether he had seen any injuries he said that he had just that second noticed a man with cuts on his arms but, 'that the first and only one that I've seen actually injured.'

He did phone back in to BBC Radio London around twenty minutes after his initial call to say that he was in a casualty room set up inside King's Cross station. Wade said, 'I'm going to have to retract what I said earlier, those that are injured are badly injured. There's a lot of blood in here.' Nonetheless, he was still talking about something hitting the front of the train as the cause for what he was seeing.

The following day, on July 8th, Ian's wife Evelyn Wade gave an interview to the Independent in which she described how, 'We heard a big blast. The lights went out, and I thought I was going to die. Everyone was saying it was a fire and I thought we weren't going to get out alive. We didn't move for 15 minutes and in that time, people were screaming, crying and banging on the windows, trying to get out. In the carriage next door, people were very injured and I saw a lot of blood on people.'[3]

How do we reconcile these two witnesses? If they were both in the same carriage on the same train then presumably they were travelling together and therefore experienced the bombing together. If Evelyn first saw badly injured people in the adjacent carriage then why did Ian not see them until later, in the casualty room? How do we account for the jocularity of Ian Wade's initial report to Radio London if he saw the same things as his wife Evelyn?

The day after, on July 9th, Ian Wade was interviewed again by the BBC. His account was now in keeping with his wife's, and he said, 'I could see there were people with their clothes burned off, people with limbs missing. There must have been at least one death in there. I have never known anything like it.' He added, 'My wife Evie really thought that we were going to die. It was just 'boom' and that was it. I couldn't think straight.'[4]

The factual contradictions and absolute contrast in tones between the interviews are quite astounding. They simply cannot be reconciled. So what did Ian and Evelyn actually see? Of course we cannot be sure, but it is doubtful that if they had seen people 'with their limbs missing' and 'with their clothes burned off' that Ian would have been phoning up citywide live radio only minutes later to make jokes about being late for work. Why would they make up a story? Curiously, in Ian's third interview with the BBC he said that, 'The explosion was on the ceiling of the carriage in front.'

There is, perhaps, a bigger question to ask about this early 'power surge' version of events. What if there was actually a large-scale electrical accident on the tube network? It is not as radical a hypothesis as it might first appear. Then mayor of London Ken Livingstone told the Greater London Authority 7th July Review Committee, 'You could have had a power surge with a quite catastrophic casualty level. We have always been aware of that on the Underground.'[5]

A considerable number of witnesses, many from inside the carriages where bombs were meant to have gone off, reported feelings of electrocution and other phenomena suggestive of electrical activity. Gracia Hormigos, on the Piccadilly line, told The Telegraph, 'My whole body was shaking. I felt like I was being electrocuted.'[6] She told the same thing to ITN news. Another witness named Ian told the BBC he remembered 'getting a sharp feeling of electrocution, like I imagine anyone who has been struck by lightning gets. I was knocked unconscious either during or after the electrocution and I maybe came round about 10 minutes afterwards.'[7]

Bruce Lait and Crystal Main were two dance partners from Cambridge who were on the train between Liverpool Street and Aldgate. Lait told National Geographic that, 'It sounded like a power generator switching on. You know that kind of pppvvvvvvv type of sound, but a million times more powerful.'[8] He also told the Cambridge Evening News that, 'It was like a huge electricity surge which knocked us out and burst our eardrums. I can still hear that sound now.'[9] For her part, Crystal Main told the Mirror that, 'all of a sudden I felt as if I was having a fit and couldn't control myself. I slipped to the side. It was as if I had been electrocuted and thousands of volts were going through me.'

Over at Edgware Road there was a train headed in the opposite direction on an adjacent track to the bombed train when the explosion happened. The train's driver, Jeff Porter, told the BBC that he saw 'a bright yellow light on the train on the other side.' He went on to explain that, 'On the underground when you see a bright light your first thought is something to do with the electricity, but normally a 630 volt arc will be a whiteish-blue light and start from the track, but this was a yellow light that was up on the level of the train.'[10]

Witnesses from inside the carriage where Mohammad Sidique Khan supposedly set off his bomb included two American sisters, Katie and Emily Benton. Katie Benton told the Christian Broadcasting Network that, 'I thought that we had derailed and hit a power line and were being electrocuted. That is kind of what it felt like. Everything was black and, yeah, we felt like we were being electrocuted.' Emily Benton also described how she, 'felt like I was being electrocuted.'[11]

There are many other witnesses whose testimony is similar, including a significant number who testified at the July 7 Inquests. It has been officially confirmed that there were power surges that morning, though they are apparently caused by the explosions, rather than caused the explosions themselves. Nonetheless, the hypothesis remains that there was in fact a huge problem with the electrical networks on the London underground. The conspiracy theory is that the explosion on the bus was staged to make the whole incident look like a terrorist attack, and thus avoid massive insurance payouts and corporate manslaughter charges.

This will seem far-fetched to some, and it is far from a complete and convincing theory. Nonetheless, on the morning of 7/7 Balfour Beatty were in court at the Old Bailey dealing with corporate manslaughter charges resulting from the Hatfield rail crash. Several days after 7/7, with the media looking elsewhere, those charges were quietly dropped. Furthermore, if the cause of at least some (if not all) of the deaths on the underground was some sort of electrical fault then that would explain why no internal post mortems were carried out on any of the victims.

Sounds on the Underground?

The official narrative as it stands today is that there were three tube train explosions, all on trains headed away from King's Cross. The Home Office says that one was on the Piccadilly line, on a southbound train headed out of King's Cross on the way to Russell Square. It also says that two were on the Circle line, one eastbound going from Edgware Road to Paddington, and one westbound going from Liverpool Street to Aldgate.

However, a large number of media reports, eyewitness accounts and official statements contradict this story. Exactly how these stories evolved into the Home Office account is far from clear. Many reports, including those put out by the Metropolitan Police Service (MPS), spoke of more than three explosions. At one stage as many as ten different stations were in the frame as possible explosion sites, though as the explosions were on trains in tunnels between stations, confusion may account for some of this.

It gets much more complex than that. The initial timeline of the three explosions had them staggered over nearly half an hour, with bombs at 8:51 at Aldgate, at 8:56 at King's Cross, and at 9:17 at Edgware Road. It was not until two days later that officials said that the tube explosions were 'almost simultaneous'. However, on the day of 7/7 the Jerusalem Post published an article by former Mossad chief Efraim Halevi titled 'Rules of conflict for a world war.' In it, he described the attacks as 'multiple, simultaneous explosions'.[12] Just like John Gibson of Fox, Halevi seemed to have the official story before British officials had it, and before anyone had evidence to substantiate it.

This revision of the timings is very strange, particularly in the case of Edgware Road. If, as we are now told, the explosion was actually at 8:50 then why was there nearly a half hour discrepancy in the early reports? Indeed, it is not just early reports. In October 2010, just as the July 7 inquests were beginning, the BBC published an 'audio slideshow' on its website, featuring clips from media coverage and emergency service communications. It included the original timeline of explosions on the underground at 8:51, 8:56 and 9:17.

The locations and directions of the trains at the times of the explosions were also subject to hugely variable reporting. In East London we were told that there was an explosion somewhere between

Liverpool Street station and either Aldgate or Aldgate East. This is a real problem, because these are not just different tube stations, but are on different lines altogether. The Circle line heading westbound out of Liverpool Street goes to Aldgate. The separate Hammersmith and City line heading westbound out of Liverpool Street goes to Aldgate East.

It gets worse. According to an article in the Independent the day after 7/7, a witness named Manjit Dhanjal was on a train heading *towards* Liverpool Street from Aldgate East. She was on her way to work in the City, i.e. heading into the centre, and hence towards King's Cross. She described how 'There were a few sparks and I thought it was just a power surge... Then I saw this fireball a few carriages in front of me, and everything went black.' The article goes on to say that, 'The blast occurred in a carriage at the front of the train, around 50 metres from the Aldgate East platform.'[13]

How could a suicide bomber on a train *from* Liverpool Street to Aldgate cause an explosion on a train heading *to* Liverpool Street from Aldgate East? They are two different trains, on two different lines, heading in two different directions. Another witness called Saira Khan wrote diary for MSNBC saying that she was stuck on a train 'between Aldgate East and Liverpool Street'. She did not describe an explosion, but merely being stuck on the train, then being taken back through the tunnel and out through Aldgate East station. She and other passengers were then taken nearer 'home' to East London, where they were let off the bus but not before police took their names and addresses and accounts of what they had seen.[14]

Complicating matters, another witness interviewed by CNN on the day of 7/7 spoke of being on a westbound Circle line train going from Aldgate to Liverpool Street. She described 'a lot of head and facial injuries' to people on her train, and when a journalist asked her if she was on the train where the explosion happened she replied 'yes'.[15] This train would have been on the right tube line for the official narrative, but headed in the opposite direction.

Even further complicating matters a witness called Will Lam was interviewed for a documentary called *One Day in London*, which is no longer available online. He described being on an affected train going from Liverpool Street to Aldgate East, the opposite direction to the train described by Saira Khan and Manjit Dhanjal. This all suggests that there were as many as four bombings on tube trains in East London - two each on the Circle and Hammersmith and City lines, one heading in each different direction. Needless to say, one suicide bomber on one train could not have caused all this.

Some will put this confusion and these contradictions down to the problems of live reporting on an unfolding event and investigation. To a certain extent this is fair, but this provokes the question of at what point unreliable early reporting becomes reliable later reporting. For instance, when the CCTV from inside Liverpool Street station was finally made public in May 2008, the Guardian made it available on their website. It is described as 'Video footage shown to the jury at Kingston crown court shows blast effect between Liverpool Street and Aldgate East stations on July 7 2005.'[16] Note: Aldgate East, not Aldgate. Nearly three years after the event, the Guardian's reporting contradicted the Home Office's narrative.

We find similar problems at the King's Cross explosion. Initial media reports said that the affected train was southbound, going from King's Cross towards Russell Square. At 14:25 Transport for London (TFL) issued a press release saying there had been three incidents on the tube, one at 'Russell Square station heading towards King's Cross station on the Piccadilly line'. This would make the train northbound, an impossible target for a suicide bomber travelling southbound from King's Cross. The same TFL release describes the East London incident as happening at 'Aldgate station heading towards Liverpool Street station on the Hammersmith & City line', which makes no sense at all, and contradicts the official story.

That evening, the Manchester Evening News ran an article saying, 'Another person to be caught in the drama was barrister's clerk, Chris Lowry, 17 from north London, was on [the] tube pulling into King's Cross when an explosion ripped through the station, killing 21 people.'[17] All these reports indicate an explosion on a train heading into King's Cross, and certainly not a southbound train heading out of King's Cross.

Two days later, when TFL updated their story to talk of near-simultaneous bombings, they also changed the direction of the Piccadilly Line train. The new version said that the incident was on, 'Piccadilly line train number 311 travelling from King's Cross St Pancras to Russell Square southbound.' This is in keeping with the Home Office story of bombers travelling away from King's Cross, but it begs the question of why they got the story wrong in the first place and why they changed it. This change in story did not stop the Independent from publishing a timeline the following day saying that, 'As the northbound train carrying Zeyned Basci approaches King's Cross there is a huge bang and shards of glass are sprayed onto passengers.'[18]

Also, the updated TFL story names the affected train as number 311. This same number appears in several media reports and in the Russell Square duty manager's log of that morning, obtained by a J7 freedom of information request. This was then changed to train number 331, though exactly when and why this change happened is unclear. The actual train 311 was at South Kensington at 8:50 that morning, several stops and many miles away. This makes it difficult to see how so many sources could have got the wrong train.

This is, unless, there were two trains involved on the Piccadilly line, one northbound going towards King's Cross, and one southbound headed away from King's Cross. Officially there was only one train directly affected on the Piccadilly line, and only one in East London, but the combination of official statements and media coverage suggest otherwise. The evidence is far from conclusive.

The Edgware Road incident is somewhat different, but the implications are much the same. This is the only site where it is officially recognised that more than one train was affected by the primary explosion. In fact, according to the statement of Deputy Assistant Commissioner Brian Paddick on the afternoon of 7/7, 'At 9:17 there was an explosion on a train coming into Edgware Road underground station, which blew a hole through a wall onto another train in an adjoining platform. In fact, it's believed that three trains were involved in that particular incident.'

This same information was issued on the MPS website at 16:30 on the afternoon of 7/7. When the MPS issued their 'one week anniversary' recap they had dropped the reference to a third train, but they still had the primary train 'coming into Edgware Road station' and they maintained that the 'explosion blew a hole through a wall onto another train on an adjoining platform.' In reality there are no separate tunnels at Edgware Road, the multiple lines simply travel through one large tunnel together before separating as they reach the platforms. This was confirmed through a J7 FOIA request. Thus, no hole was blown through a tunnel wall, and no hole could ever have been blown through a tunnel wall.

Perhaps more fundamentally, according to the MPS, even a week after the event, the bomb was on a train headed into the station. According to the Home Office it was on a train headed out of the station, and another train headed into the station (not one at a platform) was affected by the blast. At what point did the MPS realise that there was no hole in the tunnel wall, no train at a platform caught up in the explosion, and that the bomb hit a train leaving, not entering, the station? Why, even a week after the bombing, were they getting such basic information wrong?

Illogical Journeys around Edgware Road

The issues at Edgware Road become particularly perplexing in light of the fact that several of the people killed or injured in the blast should not have been on a westbound train going from Edgware Road to Paddington. They should not have been on the train that the Home Office says is the one that blew up. In most cases it would make much more sense if they were on a train travelling out of Edgware Road in the opposite direction, or a train headed into Edgware Road station, as the MPS statements describe.

Emily and Katie Benton came to visit London from Tennessee and were injured in the explosion at Edgware Road. In various interviews they have described how that day they were on their way to the Tower of London. Logically, from Edgware Road one would probably take a Circle line train that was eastbound rather than westbound to get to Tower Hill or Monument station. It is possible that two young people in an unfamiliar place might have caught a westbound Circle line train and been in the same carriage where Sidique Khan supposedly set off his bomb. But it is also possible that they were on a different train, in a different place.   Davinia Turrell is the woman seen in the well-known photograph of 7/7 with a white full-face compress, being aided by a young man (Paul Dadge). She suffered bad facial injuries but she survived and recovered, and is now married. The photo of her is an iconic and often used image from the attacks, but what is not widely reported is that she was on her way to Canary Wharf for work. Again, this would mean a westbound train out of Edgware Road would be going in the opposite direction to where she wanted to be, just as with Emily and Katie Benton.

David Foulkes was a young man from Oldham who had come down to London that morning to start his first day's work at the Guardian newspaper. He was killed in the explosion. He was supposed to get off the tube at Edgware Road to meet a colleague there, having travelled down to Euston from the North. His father Graham has even spoken of giving him very specific instructions because apparently David had never been on the tube before. Once again, it would not make sense for David to have been on a train heading westbound out of Edgware Road. If he was on a train headed into Edgware Road, as the MPS were saying even a week after 7/7, then his presence would make much more sense.

Exacerbating this worrying implication, in late 2007 the families of all 52 people killed in the explosions were sent post mortem reports on how their loved ones had died. They were given no warning, and were sent the reports regardless of whether they had asked to know the

horrific details.   David's father Graham said, 'I can't explain how
devastatingly upsetting it was to read in such detail. There was no legal
requirement for the coroner to send it out, it was his own initiative. It
makes you wonder what sort of person he is - does he have children?'
Graham also said that there were 'fundamental differences' between
what he saw when he viewed his son's body and what the post-mortem
report said.[19]

Jenny Nicholson was a young woman who apparently died on
the westbound Edgware Road train on 7/7.   The problem is that, as
reported by the Guardian, 'Her last known phone call was placed to her
father, Gregg, from Paddington station, minutes before the bombing.'[20]
The only way she could have been near a bomb on a train leaving
Edgware Road was if she had caught an eastbound train from
Paddington.   She could not have been on the westbound train that
allegedly carried Sidique Khan and his bomb.

But could she, or Davinia Turrell have been on the additional
train affected by the blast? Not according to TFL. A J7 FOIA request
sought confirmation about the number of trains affected, the supposed
hole blasted in the tunnel wall, and which trains the victims were riding
on at the time of the explosion.   The response came back that at
Edgware Road, 'No fatalities or injuries were recorded on the
Hammersmith & City line train.'[21]

Hence, even though David Foulkes, Jenny Nicholson, Davinia
Turrell or the Benton sisters should not have been on a westbound train
leaving Edgware Road, according to the Home Office they must have all
been on that train.   This leaves us with several questions.   Is TFL's
information true, or were there victims on the additional train? Was the
train actually East of the station, as the MPS kept saying, or West, as
the Home Office say? Was more than one train bombed at Edgware
Road?

Whose Hallmarks?

Around an hour after the tube bombings there was explosion on a
number 30 bus in Tavistock Square at 9:47 a.m., though Sky news and
other outlets were still reporting the 'power surge' story up to twenty
minutes later.   At a few minutes past ten the BBC first mentioned 'an
incident on a bus' and asked for witnesses to call in.   Five minutes later
the BBC reported that the National Grid had said that there were 'no
reported problems' with the electricity.   Then, reports of a bus exploding
started to reach the news.

At 10:19 BBC reporter Anna O'Neill phoned in a report from King's Cross saying that she had just seen mobile phone video footage of a bus exploding. O'Neill guessed that 'something more sinister' than a power surge was to blame for what was happening in London. She spoke of how the witness who had shown her the footage, 'had spent some time in Israel and he said that he thought that it was very similar to scenes he'd witnessed while he'd been living over there.' Shortly afterwards a London taxi driver called in to say that he had seen an explosion on a bus. Scotland Yard then issued statements to the press confirming reports of 'multiple explosions across London' and then 'a confirmed explosion of a bus on Tavistock Place'.

Over the following hour reports came in of explosions on three different buses. The locations of the buses that emerged from these reports and later newspaper coverage were Whitechapel, Russell Square and Tavistock Square. Officially, there was only one bus bombing and reports of additional explosions of buses were sporadic and uncertain. Nonetheless, these reports helped propagate an impression of lots of explosions all over London on multiple tube trains and on multiple buses.

This impression was summed up by Roy Ram, a former head of MPS Specialist Operations and the Flying Squad. He was interviewed by the BBC about an hour and a half after the bus explosion and said, 'One shouldn't speculate too much but seeing the number of incidents on the underground and now on the buses across London, and the timing of these incidents a) during the rush hour and b) following London's success as the Olympic city this is a, looks, has all the hallmarks of a very carefully structured and timed terrorist attack. One shouldn't speculate too much but those are the hallmarks that are there and that's what we're facing.'

At around 11:30, following a lengthy statement by Sir Ian Blair of the MPS on what had happened, the media got busy telling people who had done it. The BBC reported that, 'The BBC security correspondent Frank Gardner says Arab sources who monitor Al Qaeda have told the BBC they believe today's explosions in London are almost certainly the work of Al Qaeda.' A few minutes later, reporter Pete Wilson repeated the 11:30 report and said that, 'we haven't got this from any Al Qaeda source, this is from our own BBC correspondent who works closely in this field… what they are saying, effectively, it's got all the hallmarks of an Al Qaeda planned attack.'

This phrase, 'the hallmarks of Al Qaeda' itself became a hallmark of media coverage of the attack. Then Foreign Secretary Jack Straw used it in the House of Commons that evening, and it became a mantra. The same choice of words turned up time and again in news broadcasts on both sides of the Atlantic, and has since become a staple phrase for officials and media commentators.

Even though there was no evidence of who had carried out the attacks, within a few hours blame had already been apportioned. The most infamous examples was then Prime Minister Tony Blair, who on the evening of 7/7 told the press that, 'we know that these people act in the name of Islam.' However, he also promised that there would be 'the most intense police and security service action to make sure we bring those responsible to justice.' Given that in the intervening seven years no one had been brought to justice for carrying out the 7/7 attacks we should not put too much weight on the truthfulness of Blair's comments.

Even though they had no specific evidence of who carried out the attack, did they have a reasonable suspicion? The answer is no, they did not have grounds for a reasonable suspicion of who the culprits were. The London underground, and indeed train services in general, have been the target of terrorist attacks by many different groups and gangs. The tube had suffered nearly 20 bombings in the century or so prior to 7/7, and this was mostly the work of Irish militants. In particular, the scenario of multiple tube bombings was seen in 1939, 1991 and 1992, all the work of the IRA.

It is a similar story with bus bombings, which are far less common in the UK. In one of the most famous miscarriages of justice in British history, Judith Ward was wrongly convicted of three bombings, including one on a coach carrying off-duty British soldiers on the M62 motorway. The true culprits behind the coach bombing are not known for sure, but it is widely believed to have been an IRA attack.

Likewise, the only bombing on a red London bus prior to 7/7 was again the work of the IRA. On February 18th 1996 a number 171 bus exploded in Aldwych in central London. A badly injured Irishman who was pulled from the wreckage named Brendan Woolhead was reported to have been responsible. However, when the authorities discovered that the only man killed in the explosion, Edward O'Brien, was also Irish, they blamed him. It is thought that O'Brien was on his way to a target when the bomb exploded prematurely, making him a sort of accidental or unintentional suicide bomber. The parallels between the 1996 bus bombing and Hitchcock's adaptation of the Martial Bourdin story in *Sabotage* 60 years earlier are eerie in the extreme.

So, in terms of the history of terrorist attacks in the UK, the obvious suspect for multiple bombs on the tube and a bomb on a bus would be the IRA, or some offshoot or related group. Britain has endured the on-off violence of Irish Republicans over several decades, but prior to 7/7 there was no significant history of Islamic militant attacks, if any. As such, as far as Frank Gardner, Jack Straw and the rest knew on the day of 7/7, the attacks bore the hallmarks of the IRA, rather than Al Qaeda. That is not to say that the IRA were responsible, merely that given the nature of the attacks they should have been considered the most likely perpetrators.

Taking a wider range of examples, attacks on public transport networks are comparatively common across Europe in the last half-century. Many of these bombings took place as part of Operation Gladio, the NATO-sponsored terrorist campaign across Europe throughout the Cold War. The 1980 Bologna train station bombing, the 1974 Italicus Express bombing and the 1970 Rome-Messina train bombing all 'bear the hallmarks' of Gladio, and one could argue that so do the 7/7 attacks. Alternately, one could also consider the metro bombings in Paris in 1995 and Madrid in 2004. These attacks do appear to have been the work of Islamic militants, albeit militants with ties to the Algerian, French and Spanish security services.

However, the authorities were not just blaming Muslims for 7/7, but specifically blaming Al Qaeda. The only previous attacks for which Al Qaeda had been blamed were the 1993 bombing at the World Trade Center, the 1995 attack on the Khobar Towers, the 1998 East African US embassy bombings, the 2000 attack on the USS Cole in Aden, and 9/11. Whether Al Qaeda was actually responsible for these attacks is a matter of great debate, but the running theme is that these were attacks on the US, not the UK, and that the targets were military or commercial, not strictly civilian. As such, there really is no excuse for the prejudice shown by the authorities in the hours after 7/7, leaping to conclusions about who was to blame before they had even begun to count the dead.

The Bus Diversion

One of the curiosities about the explosion on the number 30 bus in Tavistock Square is that it had been diverted from its usual route. The Marble Arch to Hackney Wick route does not go through Tavistock Square, and indeed the bus driver had stopped a minute before the explosion to ask for directions. It is not at all clear when and why and how the bus was diverted, and the Home Office narrative doesn't even mention that it was diverted, let alone seek to explain it.

In part because of the mystery surrounding the bus's diversion this has inspired various alternative conspiracy theories. In Alex Jones's film *Terrorstorm* he claims that, 'the London police department orders the number 30 Hackney to Marble Arch bus to leave its normal route and park at the corner of Woburn Square and Tavistock Place'. The actual address was Woburn Place and Tavistock Square and the route going in the opposite direction, suggesting that Jones's research for this film is somewhat negligent.

Jones went on to claim that it was the only bus that the police 'take special control of' that morning. If indeed this were true then it would be extremely strong evidence of a state conspiracy, but it isn't true. Photographs from Tavistock Square shortly after the explosion show that two other buses, a number 205 and a number 390 were also in Tavistock Square at the time. Neither route normally goes through Tavistock Square, suggesting that some buses were being diverted there because of what was happening at King's Cross, just up the road.

So it is possible that the bus diversion is precisely that, a diversion, but there is a similar issue with the bus as there is with the tube trains. Its location is indisputable, but its direction is another matter. The Home Office narrative describes it as 'travelling eastwards from Marble Arch', i.e. on its way to Hackney Wick.[22] This is born out by the photographs of the bus, which show its tattered route display saying it was heading towards Hackney Wick.

However, many early media reports contradict this. The BBC, the Telegraph, the Mirror, the Scotsman, the Independent, the Guardian, the Evening Standard and other publications all reported that the bus was on its way to Marble Arch, i.e. in the opposite direction to the Home Office.[23] Despite having pictures on their newsdesks showing a bus on its way to Hackney Wick they reported it was travelling in the opposite direction. This story lasted for several days before being corrected.

What this seems to show is that the mainstream media were incapable of getting basic details right in the hours and days after the attacks. While it is not clear whether these reports of additional bombs on the underground and on buses have any basis in fact, it does establish one key point. That is, if there was a larger attack and the authorities immediately started to cover up parts of it, the mainstream media would have been none the wiser. They were quite content to report things that even their own photographs showed were untrue. Thus, the quality of their reporting about all aspects of 7/7 should be treated with caution.

It is not just the media, but also the authorities that have failed to provide an explanation for how and why the bus was diverted. Thomas Ikimi, the cousin of Anthony Fatayi-Williams, who died in the bus explosion, wanted to find out more and understand more about what happened on 7/7. His investigation was presented in his powerful documentary *The Homefront*, where he tried to find out how his cousin came to be on the bus and therefore why he died.

Anthony was last seen getting on a bus at King's Cross, so how he came to be in Tavistock Square is difficult to figure out. Ikimi initially tried to get access to George Psaradakis, the man driving the number 30 bus and one of the last people to see Anthony alive. He was rebuffed by TFL and Stagecoach, and not permitted to talk to Psaradakis on- or off-camera. Psaradakis had already been widely interviewed in the press, and was on the TV news several times during the inquests. His employers were happy for him to talk to journalists who had nothing to do with what happened, but not for him to talk to a grieving relative with questions about how their loved one died.

Ikimi did manage to get an interview with Sergeant Graham Cross of the MPS, who was one of the first officers on the scene of the bus explosion. Cross outlined how the number 30 bus was headed towards King's Cross, but was then diverted by police, presumably at the junction of Euston Road and Upper Woburn Place, which leads to Tavistock Square. He explained that to them it was 'just another vehicle' among many that they were diverting away from King's Cross.

For all the ambiguities and questions that still remain, this is more information about the bus diversion than any journalist has managed to provide, despite the journalists finding it far easier than Ikimi to get access to people. This is a sad indictment not just of the behaviour of officials and authorities, but also of the journalists of this country. One young man, with no formal training, no special contacts, managed to find out more than the entire British press combined.

Mr Jones

The stark contrast in the treatment of two different witnesses from the site of the bus explosion provides an insight into the nature and methods of the ongoing cover-up. These two witnesses are Richard Jones, a passenger on the bus who got off shortly before it exploded, and Richmal Marie Oates-Whitehead, who helped the emergency services tend to the injured.

Richard Jones is implicitly referred to in the Home Office narrative where it says, 'Witness accounts suggest 2 of the men were fiddling in their rucksacks shortly before the explosions.' It also describes the bus explosion and comments that, 'A man fitting Hussain's description was seen on the lower deck earlier, fiddling repeatedly with his rucksack.'[24]   The witness who allegedly saw Hussain on the bus, fiddling with his rucksack, was Richard Jones.

Jones was widely interviewed in the hours and days after 7/7 on both sides of the Atlantic.   His story of having seen a darker-skinned man on the bus fiddling with his rucksack helped establish the notion of suicide bombers.   Indeed, in the absence of any physical evidence it is only accounts such as Jones' that lend any credence to that idea.   Even the Home Office narrative lists it as among only seven points of 'key evidence indicating that these were co-ordinated suicide attacks by these 4 men.'

It was largely the mainstream media who framed his account in this way, for example when CBS's *The Early Show* interviewed him they introduced him saying, 'Mr Jones was actually riding that double decker bus that was hit in the terror attacks and he happened to get off the bus just moments before it was blown up. He also saw the man that police believe was responsible.'[25]

The problem is that Jones's descriptions of the man he saw have varied from interview to interview, and none of them match up with the CCTV purportedly showing Hussain from that day.   He told the BBC's *Real Story* that he noticed, 'a young lad had got on, about 25 year old, thin, six foot, olive skinned, very well dressed... This young lad kept delving into the bag, and got more and more frustrated, at least twelve, maybe twenty times in the five or six minutes that we were on the bus together.'[26]

The problem is that Hussain was eighteen years old, quite well built, and according to the CCTV he was very ordinarily dressed. According to the Scottish Sunday Mail 'The man was wearing hipster-style fawn checked trousers, with exposed designer underwear, and a matching jersey-style top.   Richard said: "The pants looked very expensive, they were white with a red band on top."'[27]   This description does not in any way coincide with what the CCTV shows Hussain wearing that day.   Jones has also given contrasting interviews on whether the man he saw was facing towards him or away from him, and whether he saw the man's face.

Most fundamentally, all of this apparently took place on the lower deck of the bus, when the explosion was clearly at the rear of the upper deck.   For Jones's story to be an account of a suicide bomber who bombed that bus a quite ridiculous set of events would have to have happened.   The bomber would have had to be fiddling with his rucksack and getting agitated for several minutes in front of Jones. Then, for no obvious reason but conveniently just after Jones had left the bus, the bomber would have to have stopped fidgeting and getting wound up, run up the stairs and to the back of the bus and immediately sat down and set his rucksack on the floor and blown himself up. All without anyone else noticing him.

It is an absurd story, but of course none of those who interviewed Jones chose to challenge him over his description not matching the alleged suicide bomber Hasib Hussain, or over the ridiculous implications of his account. He was simply presented as the man who saw the bomber. When Jones was called to the inquests as a witness, things got a whole lot worse.

At the inquests a hand-drawn diagram of the lower deck of the bus drawn by Jones for the police two days after 7/7 was entered into evidence. It shows where Jones was sitting, the location of the man with the rucksack, and two Asian ladies. Curiously, the only people Jones remembered seeing on the bus were an 'olive skinned' man and two Asian women. These were the only people he thought it was appropriate to bring to the police's attention.

Jones described the man as 'wearing light clothes, light-coloured clothes, he had a tan or was of, I would have thought, Mediterranean extraction, quite tall, about 6 feet, and very well-dressed.' He went on to confirm that the man was 'of slim build' and 'cleanshaven'. The government's lawyer Hugo Keith QC drew out the contradictions between the man Jones described and Hasib Hussain actual appearance, and an astounding reversal took place. After nearly six years of being reported as the man who saw the bomber, Jones was effectively dropped from the official story.

A. I mean, at no stage have I ever said that I actually saw the bomber. Right?

Q. No.

A. All I've ever, ever said was that somebody was acting unusually and annoying me on the bus.

Q. But I hope we've established, Mr Jones, that there appears to be no connection with the bomber and nor that that particular gentleman was doing anything other than acting as an ordinary member of the public, a passenger on the bus?

A. Correct.

Q. But your statement, I'm afraid, has been open to conjecture and surmise in the way of these things in the public domain.

A. Yes, I know.[28]

While it may be true that Richard Jones never explicitly said that he saw the bomber, he did co-operate fully with the mainstream media in propagating this idea. He never objected, for example, to how they introduced him, how they edited his comments or the slant they put on them. Though he is not named specifically in the Home Office narrative it is clearly his testimony that is cited as 'key evidence' of suicide bombings.

So we are presented with a fundamental contradiction, between a Home Office argument that cites Jones as among the key evidence proving these were suicide bombings, and the inquest testimony where he explicitly denied having seen Hasib Hussain fiddling with his rucksack. This reversal of the significance of what Jones said he saw was handled with kid gloves, with absolutely no criticism being meted out to Jones for his years of misleading interviews.

Ms Whitehead

Richmal Marie Oates-Whitehead was not so lucky. Marie was born in New Zealand in 1970 and at the time of 7/7 was in London, working as an editor for the British Medical Association (BMA). When the number 30 bus exploded outside the BMA headquarters, Marie was among those who rushed out of the building to help tend to the injured.

Her story of helping the victims alongside the emergency services despite fears of a secondary device, and of having witnessed a controlled explosion on a suspect package, made it into the media both in New Zealand and the UK in the weeks following 7/7. On the basis of her account, numerous outlets labelled her a heroine. Meanwhile, the MPS officially denied that there had been a controlled explosion on the number 30 bus. Marie then died suddenly in August 2005, seven weeks after the bombings.

At this point the mainstream media instantly turned against Marie, and began trying to cast doubt on her story, her character and her state of mind. Headlines such as 'Pathos of the bogus doctor who became '53rd victim' of 7/7' and 'The fantasy life and lonely death of woman hailed as heroine of July 7 bombing' leapt out from newspapers across the globe. The papers accused her of being a fantasist, an exaggerator and a liar. They said that she was not a doctor, and that the police had no record of a controlled explosion being carried out at Tavistock Square.

At the July 7 inquests this process of trying to assassinate Marie's character continued. A statement that she gave to the police a week after 7/7 was read into evidence. It described how she was asked to assist with the wounded by a police officer, the locations of the victims that she helped, and the location of one women that she pronounced dead. Her account was called into question, in particular her evidence on where certain victims were found on the bus. Some of Marie's evidence contradicted the MPS on where the victims were found and so, perhaps unsurprisingly, Lady Justice Hallett concluded that, 'I don't feel I can place any reliance upon that [Marie's] observation at all.'

An exchange between Hallett and Neil Saunders, the lawyer for some of the victims, followed on from this comment. Saunders pointed out that in the witness statements from Tavistock Square, 'there appears to be no reference to a lady fitting that description being on the bus.' Hallett went on to ask Saunders that, 'the fact that she may have said she was a doctor, may claim to have pronounced anybody dead or a broken neck or whatever she's done, as far as you're concerned, she's plainly made no difference?' Saunders responded 'We can see absolutely no difference.'[29]

Saunders and Hallett appeared to be trying to cast doubt on whether Marie was even in Tavistock Square on 7/7, and whether she actually helped anyone. Significantly, one women Marie described helping, Emma Plunkett, was called to testify at the inquests but was not asked if she'd seen Marie or anyone fitting her description. However, there are photographs and video footage from Tavistock Square that show a woman fitting Marie's description of herself, confirming at least part of Marie's story.

Furthermore, Marie is certainly telling the truth about a controlled explosion being carried out on the bus. Several media articles from the weeks after 7/7 also referred to the controlled explosion, and it was confirmed by several exhibits and testimony at the inquests. In particular, a report from London Fire Brigade Inspector Michael Ellis describes how, 'Secondary devices were suspected later in the incident and controlled explosions were carried out.' Ellis was never asked about this when he was called to testify at the inquests.

It is also important that Ellis's report is clearly referring to multiple 'secondary devices' and multiple 'controlled explosions'. The original official story was there was no controlled explosion, but this now seems to have been changed to there being one (and only one) controlled explosion on the bus. There is a record of a SO13 Explosives Officer Call Out Form that details a single explosion, so whether there was more than one is not certain.[30]

In any case, Marie was in Tavistock Square and did to some extent witness the suspicion about a package on the bus and a controlled explosion being carried out. She almost certainly wasn't a fully qualified hands-on doctor, but she had worked in the medical profession as an epidemiologist and had been interviewed as a medical expert for a book on pregnancy. She was also listed on an NHS website as a doctor and a medical researcher.

As such, while there may have been a few lies in her job application to the BMA, or a few details that she fudged in interviews with the media after 7/7, in essence her story is confirmed by the bulk of the significant evidence available. The concerted effort by both officials and the mainstream media to paint her as a mentally unstable liar, charges she cannot answer because she is dead, is gruesome and wholly unethical. It shows quite bluntly how the official process of investigating 7/7 has been dishonest and deceptive.

Even the question of Marie's death has not been satisfactorily resolved. Initial rumours were that she had killed herself due to the guilt of having lied and potential shame of being exposed. The official cause of death was pulmonary embolism and bilateral calf deep vein thrombosis. This is particularly odd as pulmonary embolism was one of the focal points for Marie's research for the Cochrane Institute.[31] She should have been able to spot the early warning signs, but apparently she did not.

If we directly compare how Marie was treated to how Richard Jones was treated then a simple truth emerges. Jones was a terrible witness who allowed his account to help fuel the official story of suicide bombers. His credibility was attacked for years by unofficial researchers and finally he was politely written out of the official story. By contrast, Marie is a credible witness whose account contradicts the official story that there was no second, controlled explosion on the number 30 bus. She has been systematically attacked, her claims contradicted even when the evidence corroborated her account, and been posthumously named and shamed in the major media. The simple truth appears to be that if you are a bad witness but you say something that supports the official story, you will be protected, but if you are a good witness and say something that contradicts the official story, you will be attacked.

Mysterious Origins

So amidst all this confusion, controlled explosions, dodgy witnesses, misinformation and un-sourced reporting, how did the official story emerge so quickly? Why did so many officials and reporters repeat the 'hallmarks of Al Qaeda' catchphrase when in fact the attacks bore no such hallmarks? At no stage in the first 24 hours was it even clear what happened, and so all assumptions of who was responsible were just that – assumptions.

In this context, Blair's comment about the attacks being done 'in the name of Islam' was a self-fulfilling prophecy. At that point no one knew who had carried out the attacks or what their agenda and aims were. By the very act of standing up and saying they were 'in the name of Islam', Blair was laying the foundations for an official story that would blame Muslims for what happened. All Blair was doing was naming a name, without the slightest evidence. But because that was the name, the culprits had to turn out to be Muslims.

Also, why 'in the name of' Islam? Why not 'because of a violent perversion of Islam' or some other description? Was the sole purpose of the comment to imply that the culprits would turn out to be Muslims? Or was Blair drawing attention to the possibility of someone carrying out an attack 'in the name of' someone or something else, so that the wrong culprits would be blamed?

The common counterargument used to try to dismiss these questions is that governments and journalists are not perfect, and that confusion and contradictory reporting is normal in a large-scale emergency. This is true up to a point and will account for why some of the reports must be wrong. But this only provokes a further, more important question. At what point does unreliable early reporting turn into reliable later reporting?

After all, the MPS were still reporting untrue details a week after the bombings. By that time their investigators had been over the scenes and apparently found evidence implicating Khan, Tanweer, Hussain and Lindsay. And yet the same process that resulted in the public being told that those men were responsible also resulted in the public being told that a hole was blown through a tunnel wall at Edgware Road, an event that did not happen, and could not have happened.

Similarly, the BBC and the Guardian managed to get basic details wrong four and five years after the attacks. Having accepted the official narrative without question or criticism, they proceeded to publish details of the times of the explosions and the direction of the train at Liverpool Street that contradicted that narrative. No media outlets have issued major corrections, and no apologies have been offered for the misleading information they have published, individually and en masse.

Most fundamentally, why should we believe them when they say with certainty that the four alleged bombers were responsible? That entire narrative hinges on there being only four explosions, three on tube trains headed away from King's Cross and one on a diverted number 30 bus. But both the government and the major media have repeatedly published reports that directly contradict this story, and if true would make the official narrative an impossibility. Which statements and reports should we believe?

Chapter 2: A Wider Conspiracy?

The official investigation found that four young British Muslims were the culprits – Sidique Khan, Shehzad Tanweer, Germaine Lindsay and Haslb Hussain. Officially the four men acted on their own to carry out the 7/7 bombings. The Home Office narrative says that, 'in the period immediately following the attacks, one man was arrested in connection with the investigation but he was released without charge. In subsequent weeks, a further man who had claimed to be the "5th bomber" was also arrested and later charged with wasting police time. There is no intelligence to indicate that there was a fifth or further bombers.'[1]

The fabricator was Imran Yaqub Patel, from Dewsbury. He had approached the News of the World claiming to have known the alleged bombers, to have talked with them about their 'mission', and that he was 'lined up to be the fifth 7/7 bomber'. He also claimed to have knowledge of another person preparing to launch an attack in the UK. The newspaper tipped off the police, who arrested Patel in October 2005 and subsequently charged him with wasting 4,070 hours of police time. He was jailed for four months.

The first ISC report repeats the same phrase, that 'There is no intelligence to indicate that there was a fifth or further bombers' and the second ISC report came to the same conclusion. So we have been presented with a story of the four culprits being homegrown, self-radicalising suicide bombers. There are, officially, no additional conspirators, no masterminds here or abroad, no one else left alive to face justice.

While this is a highly convenient story for the government, as it requires them to do nothing to continue investigating the crime, it is contradicted by other aspects of the official story. Three eyewitnesses to the movements of the four alleged bombers on the morning of 7/7, all of which are key witnesses for the Home Office narrative, have testified to there being a fifth and possibly sixth man alongside them.

Furthermore, three men who knew the alleged bombers were prosecuted, twice, for their alleged connection to the attacks. They were ultimately found not guilty of involvement in 7/7, but the very fact that they were prosecuted directly contradicts official claims that the four men acted alone. The three men are certainly innocent, but their case shows that the official story can be bent into any shape and in any direction required, as long as the four alleged bombers remain the culprits.

Sylvia Waugh

The alleged bombers allegedly built their bombs in a flat in Alexandra Grove, Leeds, in the weeks before 7/7. According to the Home Office, on the morning of the bombings three of the men (Khan, Tanweer and Hussain) collected their bombs and backpacks from the flat in the early hours of the morning. They then headed out of Leeds and down the M1 motorway to meet up with Germaine Lindsay in Luton.

There is only one witness, named Sylvia Waugh, who says that she saw the alleged bombers in Alexandra Grove early that morning, and no corroborating evidence. The only CCTV footage that has been released shows a car with unknown occupants several streets away. As such, a lot depends on Mrs Waugh's testimony, and yet her account is completely at odds with the official story.

She was interviewed about a year after 7/7 by ITN news, and was also called to testify at the July 7 inquests. Mrs Waugh lived in Alexandra Grove and told the court how she had seen up to seven different men going in and out of the flat in the two months before 7/7. This chimes with reports that there were as many as ten unidentified sets of fingerprints found inside the flat, and suggests that whatever was going on there was known to more people than just the four alleged bombers.

She described one as 'the Jamaican', who she identified from a photo as being Germaine Lindsay. Another she dubbed 'the schoolteacher', i.e. Sidique Khan, but she says she only called him that because she found out later that he worked in a school. A further man also visited the flat in this period who she called 'the Egyptian' and he apparently drove a Red Mercedes.

During her testimony at the inquests she got confused on several occasions, and when asked to describe some of the men she saw in Alexandra Grove she responded:

A. Just that they all looked the same to me.

Q. All right. Did you recognise --

LADY JUSTICE HALLETT: As in --

A. As they're all being coloured.

LADY JUSTICE HALLETT: Are we talking about -

A. Like the Pakistanis, to me they all look alike.

On the morning of 7/7 Mrs Waugh says that she was awoken by voices shortly after 4 a.m. and saw 'a group of Asians' loading things into two cars. When asked how many she saw she said, 'at least six.' She also said that the men were loading bags into two different cars, and that at one moment 'the Jamaican' looked up at her. Mrs Waugh said that she thought they were dealing drugs.[2]

Her prejudices aside, Mrs Waugh's account is crucial for the Home Office narrative, because no one else saw the alleged bombers in Leeds that morning, but she also contradicts it. Officially there should have been only three men at Alexandra Grove, not six. There should have been only one car, not two. The three men should not have included 'the Jamaican', i.e. Lindsay, because he met up with the other three in Luton station car park hours later.

Indeed, apart from saying 'I saw the bombers', nothing about Mrs Waugh's testimony corroborates the official account. Even the time is slightly wrong, because the CCTV showing a car on Hyde Park Road supposedly containing the alleged bombers has a timecode of 3:59, i.e. just before 4 a.m. not just after as Mrs Waugh describes. The Home Office narrative says this CCTV was captured at 3:58, illustrating once again how the author of that document clearly never actually saw the evidence.

The additional men and the extra car were never traced, and whether they even existed is not certain. However, if Mrs Waugh is considered an unreliable witness then there is literally no evidence that puts those three men at the alleged bomb factory on that morning. Strangely, the authorities also failed to trace an 'Asian lady' who Mrs Waugh said she saw throwing away bags of rubbish from the flat on the weekend after 7/7. The weekend fell on the 9th and 10th of July, whereas the police did not raid the 'bomb factory' until the 12th.

Sue Clarke

Having left Alexandra Grove, the official story says that Khan, Tanweer and Hussain drove down the M1 to Luton, arriving at the train station at 6:49 a.m. They then met up with Lindsay, who had driven across from Aylesbury a few hours earlier. They hung around in the car park apparently assembling their backpack bombs before heading into the station. Some of this story is confirmed by the CCTV footage, though the actual people and vehicles in the car park cannot be identified due to the distance from the cameras.

It is here that the story of Sue Clarke comes in. She was a commuter who regularly got on the train at Luton to travel into London. She arrived in the carpark at 7:14 and parked her car just opposite the two cars containing the alleged bombers. The maps she drew for the police, her statement to the police, and much of her inquest testimony are born out by the available CCTV images. The video shows a car arriving at the time Sue Clarke said she arrived, and parking opposite the cars apparently containing the alleged bombers.

Sue Clarke remembered seeing the two cars and the group of men around them and apparently found them sufficiently suspicious that she returned to the station car park early the following morning to look again. By that time the red Fiat Brava that Lindsay had apparently driven over from Aylesbury had been towed away, but the rented lilac Nissan Micra from Leeds was still there. She took the registration number, apparently took a photograph of the car, and wrote down the details of the hire company.

She approached the police on the morning of the 12th, the Tuesday after 7/7. Having handed the information to a policeman at St Pancras Station she was then interviewed that afternoon. The problem for the official story is that she described seeing as many as six men in and around the two cars, when there should have been four at the most. She even drew an additional map for the police showing the positions of five men around the cars as she walked past.

She said that there were one or two men in the Brava, which should have only contained Lindsay, and four in the lilac Nissan, all of whom had rucksacks. Despite this, when she testified at the inquests she could only remember four men, fitting exactly with the Home Office's story.

Q. Can you tell us, please, how many people you thought got out of the Nissan car?

A. I think three.

Q. You think three out of the Nissan.

A. Yes.

Q. What about the other car, the maroon-coloured car?

A. I don't recall. I think there might have been one.[3]

What changed Mrs Clarke's mind in between July 2005, when she described five or six men, and drew maps for the police showing the locations of five people, and October 2010 when she testified at the July 7 inquests? Perhaps more importantly, why should we place any more faith in her memory five years later than we do in her initial statements to the police?

The CCTV does not conclusively show how many people are standing around the cars at the time Mrs Clarke is shown walking past. There are two other potential eyewitnesses shown nearby, but we have no further information on who they are, if the police spoke to them or what they might have said. As such, at the second key location for the Home Office's narrative we have the same problem as at the first.

Indeed, the parallels between the two are considerable. Both Sylvia Waugh and Sue Clarke are the only witnesses who we have been presented with that remember seeing the alleged bombers at these key locations in Leeds and Luton. While the CCTV from Luton does appear to show the men entering and walking through the station, the only evidence that the CCTV from the car park shows the alleged bombers comes from Sue Clarke.

Both women apparently saw additional men alongside the alleged bombers at these two key locations. Whether they actually saw extra men is far from certain, particularly since Sue Clarke's revised testimony at the inquests contradicted her initial statements to the police. But if question their reliability as witnesses then we are left with the question of whether they saw the alleged bombers at all that morning.

Joseph Martoccia

The original narrative had the four men catching the 7:40 train from Luton to King's Cross Thameslink station in London. This scheduled train didn't actually run on the morning of 7/7, and after a ridiculously long period the Home Office issued an amendment to the narrative saying that the four caught the 7:25 train instead.

CCTV shows what appears to be the four men at King's Cross Thameslink between 8:23 and 8:26 a.m. but does not show them moving through the King's Cross underground station, or boarding the trains that were bombed. As we will see in the following chapter, this is due to a malfunctioning CCTV system at King's Cross. The key witness to their presence at King's Cross underground station, which is separate from the Thameslink station, is Joseph Martoccia.

Martoccia was a regular commuter into London, and had got confused during his journey and was finding his way through King's Cross underground station to try to get his train. He noticed a group of men who were 'in really good spirits.' He described them as a sports team, specifically thinking they were a cricket team because, 'the bags that they were wearing were pretty large, that you could actually get a cricket bat in and possibly pads, and being Asian, I -- and they were in sort of tracksuits, I thought they were a sports team.' He described how they were 'in a huddle' together and at the inquests he was asked about their demeanour:

> **Q.** Looking at the police statement that you gave, you in fact described them as hugging each other in a manner that suggested they were celebrating something.
>
> **A.** Correct, yes.
>
> **Q.** Did they appear aware of the people around them, or were oblivious to the passing passengers?
>
> **A.** They were not aware of anybody else. They were very overt in the way that they were acting. They weren't sort of - - you know, obviously, you think back, you obviously realise what had happened, but they weren't sneaking around at all. They were very, very open in the way that they were standing, crowding other commuters as well.[4]

This moment is also a key event in the Home Office narrative, which says that, 'At around 08.30am, 4 men fitting their descriptions are seen hugging. They appear happy, even euphoric.'[5] This has been used by the mainstream media as a sign that the alleged bombers were suicidal and believed they were on their way to paradise.

Indeed, journalist and mainstream terrorism expert Jason Burke wrote an Observer article saying, 'One of the last images of Hasib Hussain is from a surveillance camera at King's Cross station concourse, which shows the four bombers together at 8.26am, half an hour before the first explosions. They appear no different from any other group of young men at a station during rush hour. The twin images, of the young men swiftly saying goodbye at the station, and of the shredded bus, with its top deck peeled back by the blast, have become iconic, summing up both the new terrorism that is striking the UK and the apparent banality of the men who perpetrate it.'[6]

This image has never been presented to the public and so Jason Burke could not have ever actually seen the image he referred to, and therefore has no basis for saying it is 'iconic'. When J7 filed a complaint with the Press Complaints Commission (PCC) they received a response that included a letter to the PCC from Observer editor Stephen Pritchard. Pritchard's letter says that, 'I have checked with the Metropolitan Police, who confirm that the image exists and that they discussed it with our reporter, Jason Burke.'

When J7 pursued the issue with the Press Complaints Commission the PCC ruled in the Observer's favour, saying there was no breach of the code in claiming that the image was 'iconic' when it had not been seen by the public. They argued that 'the image existed in the public mind' and therefore could be considered iconic in the sense that it 'summed up a mass of perceptions'. As chapter 3 will show in detail, the official story has now been changed to say that the King's Cross CCTV malfunctioned, and so this moment was never caught on camera. Apparently, an image doesn't have to actually exist for it to be 'iconic', the police and mainstream media just have to pretend that it exists to make it 'iconic' in 'the public mind'.

The only source for this 'euphoric hug' is Joseph Martoccia, so like Sue Clarke and Sylvia Waugh he too is a key witness for the Home Office narrative (and Jason Burke). As with the other witnesses, there are key problems in Martoccia's story. When asked how many men were in the group hug that he saw he said 'four to six'. He also said that they were 'all Asian', when Germaine Lindsay was black.

Martoccia said that he recognised two of the men as Hasib Hussain and Shehzad Tanweer, but he said that Tanweer was 'a good deal shorter' than the others. The CCTV footage shows that this isn't the case. He described Hussain's hair as being different to the photo of Hussain that he was shown, when according to the CCTV from 7/7 Hussain's hair was the same as in the photo. He also said that the man he recognised as Hussain went towards the Piccadilly line when the group split up, when officially it was Lindsay who bombed the Piccadilly line.[7]

These inconsistencies are perhaps not as fundamental as the problems with the accounts of Sylvia Waugh and Sue Clarke but as with those two witnesses, the question has be to asked as to whether Martoccia even saw the alleged bombers. If he did see them, then he saw an additional couple of men with them. If he did not, then this 'iconic' hug did not actually take place.

All three witnesses are the only sources showing that the four men were in the locations the Home Office says, at the times the Home Office says they were there. All three witnesses say they saw at least one additional man alongside the four in each of these locations. None of these additional men have been traced, and though the Home Office makes liberal use of these witnesses in putting together its story, it makes no mention of them seeing extra men.

Alleged Co-Conspirators

Despite official claims that the four alleged bombers acted alone in planning and carrying out the attacks, a total of seven people have been arrested as part of the police investigation. Three men were arrested on March 22nd 2007. Mohammed Shakil and Waheed Ali (a.k.a. Shipon Ullah) were picked up at Manchester Airport, apparently on the verge of taking a flight to Pakistan. The third man, Sadeer Saleem, was arrested in Beeston, Leeds.

The three men did know the alleged 7/7 bombers, and can be seen in pre-7/7 home videos that also feature Hasib Hussain, Sidique Khan and Shehzad Tanweer. Waheed Ali and Mohammed Shakil were involved with the Iqra bookshop (see chapter 6) in Beeston. However, the case showing that the three were involved in 7/7 was extremely slim.

On March 28th, the police were granted additional time to continue questioning the men, under the 2006 Terrorism Act passed in the wake of 7/7. By April 5th the men were charged with 'conspiring with the 7 July bombers between the 1 November 2004 and the 29 June 2005 to cause explosions.' Strangely, this charge does not include the actual bombings themselves, on the July 7th 2005. By the time the men got to court the dates of their alleged conspiracy had been changed.

In essence, the case against the men was that in December 2004 they had carried out 'hostile reconnaissance' on potential terrorist targets during a trip to London. The men had driven from Leeds to London and met up with Hasib Hussain and Germaine Lindsay, and then travelled around the capital. According to the prosecution, the locations they visited 'bore a striking similarity' to those attacked on 7/7.

This is plainly untrue. The men never went on the underground during their visit to London. Mobile phone records from the 16th and 17th December 2004 were produced as evidence, showing where Ali, Saleem and Shakil had been. Exactly how these records were available to the police three years later is not clear. Their journeys took the men close to the King's Cross and Edgware Road stations but they never actually went inside them. This simply cannot have been hostile reconnaissance in preparation for attacks on tube trains around these stations. In fact, the men visited a series of popular attractions, including the London Eye, the Natural History Museum and the London Aquarium. This strongly suggests that the men's defence, that it was a completely innocent tourist trip, is true.

The men were put on trial in 2008 and after several months of proceedings and a lengthy deliberation the jury could not reach a verdict. Clearly not happy with their entirely circumstantial case failing to convince the jury, the Crown Prosecution Service (CPS) ordered a retrial. This took place in 2009 and the second time round the men were found not guilty of any involvement in 7/7.

Following the trial, Sadeer Saleem issued a statement through his lawyer Imran Khan that said, 'Thankfully a jury of ordinary people have unanimously been able to see this case for what it was: guilt by association... I fully understand that whilst I am allowed to continue with my life, 52 people have lost theirs. I have every sympathy with their families and support their demand for a public inquiry... Luckily I have been acquitted. Many others have not been so lucky... Even though I have been acquitted, some people will always associate me with these events. I want people to know I am totally innocent and I want there to be an inquiry as to why I was prosecuted on the flimsiest of evidence... In my view this is a prosecution that should never have happened. I need to know now why it did.'[8]

Naturally, no such inquiry has been forthcoming. The justice system has never admitted any wrongdoing in the arrests and prosecutions of these three men who had nothing to do with the attacks. In all likelihood Saleem was correct in his view that the authorities just needed 'somebody, anybody, to pay for the murder of 52 people'.

Mohammed Junaid Babar

While Saleem was found completely innocent and set free, his co-accused were not so fortunate. Shakil and Ali were both convicted of conspiring to attend a terrorism training camp, which was allegedly the purpose of the flight to Pakistan they were about to take at the time of their arrests.

The key prosecution witness against Shakil and Ali, and to a lesser extent Saleem, was Mohammed Junaid Babar, the 'Al Qaeda supergrass' and most likely an American spy. Babar ran a terrorist training camp in Malakand, Pakistan throughout most of 2003. Shakil was one of several men who travelled to the camp in mid-2003, along with Sidique Khan and several of the Operation Crevice suspects (see chapter 7). Babar testified against Shakil in this respect, helping to sell him and Ali as potentially violent Muslim radicals.

Shakil did not deny attending Babar's camp alongside Sidique Khan and the others, but he and Ali maintained that their intended trip in 2007 was primarily a holiday. They admitted to holding what many would consider extreme or at least radical views about jihad, and to sympathising with the armed struggles in Kashmir and Afghanistan.

Babar's testimony in particular helped to convince the second jury that these men were dangerous criminals. He spoke of the training he provided to Shakil and others in 2003, speaking of how Shakil fired an AK-47 rifle while maintaining a 'perfect stance'. This portrait of Shakil and Ali as hardened militants helped gloss over the fact that they had never actually planned or committed any acts of violence against anyone.

Defending Shakil, Joel Bennathan QC put it to Babar that he was only testifying in the case so he could get a more lenient sentence. He said that, 'It's possible you could be at liberty in a year or two for full co-operation. That you will serve five years - rather than 70.' 'Yes,' Babar responded, 'I hope, yes.'[9] This was, of course, exactly what happened, and Babar was released after less than five years in prison due to his 'extraordinary co-operation'.

What is important to understand is that Babar still held the same beliefs as Shakil and Ali, that jihad is or can be a violent rather than a spiritual struggle. According to the court documents from Babar's own case, where he pled guilty to being an international terrorist, he still held these beliefs when he was set free. Clearly, therefore, simply holding such beliefs does not make someone a threat to the public, or a criminal offender, at least not according to US law.

So why, exactly, were Shakil and Ali convicted? Their beliefs were, however unusual, the same as those held by the co-operator testifying against them. At the times in the past that they had attended such camps, doing so was not a criminal offence. Even if they had intended (or 'conspired') to attend another terrorism training camp, they were arrested before they went. This is in essence a thoughtcrime, a crime of intent rather than action.

This conviction was only possible because of the 2006 Terrorism Act, drafted and passed in response to the 7/7 attacks. The previous acts in 2000, 2001, 2003 and 2005 did not include 'Attendance at a place used for terrorist training' and conspiracy to do the same as criminal offences. Shakil and Ali were some of the first people to be convicted of this new offence. The others were Mohammed Hamid et al, who were jailed for going on camping and paintballing trips within the UK.

Miscellaneous Masterminds

Adding to the smoke and mirrors in this story, the mainstream media has presented us with several possible terrorists masterminds who supposedly planned the 7/7 bombings. Magdy El Nashar, Haroon Aswat, Abd al-Hadi al-Iraqi, Abu Ubaidah al-Masri and Abu Faraj Al-Libbi have all been reported as the brains behinds the attacks.

The latter three men have simply been mentioned as Al Qaeda bigwigs who were the puppeteers. No evidence has ever been presented that they had even met or spoken with any of the alleged bombers, and many of the media reports are based on tips from anonymous security service agents. Both al-Iraqi and al-Libbi are apparently in Guantanamo Bay, whereas al-Masri is reportedly dead.

As such, it is easy for unscrupulous people to spread enticing rumours about them that have no basis in fact. These figures, who have never been put before a court to tell their story, have simply been dangled before us as possible culprits. To our knowledge, none of them have been the subject of investigations by British security services for their possible connection to the bombings. In all likelihood, none of the three have the slightest connection to 7/7 except in the minds of some people who read (and write) newspapers.

Magdy El Nashar is a slightly different case. He is an Egyptian who briefly studied in the US before completing a PhD in biochemistry in Leeds. He rented the flat in Alexandra Grove that was supposedly used as the bomb factory. He then apparently sub-let the flat to Hasib Hussain, the alleged bus bomber.

El Nashar left the UK a few weeks before the bombings, and was arrested in Cairo on July 15th. Almost every news outlet simultaneously reported rumours of an Egyptian chemist having built the bombs. Ultimately, no connection was found between El Nashar and the bombings and he was released. Whether he is the 'the Egyptian' referred to by Sylvia Waugh is not clear. According to her inquest testimony, she only attributed that name to one of the men she saw at Alexandra Grove because it was, 'A description what was given to me later.'

That leaves Haroon Rashid Aswat, by some distance the most discussed of the alleged masterminds. Aswat is a British-born Indian who was arrested trying to enter Zambia on July 20th 2005 and was flown back to Britain. For the previous two weeks, police sources had been giving information to the press about a possible mastermind. The man was reported to have left the UK on the morning of the attacks, to have been in mobile phone contact at least 20 times with the alleged bombers, including one call just hours before the blasts. When Aswat was arrested the police leaked his name to the press.[10]

However, it wasn't made explicit that Aswat had actually been arrested until several days later. Almost immediately following this former DOJ prosecutor John Loftus gave an interview to Fox News in which he claimed that not only was Aswat 'the mastermind behind all the bombings in London' but also that 'one wing of the British government, MI6 or the British Secret Service, has been hiding him.' He went on to claim that Aswat was 'a double agent'.[11]

Shortly after this interview the British government said that they were no longer interested in pursuing Aswat as a suspect in the 7/7 attacks. Since then Aswat has been in maximum security prison in the UK awaiting extradition to the US for supposedly trying to set up a terrorist training school in Oregon with MI5 informant and Al Muhajiroun leader Abu Hamza. His extradition has been contested alongside that of Babar Ahmad, and his mental health has apparently severely deteriorated.

The official reports do mention Aswat. The Home Office narrative says, 'The press reported later that a known extremist figure and possible mastermind left the UK shortly before the bombings. There is no evidence that this individual was involved.[12] Almost identically, the first ISC report says, 'Claims in the media that a 'mastermind' left the UK the day before the attacks reflect one strand of an investigation that was subsequently discounted by the intelligence and security agencies.[13]

The second ISC report recounted the media reports on Aswat before saying, 'After the bombings, MI5 investigated whether or not there was a "mastermind" who left the UK before the attacks. They found no intelligence to suggest that this was the case and no indication that ASWAT had any part to play in 7/7. There were some strands of intelligence, shortly after the bombings, which led MI5 to believe that ASWAT may have been involved in the attack, but these have since been discounted.' Which was it: did they find some strands of intelligence that were later discounted, or did they find no intelligence to suggest Aswat was involved? It is truly bizarre that in one single paragraph the ISC managed to totally contradict itself.

As to the allegations of Aswat being an informant, an entire paragraph is redacted before the ISC comment that, 'It has also been alleged that ASWAT was protected from prosecution by Western intelligence services, and that he was able to leave the UK despite being on a terror watch list. We have found no evidence to substantiate these allegations.'[14] If they found no evidence then what was contained in the redacted paragraph?

A Conspiracy Theory Made in America

While the ISC's comments inspire no confidence that what they are saying is true, there is a potential pitfall in the Aswat story. It is possible that he had nothing to do with 7/7 or with MI6 and that his whole story was a deliberate diversion. Just as with the Peter Power training exercise (see chapter 10) the tale of Aswat is a ready-made alternative conspiracy theory. If the mastermind behind 7/7 really was an MI6 agent then that would, of course, heavily implicate MI6 in the attacks.

This is the stuff that alternative conspiracy theorists dream of finding out, and so when John Loftus gave that interview to Fox News it was instantly copied and redistributed by all the major alternative media outlets. The consequence of this is that aside from Peter Power, Aswat is probably the most-discussed figure in connection with 7/7 in the alternative media. The Loftus interview appears in almost every independent documentary on the bombings.

As a result, the more complex and important stories of Junaid Babar, Q and Martin McDaid are largely overlooked in favour of Aswat. Their stories are detailed in full in chapters 6 to 8 of this book. There is much more information about these other men, and they are far more likely to actually be agents or assets than Aswat is. Sadly, the ease and simplicity of only have to watch one interview to learn about Aswat has led to an uncritical acceptance of Loftus' claims.

This is despite Loftus presenting no evidence in support of the assertion that Aswat had been protected from American investigators by MI6. He made some rather flippant remarks in the interview, such as being unable to remember Abu Hamza's name and referring to him as 'Captain Hook'. In general, the magnitude of what he was alleging was not clear in his manner and style.

Furthermore, it is a truly ridiculous scenario to have a terrorist MI6 agent outed on mainstream TV by a former US government official. It is the equivalent of a former CPS prosecutor going on Sky News and claiming that the mastermind behind a terrorist attack in the US was an agent for the CIA. MI6 is even more secretive than MI5, and both are more secretive than the CIA, yet the idea of a former UK government official outing a CIA agent in a TV news interview is absurd.

Beyond that, subscribers to the alternative media and believers in alternative conspiracy theories generally don't trust what former government officials say in interviews on outlets like Fox News. If anything, they reject the majority of such interviews as propaganda, if they even watch Fox News at all. Despite this subculture of scepticism towards officials and the mainstream media, Loftus' claims about Aswat were widely accepted by these same people, almost without hesitation.

However, there is another dimension to this that has been overlooked by those seeking simple conspiracy theories implicating government involvement in the attacks. At the time of Aswat's arrest in Zambia, it was reported that a second man by the same name was arrested in Pakistan. There was no followup reporting that explained what happened to this man, and never any mention of his release. As such, there were reportedly two Haroon Aswats arrested towards the end of July 2005.

This raises the possibility of a pair of doubles, or of someone using the original Aswat's identity while in Pakistan. A hint towards this was offered at the inquests in the form of mysterious phone calls from Rawalpindi, Pakistan, to mobile phones belonging to Sidique Khan. From May 9th to June 2nd 2005, only weeks before the bombings, someone was using public payphones in Rawalpindi to call Khan on a regular basis. These calls then stopped for around three weeks, before starting again on June 24th. The last call from this phone to Khan's mobile came on the afternoon of the attacks, a few hours after Khan had allegedly blown himself up.[15]

Whoever this person in Pakistan was, they always called Khan, and Khan alone. There are no similar calls from Pakistan to Tanweer, Hussain or Lindsay. Likewise, the available phone records do not show Khan ever calling out to Pakistan, all the calls were incoming. DS Mark Stuart was asked about these calls at the inquests in a highly leading manner:

> **Q.** Did you assess that these calls, therefore, were probably connected to some guidance or some means of communicating information concerned with the manufacture of the bombs and then, ultimately, their detonation?

> **A.** Yes, I think they had to be, sir.[16]

Though there was no evidence that the calls from Pakistan had anything to do with bomb-making, as far as the police were concerned 'they had to be'. The fact that Khan was ethnically Pakistani and had recently been to Pakistan does not appear to have crossed their minds as the reason for these calls. A relative, a friend or a girlfriend on the side are all potentially innocent explanations, and all are a lot more likely than that this was some master bomb-maker giving Khan instructions.

Indeed, given that the records never show Khan calling out to Pakistan, how would this theoretical master bomb maker know to call back again after the three week hiatus in contact in June? The origins of these calls was never traced to any specific individual, as indeed it would be almost impossible to do given they were made on public phones halfway around the world. Whether they were even all made by the same person cannot be stated with any certainty.

However, the pattern of calls does fit almost exactly with the original stories about the supposed mastermind then assumed to be Aswat. So it appears those early news stories were based on these mobile phone records. When Aswat, or at least the Aswat who was arrested in Zambia, turned out to have not been in Pakistan making them he was then discounted from the 7/7 investigation. So, just as Aswat was dangled in front of alternative conspiracy theorists as a double agent, the evidence behind those allegations has been recycled to try to bolster the official conspiracy theory.

Providing one final twist to the tale of Aswat/s, a young man fighting for the Taliban was killed in Afghanistan in 2003 and he was found to be carrying a passport bearing the name Haroon Rashid Aswat. So that would make it three Aswats, further complicating the question of whether the man who is currently going insane in prison has any connection to one if not two other people using the same name on the other side of the world.

Smoke and Mirrors

The question of a wider conspiracy being behind 7/7 has been a matter of great ambiguity in the years since the attacks. The official reports deny the existence of additional bombers or a terrorist overlord but the mainstream media has repeatedly talked of co-conspirators and villainous masterminds. None of these stories has ever been backed up by anything more solid than rumour, allegations, and the occasional bit of circumstantial evidence.

This process continued at the inquests with the claim that the calls from Pakistan to Sidique Khan's mobile in the weeks before the bombings 'had to be' advice on bomb-making. No evidence beyond the records of the phone calls was produced to substantiate this claim, but the mainstream media unanimously reported it anyway.

However, when it came to the testimony of Sylvia Waugh, Sue Clark and Joseph Martoccia they either did not report it, or ignored the presence of additional men in their witness statements. None of the three are particularly reliable witnesses, and therefore we cannot be sure what they did or didn't see, but similar doubts did not stop the press reporting on the claims of Richard Jones, for example.

The possibility of other men being in contact with the alleged bombers on the morning of 7/7, however tenuous, is of great significance. If there were additional men not just at one stage in the journey, but at all three stages then we should be asking who were these additional men? Handlers? Masterminds? Provocateurs? Double agents?

The three men arrested and prosecuted twice for their alleged involvement in the bombings were found innocent. In their part of this story, we can find the same contradictions between official statements as everywhere else. When they were first arrested Lord Carlile stated that, 'Anybody who imagined that this had simply been treated as four lone wolves, or a lone pack of wolves on July 7, 2005, is very wrong.'[17]

This directly contradicts the Home Office's conclusion that the four alleged bombers acted alone to carry out the attacks. Similarly, when DAC Peter Clarke announced that the men had been charged he commented, 'I firmly believe that there are other people who have knowledge of what lay behind the attacks in July 2005, knowledge that they have not shared with us. In fact, I don't only believe it. I know it for a fact.'[18]

How could Clarke know 'for a fact' that there are other people who know 'what lay behind the attacks'? If the police have any additional information proving that other people knew what was going to happen then why haven't they arrested them? Why have they spent their time and millions of pounds of public money prosecuting three men who had nothing to do with 7/7?

Were these statements by Clarke and Carlile just bluster, or alternatively an attempt to encourage people to assume the guilt of the men who had been arrested? After all, the authorities had to be seen to be holding someone responsible, as Sadeer Saleem rightly observed after he was acquitted. Or is there more to it than that? The suggestion that there was a wider conspiracy, albeit one that invariably includes the four alleged bombers, has not gone away.

Indeed, as long as the supposed conspiracy involves Khan, Tanweer, Hussain and Lindsay the authorities seem perfectly happy for the media to speculate about co-conspirators. The only exception to this is speculation that leads back to one of the probable double agents discussed in detail in later chapters. This can be seen in the contrasting responses to J7 freedom of information requests to the Foreign and Commonwealth Office (FCO) regarding Junaid Babar and Haroon

Aswat. The FCO initially rejected the request for information they held on Babar, before eventually relenting and releasing one single document that tells us almost nothing. They refused to release any other information that they had on Babar on the grounds that it would be an invasion of his privacy.

By contrast, when an identical request was filed regarding Aswat the FCO gave up a large number of documents, though naturally nothing in the files connected him to either 7/7 or MI6. My own FOIA requests to the FBI for information they had on Babar prior to his return to the US in March 2004 met with the same response, a refusal on privacy grounds.

Why were the Aswat files not protected by Aswat's right to privacy in the same way as the Babar files? Is it because with Aswat was always a diversion, a man who had nothing to do with 7/7, whose name was fed to the papers as a distraction? The absurdly public nature of Loftus' claims that Aswat was an MI6 double agent does suggest that the Aswat story was used to create a false conspiracy theory. This apparently false theory assumed the guilt of the four alleged bombers, as do all the official hints towards a wider conspiracy. As we will see in the following chapters, conspiracy theories that do not assume their guilt, or actively proclaim their innocence, have met with a very different response.

Chapter 3: The CCTV

The Metropolitan Police Service (MPS) investigation into 7/7 has been a shambles, and an expensive shambles. Codenamed Operation Theseus the process has cost around £100 million and has led to only a handful of arrests and a total of three convictions (Waheed Ali, Mohammed Shakil and Khalid Khaliq - see chapters 2 and 6). These convictions were not directly connected to 7/7 and are mirrored in the convictions of several police officers working on Theseus who were fiddling their expenses.

Much of the controversy about the police investigation has focused on the CCTV evidence, which was central to how the alleged bombers were quickly identified and then presented to the public as the culprits. Police terrorism coordinator Andy Hayman said only two days after the attacks that, 'The bombers are all certain to have been caught on many cameras during their journey to and on the Underground. They were not masked so we will end up with very good pictures that will identify them.'[1]

Similarly, on the same day deputy chief constable of the British Transport Police Andy Trotter said that, 'If they weren't suicide bombers, then they must have got on and off these trains. That means their pictures can be grabbed from CCTV cameras. The Underground network is a CCTV-rich environment, and so this is going to be an intense investigation to look at the images.'[2]

However, a few days later the police released just three still images of the alleged bombers that morning. The first shows four men entering Luton station at 7:21. Three of the men cannot be positively identified as Khan, Tanweer and Lindsay but Hussain is more easily recognisable. The other two images only show Hussain, one of him outside Boots at King's Cross at about 9:00 a.m.. The third picture purportedly shows Hussain in the ticket hall at Luton station, but it has been cropped to exclude the other three men who should be around him. The image has no date or timestamp or indeed anything that would identify when or where it was captured.

For three years those three still pictures were the only CCTV images we had from the day of 7/7 itself. In the absence of moving video from the 7th, the mainstream media often made use of video footage from the 28th June 2005, when Khan, Tanweer and Lindsay took a trip to London. They rarely made it clear that the video being shown was from a different day.

The trip on the 28th has been dubbed the 'dummy run' for the attacks, though there is no evidence supporting this claim. Only three of the alleged bombers went on the journey, and they did not split up when they reached King's Cross. They did not visit Edgware Road, Liverpool Street, Russell Square or Tavistock Square. They also took the trip down to London over an hour later than their repeat trip on 7/7. None of this makes sense if it was a 'dummy run' or reconnaissance mission.

In 2008, after the first trial of Waheed Ali, Sadeer Saleem and Mohammed Shakil more CCTV was finally released in response to Freedom of Information requests. The videos were made available for a few weeks on the MPS's website and were published on a Friday afternoon before a bank holiday weekend. As such, they received little attention in the press, and have not been publicly archived by any official body. The webpage where you could download the material is no longer accessible, though I was one of a handful of people who downloaded copies while they were still up.

In 2010, further CCTV and other video material was made available on the website of the July 7 Inquests. The new frames and sequences include brief clips of when Sidique Khan took his wife Hasina Patel to the hospital due to problems with her pregnancy on July 5th. It also shows some of the alleged bombers buying bags of ice cubes and similarly mundane items. The footage was exceptionally difficult to download as the site used a particularly rare type of streaming software. With some help, again I was able to download copies of all of these video files. As such, accessing this material has not proven to be a straightforward, simple process. It will become clear why this is the case.

What the CCTV does and doesn't show, and Why

In broad terms the CCTV does back up many of the more innocuous claims in the official narrative about the movements of the four alleged bombers that morning. The footage shows a Nissan Micra in Leeds just before 4:00 a.m., and shows the car stopping at Woodall Services on the M1 at around 4:54. A man recognisable as Shehzad Tanweer can be seen filling up the car with petrol before entering the shop to buy snacks.

Another man can be seen sitting in the front seat of the car, but it isn't clear who they are. The back seat of the car is not visible due to the camera angle. Tanweer is shown going into the shop, selecting some food, and paying at the till. Even the Home Office concede that he argued with the cashier about his change, which was confirmed in testimony at the inquests. This is truly strange behaviour for someone supposedly on his way to commit murder-suicide.

Meanwhile, a car supposedly carrying Germaine Lindsay is seen arriving at Luton train station at 5:07. Lindsay himself is not seen until 6:40. What happened in the hour and a half in between is not clear. There is no CCTV available from this period. At 6:40, Lindsay is seen wandering around the station and checking departure times before going back to the car park. He then gets into his car and moves it to another space, parking at 6:49. Shortly afterwards the Micra apparently carrying the three others down from Leeds arrives and parks next to Lindsay's car.

Around this time the video is edited in an apparent attempt to obscure the movements of a Jaguar, which is dealt with in detail below. The footage then cuts out at 6:54 and the two CCTV releases start to seriously differ. In the original release we are briefly shown someone opening the boot of the Micra at 7:01 and again at 7:03. There is then another cut, which restarts at 7:13 and shows Lindsay going into the station again and checking the departures board. The second release does not include the clips of someone opening the boot, and after cutting out at 6:54 it doesn't come back until 7:15. It shows Lindsay returning to the car, the four putting on rucksacks and then walking into the station.

Both releases show the men walking into the station just before 7:22, walking through the station and down onto the platform before catching a train. The timecodes in the original version are obscured but in the new version they can be seen throughout. The alleged bombers are then seen walking through King's Cross Thameslink station (not the underground station) at 8:25 to 8:26. Three of them are never shown again on the CCTV.

There is a brief clip of a train at Liverpool Street station arriving, people getting on and off, the train departing and pulling into the tunnel, and then a short while later smoke coming from the tunnel and people running. Bizarrely, that clip has a timecode from 7:44 to 7:48, which even accounting for an hour's error due to British Summer Time is still several minutes out from the official version.

Aside from this Liverpool Street station video there is no CCTV from 8:26 until 8:54. There is no footage showing Khan, Tanweer and Lindsay moving through King's Cross underground station, or approaching the trains they supposedly bombed, or on the platforms, or getting onto the trains, or riding on the trains. The reason for this, we are told, is that the CCTV system at King's Cross, which was a temporary system, mysteriously experienced an error. For the exact timeframe when the alleged bombers should have been there, at least according to the official story, the system was stuck on one camera.

At the inquests Detective Inspector Ewan Kindness, who was in charge of 'coordination of CCTV analysis' for Operation Theseus, outlined this fault for the first time. He was not pressed on the question of what caused the malfunction and caused the recorder to only capture video from one camera instead of all the cameras on the system. Not only that, but he tried to claim that it was 'fortunate' that this had happened because the one camera that was recording captured the four alleged bombers walking towards the underground.

At 8:54 the video begins again, and the original release shows Hasib Hussain wandering around in the King's Cross area for a few minutes, going into WH Smiths and buying something, possibly a battery. The second release included extended highlights of Hussain meandering about in central London, not really doing anything, until 9:22.

There is no footage of his reported trip to McDonalds, which would have been a bizarre choice of breakfasting locations for a fanatical Muslim suicide bomber. At the inquests we were told that once again the CCTV was not working – the manager had apparently switched it off just before Hussain entered. Though some witnesses claim to have seen Hussain on a number 91 bus, there is no footage of him boarding or riding on it, because the bus did not have any cameras.

The Home Office claim that, 'It was almost certainly at Euston that Hussain switched to the no 30 Bus'[3] but the Euston CCTV does not show Hussain getting on the number 30. There is no video of him riding on the number 30, which we were told immediately after the bombings was due to a fault with the CCTV system. There is some external CCTV from various buildings and other cameras, showing the number 30 moving from Euston to Tavistock Square. The moment of the actual explosion on the bus is only seen from interior cameras in buildings on that street, and they show nothing significant.

So, the CCTV record shows four men, almost certainly the four alleged bombers, travelling from Luton to London. Exactly what happened to three of them – Khan, Tanweer, and Lindsay – after the 'fault' in the King's Cross system at 8:26 is not shown. Hussain does appear to have been alive and moving from 8:54 to 9:22, walking around the King's Cross area, but like the others what then happened to him was not recorded.

The failure of these CCTV systems is extremely suspicious. To have one camera system fail could be considered unfortunate, to have two fail could be considered careless, but three or more looks like sabotage. Fundamentally, this means that we do not know what happened to three of these men after 8:26, and the other after 9:22. There is nothing showing the men within even 200 yards of the targets they supposedly bombed. Likewise, there is nothing showing them in the areas within 20 minutes of the bombings that they allegedly perpetrated.

The Luton Station CCTV Fiasco, part one

The most telling aspects of the CCTV are not from London, but instead are from Luton train station. The original timeline in the Home Office narrative had the four men catching the 7:40 train from Luton to King's Cross Thameslink. As many people are now aware, the 7:40 train never ran that day. This was eventually corrected by an amendment published by the Home Office but no longer available on their website. If you look for the narrative today then you will find the uncorrected version.

The amended version is not much of an improvement, and the problems extend well beyond the matter of the train time. Both versions say that the second car, the Micra from Leeds, arrived at 6:49, but the CCTV shows it arriving at 6:52. They say that the men then put on their rucksacks just after arriving, but the CCTV does not show this.

The first narrative has the four men walking into the station at 7:15, but the CCTV shows this happening just before 7:22. The Home Office document includes the original single frame of CCTV from Luton that was publicly available at the time. However, the timecode of 7:21:54 is cropped out of the Home Office version of the image, allowing them to get away with saying this happened 7 minutes earlier.

The amended narrative does include Lindsay checking the departure board for a second time at around 7:14, and then describes the men putting on their rucksacks (for a second time) and walking into the station. This is shown in the CCTV, but it only begs the question of why similar mistakes were not corrected in the amendment.

For example, there is no change to the original narrative's claim that at 7:21 the four were 'caught on CCTV together heading to the platform for the King's Cross Thameslink train.'[4] The CCTV shows them entering the station at 7:22, so obviously it does not show them in the station moving towards the platform a minute earlier. Finally, the CCTV shows the four catching a train at 7:25, not at 7:40, raising the question of how they could have got the time wrong in the first place.

The explanation for these discrepancies that has been offered is that some of the timecodes from some of the Luton station cameras may have been out by a few minutes. This is unrealistic for several reasons. A train station, whose functioning relies on accurate timing, would probably not have several cameras showing the right time, but one that was 3 minutes out and one that was 7 minutes out. Furthermore, it is clear from the continuous sections of footage across different cameras that they were all on the same central system and all had the same timecode.

What is abundantly clear from this is that whoever wrote the Home Office narrative had never actually seen the CCTV footage they were writing about. Either that or they did see the video but paid little attention to the details. The basic times and even sometimes the order of events is not borne out by the video images, which possibly explains why the CCTV has been so difficult to obtain.

There is also the question of how fast the men moved through the station to catch the 7:25 train. On June 28th, the day of the 'dummy run', it took the three of them nearly five minutes to get from entering the station to the platform to catch the train. They walked through the door at 8:10:39 and arrived on the platform at 8:15:20. On July 7th they walked through the door at 7:21:58 and arrived on the platform at 7:23:30. That is less than a third of the time – 92 seconds rather than 281. How did the men, carrying large and heavy rucksacks supposedly full of explosives, move three times quicker through the train station than they had only a few days earlier?

The Luton Station CCTV Fiasco, part two

The problems only got worse as the inquests broached the question of how the CCTV footage from Luton was recovered by the police. The official story says that on July 12th, five days after the bombings, 'By lunchtime, police (...) identify a CCTV image of 4 men with rucksacks at King's Cross. They recognise Tanweer first from a DVLA photograph. The police identify CCTV images of the same 4 at Luton Station.'[5]

The problems began at the inquests when Hugo Keith asked DI Kindness about the footage of the four walking through King's Cross around 8:25 on the morning of the 7/7. Keith asked, 'Can you recall on what day you first spotted a number of men walking through the King's Cross area, in particular through the Thameslink station carrying rucksacks?' Kindness replied, 'It was on 11 July 2005, sir.' Once again, sworn testimony contradicted the Home Office, saying that it was the 11th, not the 12th, when the four were noticed on the King's Cross CCTV.

According to DI Kindness' account, after finding the footage of the four at King's Cross they then followed the Thameslink line north 'up through Bedford and Luton and looking for fast-time CCTV recovery of those stations to see where the bombers had access to rail network.'

Q. What did you discover?

A. We were able to identify that the individuals had arrived at Luton underground station earlier that morning and boarded a train to London.

Q. Can you recall when it was that you discovered that they had boarded the railway network at Luton?

A. I think it was on the 12th, sir.[6]

So, the new story is that the four were first noticed on the King's Cross footage on the 11th and then the following day the police found the CCTV showing the four getting onto the train at Luton. A relatively plausible story, perhaps, though there is the question of how it only took them a day to review the CCTV from at least the seven stations between King's Cross Thameslink and Luton.

It is possible that they focussed their efforts on Luton because of the account of Sue Clarke, the witness from Luton station car park discussed in chapter 2. She spoke to the police on the afternoon of the 12th and so could be the reason why they then checked the tapes from Luton later that day. When counsels for the bereaved tried to get more details out of DI Kindness the coroner Lady Justice Hallett said, 'I think this is a fuss about nothing.'

It certainly proved to be a fuss about something because even with the account of Sue Clarke there is a critical problem with this version of events. A CCTV viewing log cited by a lawyer for some of the bereaved families notes that the Luton footage was watched by a DC Stephen Bain, commencing '10 July 2005, 20.00 hours'. The lawyer, Caoilfhionn Gallagher, asked DI Kindness, 'So is it possible that, in fact, that information was received on 10 July rather than 11 July, Inspector?' Kindness responded, 'That's absolutely correct. It's an error. It should have been the 10th.'[7]

This is the third different story we've been told about when, how and why the four alleged bombers were identified as possible culprits from the CCTV images. The Home Office say the four were identified at King's Cross on the 12th, then at Luton later that day. Kindness said they were identified at King's Cross on the 11th, but somehow that they were identified at Luton on the 10th. Why were the police watching the CCTV from Luton two days before the Home Office says they were, and a day before they had any reason to?

This CCTV viewing log was not actually presented as a public exhibit at the July 7 Inquests, making it very difficult to make sense of this story. A Freedom of Information request submitted by J7 was ultimately rejected on the grounds that the Metropolitan Police Service (MPS) claim they have not received a copy of it back from the inquest proceedings. In short, they are saying it has been lost.

Did someone else or something else give the MPS a reason to be in Luton before they had identified the four on the King's Cross tape? It is perhaps ironic, if not chilling, that the police investigation is codenamed Operation Theseus. The Theseus of Greek mythology fought the minotaur in the labyrinth on the isle of Crete. In order to navigate the labyrinth, he took a ball of string into the maze to lay down behind him so he would be able to follow it and find his way back out. He laid down a trail for himself to follow. Is this what the police wanted to evoke when they named their 7/7 investigation?

Possibly confirming this is Andy Hayman's statement on July 9th, another day before even DI Kindness's revised testimony, that the perpetrators 'were not masked'. If the alleged bombers were not identified on the King's Cross CCTV until the 11th, or at best the 10th, then how could Hayman be so sure they were 'not masked' on the 9th? At that point the police, at least officially, had no CCTV footage of the four alleged bombers.

The Mystery Jaguar

By far the most suspicious element in the Luton station videos, and one that has never been officially discussed in any way, is the presence of a Jaguar in Luton station car park. On June 28th, the day of the 'dummy run' that wasn't a dummy run, Khan and Tanweer arrived at Luton station at 8:05. They met up with Lindsay and went into the station, walking through the door at 8:10.

Sat in the South Eastern part of the station car park throughout this period of time is a Jaguar. It is there when the footage begins, showing Khan and Tanweer's arrival. The car can also be seen in the background of the video from a different camera as the trio are shown walking towards the station entrance. The spooky thing is that an identical-looking car was parked in the same exact spot on the morning of July 7th, at the exact time that Khan, Tanweer and Hussain arrived and met up with Lindsay.

CCTV from Luton station on 28/6 and 7/7

In both images the Jaguar can be seen in the foreground, parked on the double yellow lines at the edge of the grass verge. Though the CCTV does not make this clear, the ground actually slopes upwards towards that area and so the Jaguar has a vantage point from which it can see the rest of the car park. Specifically, in the image from the 28th, people inside the Jaguar could see across the road where two of the alleged bombers were walking on the pavement.

The image from the 7th shows the Jaguar in the exact same spot, again in the area from which the occupants of the car could watch over the rest of the car park. This time, and perhaps due to the early hour, the car is even more isolated away from the rest of the cars that are parked much nearer the station. Lindsay's Brava is the nearest car parked in the right hand row of cars directly behind the Jaguar. The vehicle in the distant background driving between the two rows of parked cars is the arriving Micra carrying Khan, Tanweer and Hussain.

The two different releases of the Luton CCTV from the morning of 7/7 are somewhat different and both versions obscure the movements of this Jaguar in slightly different ways. The 2008 release shows Lindsay moving his car to a different parking space at 6:49 to 6:50. The camera clearly shows that there are no cars parked in the South East area of the car park at this time. The video then cuts out, inexplicably, at 6:50:11 and comes back at 6:51:39. During this 88 seconds, a Jaguar that looks the same as the one in the June 28th footage has entered the car park, and parked in the South East area.

Less than a minute later, at 6:52:15, the Nissan Micra arrives from Leeds and enters the Western end of the car park. Just as it enters, the Jaguar flashes its lights, starts up, and begins moving. The footage again cuts out at 6:52:38, just as the Micra parks next to Lindsay's Brava, and as the Jaguar is driving past both cars. The video comes back at 6:53:54 and in that 76 seconds the Jaguar has disappeared. It is possible that a newly parked car a couple of spaces up from the alleged bombers is the Jaguar, though this is not certain. The quality of the CCTV images makes it impossible to tell, or for that matter to figure out the registration number on the suspect car.

The second release of video from Luton station car park accomplishes much the same effect through a slightly different method. In the 2010 release we are shown Lindsay moving his car from a different camera at the opposite end of the car park. From this angle it is impossible to tell that the South Eastern part of the car park is empty (i.e. that no Jaguar is parked there). This time, the footage cuts out at 6:49:52, but again comes back at 6:51:39 and it comes back on the same camera as the original release.

Once more, the Jaguar is sitting pretty and waiting, and the footage continues to show the same as the original release – the other three arriving and the Jaguar starting up as soon as they enter the car park. The same second edit of 76 seconds that makes it impossible to see where the Jaguar went was also made to this second release. So, by using two different cameras at two different ends of the car park, and some rather obvious editing, the police have managed to obscure what happened to the Jaguar.

We know it arrived sometime during the first edit of 88 seconds, despite the editor's efforts at hiding this in the 2010 release. The later release can still be accessed through an official website, unlike the 2008 release where the Jaguar's arrival is more obvious. We do not know when the Jaguar left the car park, but fundamentally it was there on two separate days, at two separate times, that just so happened to coincide with when the alleged bombers from Leeds arrived at the station. Clearly, the chances are that the Jaguar was somehow connected to those men.

That it was parked in the exact same position on both days, and that our attention was drawn to activity taking place elsewhere on the screen only fuels these suspicions. That the police went to such lengths to try to obscure its movements all but confirms that they were trying to hide the connection between the Jaguar and the alleged bombers. That this has never been discussed by the mainstream media, despite the televisual nature of the story, just illustrates how uninterested they are in asking serious questions.

Who Moved the Cameras?

There is one further aspect to this mystery. The videos from both June 28th and July 7th that clearly show the Jaguar are both from the same camera – number 26, which is attached to a lamppost on the Eastern edge of Luton station car park. But the videos, shot only days apart, do not show images from the same angle. The following CCTV captures show that in the first image, from the 28th, the camera is pointed more to the right, slightly more North, than in the second image, from the 7th. Did someone move the camera in between the 28th of June, when it captured the alleged bombers (the highlighted car in the upper right centre) and the 7th of July?

Curiously, both images appear to have multiple electronic stamps on them, one in the top left saying 'camera 26' and the time and date. But the image from June 28th also bears a mark saying 'CAM 10' and both have the serial number 3-10-41071 down the right side. In the first image, from June 28th, this number is partially cut off at the top of the frame, suggesting that the camera may not have moved at all and that the images have been digitally cropped. Alternatively, perhaps the cameras ran into two separate systems that added two separate electronic stamps. In the 7/7 video the time code on the left is slightly lower than in the June 28th video. This suggests a small problem on the 28th that cut off a thin strip from the top of the video.

CCTV from 28/6, Eastern part of Luton Station car park

CCTV from 7/7, Eastern part of Luton station car park showing how the camera was re-positioned since 28/6

If we look at the footage from both days from camera 24, at the opposite end of the carpark (opposite page), we are provided with some answers. In the first picture you can just glimpse the parked Jaguar in the background, partially obscured by the footbridge with the triangular frame. The 28th June video also bears a second camera number, and the incomplete serial number down the right side. This seems to confirm that the cameras did run on two systems that put two electronic stamps on the images. The same problem with the top of the serial number being cut off can also be seen on this camera.

CCTV from 28/6, Western part of Luton station car park

CCTV from 7/7, Western part of Luton station car park, which was also re-positioned between 28/6 and 7/7

However, this doesn't resolve the problem of why the two images from the first camera, camera 26, do not show the same scene when the same supposedly static CCTV camera captured them only nine day apart. Strangely, this issue of the camera being moved also seems to affect camera 24, which also shows a different angle across the two days. The other cameras on the system, showing the entrance to the station, inside the station and the platforms, do not show any difference in angles across the two days. It is only the two cameras at either end of the car park, i.e. those cameras that could most easily be accessed by someone outside of the station.

Exactly who this was and why they apparently altered the angles of these CCTV cameras is not known. What is clear is that both cameras were pointing more towards the station on the 28th of June than they were nine days later on the 7th of July. The fence and pavement running between the car park and the road in front of the station make this easy to see. It may be significant that on the 28th the alleged bombers did not park in the same places as on the 7th, but that does not explain moving the cameras. They were apparently moved after capturing the alleged bombers on the 28th, to angles that made no practical difference to them capturing the alleged bombers on the 7th. So who moved the cameras, and why?

The only appreciable effect that I can see is that it means that the Jaguar that is parked in the foreground in both images does not appear in the exact same place on both videos, which would have made it easier to notice. Because the camera has been moved the Jaguar, in relative terms, has moved from left of centre in the June 28th CCTV to right of centre in the July 7th video. As tempting an explanation as this might be, this does not explain why camera 24 at the opposite end of the car park was also adjusted, because the video from there barely shows the Jaguar or that area of the car park.

Closed Conspiracy TV

The CCTV evidence from and around 7/7 has been the focus of much debate and controversy. The drib drab, incremental process by which the images and video footage have been released, and the failure of the state or the mainstream media to archive this evidence, have only contributed to this. The initial image from Luton, released just days after the attacks, has been accused of being a fake.

On close examination it is not a particularly convincing image. It apparently shows (from left to right) Hasib Hussain, Germaine Lindsay, Sidique Khan and Shehzad Tanweer. The latter three aren't positively identifiable, though it probably is them. There are also a number of anomalies, such as Tanweer's left leg trailing away into nothing, and the railings behind the men appearing to go through Khan's head and in front of his left arm.

CCTV from 7/7, entrance to Luton station

As evidence in favour of the official narrative it is extremely weak, though this did not stop it being used as such by the major media. However, this argument was not enough for some people, who instead claimed conclusively that the picture was a fake. In constructing this argument some of the alternative conspiracy theorists have looked for corroboration from any source they can find.

For example, in Nick Kollerstrom's book *Terror on the Tube* he cites a 'professional image-analyst' and quotes a series of comments supposedly proving the original Luton CCTV image is faked. The footnotes reveal that the comments are being quoted from an anonymous posting on an internet forum.[8] Perhaps the poster is or was a professional image analyst, but perhaps they are not. To cite such loosely sourced information as central evidence only shows that in fact, there is no graphical professional or expert willing to put their real name to the claim that the original Luton image is a fake.

Similar claims have been made by other alternative conspiracy theorists. Richard D Hall is the presenter of a 'truth' TV show that is set on a computer-generated spaceship that is supposedly orbiting the earth. While interviewing Kollerstrom about the CCTV image, Hall claimed that, 'All photographic experts agree, or photoshop experts, that photograph is a fake, it's a forgery.'[9] This is simply untrue, though that did not stop Kollerstrom agreeing with Hall on the show.

Likewise, the film *7/7 Ripple Effect* calls the image a 'very badly doctored official single frame, time-stamped photo'. It goes on to claim that the authorities, 'can't show them moving, because it has been faked, that's why they show only one single frame still photo.' Showing how this is something of a closed shop of conspiracy theorists, Kollerstrom devotes great lengths of his book to extolling the virtues of *7/7 Ripple Effect*, and it is the only 7/7 film that Richard D Hall has shown on his TV show. Indeed, *7/7 Ripple Effect 2* (the sequel) premiered on Hall's show.

Fuller sequences of CCTV were released in 2008 and 2010 that show the alleged bombers moving, and from camera angles where they are more in focus and easier to identify. So how did the alternative conspiracy theorists react to this new evidence that contradicted their prior claims? They either pretended it didn't exist or dismissed it as a fake. The third edition of *Terror on the Tube* was published in May 2011, months after new edits of the 2008 footage had been released in late 2010. In the book Kollerstrom writes of 'CCTV images which no one has seen' when in fact we have seen them.

Likewise, in the show where Richard Hall claimed that the original single frame was a 'forgery' the original image is shown, and suspicious bits highlighted, but not the full moving sequence around that single frame, which had been available for three years. Nor did he elect to include the somewhat different edit of the Luton footage that had been available for several months. Incidentally, or perhaps not, the show was one of a pair of programmes that coincided with the release of the third edition of Kollerstrom's book.

Similarly John Hill, the maker of the *7/7 Ripple Effect* films, has also been interviewed on Richard Hall's show. In his 2007 film he argued that the CCTV image was fake, but in his 2012 film he chose to completely ignore the additional CCTV releases. Instead, he used a clip of Nick Kollerstrom talking about how the CCTV was faked.

Hypocrisy

This behaviour, whereby exaggerated and unsubstantiated claims are made about evidence having been faked, poses several problems. As we will see in the following chapter, it leaves those alternative conspiracy theorists wide open to counter-attack by the mainstream media. It also means that the evidence that is actually contained in the released CCTV has largely been ignored, because this clique of 'truth' advocates has dismissed it all as fake.

This is, for example, why the mystery Jaguar and the editing of its movements were not discovered by Nick Kollerstrom or John Hill or

Richard Hall. They had already decided that there was nothing to find in the CCTV footage and so they never really looked at it. Instead, the discovery was made by the July 7th Truth Campaign, who have raised doubts about the authenticity of the CCTV images but never exaggerated that into a positive claim of fakery. The question of the cameras being moved is my own development from J7's original discovery, and has been completely overlooked by Hill, Hall and Kollerstrom.

However, in a demonstration of utter hypocrisy, all three men jumped on the Jaguar bandwagon and tried to fit this new evidence into their existing mishmash of claims and conclusions. They all pretended that they hadn't ever dismissed this CCTV as a meaningless fake, and turned it into another means of claiming that they were right all along.

The same basic theory about the Jaguar was expounded by all three of the alternative conspiracy theorists that have declared that the Luton CCTV is fake. Shortly after J7's discovery, Richard Hall devoted a significant proportion of one of his shows to 7/7, featuring the new CCTV evidence. He concluded his coverage by saying that, 'It is suspected by some that the driver of the Jaguar was none other than terror drill maestro Peter Power.'[10]

Similarly, in his book Kollerstrom devotes several pages to the Jaguar but focuses on the idea it parked next to the cars of the alleged bombers. The book largely ignores the way in which the CCTV obscures the Jaguar's suspiciously timed arrival just after Lindsay moved his car and just before the car from Leeds arrived. Kollerstrom asks, 'Did Peter Power then own a Jaguar?'[11]

The same basic insinuation – that the Jaguar had something to do with Peter Power – was made in the second *7/7 Ripple Effect* film. The only mention of the Jaguar comes in the section on Peter Power, as part of the theory that the four alleged bombers were recruited as part of his terrorism training exercise (see chapters 10 and 11). This clique of Hill, Hall and Kollerstrom have tried to turn the question of the Jaguar and the Luton CCTV from one of fakery, into one that happily merges with their desired theory about Peter Power.

As discussed in chapter 11, there has never been any evidence supporting this theory that the alleged bombers were recruited by Power as part of his exercise. There is also no evidence connecting the Jaguar to Power except wishful thinking on the part of alternative conspiracy theorists. Instead of admitting that they were wrong to decry and dismiss the Luton CCTV evidence and then undertaking a sober analysis of what it contained, they simply folded the Jaguar into their desired version of events. Exactly where they stand on the authenticity of the Luton footage is difficult to say, precisely because they have made quite contradictory statements about it. This has muddied the waters of the unofficial investigations, and contributed greatly to the confusion and apathy about 7/7. For that, Hill, Hall and Kollerstrom bear some responsibility.

Beyond the Controversy

The question of the reliability and accuracy of the Luton CCTV system was brought up at the inquests but in a largely misleading way. When DI Kindness was on the stand, and as they watched the CCTV frames from June 28th, Hugo Keith commented that, 'there's been a great deal of comment on certain websites and on the internet about the accuracy of that, amongst other pictures, the pictures of the three men outside the station on 28 June. There's been comment about the accuracy of the CCTV that we've seen there.'

There has been some commentary about the authenticity of the June 28th footage, but by far the most controversial and most discussed footage is that from July 7th itself. Why Keith was discussing the June 28th images, but not the July 7th images, is not at all clear. Nonetheless, he asked DI Kindness 'Do you have any grounds whatsoever for doubting the accuracy of the images recorded and retained by the CCTV system?' Kindness did not explicitly answer the question but responded, 'This CCTV system? 100 per cent confident, sir.'[12]

There was no discussion of the mystery Jaguar, and so as far as we know the car and its occupants were never traced. Just like the additional men apparently seen at every stage of the alleged bombers journey, this suggestion of a wider conspiracy was never followed up. It may be significant that the more reliable of the three witnesses was Sue Clarke (see chapter 2), who says she saw one or two extra men in Luton station car park in and around the cars of the alleged bombers. This is some time after the Jaguar had arrived at Luton, and so may be connected.

Similarly, there was no discussion at the inquests of why there were multiple faults in multiple CCTV systems that meant that the alleged bombers were never seen within 20 minutes of their supposed targets. No one seemed to notice that two of the cameras at Luton station had been moved between the 28th and the 7th, so there were no questions about that. The issue of when, how and why the police first got the video from Luton was pursued, but to a completely unacceptable conclusion.

Many of these questions have also been overlooked by the unofficial investigations and the web-based 'alternative' media. The only significant issue they have picked up on, the Jaguar, has mostly just been filed under 'things to arbitrarily connect to Peter Power'. This is also unacceptable, given the noise these very same people and very same media have made about the failings of the mainstream media and the official investigations. To simply replicate the same shoddy standards of proof in their own work as they criticize in the official account is a categorical error of judgment.

So what of the claim that the original Luton CCTV image is a fake? In my opinion it is simply a poorly replicated digital image. In any CCTV images released to the public there are at least three stages of production and reproduction. The first is the camera, capturing the images from the light bouncing off the things it can see. If the camera is of poor quality, then it will capture poor quality images. Second, there is the recording device, sat in an office somewhere converting the live feeds into recorded videos. There is tremendous variance in the quality of these devices, as there are with cameras.

Third, there is the process by which the recorded video on the office machine is reproduced by the police. Whether it is burned to disk or, as I once saw, the police simply photograph the paused video on the monitor, that is one more step that can reduce quality, and introduce anomalies and inaccuracies. If the image is then rendered as part of a TV news broadcast then that is yet another step, though one that is less likely to produce such problems.

So, at Luton we could have an video stream shot by a mediocre camera, recorded by a mediocre recorder, reproduced imperfectly and then uploaded to the MPS website. That the resulting image is of poor quality should actually come as no surprise, though of course it is still ridiculous to use such a poor image as evidence. Indeed, the image is so poor, so unconvincing when subject to the slightest scrutiny, that we are left the possibility that the whole question of it being faked was a trap set on purpose. This possibility is explored in further detail in chapter 5. Likewise, we must bear in mind that however spooky the Jaguar might seem it too could be a deliberate diversion. After all, we cannot really go any further in investigating it, because the number plate and occupants cannot be identified in any way.

The angle open to us is one I have tried to pursue. I filed a Freedom of Information request to the MPS asking for the sequences of CCTV that have been edited out (from cameras 24 and 26) of the existing releases from Luton. Initially my request was rejected on the grounds that the footage was already in the public domain, and I was provided with a link to the website of the July 7 Inquests. This being a complete nonsense, I registered a complaint and despite numerous follow-ups they have refused to provide me with an answer and have stopped responding to my emails.

At base, beyond the controversy, the disputes, the allegations of forgery and the conspiracy theories, the CCTV evidence against the four alleged bombers is non-existent. All the available footage shows is a group of four young men taking a trip to London on the morning of 7th July 2005. The exact process by which this evidence was found and made part of the conclusion that the four were guilty of these bombings is a story of contradictions.

Why and how did the police obtain the CCTV footage from Luton on July 10th, just three days after the bombings? According to DI Kindness, the man overseeing the CCTV part of the police investigation, this was a day before the men were even identified from the King's Cross video. It is also two days before the Home Office narrative say they were identified from that video. Did someone else tell the police where to look? If they did, then did that someone have anything to do with the mystery Jaguar and the moving CCTV cameras at Luton station?

Chapter 4: Suicide Bombings

The story told by the police, the Home Office and the security services fundamentally relies on the idea that the attacks of 7/7 were suicide bombings. They say that four men knowingly carried the bombs to the targets and deliberately blew themselves up and killed another 52 people. While many aspects of the official story have been subject to speculation in the mainstream media, this one has passed by almost unquestioned.

The possibility of them being duped somehow was raised by The Mirror only 9 days after the attacks in an article titled 'Was It Suicide?'. The article suggests that the four were told the bombs were on timers but that some shady mastermind double crossed them and gave them bombs that exploded as soon as they pressed the buttons. A fiendish scheme, no doubt, but also a distinct possibility.

The Mirror wrote that 'the evidence is compelling: The terrorists bought return rail tickets, and pay and display car park tickets, before boarding a train at Luton for London. None of the men was heard to cry "Allah Akhbar!" - "God is great" - usually screamed by suicide bombers as they detonate their bomb. Their devices were in large rucksacks which could be easily dumped instead of being strapped to their bodies. They carried wallets containing their driving licences, bank cards and other personal items. Suicide bombers normally strip themselves of identifying material.'[1]

However, this was the last time any such argument was made in the mainstream media. At no point has any article gone as far as the Mirror in actually showing how easy it is to come up with alternatives that fit at least as much of the evidence as the official story. A few newspaper articles since then have mentioned some of the outstanding questions and alternative conspiracy theories, as have several TV shows (see chapter 5), but never made such an argument in favour of an alternative. Of course, the Mirror did not follow up on this story in any depth.

There is a more basic question: were the four men even on the four vehicles that were bombed? Three trains left King's Cross and then exploded but there is no CCTV of three of the men walking towards, getting on or riding on those trains. Similarly, there is no footage of Hasib Hussain approaching, boarding or riding on the number 30 bus. Witnesses to their presence are few and far between, and like Richard Jones (see chapter 1) they are highly questionable. However, there is perhaps an even more basic question that threatens to undermine the whole official story.

What Type of Explosive?

Exactly what kind of explosive was used in the 7/7 bombings has been a contentious matter. It is critical to the official story. In any murder inquiry finding out the precise weapon that was used to kill is crucial. In the initial days after 7/7 the mainstream media were unanimously reporting that high explosives or even military explosives had been used in the bombings. Some papers even named the explosive as either C4 (Composition 4) or RDX (Research Department Explosive or Royal Demolition Explosive).

That left open the question of where four alleged suicide bombers got their hands on such explosives but according to the New York Times, 'British intelligence officials have asked their counterparts elsewhere in Europe to scour military stockpiles and commercial sites for missing explosives.'[2] Another possible source of military grade explosives that was suggested in media reports were arms dealers or terrorists in the Balkans.

This reporting continued until a couple of days after the police discovered the 'bomb factory' in Alexandra Grove and the Nissan Micra in Luton station car park. Then the mainstream media unanimously forgot the old story and reported the new one, that the bombs were homemade. However, even the official reports are not certain about this 'fact'. The Home Office narrative of 2006 says that, 'Expert examination continues but it appears the bombs were homemade'.[3] Why was examination still going on almost a year later? Finding explosive residues and analyzing them is not an especially difficult task.

The ISC's first report is somewhat more certain, even though it was published at the exact same time as the Home Office narrative. It says, 'Post-incident forensic analysis has shown that the explosions were caused by home-made organic peroxide-based devices, packed into rucksacks.'[4] So the 'post-incident forensic analysis' was complete and conclusive but the 'expert examination' was not?

The current explanation is that HMTD was used as an initiator or trigger explosive and the main charge was made up of a mix of concentrated hydrogen peroxide and piperine, a substance found in black pepper (and, according to *Newsnight*, in powdered Masala Spice). This is a unique and unprecedented explosive mixture, never seen before in the history of bombs. This explanation is doubtful for several reasons.

The first reason is that the story has changed so much over time, from military explosives to homemade explosives and then from one recipe to another. There are many contradictory statements on whether HMTD, TATP or some other peroxide-based explosive made up the main charge. The idea of piperine, black pepper and/or Masala spice being part of the recipe was not mentioned until years after the bombings, even though they should have had the evidence within days (or at most weeks).

There are significant differences between the testimonies on what explosives were found and where, depending on which proceedings you look at. Some of this testimony was given during the inquest into the death of Jean Charles de Menezes. A former army man who works as an explosives officer for the MPS was known as 'Codename NEIL' at the Menezes inquest. He said that the main charge of the explosive was a form of organic peroxide, but said that in his army experience he had never used peroxide based explosives. NEIL said that, 'If you were to put your hand on a small amount of organic peroxide explosive it can cause it to detonate. So it's just far too unsafe for us to manufacture.' Far too unsafe for an army explosives expert, but safe enough for an amateur home-based bomb-maker?

NEIL went on to say that 'there was evidence of TATP explosive at the bomb-making factory in Leeds' and how he had carried out controlled explosions on 'pure' peroxide explosives found in the Nissan Micra at Luton station. He confirmed that by 'pure' he meant 'TATP explosives.' The explosives found, and destroyed, in Luton consisted of another rucksack that contained 12 small explosive devices. In the opinion of NEIL and many media commentators these smaller bombs were for self-defence.[5] But if that is true then why were they left behind?

DAC John McDowell elaborated on this, saying that, 'In the bomb factory in Leeds that was discovered, we found TATP literally sprayed around the premises and on the floor.'[6] Why would the alleged bombers have taken the time and incredible risk to spray an entire flat with this highly volatile substance? Indeed, if simply standing on it could set it off then how could they do it?

McDowell went on to talk of the 'very great magnitude' of 'explosive left behind', describing it as 'a bathful and more of the main charge'.[7] This is in keeping with numerous press reports and video items saying that the alleged bomber brewed up their bomb mixture in the bathtub, usually complete with pictures from inside the 'bomb factory'. The pictures show a brown sludge inside numerous circular Tupperware containers, and a bathtub with a more liquid brown sludge in the bottom.

In contrast to McDowell's testimony DCI Gregory Purser, was only asked about the sludge in the bath. He confirmed that, 'Examination indicated that it was not explosives. Porton Down had indicated that it was not a biological substance but they weren't sure what it was, and had said it might be some kind of insecticide'.[8] So was the concoction in the bath TATP or some kind of insecticide? All the testimony from 2008 described TATP as being widely present at the bomb factory and in the Nissan Micra in Luton. None of the witnesses testified to the presence of traces of TATP at the actual explosion sites.

By the time of the July 7 Inquests in 2010-11 the story had changed again. The court heard from Forensic Explosives Laboratory expert Dr Clifford Todd who only spoke of TATP in order to clarify that, 'At Russell Square, none was found, no traces of HMTD or TATP or, indeed, any other explosive was found.' Todd went on to say that tiny traces of HMTD were found at Tavistock Square, Edgware Road and Aldgate, but that no piperine was found anywhere in London. Indeed, according to Todd, no trace of the main explosive was found at any of the explosion sites.

This is wholly unacceptable. While the bus explosion was a large, outdoor scene making it harder to preserve and locate evidence, three of the explosions were on tube trains. There should have been traces of the main explosive somewhere on those trains. This is particularly true of homemade explosives, because as an imperfect mixture they are less likely to be wholly consumed in the detonation.

Furthermore, if only HMTD was found at the explosion sites, but TATP was found in the Micra in Luton and the flat in Leeds, then what connects the different locations? No trace of the substance found in Luton and Leeds was found in London, at least according to the sworn testimony of the different experts and police officers involved in the case. That the actual type of explosive, the weapon used in this mass murder, remains unknown after more than 7 years is a sad indictment of this critical part of the official investigation.

Todd went on to talk about the 'bulk explosive' that was 'left behind' at the supposed bomb factory. The plastic tubs of brown sludge contained at least two different mixtures, a lighter-coloured type and a darker-coloured type. Todd outlined that, 'The darker brown material, after various tests done at the laboratory, was found not to be energetic, so would not work as an explosive. The lighter, sandy-coloured material, that was shown, in at least one specific case, to be a high explosive.'[9] So of these numerous tubs of different coloured sludge, adding up to dozens of kilos of material, they only found that it had explosive properties in 'at least one specific instance'.

Forensic links to the Micra and the 'Bomb Factory'

There are significant problems with the evidence connecting the three locations – Leeds, Luton and London – in terms of the bombs' composition. There are equally huge problems with the evidence connecting the alleged bombers to the three locations. The bomb sites themselves are dealt with in detail below.

Exhibits presented at the July 7 inquests detailed what the police found in the Nissan Micra in Luton station car park, and how they were connected to the alleged bombers. By some distance Khan's fingerprints and DNA were the most commonly found, with traces of Tanweer and Hussain only found on a few items. All of the items linked to all three men were essentially trivial, such as plastic bags, plastic pens, sticky tape, a water bottle and sweet wrappers.[10]

The implied official story is that the four men assembled their bombs in the boot of the Micra in the car park at Luton. However, none of the four men, not even Khan, were linked by fingerprints or DNA to the more suspicious items such as batteries, light bulbs, cool boxes and the small explosives. Beyond the lack of positive evidence for this story, it is inherently ridiculous. No would-be suicide bomber would assemble their bombs in the car park of a busy commuter station, in front of CCTV cameras and members of the public.

The story at the alleged bomb factory was more complicated. The inquest exhibits detailing forensic links of note show that at 18 Alexandra Grove, Hussain's traces were the most common. All four men's fingerprints and DNA were found, but again the items linked to them were innocuous. Saucepans, extension cables, plastic bags, scissors, household appliances and CDs are all items with completely innocent uses.[11]

By contrast, none of the tubs of brown sludge that supposedly made up the main explosive were linked to any of the four alleged bombers. There is no reason for them to have always worn gloves, and it is highly unlikely that they would have been able to produce 20 tubs of the stuff without leaving a DNA trace on some of the containers. The MPS did link Hussain by DNA to one very small container of HMTD, but contradicting the police testimony at the Menezes inquest none of the July 7 inquest exhibits mentioned TATP anywhere in the flat.

A 9-volt battery was found in Tavistock Square showing signs of 'possible explosive damage' and some short wiring was found at Edgware Road and Aldgate. A small device that is redacted in the publicly available inquest exhibits was found at the 'bomb factory', made up of a halogen light bulb, wiring and HMTD wrapped in tin foil. This device was not linked to any of the four alleged bombers, but Clifford Todd presumed it to be the bomb initiator. Some other items such as rubber gloves and respirators were linked to Khan, but these exhibits are not available even in a redacted form.

From all this, Todd explained that, 'the conclusion that it's likely that it was HMTD and hydrogen peroxide and pepper comes from the accumulation of all the other evidence from Alexandra Grove and the various components that were physical items that were actually found from Russell Square and, indeed, the other scenes.' Note, he only says 'likely', leaving this latest version of the bombs open to further changes at a later date.

Even this is overstating the case. None of the four alleged bombers were linked to the small bombs in the Micra in Luton or the 'bulk explosive' in the flat in Leeds. If these were homemade, handmade bombs then the men would have been handling them, which would have left detectable traces. Likewise, if these were homemade bombs then it is extremely unlikely that they would have been entirely consumed in the blasts, so they should have left detectable traces at the explosion sites. In short, the entire official story of what the bombs were made of and how they were made is drawn from items and evidence that they did not link to the four alleged bombers or in most cases any of the four bomb sites.

Identifying Property at the Bomb Sites

The Home Office account from 2006 details how and when property belonging to the four men was found at the various bomb sites. There is also a timeline in the second ISC report answering their own question of 'how were the bombers identified?'. There is a conflict between the two timelines, a conflict that is only exacerbated by testimony at the inquests.

A visa credit card was found at the Edgware Road bomb site bearing the name 'Mr M S Khan'. Some of Khan's property had already been found at Aldgate, and so according to the Home Office narrative, on July 8th 'At 23.59, Khan [was] identified as the account holder for a credit card found at a second scene, Edgware Road.'[12] So according to the Home Office the card was found on the 8th and checks performed later that day identified it as Khan's. This is not the story told by the ISC. Their timeline says the card was found at 19:50 on July 8th, but that the message containing details on the cardholders was not collated until 23:59 on the following day, July 9th. So which was it?

DC Malcolm Wilson, who was the forensic scene examiner for the MPS at Edgware Road, testified as to when this card belonging to Khan was found.

> **Q.** Once the deceased had been formally removed from their locations, was a credit card found in the near vicinity of the underneath of the westbound train under the blast hole?
>
> **A.** Yes, there was.
>
> **Q.** Was that a visa card, MW85, in the name of Mr S Khan?
>
> **A.** Yes, it was.
>
> **Q.** The card was entangled with human debris near the location of the explosion?
>
> **A.** That is correct.[13]

The problem is that the bodies of the deceased were removed on July 9th, so if the visa card wasn't found until after that happened then both the ISC and the Home Office reports are wrong. Also, note that name on the card given at the inquests is 'Mr S Khan', not 'Mr M S Khan' as in the ISC report. Wilson went on to explain how another bank card in Khan's name was found on July 13th, a Halifax debit card. This find is not mentioned by either the Home Office or ISC reports. Another Halifax card in Khan's name had already been found at Aldgate on the evening of the bombings, according to the statement of DC Richard Hall.[14]

Why did Khan have two Halifax bank cards? Why would he have given one to Tanweer to take to Aldgate? The Home Office report says that in fact Khan's property was found at three different sites – Aldgate, Edgware Road and Tavistock Square. For some reason they missed out the Piccadilly Line though according to Hugo Keith's opening statement at the inquests Khan's mobile phone 'was recovered from the tunnel between King's Cross and Russell Square'.[15] Also, at least one if not two of Khan's mobile phones were found at Edgware Road, depending on which of DS Stuart's testimonies you read. As such, Khan's property was, officially, recovered from all four bomb sites.

This is not only contrary to the behaviour of most Islamic suicide bombers, it also smacks of planted evidence, albeit not very sensibly planted evidence. The amount of Khan's property that was allegedly found – two mobile phones at Edgware Road, another phone at Russell Square, numerous bank cards and other ID at both Edgware and Aldgate – is vast. If we assume the official version, that Khan and the others left evidence at the scene to identify themselves, then why did they kill themselves? Why not, as Anders Breivik and many previous terrorists have done, carry out an atrocity and use the resulting media exposure and trial to project their ego and promote their views?

The whole story about leaving ID behind to ensure that they were blamed for the attacks doesn't ring true. From the four men's perspective they couldn't know that the CCTV would fail while they were still 25 minutes away from their supposed targets. There is no reason for them to have been so concerned about being identified that they each of them took along some of Sidique Khan's property.

While other documents belonging to the three other men were found, the most significant problem is the condition that the various items were in when they were found. Even at the inquests it was stressed how, 'some of the documents appeared not to have been as damaged as you might have expected.' No witness saw any of the four men throwing identifying documents on the floor before setting off a bomb. As such, this was quite a problem for explosives expert Clifford Todd to try to explain. He was asked if there was a 'sensible explanation' and he replied, 'Well, no, I would still say that it suggests to me that they'd been placed - that they were neither in the rucksack nor on the person of the perpetrator simply because, in a lot of cases, they weren't as damaged as they should have been, had they been that close.'

Todd went on to guess that 'it would only take, you know, a separate carrier bag, for instance, with those materials in, just to be put next - put down next to the rucksack or maybe slightly away from it to one side.' Lady Justice Hallett, completely departing from her powers and responsibilities as laid in out in the Coroners and Justice Act, actively encouraged this speculation, asking, 'you'd say that might suggest a concerted effort to ensure identification?' Todd replied, saying it was 'the most likely suggestion that I could give for that being the case.' In summary, Todd doesn't know, Hallett doesn't know, but they aren't willing to entertain the possibility of planted evidence.

Modelling the Unknown

That leaves the question of whether the men were at those locations at the times of the explosions and whether their bodies were found at the scenes. Officially, of course they were, but even the Home Office give cause for doubt in their report. It says, 'DNA has identified the four at the four separate bombsites. The impact on their bodies suggests that they were close to the bombs.'[16] The ISC's timeline of how the men were identified says that on July 10th 'Pathologist reports suggest that the men later identified as HUSSAIN, KHAN and LINDSAY were in possession of, or in close proximity to, the bombs at the times of the explosions.' The following day, 'Pathologist report suggests that the man later identified as TANWEER was in possession of the bomb at the time of the explosion.'

None of the official reports explicitly say that there is hard evidence that the men were in possession of the bombs at the times of the explosions. They only say that this is 'suggested' by the evidence, and sometimes that the four were just 'close to' to the bombs, as could be said for any innocent victim of a bomb explosion. This cryptic language should not inspire confidence.

Perhaps the most astounding revelation of all at the July 7 inquests is that no internal post-mortems were performed on any of the victims of the bombings. This was a major limitation on the inquests' ability to make judgments on, for example, whether people could have survived had emergency services been better equipped and organized. As a result, nothing and no one were blamed.

This lack of internal post-mortems also meant that there was little detailed information to feed into computer models of the explosions. Despite the existence of models of the explosions that had been done shortly after the attacks, in August 2010 Colonel Peter Mahoney of Porton Down was commissioned to do a new modelling study. Why the earlier models were not used isn't clear, but Mahoney's study was commissioned specifically for the inquests.

Mahoney was asked to look at whether 18 of the victims who were assessed as having still been alive after the explosion could have survived. Mahoney explained that there were numerous caveats, such as 'there was no invasive post-mortem in any case', 'X-ray examination was limited, as you've just said, to fluoroscopy' and 'in some cases the photographs were difficult to interpret'. He also said that because the given peroxide and piperine recipe was previously unknown, 'we had to make assumptions on the explosive output of the device.' Mahoney was not kidding. For the computer modelling they simulated the explosion using the mathematically equivalent amount of TNT, about 2 kg, but how did they come to this amount? If they didn't know the properties of the given explosive then they could not assess what would be the equivalent amount of TNT.

Furthermore, if these bombs were made, as they are so fond of telling us, from things you can buy on the high street then why didn't they whip up a batch and find out the properties of this unknown explosive? If the plastic tubs of brown sludge did contain explosive then they could have taken a sample from that and replicated it to find out exactly what it did when detonated on a rucksack-bomb sized scale. Instead of doing any of this, Mahoney admitted most of these limitations before offering his conclusion that none of the victims could have survived the explosions.

Alongside Mahoney's models and those done back in 2005 by the Defence Science and Technology Laboratory, the MPS also put together detailed pictorial diagrams of the explosion sites. They are based on eyewitness statements and three of the four show the locations of all the people within the carriages and the bus at the time of the explosion. The one exception to this is the Piccadilly Line.

The Piccadilly Line

The Home Office narrative says that, 'On the Piccadilly Line, Germaine Lindsay was in the first carriage as it travelled between King's Cross and Russell Square. It is unlikely that he was seated. The train was crowded, with 127 people in the first carriage alone, which makes it difficult to position those involved. Forensic evidence suggests the explosion occurred on or close to the floor of the standing area between the second and third set of seats. The explosion killed 27 people including Lindsay, and injured over 340.'[17]

Initial media reports had the explosion in the Piccadilly Line train happening in the standing area between the first set of double doors in the first carriage. This was then changed, possibly as a result of Rachel 'North's account in her diary for the BBC, to the standing area between the second set of double doors. The MPS diagram shows the explosion in this area, but it does not show the location of Lindsay or the 26 victims of the blast.

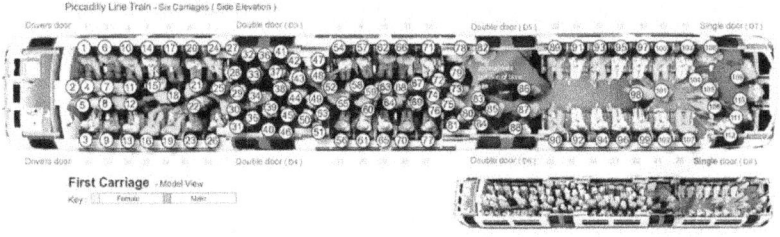

First Carriage - Model View

One of the immediate problems with this is that the train is clearly at crush capacity, but it shows 112 people in the carriage. Even if they were all injured in the explosion, it would take almost another two full carriages of people to all be injured to get up to the narrative's number of 340. Similarly, if we add the 112 survivors to the 27 people who were killed, we get 139 people in total in the carriage, rather than the 127 the narrative says were there. If we compare the above image to the MPS's diagram of where the victims bodies were found then we are presented with an even more critical problem.

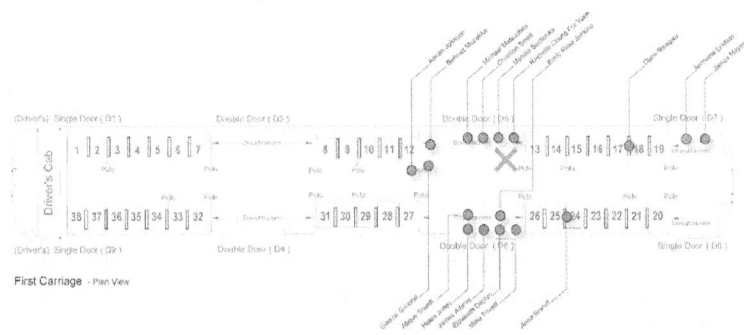

First Carriage - Plan View

According to this, Lindsay's body was found on the right side of the image, at the rear of the carriage. The X marks the centre of the explosion and most of the victims' bodies were found in that area, so how did Lindsay's body end up so far away? According to the original MPS diagram there are numerous people sitting and standing in the space in between the centre of the explosion and where Lindsay's body supposedly landed.

Detective Inspector Brunsden, part of the forensics team at King's Cross/Russell Square, testified at the inquests. A diagram he drew, dated 10.11.2006, shows the Piccadilly Line carriage. It shows the 'bomb crater' close to where the MPS diagrams show it, and 'area Z' is where Brunsden says they found Lindsay's body. He also said this is where they found several documents identifying Lindsay, and part of a plastic bottle that was spuriously thought to have been part of the bomb.[18]

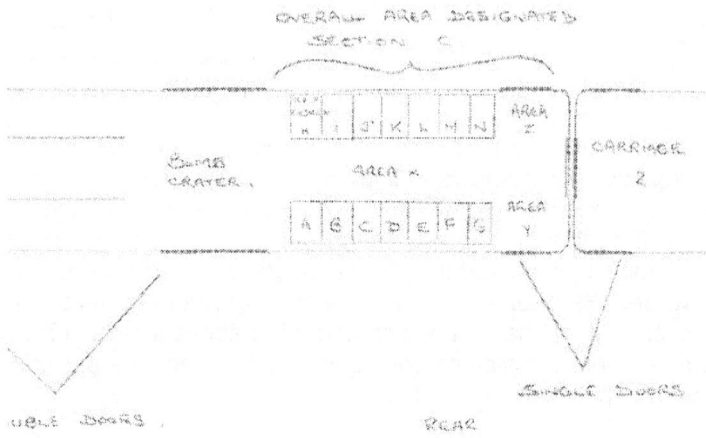

For this story to be true, Lindsay would have had to enter a packed tube train using the single door at the rear of the carriage. He would have had to throw the identifying documents down on the floor in area Z and then push past numerous people to get past the row of seats to the area where the 'bomb crater' was. Lindsay would then have had to remove his backpack bomb in extremely cramped conditions, put it on the floor and set it off. Somehow, this then catapulted his body, and the bit of the plastic bottle, over a dozen feet past several people to land in area Z, all without a single witness on the train remembering him doing any of this.

Liverpool Street

On the bombing between Liverpool Street and Aldgate, the narrative says, 'Forensic evidence suggests that Tanweer was sitting towards the back of the second carriage with the rucksack next to him on the floor. The blast killed 8 people, including Tanweer, with 171 injured.' The MPS diagram contradicts this, showing Tanweer (number 5) and the explosion happening in a standing area, not in front of a seat.

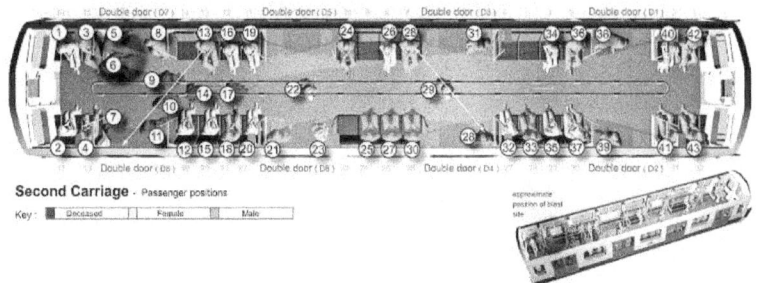

Second Carriage - Passenger positions

Key: Deceased | Female | Male

This part of the standing area is where a witness named Bruce Lait says he saw a hole in the floor. In an interview with Cambridge Evening News only days after the bombing he spoke of how they were being helped off the bombed train by a policeman, 'The policeman said 'mind that hole, that's where the bomb was'. The metal was pushed upwards as if the bomb was underneath the train. They seem to think the bomb was left in a bag, but I don't remember anybody being where the bomb was, or any bag.'[19]

Years later, when Lait was interviewed for the BBC's *Conspiracy Files* show on 7/7 he reiterated all of this and pointed to the same area where the MPS diagram says the explosion happened. Lait is number 18 in the diagram, one of the closest survivors, and therefore a consistent and important witness. It appears the police took him seriously when he said that's where the explosion was, but not when he said he doesn't remember anyone, let alone Tanweer, standing there.

There are people even closer than Lait who managed to survive. Person number 3, William Walsh, is an Irishman who suffered only minor injuries. He broke through the window behind him to escape the carriage immediately after the bombing. If the MPS diagram is realistic then Walsh should be dead, particularly when people as far away as Carrie Taylor, number 17, were killed.

The MPS diagram shows 43 people in the carriage, 35 of which survived. At that rate of occupancy it would require everyone in another three full carriages of people to also be injured to get up to the Home Office number of 171. If the bomb was so destructive that it injured four whole carriages of people then how did Greg Shannon, number 8 in the MPS diagram, survive when he was only a few feet away from it?

The diagram of where the bodies of the victims were found only emphasizes this problem. Carrie Taylor was clearly thrown away from the explosion, despite being some distance from it, yet the majority of those in the bomb's immediate vicinity survived.

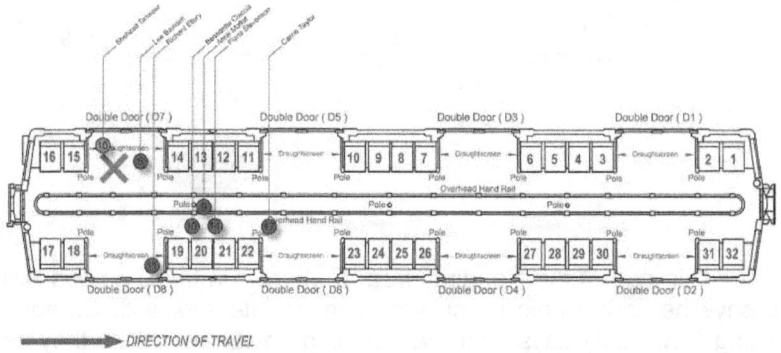

Edgware Road

On the Westbound Circle Line train the Home Office says, 'At Edgware Road, Mohammad Sidique Khan was also in the second carriage from the front, most likely near the standing area by the first set of double doors. He was probably also seated with the bomb next to him on the floor. Shortly before the explosion, Khan was seen fiddling with the top of the rucksack. The explosion killed 7 including Khan, and injured 163 people.' The lack of clarity is typical of the official narrative, saying Khan was 'near the standing area' but 'probably also seated'.

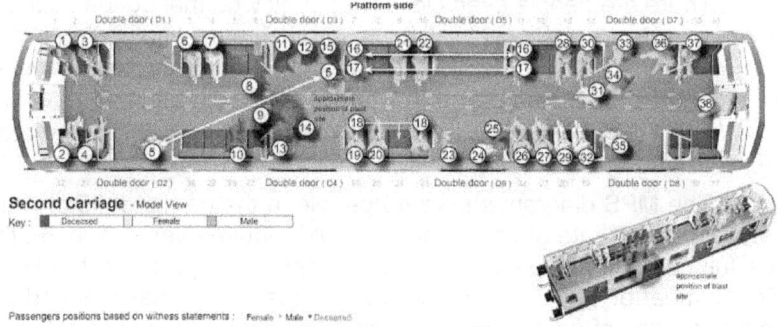

The MPS diagram reflects this, showing the explosion happening in the standing area but Khan (number 10) sat down. Khan isn't even in the seat closest to the explosion. The same questions from the other diagrams apply to the one for Edgware Road. How was David

Foulkes, number 15, killed but Elizabeth Owen and Catherine Al Wafai, numbers 6 and 7, were not?

Elizabeth Owen was quite badly injured, but not so badly that it stopped her tending to another victim, Laura Webb (number 8). Catherine Al Wafai suffered relatively minor injuries, and managed to walk home, though she describes doing this in a state of severe shock. The same question as to the number of injured people also applies here. How was Al Wafai capable of walking home when 163 people – again around four carriages full of people – were injured in this one explosion that took place only a few feet away from her? However, if the explosion was in the middle of the standing area then a lot of this makes more sense, but that means that it couldn't have been Khan, or indeed anyone, blowing themselves up where the MPS say Khan was. Fundamentally, the MPS diagram for Edgware Road does not show a plausible scenario. The diagram of where the bodies were found after the explosion makes this story even less credible.

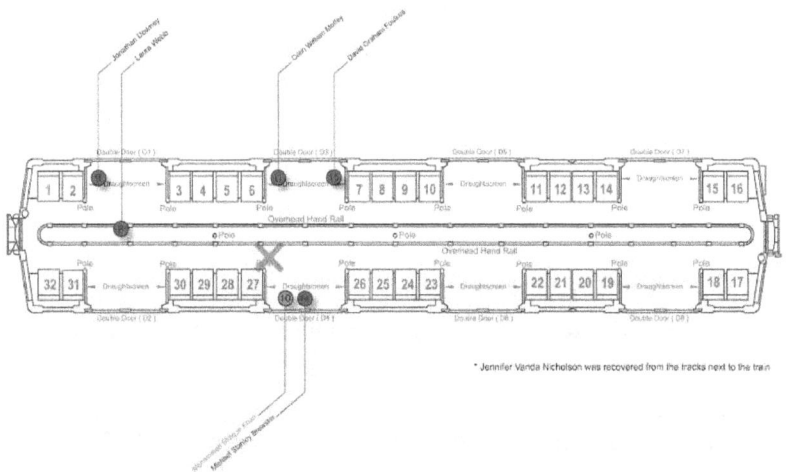

The centre of the explosion is the X, but what is particular inexplicable is where Khan's body was supposedly found. If Khan was sat in seat number 28 in this image, and the explosion happened to his right, where the X is, then how could he (number 10) end up on the other side of the explosion?

According to the inquest testimony of DC Wilson, the human remains logged as exhibit MW84 and later identified as Khan were found 'on the westbound line of the track', not within the carriage as shown on the MPS diagram. How do we reconcile this testimony with the image produced by the MPS to show us what happened? The diagram even notes that the body of Jennifer Nicholson was found on the tracks, but not Khan's. It also overlooks the fact that Stanley Brewster fell into the hole in the standing area created by the explosion and likewise, his body ended up on the track.

PC Geoffrey Potter of the British Transport Police, who one of the first officers to reach the scene, found this when he arrived. His diagram of what he found shows the crater much more centrally in the standing area. It also shows the bodies he found at the scene, none of whom were Sidique Khan, and numbers the bodies from one to six.

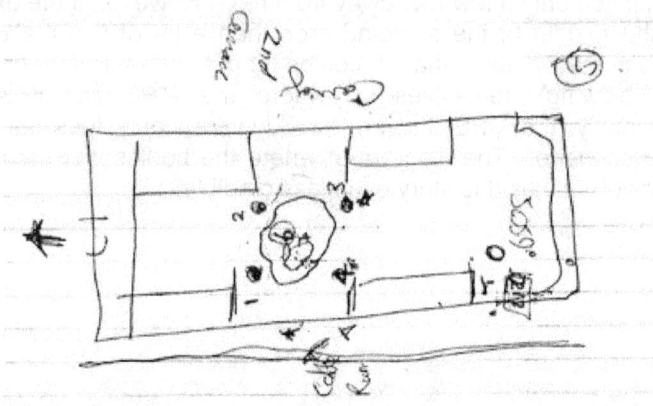

Q. Who was number 6?

A. Number 6 was what I took at the time to be the centre of the explosion, I took him to be the bomber.

Q. Obviously, and there's obviously no question about it, that's quite wrong, but that was what it appeared to be?

A. Yes, sir.

Q. Was he inside the hole or beneath the hole?

A. He was through the hole, yes, he was on the floor underneath the train.[20]

Tavistock Square

The case at Tavistock Square is somewhat simpler, because of the existence of video footage and photographs showing the bus immediately after the explosion. It is clear from these that there was an explosion towards the back of the upper deck of the bus that had torn off the roof, shattered the windows and blasted open the rear and side panels of the top deck.

The Home Office say that, 'Hussain sat on the upper deck, towards the back. Forensic evidence suggests the bomb was next to him in the aisle or between his feet on the floor... The bomb goes off, killing 14 people, including Hussain, and injuring over 110.' The MPS diagram reflects this, showing Hussain (number 53) in the relevant seat.

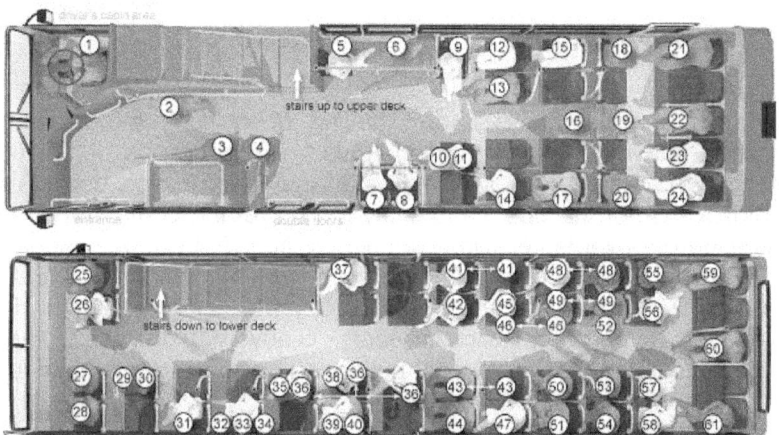

Once more we are left to speculate as to how three of the ten people closest to Hussain (56, 57, 58) survived, but others further away (55, 61) were killed. To make up the 110 people injured by the explosion, even if all 60 people on the bus were hurt then another 50 on the street nearby were also injured. In the pictures and photos from the scene it is difficult to find that many people, let alone that many people showing signs of being hurt.

One of the most noticeable things about the photos and video of the bus is that while the roof, sides and windows have been blown out, the floor remains largely intact. The last few feet of the top deck of the floor were bent down, but it was still essentially one continuous piece of material. How is this possible, if the bomb was planted on the floor? Why were so many people on the lower deck of the bus killed and injured without the force of the explosive hitting them through the floor between them and the bomb? These problems only get worse when examining the MPS diagrams of where the victims' bodies were found.

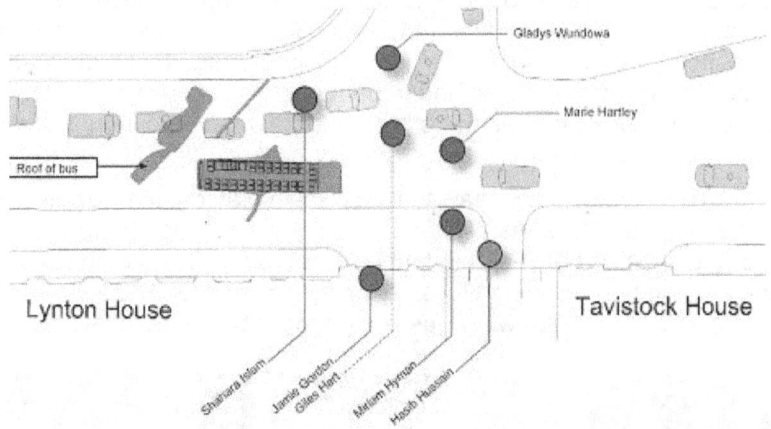

Hasib Hussain's body is shown having been flung a considerable distance, maybe 30 feet, from the bus. The locations of the other victims make little sense. Miriam Hyman (number 50) was, according to the MPS plan of the bus, sat directly in front of the bomb, yet she too was flung backwards. Similarly, Jamie Gordon (51) was apparently sat next to Miriam Hyman, yet was also flung towards where the police say the explosion came from. Giles Hart (52) was sat to the right of the bomb but was thrown mostly backwards. Gladys Wundowa (61) was sat behind and to the left of the bomb but ended up some way to the right.

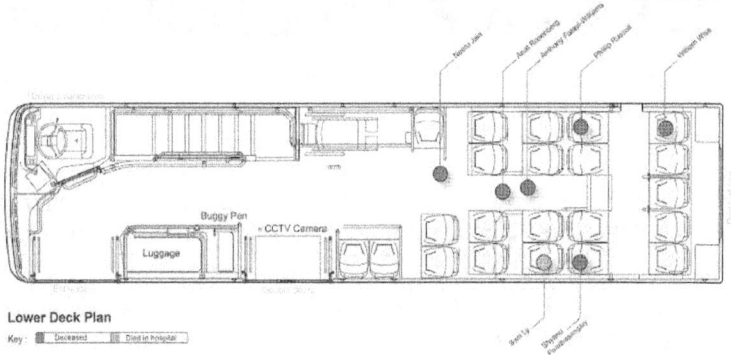

The diagram of the bodies found within the bus also has a critical problem. Most of the victims are in the same locations that the first MPS diagram has them, except for one. Neetu Jain's body was apparently found on the lower deck, essentially in the middle of the bus. But before the explosion the MPS have her sitting in the window seat next to

Hussain (number 54). From the pattern of where the people around her were found, she should have ended up outside the bus, back and to the left. Instead, she was thrown forward and somehow was found on the lower deck, even though there was no hole in the floor for her to fall through.

Indeed, why was there no hole in the floor of the upper deck? In each of the trains the bombs blew a substantial crater, and in at least two cases additional holes in the floors of the carriages. Yet supposedly the same sort of bomb produced very different results when detonated on the bus. Was the same type of bomb used on the bus as on the trains? The simple photographic evidence suggests not. The diagrams produced by the MPS yet again tell a story that is not even remotely plausible.

Witnesses

Very few eyewitnesses have claimed to have seen the alleged bombers in the trains and bus shortly before the explosion. The MPS reconstruction diagrams of the explosions shown above rely heavily on eyewitness accounts. They never make clear just how few witnesses have testified to the presence of the alleged bombers.

On the Piccadilly Line, not a single witness at the inquests or interviewed in the mainstream media remembered seeing Lindsay on the train before the explosion. From Aldgate, one survivor from the next carriage called Michael Henning was called to the inquests, but gave a very vague description of a man he remembered. The man was sat in the seat that the MPS say was occupied by William Walsh, and so almost certainly was not Tanweer. None of the surviving witnesses from the bombed carriage remember anyone where the MPS diagram shows Tanweer.

At Edgware Road only one man remembers seeing Khan – Danny Biddle. Biddle is person number 13 in the MPS diagram, stood in the standing area where the explosion happened. He was close to where he says he saw Khan, and indeed is apparently the only reason Khan is placed where he is in the MPS image. As you might expect, Biddle was terribly injured in the explosion, losing both legs and one eye, and he was in a coma for several weeks.

After waking from the coma he recognised Khan from a news broadcast and recalled seeing him on the train at Edgware Road. Biddle was interviewed by a number of press outlets and told them that he recalled the man looking up and around the carriage, then making a quick movement before the bomb went off. Unsurprisingly, this story very much helped reinforce the notion that suicide bombers were to blame. This was always presented as solid eyewitness testimony, despite the terrible and mentally compromising nature of his injuries. Biddle was called to the inquests where he told his account once more. He was asked about what the man was carrying.

Q. Do you recollect him carrying anything?

A. He had a rucksack, like a small, black camping rucksack.

Q. Was he holding it or carrying it in a particular way that you can recall?

A. I remember it being on his lap.[21]

This is completely at odds with the CCTV showing Khan carrying a large rucksack, and the official story saying he had it on the floor at the time of the explosion. Thus, the only witness to Khan's presence on the Edgware Road train contradicts the Home Office on what he was carrying and how he was carrying it. Aside from Richard Jones (see chapter 1), Biddle is the only person who remembers seeing one of the alleged bombers 'fiddling with his rucksack' shortly before the explosion. As such, he is part of the 'key evidence' cited in the Home Office report, despite the fact he contradicts the other 'key evidence' that is the CCTV footage.

At Tavistock Square, with Richard Jones having been quietly dropped as a crucial eyewitness, there is only one account suggesting Hussain was there. Lisa French boarded the number 30 bus at Euston and was talking to the driver as others pushed on behind her. She recalled how, 'the man with the big backpack, he actually took his backpack off his shoulder and held it like I was holding my laptop to squeeze past, and that's the reason I really noticed him because I can remember thinking, "Oh, there's one polite person left boarding this bus today".'

As she followed the man upstairs to find a seat, she looked again at his bag and described it as, 'quite large, sort of square, so I think that's why I thought it was a laptop bag rather than a camping rucksack because it was still quite square for being a rucksack.' She said that the man 'went towards the very back row' of the bus and sat down there.[22] Other witnesses vaguely remembered an Asian man heading towards or sat at the back of the top deck of the bus.

There are four critical problems with Lisa French's account, in terms of how well it supports the Home Office's story of 7/7. First, she was unsure about the bag, initially calling it a 'big backpack' and then a 'laptop bag'. Second, she did not positively identify the man as Hussain. Third, there was an Asian man, a Sri Lankan called Prevshan Vijendran, who was on the bus that day. He was dressed similarly to Hussain and was carrying a shoulder bag and he was sat on the very back row of the bus, whereas Hussain wasn't. Did Lisa French see Hasib Hussain or Prevshan Vijendran?

Furthermore, French has suffered from PTSD, and even appeared on a 'overcoming their fear' reality TV show where she did a sky-dive for charity. She has spoken at some length about how she suffered only minor physical injuries but also considerable mental pain and confusion. She admits that her memories of what happened before the explosion are imprecise and uncertain. As such, the only witness to Hussain's presence on the bus admits she is deeply uncertain, and could well be remembering a different man.

The Bodies

The process by which the bodies were found at the scenes, recovered and identified was ruled 'outside the scope of these proceedings' by Lady Justice Hallet. Even though the Coroners and Justice Act requires inquests to establish who has died, this process was largely ignored. Some information was provided, but once again the official story does not add up.

As the diagram above shows, Hussain's body was apparently found around 30 feet from the back of the bus, outside the front of the British Medical Association building. The photos from the scene do show what appears to be a body covered in a blue blanket or sheet. Some witnesses at the inquests did testify to seeing a body there, but no one recalled covering it with a blanket or logging it as a human remains exhibit for the investigation. As such, we know virtually nothing about how it was identified as Hussain.

Two days after 7/7, the Times ran an article, 'The grim signs that say suicide bomb', that outlined some of the tell-tale signs of suicide bombings. It explained that Israeli investigators often found that suicide bombers were decapitated by the blasts. Three days later, the Times reported that Hussain's body had been found, decapitated, at the scene of the bus bombing. This, they said, was proof he was a suicide bomber. According to the photographs and the MPS diagram, Hussain's body was on the pavement outside the BMA building, so it should have been found almost as soon as crime scene investigators arrived on the afternoon of 7/7.

On the Piccadilly Line, Lindsay's body was apparently found and given both an exhibit number, JB3, and a disaster victim identification number, 60022242. However, no witness at the inquests explicitly spoke of finding his body at the back of the carriage as indicated on the MPS diagram. DI Brunsden said that he found other items in that area, mostly days later, that identified Lindsay. He was asked about the body:

Q. Did that person, JB3, turn out subsequently to be the bomber --

A. Yes, that is correct.

Q. -- Lindsay?

A. Germaine Lindsay.[23]

But there was no explanation of how the body was identified as Lindsay's. In two cases we simply weren't told who found the body, when, and how it was identified. The other two cases were even stranger.

At Edgware Road, Sidique Khan's remains were found, though exactly when and where is not clear. The MPS diagram shows them being found inside the carriage, but DC Wilson says they were found on the tracks. Curiously, the remains were given the exhibit number MW84 but a visa card belonging to Khan was given the next number in the sequence, MW85. The card was not found until after the bodies had been formally removed on July 9th, suggesting that Khan's body was not found until after all the other bodies were removed.

Unlike Hussain and Lindsay, at least as far as we know, only pieces of Khan's body were found. A small sample of muscle tissue from these pieces was sent for DNA analysis and identified as being Khan's. According to a pathologist's report by a Dr Djurovic, MW84 was the, 'severely damaged and fragmented parts of what appeared to be the body of a young adult male'.

The pieces of the body left were, 'Most of the scalp tissue, but separated into two larger fragments... several large fragments of broken vault of skull... The facial skeleton was absent. There were multiple fractures on the base of the skull. The upper segment of the spinal column was present... The spine was separated at the level of the upper thoracic spine...Attached to the back of the neck was a large fragment of the skin of the back of the torso. There was a further large fragment of skin, probably part of the lower part of the back and the upper buttock. There was a separate large fragment of skin... there was a large section of spinal column with the sacrum consisting of the lumbar and most of the thoracic spine up to the fifth thoracic vertebra.'[24]

This near-total disintegration may explain why Khan's body was not found and removed with the others at Edgware Road. Indeed, when PC Potter of the BTP arrived, he found only six bodies – four within the carriage, one fallen under it, and one on the tracks. If Khan's body was there, he should have found seven bodies. Likewise, Dr Morgan Costello, a consultant psychiatrist who was sent to the Aldgate and Edgware Road scenes late in the evening of 7/7, only pronounced six bodies dead at Edgware Road.

Similarly, Dr Costello only pronounced dead seven people at Aldgate, when if Tanweer was there then there should have been eight bodies. Along with Lindsay and Hussain, that means that none of the alleged bombers were pronounced dead at the scenes of the explosion. Nor were many of the other victims – out of a total of 56 people, only 15 were pronounced dead at the bomb sites. No wonder Hallett ruled that this process was outside of the scope of the inquests.

Other testimony, including from DI Robert Munn of the BTP and London Ambulance Service paramedic Steven Jones, also said there were only seven bodies at Aldgate. This is also backed up by transcripts of police communications recordings, which repeatedly refer to seven bodies. So where was Tanweer's body?

Two days later, at around 9:30 p.m. on July 9th, a piece of Tanweer's spine approximately 30cm long and weighing nearly two kilos was found 'in the front of a rear bench seat in carriage 2' on the Aldgate train. How was such a large piece of body not found earlier? DI Neil Kemp, one of the first responders on the morning of 7/7, said that he saw something that looked like a human spine when he got to the scene. So why did Dr Costello and the other police officers and investigators manage to not see it for two and a half days?

Other pieces of Tanweer's body were apparently found and some were sent for DNA testing, though exactly which parts were used for testing was not made clear at the inquests. A pathologist's report by Dr Nathaniel Cary only describes the piece of spine, and alludes only to paperwork saying that other body fragments were found. It appears that Tanweer's body disintegrated to an even greater extent than Khan's.

This is very strange. According to the Home Office, the four bombs were virtually identical, of the same recipe and strength and therefore should, if they had all been set off in suicide attacks, produced relatively similar results. In Hussain's case he was reportedly decapitated, even though he was allegedly carrying a bomb in a rucksack, not in a suicide vest. As such, his decapitation doesn't make much sense. According to the inquest testimony, Lindsay's body was found almost entirely intact, but Khan and Tanweer were blown to bits.

Dr Roberts

Things only got more problematic when forensic anthropologist Julie Ann Roberts took the stand. In the days after 7/7 she was tasked with reassembling the various body parts of the four alleged bombers 'so that we could look at the entire remains of each individual bomber for the specific purpose of assessing the injury patterns to look at any bones that were missing and, by doing so, to try to make inferences about the relative position of the bomber to the device, to the explosive device.' As she explained, she was only provided with the remains of the four men said to be the alleged bombers. As such, the conclusion, that these were suicide bombers, was to a large extent presumed by the very nature of the task she had been given.

Hugo Keith QC went to some length to build up her appearance of authority, noting how, 'you describe yourself very modestly as a forensic scientist in your witness statement, but you're very much more than that.' This 'modesty' continued as Dr Roberts played this down when asked about how she'd gone about making her assessment. When asked, 'Were you able to distinguish between degrees of explosive damage to parts of the body or not?' she answered, 'I'm not qualified in that area of expertise.'

In essence, she had never performed this task before, as indeed no one in Britain had. While certainly a very accomplished person, Dr Roberts has no background in terrorism, explosions, suicide bombings or anything particularly relevant to the job she was given. As far as we can tell from her brief testimony, she did the task as well as it could be done within the imposed limits.

In fact, she did a remarkable job, managing to reassemble four bodies, two of which had been blown to pieces, in only three days. How was this possible? Furthermore, she described remains that were more complete and, it seems, intact than are described earlier in the recovery process. The only piece of Tanweer that was reported found and that is noted in the pathologist's report was his spine, but Roberts said she was looking at considerably more of him.

She confirmed that 'some significant parts of his body were entirely missing: the cranial vault and facial bones, both wrists and hands, the breast bone and the bottom half of the pelvis on both sides.' However, 'some parts had remained' that were not described by anyone at the Aldgate scene, namely, 'the front and sides of the rib cage, the lower jaw, the right radius and the shafts of the right and left lower limbs.' How were all these body parts missed by initial investigators, and at what point were they found?

When asked about the parts of Hussain's body that were missing she replied, 'Completely absent was the right hand and the toes from the right and left foot, and then almost entirely absent were the facial bones, the right forearm and the right lower leg.' She made no mention of him being decapitated. Similarly, she said of Lindsay's body, 'entirely absent were the left wrist and hand, the left knee, the lower part of the right and left pelvis and the right wrist, and almost entirely missing were the right hand, the bones of the lower legs on both sides and the bones of the upper part of the face.' This loosely confirms the other inquest testimony that Lindsay and Hussain's bodies were found with the torsos essentially intact but the limbs partially or mostly destroyed. This only begs the question of why with Tanweer the opposite was the case.

Her description of Khan also differs in key ways from the pathologist's report. Roberts said, 'The body parts that were completely missing from Khan were all the upper and lower dentition, the left forearm, wrist and hand, the lower half of the pelvis on the right and the left sides, and those parts that were almost entirely missing were the right and left upper jaw, the right hand, with the exception of one hand bone, the left knee, the lower half of the right and left lower leg, and the left foot, with the exception of one toe.'[25]

That leaves the left upper arm, most of the torso, the right arm, both upper legs and the right knee, none of which were described in Dr Djurovic's pathology report. Furthermore, Dr Djurovic's report says that 'the facial skeleton was absent' whereas Dr Roberts says that 'all the upper and lower dentition' was absent and 'the right and left upper jaw' were almost entirely absent. That leaves about half of Khan's face unaccounted for in Djurovic's examination but present for Roberts' later examination.

Compounding all this, in Roberts' assessment she said of Khan, 'I thought it was perhaps possible that the device was situated further to the left than the right. But again, that's - that's speculation.' It was speculation, but it is a speculation that contradicts the official story. For the MPS diagram to be even close to what happened, Khan would have had to push the bomb to his right before setting it off, not his left. This shows once again how fundamentally unrealistic the MPS diagrams are.

With these questions as to where and when and how much of the alleged bombers bodies were recovered from the bomb sites we are bound to ask another critical question: were the four men even in those places at the times of the explosions? After all, if they weren't then the official story is simply untrue and the bombings were carried out some other way. Even if their bodies were found there, that doesn't prove they caused the explosions. This is particularly true when the assessment that they were 'in close proximity' to the bombs was the conclusion of a process riddled with contradictions.

Explosions Under the Carriages?

While much of the speculation by the alternative media has been baseless and sometimes counter-productive, the popular idea that the bombs were somehow built into the trains (and possibly the bus) has a wealth of evidence supporting it. As Nafeez Ahmed noted in his 2006 book *The London Bombings: An Independent Inquiry*, 'reports from survivors and witnesses in the public record largely suggest to the contrary that the bombs exploded from underneath the carriages, rather than from bags placed upon the floor.'[26]

These reports include statements that at least some of the bombed trails had derailed, indicating an upwards force from underneath the train, of metal twisted upwards from holes blown in the carriage floors, and of widespread damage to the carriage floors over large areas. Ahmed cites many of the reports that were available at the time, for example Angelo Power saying that people on the Piccadilly Line were 'physically ejected' from their seats, the accounts of Aldgate survivor Bruce Lait and Anita Kinselley from Edgware Road who said that, 'The tiles on the floor of my carriage suddenly shot up'.

There are other accounts, for example a man interviewed for Sky News Ireland under the name Peadar O'Sullivan, but who is probably William Walsh, said, 'The explosion was like hearing it but feeling it as well, tremors shivering all the way up through your body, my whole body shook and then this floor panel came up underneath my feet.'[27] Similarly, Katie Benton who survived the Edgware Road bombing said that 'I thought that we had derailed' and that, 'There was a huge crater in the floor, the bottom of the train was just rubble.'[28] Bruce Lait has also repeated his same account of metal pushed upwards at the edge of the bomb crater on the BBC's *Conspiracy Files* show.

The account of one survivor from Edgware Road, Susanna Pell, is particularly at odds with the official story. She was in the carriage adjacent to the one that was bombed, and despite being injured by flying glass and debris she crawled through to the next carriage to help people. She called in to BBC Radio London that morning and described how after the explosion, once the smoke had cleared, 'I tried to get up and nearly fell down a hole in the bottom of the tube.' How could there be a hole in the bottom of the tube in the next carriage along from the bomb?

In fact, testimony and diagrams from witnesses at each of the scenes shows additional holes blown in the floors of the carriages, too far apart to have been from a single backpack bomb. Elizabeth Kenworthy was an off-duty police officer who was on the train headed towards Aldgate. After the explosion she walked through the train and into the bombed carriage to help the injured. As such, she is an extremely reliable witness – trained in observation, she kept her cool and helped save lives. What she says, therefore, is significant.

In an interview with the Independent shortly after 7/7 she essentially corroborated Bruce Lait's account of metal twisted upwards and a big hole in the floor of the carriage. She was called to testify at the inquests and repeated this, saying there was 'twisted metal' 'shattered metal' and 'the door was twisted and something had obviously happened to the door.'[29] The door was some distance away from where the MPS say Tanweer was, in the standing area. William Walsh and others in between suffered relatively minor injuries, so how was the door so badly damaged?

The diagram drawn by an officer based on Kenworthy's account only poses further questions. The 'twisted' and 'shattered' metal she described is shown just inside the carriage, between the last few seats and in front of where William Walsh was sat. It shows a big 'hole in floor' where Tanweer supposedly was, and where Bruce Lait said that the metal was pushed upwards. It also shows another hole in the other side of the carriage further up. How could one bomb cause all this damage but leave the people and much of the carriage interior in between intact?

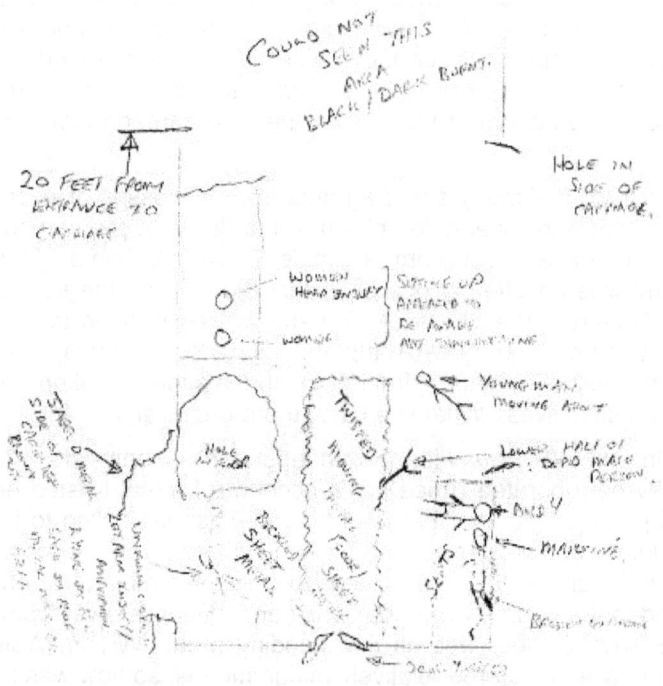

On the Piccadilly Line a standard schematic annotated by Russell Square station supervisor David Boyce also indicates an additional hole in the floor of the bombed carriage. Boyce, along with Russell Square Duty Manager Ray Stephens, was one of the first people to arrive at the Piccadilly Line train after the bombing.

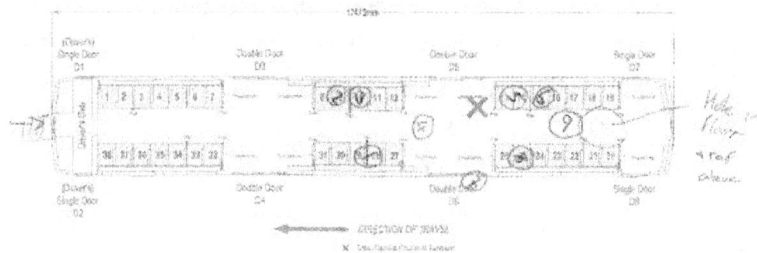

The diagram shows a 'hole in floor + roof above' between the last row of seats, not in the standing area between the double doors. Boyce said, 'Looking at that plan, I now know that obviously where I've put the hole in the floor was wrong, but obviously this was 19 months after it happened'.[30] He also said that he has 'been trying to forget it' so like Lisa French he is not a particularly reliable witness.

However, at Edgware Road there are numerous witnesses who testified to additional holes in the floor. The driver of the bombed train, Ray Whitehurst, testified to there being a large hole in the floor near the connecting doors between the first and second carriages, but it is not clear exactly where this hole was. Danny Belsten, a survivor from the front end of the second carriage (number 3 in the main MPS diagram), said that as the bomb went off he felt like he was falling through a hole in the floor and being electrocuted. However, his diagram shows the bomb crater between the first main row of seats, in front of where Khan was supposedly sat but not in the next standing area where the MPS say the bomb was.

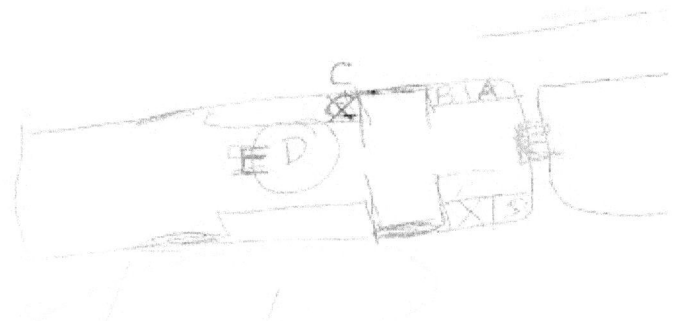

Belsten did not draw the hole he 'felt like' he fell into, but he did say, both on the BBC website and in his inquest testimony that some of the carriage doors had landed on top of him. Why would the doors be blown inwards? As he was helped out of the train by Susanna Pell they went through the first carriage, where Belsten noticed that, 'all the manholes in the bottom of the carriage were blown out', essentially confirmed Pell's account of holes in the floor of the adjacent carriage.[31]

John Tulloch, person number 16 in the MPS diagram, was sat on the opposite edge of the standing area from where Khan supposedly was. He has consistently described a hole in the floor just to his right. When he was shown the diagram of where the bodies were found, he said 'it seemed to me to be closer than that red cross'. Hugo Keith responded, 'Professor, don't worry about the X, because we have heard evidence from some witnesses which suggests that there's other disruption and potentially other holes in the floor as well as the bomb crater, so it may in fact be a different hole that you're referring to.'[32]

A man named John McDonald who was sitting at the far end of the carriage moved towards the injured after the explosion. He drew a sketch showing a small hole between the rows of seats where Tulloch was sat. McDonald says he half fell in that hole in front of seats 25 and 26, which would have been in front of Tulloch. He confirmed that this was a different hole to the one in the standing area that Stanley Brewster fell into.

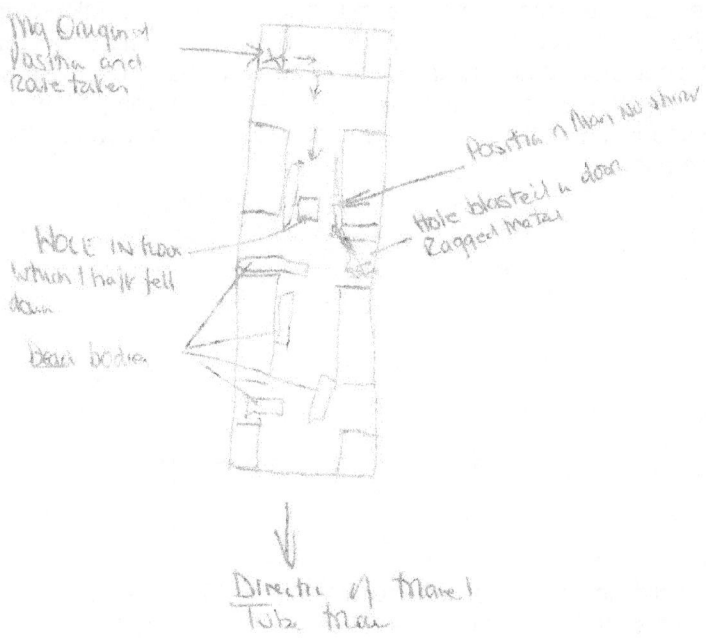

Bill Mann also moved from the far end of the train to try to help people after the explosion. His statement was read into evidence so he was not questioned on precisely what he saw but the statement said that, 'There seemed to be a bloody great hole. The door seemed to be gone, a big hole, I assume that is where the bomb was.' Mann's diagrams do not make it clear whether this hole was in the doors on the edge of the standing area where the MPS say the explosion was, or the doors closer to where he was originally sitting.

So how many holes were blown in the floor of the Edgware Road carriage? The exact number cannot be ascertained from these diagrams and witness accounts, but in any case several reported holes were too far away for Khan to have caused it by blowing up a bomb at his feet. These additional holes, however many there were and whatever their exact location, are far more in keeping with a bomb or bombs built into the floor of the carriage than with a single backpack bomb carried by a suicide bomber.

Who Bombed London?

Reviewing all this evidence, it is hard to believe that the four men were real suicide bombers and therefore that they were the culprits of this mass murder. The case proving their guilt should be relatively simple, and indeed is presented in a simple way by the Home Office. A closer look at the core aspects of the case show that the truth is clearly not so straightforward.

The exact means for the crime – the type of explosive used and how it was detonated – has never been conclusively established. It is the equivalent of blaming someone for a murder-suicide but not being able to find the gun they used to shoot themself and others. The most incriminating evidence that was found in the car in Luton and the 'bomb factory' in Leeds could not be linked to any of the alleged bombers by fingerprints or DNA.

Whether the men were even in the trains and bus at the time of the explosions in not at all clear. Exactly when their bodies were found, where, and how complete the bodies were was subject to much contradiction between the testimonies and inquest exhibits. The MPS diagrams of the explosions are especially ambiguous and unrealistic.

Even the mechanism by which the bombs were set off had never been properly explained. A Guardian article from August 2005 - just as scepticism was growing about the official story - says that according to 'senior police sources' the alleged bombers, 'triggered the bombs themselves by pressing a device similar to a button'.[33] However, no such triggers (buttons, switches or otherwise) have been officially reported found at the bombs sites. So what caused the explosions?

The carriages in which bombs are said to have gone off have all been scrapped. Other carriages from the affected trains were sent all the way to Hungary to be repaired. Very few photos from inside the carriages have been made available, and the crime scene video is heavily edited. As such, we cannot confirm at this stage the large number of witness accounts suggesting multiple holes blown in the floor, and metal pushed and twisted upwards, into the carriages, by the blasts.

So who bombed London? The evidence that it was Khan, Tanweer, Hussain and Lindsay is far from conclusive. If they were not responsible, then the actual perpetrators are probably still out there, and have gotten away with mass murder.

Chapter 5: Debunking 7/7 Debunking

The mainstream media have largely ignored the important questions posed about the 7/7 attacks. There are some exceptions. A year after the attacks, the Guardian newspaper devoted an issue of their G2 supplement to the evidence and questions being pursued by J7, including a lengthy interview with two of the group's members.

The supplement discussed a wide range of concerns about the evidence that was available at the time, from the times of the various trains the alleged bombers caught that day, to the possibility of the single CCTV image of the four being faked or manipulated. However, since then there has been very little press coverage devoted to these issues.

The Guardian has not returned to these questions, save for some strong coverage of the Junaid Babar controversy following his sentencing in late 2010. The Daily Mail, whose pages are filled with conspiracy theories that are both significant and trivial, also briefly touched upon the 'rise' of 'conspiracy theories' about 7/7.

Following the Guardian article, in early 2007 Channel 4 broadcast a show called *Conspiracy: Who Really Runs the World?*. The show did not answer this question, but instead looked at four different 'conspiracy theories' – concerning UFOs, the murder of Princess Diana, 9/11 and 7/7. Then the media went quiet on the issue of 7/7 for a year. After the 2009 retrial of three men accused of being part of the 7/7 conspiracy (see chapter 2) the ISC published their second report, provoking much media commentary. A few weeks later, the BBC put out a 7/7-based episode of their popular but heavily criticised *Conspiracy Files* series.

The running theme throughout this major media coverage of questions and alternative theories about 7/7 has been the attempt to 'debunk' these theories and criticise the people who ask the questions and/or believe the theories. These debunking efforts have employed a series of weak or illogical arguments that focused on easy targets and weak evidence, and failed to address the core issues.

This process began in the G2 supplement in June 2006, which was comparatively even handed. On the morning of 7/7 Guardian journalist Mark Honisgbaum was sent to Edgware Road station. He interviewed passengers and survivors all morning and at 11 a.m. phoned in a report. The report described the explosion as being 'under the train', and that eye witnesses had reported that at the moment of the explosion, 'the tiles, the covers on the floor of the train, suddenly flew up, raised up.'

The audio recording of this report was made available on the Guardian's website and it was downloaded and replicated across the internet. The idea that the explosions came up through the floor, rather than out from a rucksack wielded by a suicide bomber, has become widely believed in the web-based 'alternative media' community. Along with an interview with Aldgate bombing survivor Bruce Lait, the Honigsbaum report is cited by almost all of the alternative conspiracy theorists.

Yet in his 7/7 article in 2006 Honigsbaum explained that, 'It later became clear from interviewing other passengers who had been closer to the seat of the explosion that the bomb had actually detonated inside the train, not under it, but my comments, disseminated over the internet where they could be replayed ad nauseam, were already taking on a life of their own.'[1]

This is a perfectly sound argument, and a reasonable debunking of the idea that his report was proof of an explosion under the train at Edgware Road, but it begs a significant question. As the previous two chapters have shown, there were a great many wrong or false media reports on and immediately after 7/7. Some of these even referred to CCTV images that do not exist and could not have existed. None of these demonstrably false reports have provoked a public retraction or clarification. The only one that has been retracted is the report from Honigsbaum that suggested a scenario that is very different to the official story.

The 'Psychology' of Conspiracy Theories

Honigsbaum was interviewed for the 2007 *Conspiracy: Who Really Runs The World?* show on Channel 4 and repeated the same story as in his 2006 article. He recounted how he arrived to a scene of massive confusion, and just started interviewing survivors and asked them what they saw. He explained how his audio report 'was picked up by various conspiracy sites' and that he 'became quite disturbed that my report was being used in this way'.[2]

What this debunking of the significance of Honigsbaum's report overlooks is the dozens of other witnesses to the explosions and what they have said in interviews. Many of the surviving witnesses also gave descriptions consistent with explosions from within the floor or underneath the trains (see chapter 4). Honigsbaum's report is just a weak example of a strong and clear pattern in the eyewitness accounts.

The Channel 4 show was subtitled *The Psychology of Conspiracy Theory* and was produced as part of their 'Learning' programming on 'Citizenship'. The Channel 4 website makes it clear that the show is aimed at 14-19 year olds and claims it is relevant to relevant to those doing GCSEs or A levels in Sociology, Psychology, Media Studies, Government and Politics. As the programme progressed the agenda became clearer.

The second half of the show was largely dedicated to two psychologists who sought to reduce all beliefs in 'conspiracy theories' to, in effect, mental illness. They carried out an 'experiment' whereby a whopping 30 students were given a written question and answer test that apparently assessed the degree to which they exhibited three personality traits. The traits were: a lack of trust in those around them, a feeling of alienation from society, and being prone to assumption based on partial evidence.

The psychologists predicted that those who exhibited these traits to a greater degree would be more likely to believe in 'conspiracy theories'. They split the 30 students into two groups based on the results of the paper tests, taking the six with the highest scores and the six with the lowest. They then got the groups together and gave them a 'brand new' conspiracy theory to see how they would react, and whether or not they would believe it.

The 'new' conspiracy theory was the idea that the government uses mobile phones to track people's movements. Even in 2007 this was hardly an original idea that no one had ever heard of or considered before, so this was not in any way a test of reactions to a new idea. As predicted, the six who scored low on the test did not believe the 'new' conspiracy theory, but the six who scored highly did believe that it was 'quite likely'.

As far as tests go, it was a shambles. The participants were tested individually for their character traits, but in groups to see if they believed in 'conspiracy theories'. The very fact of being asked while in a group might influence the responses, so for consistency they should have asked the people individually, in the same way as the test to determine their personality. The method is unscientific, if not downright manipulative.

Likewise, the 'new' conspiracy theory was presented in different ways to the two groups. The low scoring group was asked if they believed that, 'the government is using mobile phone technology to track everyone all the time.' The high scoring group was asked, 'Do you think the government is using that technology to track where you are at different times?' The two propositions are quite different, the first being the very specific idea that everyone is being tracked, everywhere, at all times. The second is that some people, or rather 'you' are being tracked in some places at some times, a much more general idea. As a result, the test wasn't remotely fair and was deliberately skewed to help produce the desired result.

Furthermore, even if the test were done properly and did produce this result, what would it prove? It would prove that people who believe in 'conspiracy theories' are less trusting and feel more alienated. That much should be obvious to anyone who has ever thought about the subject, but it only begs the question of which is cause and which is effect? Are people less trusting because they believe in conspiracy theories, or do they believe in conspiracy theories because they are less trusting? After all, someone whose lover has cheated on them is going to find it harder to trust that person not to do it again, but this is perfectly natural and in many ways rational.

Likewise, being prone to assumption based on partial evidence is difficult, if not impossible, to measure objectively. What one person considers an assumption might be taken as an established fact by another person, and so the judgment as to who is more prone to assumption is essentially subjective. Also, as in the above example, if someone has been cheated on in the past then they might be more prone to the assumption that their new lover could be cheating on them. Likewise, someone might suspect their lover for no good reason.

Applied to terrorist attacks, this logical sleight of hand becomes even more stark. After all, any belief about 7/7 is a belief based on partial evidence, and therefore involves some assumptions, because so much of the evidence is being kept out of the public domain. The psychologists employed for the show presumably wrote the test. They assumed, based on partial evidence, the truth of official conspiracy theories, to the extent that they did not even recognise their own beliefs as conspiracy theories. However, as these psychologists and this TV show would have it, it is only those who believe that the state was somehow behind the attacks that are making assumptions.

In the same way, it is true that alternative conspiracy theories can be psychologically appealing but that argument conveniently ignores that the official conspiracy theory is also psychologically appealing. Given the choice between believing that the culprits died in the attacks and believing that the culprits are alive and well and in positions of power, the former is more appealing to most people. It provides closure, and an excuse for not investigating further.

Conspiracy: Who Really Runs the World? was a truly shameful production that made crude generalisations and used an incredibly unscientific, logically fallacious 'test' to prove a desired conclusion. That this programme is presumably being shown to teenagers to help shape their notions of 'citizenship' is particularly worrying. The core message of the show is that trusting authorities is rational and that distrusting them is irrational, and the implication is that being a good citizen means believing what the government tells you. Sadly, it was by no means the last TV show to do this.

The *Conspiracy Files*

At the end of June 2009, a week before the fourth anniversary of the attacks, the BBC finally broadcast their episode of *Conspiracy Files* devoted to 7/7. They had begun working on the show in mid 2007, and clearly the show was intended to air after the 2008 trial of the three alleged co-conspirators. Because their first trial resulted in a hung jury, the show was not broadcast until after their re-trial. The same is true of the ISC's second report, which was published just weeks before *Conspiracy Files* aired.

When the BBC began making the show they contacted J7 and the filmmakers behind what is arguably the best independent documentary on 7/7, *Ludicrous Diversion*. They were initially told that the production was a serious documentary, but it emerged that it was going to be part of the *Conspiracy Files* series. At that time, the whole four-episode first season of the show had broadcast, and in particular its episode on 9/11 had been heavily criticised by the web-based media.

Both J7 and the makers of *Ludicrous Diversion* refused to get involved once they found out that the planned documentary was part of the same series. That left the BBC in the position of having to look elsewhere for participants, but fortunately during the exact same timeframe another internet-based documentary had been released – *7/7 Ripple Effect*.

7/7 Ripple Effect and its sequel outline an alternative conspiracy theory whereby the alleged bombers were lured to London as part of Peter Power's training exercise, and then disposed of by police snipers at Canary Wharf. The basis for the theory, as presented in the films, is a lot of rumour and anonymously sourced media reports. There is not a single named witness or document or photograph or any other piece of evidence that supports this hypothesis.

This alternative story is so speculative that I consider it to be a distraction from more serious questions and lines of inquiry. It also provided an easy target for the BBC in their *Conspiracy Files* show, and much of that show was devoted to refuting the poorly sourced claims in *7/7 Ripple Effect.* The makers of *Ripple Effect* did not apply the scepticism to their own theory that they had applied to the official version. Thus, it was full of the same sorts of gaping holes as the Home Office narrative.

Much of the argument revolved around a training exercise being run by Peter Power of Visor Consultants on the morning of 7/7. A fuller explanation of this is saved for chapter 10 but critically, *Ripple Effect's* theory is that the four men were recruited to play the role of mock terrorists in Power's exercise.

The BBC refuted this by interviewing Power, who claimed that it was a desktop simulation for a small room full of people in one office, not a suited-and-booted exercise on the ground at the tube stations. As such, there was no need for people portraying mock terrorists. While some will not be convinced by this explanation, the makers of *Ripple Effect* have no evidence contradicting it. As such, the argument is effectively a stalemate. Neither side can convince the other that they are wrong.

The *Conspiracy Files* described Power as a 'crisis management consultant', and glossed over his history working for the MPS. They also neglected to mention his appearance on a May 2004 episode of *Panorama* that predicted many aspects of the 7/7 attacks. As such, their refutation may be perfectly true but was done in such a way that only engenders further suspicion. If Power has nothing to hide, then why were the BBC so careful about how they presented him?

Similarly, *Ripple Effect's* alternative conspiracy theory puts a lot of stock in the presence of a small white van that was next to the number 30 bus when it exploded. The van bore the logo of the firm Kingstar, whose website lists among their services 'controlled demolition'. The makers of *Ripple Effect* speculated that the company were involved in blowing up the bus.

The BBC interviewed Mick Barnard, an Operations Manager for Kingstar who explained that they didn't do the types of controlled demolition that use explosives. Instead, they work with diamond tipped drills, pneumatic tools and so on. Once again, because the makers of the alternative story had not even bothered to ask the firm what kind of controlled demolition they did, their argument was left open to this easy and simple refutation.

The makers of *Conspiracy Files* had less luck when they talked to one of the survivors of 7/7 whose account is consistent with an explosion under the train. This is the one part of the *Ripple Effect* narrative that is born out by much of the available evidence, though neither the first nor the second film make clear the sheer number of witnesses and diagrams that support this idea.

The first *Ripple Effect* film mentions the account of Bruce Lait, the dancer from Cambridge who was in the carriage of the bombed train near Liverpool Street. The BBC interviewed Lait for the *Conspiracy Files* show, and he repeated to them his memory of seeing metal in the floor pushed upwards, into the carriage, as though the bomb were underneath the train. In the broadcast show as soon as Lait says this the voice-over interjected saying that Bruce 'doesn't know if he actually saw evidence' that the bomb was under the train. No other witness in the show was subject to such caveats.

Lait had been sent a copy of *Ripple Effect* on DVD, and the BBC asked him about his reaction. In a moment that ran completely against the BBC's slant on the subject, Lait responded, 'If what the *Ripple Effect* says is true, then we should know about it, and it should be looked into in a massive way, because like I say, it basically is saying that "somebody is to blame other than those suicide bombers, who is it?"'

The final, bizarre part of the BBC's refutation of *7/7 Ripple Effect* was to 'unmask' its maker, who in the film goes by the name Muad Dib. They described how he was 'waging a propaganda war' to advance his 'distorted vision of reality' and that he had so far evaded scrutiny. The *Conspiracy Files* voice over claims that the BBC tracked him down, even though by the time the show was broadcast everyone knew that 'Muad Dib' was actually Anthony John Hill of Kells, County Meath.

Showing their out of date footage as though it were recently recorded, the BBC interviewer is seen confronting Mr Hill in the street and claiming, 'You have made a film that is undermining trust in the British government and damaging community cohesion, is that your intention Mr Hill?' The interviewer didn't get a response to his rather loaded and biased line of questioning. In the absence of an answer, they explain how Hill believes he is the messiah.

It was an extremely lame piece of theatre, designed to portray Hill as representing those who question the official version of 7/7, and as a reclusive madman. As one commenter on the BBC website who identified themselves as a non-sceptic of the official account put it, 'The government doesn't need a beardy weirdy who thinks he's Jesus to bring it into disrepute, its already doing a splendid job by itself.' That is as true now as it was back in 2009, at a time when the expenses scandal and the financial crisis were front-page news.

Provoking Extremism?

Throughout the *Conspiracy Files* show the BBC focused entirely on that group of people who form alternative explanations on the basis of suspicion rather than evidence, and who make unfounded accusations. The implication is that they are representative of all people asking questions or posing alternative theories of what happened. Just as in *Conspiracy: Who Really Runs the World?* the conclusion they were trying to get across is that all such people are mentally deficient, if not also emotionally troubled.

This was done in the context of arguing that such theories encourage extremism, and the show interviewed Rachel 'North', a survivor from the Piccadilly Line explosion. Rachel was thrust into the public eye immediately following the bombings, and wrote a diary for the BBC's online coverage in the days after 7/7. She has since appeared on TV, in numerous press interviews and has written a book about her experiences. She has campaigned at great length for an independent public inquiry in 7/7, but, oddly, has been very hostile to any suggestion that the official version might not be true.

On the *Conspiracy Files* Rachel said, 'We have a small minority of people spreading a big powerful idea. The big powerful idea is there is a war on Islam, there is a war on Muslims, it is your duty to fight against those who strike at our people. The idea that the government actually faked the 7/7 bombings, in order to demonise Muslims, is just throwing petrol onto the flames of this idea.'[3]

This is a dangerous and deceitful portrait of the world. It implies is that you shouldn't hold suspicions or make accusations against the government in case you help to inspire and encourage terrorism and other violence. It suggests that there is no truth to the idea that Muslims are being attacked through wars and 'counter-terrorism' operations, when it is abundantly clear that there is some reason to think that.

Of the tens of thousands of young Muslims stopped and searched under so-called anti-terrorism powers, not a single one has been found to have any involvement in terrorism. Of the well over a thousand people, mostly Muslims, arrested in the wake of 9/11, only a handful have been convicted of terrorist offences, and many of those convictions are suspicious (see for example the convictions of the 21/7 'bombers' explored in chapter 11). The shooting at Forestgate, the 'extraordinary rendition' of 'terror suspects' and much much more point to an aggressive, organised targeting of Muslims as a designated enemy of 'National Security'.

In reality, if such alternative conspiracy theories did tend to inspire terrorist attacks then we would have had a lot more attacks in the UK since 7/7, as such theories are quite prevalent. Rachel's position as a survivor of the attacks may make it unseemly to attack her views, but it does not qualify her as an expert in the mindset of a targeted ethnic minority. However, she has repeatedly argued in interviews and articles that the use of 7/7 as an excuse for new legislation and 'counter-terrorism' powers is wrong and exploitative. This suggests that she is well aware of how terrorist attacks can be used to advance state power and as an excuse for targeting innocent people.

One has to wonder, therefore, at the contradictions in the views she has made public. She is wholly in favour of an independent public inquiry, but wholly against the idea that the official version of 7/7 is not true. She objects to the view that there is a war on Muslims, but seems very aware of how Muslims have been mistreated and even killed in the name of fighting terrorism. In her writings and interviews she makes it clear that the traumas of her life have caused her to suffer from shell shock, now known as posttraumatic stress disorder or PTSD. What is clear from her assorted and often contradictory views on these issues is that when it comes to 7/7, she remains understandably emotionally conflicted.

Theorising Truth

Perhaps unsurprisingly, the BBC's *Conspiracy Files* show did nothing to dissuade those who doubt the official version of 7/7 or advance alternative versions. If anything, it had the opposite effect. It resulted in those who believed in the alternative theory espoused by *Ripple Effect* becoming ever more dogmatic in their views, and in them seeing themselves as victimised.

In the wake of the show being broadcast, a new voice entered the discussion about 7/7 that was taking place largely online. Dr Rory Ridley-Duff, a lecturer in Business Studies at Sheffield Hallam University, published an essay on the internet explaining why he thought that the story posed by *Ripple Effect* was more truthful than the story implicitly told by the *Conspiracy Files* show. It may or may not be significant that John Hill, the public face of *Ripple Effect*, is also from

Sheffield, as is 'former' police intelligence analyst Tony Farrell who also endorses this alternative version of events.

Ridley-Duff's paper is titled *Theorising Truth: What Happened at Canary Wharf on 7th July 2005?* It is riddled with basic factual inaccuracies, such as when Peter Power first appeared on TV and radio on 7/7 and announced that he was running a training exercise that morning. Ridley-Duff's paper says this was in the morning, whereas in fact it was in the afternoon.

Likewise, he repeats the claim from *Ripple Effect* that if the alleged bombers did not catch the 7:40 train from Luton - which was cancelled - then the next train was at 7:56 - the delayed 7:48 train. Strangely, he also cites the July 7th Truth Campaign website that includes an actual timetable of the Luton-King's Cross trains on 7/7, which shows there was a train at 7:42 - the delayed 7:30 train. Given that the essay does not even get such basic facts correct all the talk of theories of truth (correspondence, coherence, constructivist) seems a little premature.

The essay focuses on the final key part of the *Ripple Effect* conspiracy theory – the claim that some if not all of the alleged bombers were shot dead at Canary Wharf on the morning of 7/7. This is based on a relatively widely reported rumour on the day of 7/7 that was explicitly denied by the MPS in a press conference. It is a central part of the *Ripple Effect* narrative because it supposedly accounts for what happened to the alleged bombers if they did not kill themselves in suicide attacks.

Ridley-Duff's method of testing the accuracy of this theory was to use the Nexis UK news database, and Google searches for blogs, forums and other websites talking about Canary Wharf on 7/7. These searches found two things: a large number of media reports detailing the Canary Wharf story as a rumour, and a handful of named witnesses to a police presence at Canary Wharf and a lockdown of buildings in the area.

Crucially, there is not a single named witness to the presence of supposed terrorists in Canary Wharf, or of police snipers, or of anyone being shot. Ridley Duff avoids this issue by saying that the bloggers and forum posters are 'verbatim first hand reports, carrying more credibility than second-hand BBC reports. Their credibility does not depend on endorsement or confirmation by a government or state authority.'[4]

The point is that regardless of their credibility as sources, none of them actually saw anyone being shot at Canary Wharf. It is all second-hand 'the radio said this', 'a friend of mine said that', which isn't credible evidence of anything. The only evidence Ridley-Duff could find through this method is a load of anonymously sourced mainstream media reports and hearsay – precisely the sort of thing someone skeptical of official sources would normally reject. The entire case Ridley-Duff makes is intellectually dishonest.

It is also thoroughly implausible. Let us imagine for a moment that John Hill is correct, and the alleged bombers were duped into travelling to London to play the role of mock-terrorists in a training exercise. Why would the conspirators who have set them up decide not to intercept them prior to the bombings that were to be blamed on them? Why would they have simply got them to London and then left them to hang around while bombs were being set off in their name?

Let us imagine that for some completely irrational and stupid reason this is actually true, and that the four were in London as the crisis unfolded. According to Hill they became suspicious, fled to Canary Wharf to try to reach newspaper offices so they could reveal their story, but were shot by police snipers as they arrived. Why would the police not simply arrest them? The four could then be easily disposed of in secret without any risk of blowing the operation. Why would they shoot them dead in the street, in one of the busiest parts of London?

Furthermore, how could they manage this without even a single eyewitness seeing the shootings? The streets were filled with people unable to get tube trains because the network had been halted shortly after the bombings. Yet, so Hill would have us believe, the police shot two, three or possibly even all four alleged bombers at Canary Wharf without anyone realizing it had happened, beyond it becoming an office rumour.

There was a lock down at Canary Wharf that begun at around 10 o'clock on the morning of 7/7 that lasted for several hours. However, this is not particularly suspicious because Canary Wharf (both the area and the skyscraper at One Canada Square often called 'Canary Wharf') was the target of a major bomb attack in 1996. The explosion killed two men who had been missed in the evacuation, injured dozens more, and caused tens of millions of pounds worth of damage.

Ridley-Duff concludes that, 'After deploying three different theories of truth to develop insights into new and existing evidence, it is the BBC / Government theory that has a lower level of correspondence with known 'facts', is incoherent to the point of being implausible, and is more likely to distort its reports because of institutional controls and political pressures.'

The 'facts' he refers to are not by any means known, and his generally lax approach towards factual information throughout the essay renders this an unconvincing argument. The government's narrative is extremely incoherent and implausible, but no more so than *Ripple Effect*'s narrative. Ridley-Duff assumes that the filmmaker behind *Ripple Effect* is freer from 'institutional controls and political pressures' that those working for the Home Office. Given that the man in question has consistently lied about being the only person behind the film (there were others), and believes himself to be the messiah, it is somewhat absurd to suggest that he is a more credible authority than the government, or indeed than just an ordinary, sane person. Of course, the essay neglects to mention these facts.

Throughout Ridley-Duff's paper he commits a logical fallacy that is common among those with no philosophical background – the fallacy of sophisme de l'opposition or the false dilemma. He presents the argument entirely in terms of a choice between the official Home Office story being true or the alternative *Ripple Effect* story being true. It is a black and white choice that ignores the rather obvious possibility that neither story is true.

In approaching the dialogue about 7/7 in this way, Ridley-Duff actually exacerbated the division between the two opposing views, making those that believe the *Ripple Effect* story all the more dogmatic in their claims of truth. He engaged the BBC using their terms, their types of information sources, and their level of intelligence. In doing this, he failed to advance the discussion beyond simply scouring media reports and cherry picking those bits that support one's theory, something both *Ripple Effect* and *Conspiracy Files* are guilty of doing.

The ISC and the Saudi warning

Just after the second trial of the three alleged co-conspirators the Intelligence and Security Committee (ISC) published their second report. Like the *Conspiracy Files* episode, it had been delayed because of the trial and re-trial of Ali, Saleem and Shakil. With those proceedings over, and with the accused cleared of any involvement in the attacks, the attempt to debunk scepticism and alternative views of 7/7 was obviously a priority.

The ISC's second report on 7/7 tells a tale of MI5 being swamped with potential suspects and lacking the resources to investigate them all satisfactorily. This meant that some people who appeared on their 'radar' during their various pre-7/7 operations were not properly followed up, and this apparently included the alleged bombers.

The details of this part of MI5's excuse are dealt with in details in chapters six to eight, but the ISC also explicated attempted to put down what they describe as 'other allegations'. By far the most extraordinary example of this was the claim in an Observer newspaper report that Saudi intelligence had warned the British about an impending attack only months before 7/7.

The story first appeared in the Observer in August 2005, but by September more details had become available. According to 'highly-placed Saudi security sources' a warning was sent to MI6 in December 2004 saying that a 'cell of four people' were planning to attack the London tube network in the following six months.[5]

These claims were repeated by Saudi King Abdullah when he made a visit to the UK in autumn 2007. The specific nature of the warning and the way it predicted at least the official version of events have made it a focal point for sceptics and those who believe alternative theories. The ISC dealt with this in a very strange way.

They redacted several paragraphs on what the December 2004 warning to MI6 actually contained, cited the Observer article and then said, 'We cannot comment on the accuracy of this report, compared with the actual intelligence relating to the Saudi warning, without disclosing the details of the intelligence.' This tells us that the Observer report and the actual warning must at least be similar in content because if they were wholly different then the ISC could say so without revealing any details of the actual warning.

The ISC went on to reiterate their assessment in their first report that the warning 'was materially different from what actually occurred on

7 July and clearly not relevant to these attacks.' This may be true, after all it is far from certain the attackers were a cell of four people, and the date of 7/7 lies just beyond the six month period cited by the Observer. However, this only provokes a different kind of question.

A month before 7/7, just as the Saudi warning was expiring, MI5 downgraded the terror threat level to the UK. At that time the information was only passed to businesses and government departments, and not the public. One of the post-7/7 changes is that now the assessed threat level is made public on MI5's website and elsewhere. But if MI5 and MI6 were under-resourced in the years before 7/7 then how were they in a position to make a valid assessment of the threat level? Either they were in a position to assess the threat, and therefore to recognize the importance or triviality of the Saudi warning, or they were not. To claim both at the same time is doublethink, or doublespeak.

The very fact that they downgraded the threat level at the end of the period when the Saudis warned there would be an attack suggests that they took it seriously. In any case, to present such a self-contradictory and bizarre argument while refusing to clarify what was in the Saudi warning has, like the other debunking efforts, only fuelled the fires of scepticism and suspicion.

Debunking 7/7 at the Inquests

This process of attempting to debunking 'conspiracy theories' about 7/7, by which they mean legitimate questions and alternative views of the evidence that is available, did not stop in 2009. At the end of 2010, over five years after the attacks, the government finally decided to hold some inquests into the deaths in London's greatest ever peacetime mass murder.

Initially, and legally, the deaths of the alleged bombers were going to be examined at the same time as those of the victims of the bombings. This decision was rejected by the bereaved families and they appealed to the coroner Lady Justice Heather Hallett, successfully. The inquests were then divided into the 52 victims and it was ruled that the deaths of the four alleged bombers would be examined later.

The bereaved families of the alleged bombers, some of whom have made public statements expressing their disbelief at the official version of events, were denied legal aid. This prevented them from being able to be present at the inquests into the 52 deaths, and from challenging the evidence and the assumptions drawn from it.

At the end of the inquests in May 2011, Hallett ruled that there was no need to hold inquests into the deaths of the alleged bombers, which makes the rest of her conclusions logically and legally absurd. It has never been proven, to any standard of legal satisfaction, that those four men were on the trains and the bus, killing themselves and others with bombs. Not only that, but it makes no sense.

None of the men had any reason to kill themselves, and if they simply wanted to commit mass murder they could have done so without killing themselves. None of them were known as particularly political or religious. There is no evidence of murderous intent in their behaviour, and no history of violent crime. Of course, this is not how the men were portrayed at the inquests.

The proceedings were largely controlled by Hallett and Hugo Keith QC, the government's lawyer. He directed the questions, explained the evidence and generally directed the examination and investigation. Keith has an interesting background, having helped defend the Royal family at the inquests into the deaths of Princess Diana and Dodi Al Fayed. He also helped defend Silvio Berlusconi and David Mills in a major money laundering case. He also helped defend the Director of Public Prosecutions decision not to prosecute anyone for the killing of Jean Charles de Menezes.

Keith's other jobs have included helping the Secretary of State try to extradite Gary McKinnon, the hacker who broke into the Pentagon's website looking for evidence of UFOs and extraterrestrials. He defended the police at the inquest into the death of barrister Mark Saunders, who was shot five times by the police in a case that was ruled to be 'self-defence'. Keith's activities likewise include assisting the Serious Fraud Office in protecting the decision to end an investigation into allegations of bribery involving BAE Systems contracts in Saudi Arabia. In sum, Hugo Keith QC has spent most of his career defending the rich and powerful against allegations of conspiracy, corruption and criminal negligence. The perfect man, you might say, to host inquests into the deaths of the victims of England's most lethal terrorist attack.

On the first day he got to work, admitting that, 'It is not a proper function of an inquest to attribute blame or apportion guilt, or a proper function of mine to express opinions on impermissible areas.' This admission is in keeping with the 2009 Coroners and Justice Act, under which the July 7 Inquests were held. Nonetheless, Keith then set about doing the exact opposite, describing the death, devastation and mutilation' that unleashed an unimaginable tidal wave of shock, misery and horror'. The bombings, he said, 'were acts of merciless savagery and one can only imagine at the sheer inhumanity of the perpetrators'.

There is no doubt that the suffering of the bereaved has been tremendous, but these are not words of sympathy. They are in effect slogans, designed for the maximum psychological impact on those listening. In the days after Keith made these comments, the same exact phrases appeared in national newspaper headlines. He went on to outline how debunking 'conspiracy theories' was one of the key aims of the proceedings.

Keith said, 'it is to be hoped that these inquests, however unpleasant and distressing, as they will be, will assist in answering the families' questions in allaying some of the rumours and suspicion generated by conspiracy theorists... a number of unlikely conspiracy theories have been aired in the press and on the internet... We consider it important that such claims are identified and addressed... Where such claims do not appear to be supported by the evidence that has been gathered, there is, we feel, a danger that the continuation of such claims might needlessly distress the bereaved families as well as detracting attention away from the issues that you have identified as being worthy of further investigation.'

Having told us of the 'sheer inhumanity' of the perpetrators of 7/7, Keith tried to lay some of the blame for the 'unimaginable tidal wave of shock, misery and horror' on the shoulders of 'conspiracy theorists'. While the behaviour of some alternative conspiracy theorists has been reprehensible, that does not compare to the behaviour of the state. It is the police, the Home Office and MI5 who keep changing their story. It is three consecutive Prime Ministers who have refused to hold any kind of public inquiry. It they who took five years even to hold inquests into the deaths of the victims of the attacks. However crazy some people's speculations might be, they have not caused anything like the degree of suffering that the security services and the state in general have caused to the bereaved.

Keith went on to claim, 'There is no evidence at all that we have seen to suggest that the bombers were duped in some way so that they did not know that they were going to die or, even more absurdly, that they did not know that they were carrying explosives at all.' They have seen such evidence, for example the fact that Shehzad Tanweer argued with the cashier at Woodall Services on the M1 only a few hours before the government say he blew himself up. Tanweer was a wealthy young man. Despite being only 22 when he died, he apparently left a fortune in the order of £100,000. Even if he were poor, he should not have been bothered about his change while on his way to kill himself.

This sort of behaviour, and this is far from the only example, is evidence that the men were not planning to kill themselves. Hugo the

Hatchet dealt with this by claiming that they must have simply been covering their tracks, pretending to not be suicidal so no one would suspect them. He said, 'It is right to say that the bombers were surprisingly effective, it would seem, in concealing their intentions from those around them. Tanweer played cricket in the evening before putting the terrible plot into effect and seemed more concerned, according to his family, by the loss of his mobile phone.' This is, of course, completely circular. By this argument, behaviour that indicates that you intend to survive isn't actually that, it is behaviour that indicates that you are concealing your intention to kill yourself.

Keith's final attempt to prove that the four were intentional, premeditated suicide bombers is lifted from the 'key evidence' in the Home Office narrative. He proclaimed that, 'If there were any residual doubts, these are further answered by two other pieces of evidence: Tanweer's so-called last will and testament, which appeared a year later on the internet, in which he seeks to justify attacks, and the footage of Khan which appeared on Al Jazeera, on 1 September 2005, to similar effect. Those parts of the videos that showed them at any rate must of course have been prepared prior to 7 July, and thus, on account of their content, demonstrate that their views had been held for some time. Indeed, the release of the videos reinforces the terrorist dimension of the attacks. They were made to be released following the attacks themselves.'[6]

These supposed 'martyrdom videos' contain no mention of suicide, or terrorist attacks, or London or the tube network. As far as proving intent to carry out the 7/7 attacks, they are ambiguous at best. Furthermore, this argument overlooks several vital questions. If the alleged bombers were dead on July 7th 2005, and they were working alone, then who sent the video to al Jazeera? Who posted Tanweer's video on the internet a year later? If the videos were made with the intention of releasing them following the attacks, then who made them, kept them and released them? By citing this as evidence of the four men's intention to kill themselves, Keith's argument requires that there must be at least a fifth if not more conspirators.

Perhaps most fundamentally, if the men were a self-radicalising group of suicide bombers then where are the equivalent videos for Hussain and Lindsay? Why would only two of them make 'martyrdom videos'? Why not all four? Regardless, knowing someone who has signalled their intention to kill themselves is not evidence of you being a suicide bomber, so even if Khan and Tanweer's videos are seen in that way they are not evidence of Hussain and Lindsay's guilt.

The *Conspiracy Roadtrip*

In spring 2012 a new programme was commissioned on the subject of debunking 7/7 'conspiracy theories'. The inaugural *Conspiracy Roadtrip* show in 2011 had seen a small number of young 'conspiracy theorists' taken to America to be confronted with evidence and 'experts' that were against their 'conspiracy theories' about 9/11.

It was a remarkably infantile show. One highlight was the use of a lego tower to try to demonstrate why the twin WTC towers collapsed largely straight down into their own structures, the path of most resistance. Another moment saw the five participants dropping stones into piles of flour, to show that that Flight 93 could indeed have buried itself underground without leaving a large hole or crater.

However, the show was a huge success, garnering the highest audience ever for a BBC3 broadcast. It also garnered arguably the most online criticism for any BBC show ever broadcast on any channel. The participants were angry at how they'd been portrayed, with few if any of their questions and discussions with the 'experts' making it into the broadcast show.

So when I saw that the same production company were seeking participants for a related show on 7/7, it was with some trepidation that I approached them to provide them with links to my films on the subject. It became clear in dialogues with one of their researchers that the company had received a lot of critical and abusive feedback from their first show.

Throughout my discussions with their researchers and one of their producers they consistently tried to persuade me to agree to be involved in the show. I provided them with a list of people I believed would be the most important to talk to – including DAC Peter Clarke, who led the police investigation and the head of the ISC Paul Murphy MP, who led their two investigations. I also suggested Clifford Todd, the government explosives expert who has repeatedly testified about 7/7, the original coroner Dr Andrew Reid, the forensic anthropologist Dr Julie Ann Roberts who examined the alleged bombers bodies and others. None of these people were interviewed as part of the show.

I also asked that if I were to agree to be on the show that I could run my own camera. I am, after all, a researcher and filmmaker. I was never given a straight answer to this request. I was constantly flattered and told how important it was that I be on the programme. I was also told some odd things (including that Tony Blair might be available to talk to) that struck me as unbelievable.

I raised one criticism with the makers of the show that I had seen made by a J7 member and astute critic of their 9/11 broadcast. The show's presenter Andrew Maxwell, a comedian, is Irish and thus would presumably be familiar with the British state's collusion in the Patrick Finucane murder and similar acts of terrorism. I asked about this and was told that the presenter was very much aware of British state collusion with terrorists in Ireland and this was partly why he was interested in 7/7. I tried to press further on why it was that none of this came across in their 9/11 show but was told by the researcher and producer that they couldn't speak for Mr Maxwell.

In the end, it became impossible to reconcile what they were telling me they were making (a sincere documentary) with what I knew they were actually making (a reality TV show) and I made my conditions clear. I wanted to talk to people in real positions of authority in the official 7/7 investigations, not commentators and people who had nothing to do with the case, and I wanted to be able to run my own camera. I said that I did not want to hear back from them unless these conditions could be met. As a result I did not hear back from them.

The show's producers opted for four participants. One was Tony Topping, a relative well-known figure on the British conspiracy circuit, who also appeared on the *Conspiracy: Who Really Runs the World?* show talking about UFOs and alien abduction. Another was a young Muslim woman called Davina who didn't get much screentime and didn't seem particularly interested in 7/7. Third was Jon Scobie of activist group WeAreChange Birmingham, who evidently tried to ask some important and informed questions but was largely shot down and left on the cutting room floor. Fourth was Layla, a young lady who is a part-time witch and Tarot card reader, and also a nude model and low-budget film actress.

When it initially broadcast, the *7/7 Conspiracy Roadtrip* included a rundown of the alleged bombers and the official version. There was one glaring error – the picture they used of Mohammad Sidique Khan wasn't a picture of the right man. It was a picture of one 'Siddique Khan' taken from a Johns Hopkins University in Baltimore webpage from their maths department.[7] Note the two ds in 'Siddique', unlike the alleged 7/7 ringleader whose name only had one d. The only way the makers of *Conspiracy Roadtrip* could have found this picture in a Google image search is if they spelled the man's name wrongly.

Apparently the Siddique Khan shown on BBC3 was teaching in Maryland for several years from 2005 to 2009. As such, there is no excuse for the show using the wrong picture. They could only have mistaken it for the desired Sidique Khan if they never looked at the webpage that hosted the picture. In subsequent broadcasts the image was changed, but it is nonetheless a terrible indictment of the inaccuracy and casual nature with which this programme approached accusing these men of mass murder.

The show largely focussed on four experts, people chosen by the production company to try to persuade the four participants that they were wrong to believe that there was something wrong with the official story. Expert talking head number 1 was Russell Razzaque, whose job it was to explain how four men with no apparent motive for suicide or outward indication of suicidal intent became suicide bombers.

Razzaque claimed that the four radicalised each other through secret late night meetings at the Hamara healthy living centre in Leeds. Some of the four men are known to have visited the Hamara centre, but how did Razzaque know that they met there together in secret? If they were the only people there, and they are all dead then how did he know about the supposed secret meetings? Even if those meetings did take place, Razzaque had no way of knowing what was said at them. It was an entirely spurious argument.

The four participants were then shown attempting, and failing, to reconstruct the supposed journeys of the alleged bombers on the morning of 7/7. The fact that the improbable but possible movements of the four could not be exactly replicated was, bizarrely, treated as a success and largely helped convince Layla that the official story was true.

Expert talking head number 2 was the disgraced former Met Police officer Brian Paddick, who also appeared in the *Conspiracy Files* show, and led the MPS press conference on the morning of 7/7. He was responsible for explaining why there was so little CCTV footage showing the alleged bombers movements. His answer was, in essence, 'I don't know', before reiterating that the men's DNA had been found at the scenes (not their bodies, their DNA), and that this negated any questions about the CCTV. This managed to convince Layla and Davina that their scepticism towards the official story was unfounded.

After going over some well-trodden ground with Dr Naseem of the Birmingham Central Mosque, a repeat of the *Conspiracy Files* show, the *Conspiracy Roadtrip* took another turn down Expert Lane. Expert talking head number 3 was Chris Hunter (not his real name), a former security services agent and, so they claimed, a bomb expert. It was his job to contradict the abundance of evidence indicating explosions from within the floors or underneath the trains.

This question, one of the most contentious and important in the entire 7/7 story, was presented by Layla in a misleading way. She explained that she'd heard that on the trains that those sitting down were more badly injured than those standing up. 'Chris Hunter' countered by explaining that his interpretation of photographs of the Aldgate train explosion showed the damage going mostly upward and downwards. Exactly how this refuted the idea of an explosion from within the floor or under the train wasn't made clear.

Furthermore, the photograph 'Chris Hunter' was shown holding as he explained this was not from the Aldgate train, but from the Piccadilly line train. That he didn't even know which train he was looking at shows that he is no expert on the 7/7 explosions. 'Hunter' also claimed that the bombers on 7/7 attached nails and other shrapnel to the outside of their devices so as to maximise casualties. This statement, which appeared to seriously shock participant Tony Topping, is not true, or at least if it is true then it is strange that it doesn't appear in any official report or testimony of those who examined the scenes.

The final theory that the show sought to rebuff was the claim that you can't blow up a bus with homemade explosives. Of course, this isn't a claim made by any serious 7/7 investigator because with the right kind of homemade explosive, and enough of it, you can of course blow up just about anything. Enter expert talking head number 4, Sidney Alford. Alford is a darling of TV shows about explosions, his charmingly doddery manner proving popular. However, his contribution to the *7/7 Conspiracy Roadtrip* was quite deceitful

Alford was shown assembling a bomb that he then planted on a double decker red London bus like that blown up on 7/7. He said that he was including large amounts of black pepper, because a policeman reported smelling pepper at one of the bomb scenes. If that is true then like 'Chris Hunter's fantasy about shrapnel, it is the first mention of it. Alford then mixed the pepper with, apparently, some concentrated hydrogen peroxide, though there is no explanation of how he concentrated it down from the commercially available type.

This concoction, which looked nothing like the sludge found in plastic tubs in the flat in Alexandra Grove, was then sealed up in a biscuit tin and supposedly used to blow up the bus. It was a dramatic, psychologically effective finale to the show, but it proved nothing of significance. For one thing, the bus was clearly an old and worn-out model, presumably bought on the cheap for the sake of being blown up in a quarry by the BBC. For another, Alford placed the bomb in the wrong location, at least according to the official diagrams. Thirdly, Alford's bomb blew a large hole in the floor of the bus, unlike on 7/7.

Perhaps most importantly, is it even fair to call this a homemade bomb? After all, the bomb was made not by the show's participants or any of the production staff but by a career explosives expert.

The very end of the programme showed presenter Andrew Maxwell meeting up with the participants in the middle of Westminster. Three of the participants – Layla, Davina and Tony Topping – renounced their views and expressed some adherence to the official story. Only Jon refused to believe that anything he had been shown was a reason to abandon his suspicions. It was a dreadful piece of television that I am glad I did not participate in, and that did nothing to advance a rational understanding of 7/7.

The Argument Rages on

The efforts made to debunk questions and alternative conspiracy theories about the 7/7 bombings have been crude and misleading. The fundamental issues have consistently been avoided. The discussion has focussed on the people who ask the questions and believe the theories, rather than on the questions and theories themselves, and the evidence that could resolve them.

The unsayable truth is that many people ask these questions and believe these theories because of the evidence available to them. For some it is a matter of personal prejudice, intellectual laziness and political persuasion but for others it is a recognition of the simple fact that we have been lied to about 7/7. While I do not endorse the alternative conspiracy theories proposed by the makers of *Ripple Effect* and their associates, nor do I dismiss what they are saying without looking at their evidence.

Sadly, when I did look I found the same cherry picking, the same contextless quote-mining, the same vague and contradictory use of sources as I saw in the official Home Office explanation. The films, and their advocates, have done nothing to advance the discussion. If anything, they have simply polarised it, assuming just as the BBC have done that either you believe the official story, or you believe their own narrow, baseless alternative story.

In seeking to debunk only the weak alternative explanation offered by *Ripple Effect*, the BBC chose an easy target. Their refutations of some of the key aspects of the alternative story outlined in the film were so poor that they did nothing to convince those who believed that alternative story. On the contrary, it simply encouraged those people to think that they were on the right track and become more adamant about what they believed.

Into this dispute came Rory Ridley-Duff, whose refutation of the BBC's refutation of *Ripple Effect*'s refutation of the Home Office only exacerbated this polarisation and dogmatism. The divide between those who believe the official story and those who question or disbelieve it got wider, and the quality of the evidence cited and standard of argument employed only got lower. None of this two-sided, polarised discussion got us any closer to the truth.

In particular the dispute caused by Mark Honigsbaum's early report indicating an explosion from under the Edgware Road train has continued. In David Aaronovitch's 2010 book *Voodoo Histories*, he sought to dispel any and every alternative conspiracy theory that he could. He made use of Honigsbaum's retraction of his early audio report, commenting that, 'if the bombs could be shown to have detonated somewhere else -underneath the trains, for example- then they couldn't have been associated with the so-called terrorists. This, stated the theorists, was exactly what eyewitnesses had claimed to see happen when the bombs exploded.'[8]

Aaronovitch went on to claim that, 'Ultimately, all such reports could be traced to one source - Guardian journalist Mark Honigsbaum.' His argument is that because Honigsbaum retracted his audio report that there is no evidence at all supporting the 'bombs under the trains' idea. As we saw in the previous chapter, this simply isn't true. In particular, Bruce Lait's account is entirely consistent with an explosion from under the train, or within the floor of the train. Aaronovitch must be aware of Lait's comments because he references two 7/7 documentaries that include Lait's story. As such, it appears he knowingly ignored Lait in favour of trying to dismiss all 7/7 'conspiracy theories' in one fell swoop.

In 2011, 7/7 alternative conspiracy theorist Nick Kollerstrom published the third edition of his book *Terror on the Tube*. In stark contrast to Aaronovitch's argument Kollerstrom makes copious use of Honigsbaum's early report, and only briefly mentions the retraction. He describes this as Honigsbaum attempting to 'back out from this early report... without suggesting what was wrong with it.'[9] On the contrary, Honigsbaum did say what was wrong with it, namely that other witnesses had said the explosion came from within the carriage. Just as Aaronovitch overstated the importance of and misrepresented Honigsbaum's retraction, Kollerstrom understated its importance and also misrepresented it.

We cannot solve the 7/7 mass murder through arguing about how to interpret mainstream media reports. Indeed, we cannot solve the case via media reporting in general. It has proven itself too unreliable, too inconsistent and too self-contradictory. What the polarised discussion about 7/7 conspiracy theories shows is that the web-based alternative media is capable of just the same poor standards and bias. Because of this, we must look elsewhere so we can understand what happened on 7/7, and why.

Chapter 6: The Iqra Bookshop

It is impossible to understand what happened on 7/7 without looking at what came before, in particular the 'intelligence failures' in the years leading up to the attack. The security services have been widely accused, particularly by the mainstream media, of having failed to prevent the attacks. This accusation is one of the few that have been officially investigated in a significant way. Two reports by the Intelligence and Security Committee (ISC) discussed the allegations, and then a significant portion of the inquests was devoted to the question of 'preventability'.

The official investigations by the ISC have been woefully inadequate, based on a story of how MI5 classified its intelligence targets that is simply untrue (see Introduction). Further documents that became available at the inquests and elsewhere now cast doubt on the official timeline presented by the ISC. In exploring this timeline of what the security services knew, and when, and what they did about it, what emerges is a tale of ridiculous excuses for the 'failures', and an ongoing cover-up.

The allegation that the security services had somehow failed to stop the supposed 7/7 bombers surfaced within a week of the attacks. It began when then French interior minister Nicolas Sarkozy said that then Home Secretary Charles Clarke had told him that some of the alleged bombers had been subject to 'partial arrest' in 2004. Clarke then explicitly denied this, saying that the four were previously unknown to the security services. The phrase 'clean skins', meaning people who were not previously known to the security services, was widely circulated through the mainstream media.

It soon became obvious that this wasn't true. Only three months after 7/7 the BBC's *Newsnight* show detailed various links between the alleged bombers and wider Islamist networks such as Jemmah Islamiyah and Al Muhajiroun. Many of these stories, such as Mohammad Sidique Khan meeting with renowned international terrorist Hambali, have since been shown to be untrue. The *Newsnight* piece rather laughably asserted that, 'If British intelligence knew nothing of these links, it was because they had too few agents inside groups like Al Muhajiroun.'

Echoing the 9/11 Commission Report, former chairman of the Joint Intelligence Committee Sir Paul Lever told the BBC: 'I suppose you could characterise it as a failure of intelligence; I would put it more as perhaps a failure of imagination. It really didn't occur to people that young men, born, educated, sometimes from middle class backgrounds, in Britain, would go down that path.'[1]

This is a strange assessment of the pre-7/7 attitude towards terrorism within British security institutions and certainly not an accurate one. At that time, officials and commentators were referring to the general threat from terrorism on a near-daily basis. This was backed up by hundreds of arrests, albeit arrests that resulted in very few charges or prosecutions. If anything, the security services were imagining a threat that wasn't really there, or was in reality far smaller than they believed.

Alternatively, if Lever is referring to the specific idea of suicide bombings then an MI5 document from the July 7 inquests that outlined their quarterly summaries in the months before 7/7 shows otherwise. The quarterly summary from June 2005, only weeks prior to the bombings, said that in MI5's view there were five potential suicide bombers in the UK. Put simply, Lever's assessment contradicts all the publicly available data, and looks like a misleading attempt at an excuse.

Nonetheless, some of the BBC's material was accurate, enough to start refuting the 'clean skins' tag. They outlined the alleged bombers' connections to two men who weren't identified for legal reasons, but who we now know as Mohammed Junaid Babar and Omar Khyam. They also showed that alleged 7/7 ringleader Mohammad Sidique Khan had been monitored by the security services during 2003 and 2004 as part of a surveillance operation - Operation Crevice - that focussed on Khyam.

The question being asked was 'why did MI5 and the other security services fail to stop the bombings?' The original ISC report in 2006 dealt with this question by saying that:

> 'We have been told in evidence that none of the individuals involved in the 7 July group had been identified (that is, named and listed) as potential terrorist threats prior to July...

> It has become clear since the July attacks that Siddeque Khan was the subject of reporting of which the Security Service was aware prior to July 2005. However, his true identity was not revealed in this reporting and it was only after the 7 July attacks that the Security Service was able to identify Khan as the subject of the reports...

> It is also clear that, prior to the 7 July attacks, the Security Service had come across Siddeque Khan and Shazad Tanweer on the peripheries of other surveillance and

investigative operations. At that time their identities were unknown to the Security Service and there was no appreciation of their subsequent significance.'[2]

In effect, the ISC said that MI5 never actually identified Khan and/or Tanweer and had no intelligence indicating any intent on their part to carry out a terrorist attack.

Unfortunately for the ISC and MI5, a lot more information became available after the Operation Crevice trial in 2007, where Omar Khyam and several others were put on trial for plotting a fertiliser bomb attack in Britain. On the evening of the guilty verdict for five of the seven defendants, including Khyam, the BBC *Panorama* episode *Real Spooks* discussed the Crevice connections to 7/7.

Among the new information were transcripts of bugged conversations, including conversations between Khan and Khyam where they talked about terrorism. It showed that as part of the Operation Crevice surveillance security service teams followed Khan all the way from Crawley to Leeds, a distance of over 200 miles, on multiple occasions. They took photos, took down the registration numbers of the cars, and listed the addresses where the cars stopped. This included Khan's home in Dewsbury. So much for the alleged bombers being 'clean skins'. It subsequently emerged that the video and photos from this surveillance were never seen by the ISC during their first investigation. This eventually led to a second ISC investigation and their second report, published in 2009.

A fuller analysis of the Operation Crevice aspects of the 'intelligence failures' question is detailed in chapter 7, but the slightly earlier surveillance and intelligence operations in and around Leeds also require scrutiny. The first ISC report made no mention of this earlier surveillance, which came across Khan on several occasions. The second ISC report only made a few references to this earlier surveillance; references that under close scrutiny appear inaccurate and self-contradictory.

As with Operation Crevice, much of what is now known about the earlier surveillance operations has not come directly from the government. Instead, it has come through the filter of the mainstream media, and particularly the BBC. The October 2005 *Newsnight* mentioned the Iqra bookshop, but didn't explain its significance. Further *Newsnight* episodes, various newspaper articles, and exhibits and testimony from the July 7 Inquests have shed more light on the bookshop and the surveillance operations around it.

The Iqra Bookshop and Learning Centre was on the corner of Bude Road in Leeds, not far from Shehzad Tanweer's home. From 2002 to 2005 it was the premises for a registered charity, with both Khan and Tanweer listed as trustees. The organisation was largely funded by government grants, and among its trustees were Sadeer Saleem and Waheed Ali, two of three men who were tried and acquitted of involvement in the 7/7 conspiracy. Their co-accused Mohammed Shakil was also involved with the bookshop and its activities.

Iqra has been portrayed as a local hotbed of Islamic radicalism, a hub for the spreading of extremist literature. It is widely suspected, implied or claimed to have played a key role in radicalising at least Khan and Tanweer. It is also the focal point for many of the 'intelligence failures' preceding 7/7, and the story goes back to even before 9/11.

Martin 'Abdullah' McDaid

One key figure in the tale of the bookshop is Martin McDaid, a white convert or revert to Islam who, at least according to mainstream newspaper reports, was former member of the Special Boat Service (SBS). For several years before 7/7 McDaid was subject to sporadic surveillance by the security services. The key agencies involved in this surveillance were West Yorkshire Police (WYP) Special Branch and MI5. The 'intelligence failures' around this surveillance concern leads not being followed up and information not being shared between agencies.

A WYP document submitted to the July 7 Inquests explains that McDaid first came to the attention of the security services in 1998. It says that 'he was suspected of being an Islamic extremist, and of possible involvement in extremist activities including Jihad Training since at least 1998.'

According to the document, in January 2001 a 'training camp' in the Dalehead region of the Lake District was put under surveillance by WYP in an operation codenamed Warlock. Other camps were also monitored later. MI5 and WYP were aware that McDaid was one of the organisers of the Dalehead camp, which was attended by around 45 people. Surveillance photos were taken of the various men and subsequently shown to various sources. Nine of the 45 men were identified, including Tafazal 'Taf' Mohammed, who would later become one of the trustees of Iqra. Another man whose photo was taken but who remained unidentified until after 7/7 (at least officially) was Mohammad Sidique Khan.[3]

It is strange that Khan was not identified at this stage, as many of the figures around him were not only identified but were placed under additional surveillance. Nonetheless, officially he was not identified, and the first ISC report does not even mention McDaid, Taf Mohammed, the 2001 trip to the Lake District, or the surveillance photo resulting from it. This is a bizarre omission from the 2006 report given that some of the story about McDaid was in the newspapers only days after 7/7.

The information about McDaid, his former position as an elite British soldier and his connection to the alleged 7/7 bombers first appeared in the Daily Mirror only two weeks after the bombings. The article featured an extensive interview with McDaid, who spoke openly about having been in the Royal Marines and then in the SBS in the 1970s and 80s. He explained that he now called himself 'Abdullah' and that he was involved at the Iqra bookshop and knew all four of the alleged suicide bombers. However, he denied that the Iqra bookshop was important because 'They left the bookshop before I even joined'.[4] How the Mirror gained access to McDaid so quickly and why he was apparently so willing to talk to them is not clear.

The second ISC report only poses further questions. It says that Khan was identified from the Operation Warlock -Dalehead camp photograph by a WYP officer in 'Late July/August 2005', i.e. shortly after 7/7. For no obvious reason, this information was apparently not shared with MI5, or presumably with the Metropolitan Police investigating 7/7, until much later. The second ISC report says that, 'this information comes to the attention of MI5 in May 2007 as a result of this review'.[5] The ISC claim that MI5 only became aware of the WYP identification of Khan in the Dalehead photograph during the ISC's second investigation, nearly two years after the attacks.

This makes little sense, regardless of whatever 'failure of imagination' might have afflicted the security services before 7/7. Surely in the aftermath of the worst terrorist atrocity in London's history such significant information would be shared immediately between the relevant agencies. If this failure to share information is actually true then it points to serious ongoing problems even after 7/7.

Yet, on the same page of the ISC's report they go on to say that photos from Operation Warlock were shown to two MI5 sources in December 2005, and that the sources identified Khan as one of the attendees. This poses some important questions. Regardless of whether WYP Special Branch shared their identification of Khan from the 2001 photograph, MI5 sources identified him in December 2005 from that photograph. So why did the ISC not mention anything about any of this in their report of May 2006?

In their second report the ISC knowingly admit that MI5 had sources who identified Khan from the 2001 image in December 2005. So why did they say in the same report that MI5 were not aware of WYP's identification of Khan until May 2007? What difference did it make? If MI5 knew in late 2005 that it was Khan in the 2001 picture then it doesn't matter than they didn't know until later that WYP had already figured that out months earlier.

So why did the ISC mention it? Were they just trying to portray WYP as useless for failing to give important information to MI5? Perhaps more importantly, given the inconsistencies in the ISC, MI5 and WYP accounts on what they say happened after 7/7, can they be trusted about what they say happened before 7/7? If they are not telling the truth about which point after 7/7 they realised that they had a photograph of Khan from 2001 then are they telling the truth about not identifying that photograph as Khan before 7/7?

Honeysuckle

Operation Warlock was not the end of surveillance on McDaid and the people around him. In April 2003 a surveillance operation codenamed Honeysuckle followed McDaid around for two days. The WYP document on McDaid said, 'In the course of surveillance on 14 April McDaid was seen to get into and be given a lift in a blue BMW car registration J729 EUB. The lift lasted for 3 minutes. Subsequent checks on the car showed it was registered to Mr Sidique Khan of 11 Gregory Street, Batley, West Yorkshire, WF17 6NH. Checks on police record systems revealed a reference to a previous caution. There was no previous record of Sidique Khan on WYP Special Branch systems.'[6]

The 'reference to a previous caution' relates back to 1992 when Khan was cautioned for assault, but otherwise the WYP's checks revealed nothing significant about him. But what about the MI5 databases? According to testimony at the inquests, they were never checked. John David Parkinson, assistant chief constable of the West Yorkshire Police, was asked about the checks that took place following the surveillance of McDaid being given a lift in Khan's car.

> **Q.** At the time, would that meeting between McDaid and a BMW car registered to someone called Sidique Khan of 11 Gregory Street been of sufficient importance as to have led any officer in the West Yorkshire Police to tell the Security Service about it?
>
> **A.** I don't believe it would, no.

Q. Even though it was a joint operation?

A. Yes, I don't believe it would have done.

Q. Why would that sort of encounter -- which was, of course, noted on the surveillance log of the surveillance officers, the fact of the car giving McDaid a lift -- not be something that would routinely be expected to be passed to the joint holder of the operation the Security Service, rather the fact that you had then interrogated your own systems and found out that it was a registered keeper of 11 Gregory Street?

A. Because the activity was delineated by the operational purpose.

Q. You'll have to forgive me, I'm not sure I follow you.

A. Well, I can't expand on the operational purpose that's outlined in the gist, but there was -- that wasn't the only event that was recorded on the log. There was other activities. It proved no significance to the reason for the operation.

LADY JUSTICE HALLETT: So it was irrelevant to the -

A. Yes.

LADY JUSTICE HALLETT: -- operation --

A. Yes.

LADY JUSTICE HALLETT: -- as far as you were concerned at the time?

A. Yes, my Lady.[7]

This is a truly bizarre explanation, for several reasons. The WYP document does not explicitly outline an operational purpose for Honeysuckle. It merely explains that McDaid was a suspected extremist, possibly involved in jihad training. McDaid had been photographed in 2001 at a 'training camp' that he organised in the Lake District, and most of the others at the camp had been photographed but not identified. From this we can only assume that part of the purpose of the Honeysuckle surveillance operation was to follow up on McDaid and his 'trainees', to help with the process of identifying them. If this is the case then it makes no sense to say that finding out more about the owner of a car that was seen giving a lift to McDaid was irrelevant. If this is not the case then what *was* the purpose of Operation Honeysuckle?

For another, the lift might have only been short, but it was considered significant enough for WYP to carry out an immediate check on the car's registration. The day after the Honeysuckle surveillance was finished, WYP carried out a check on the number plate of the BMW they had seen giving McDaid a lift.[8] So it was important enough to immediately follow up to obtain more information, but not important enough to tell MI5 about even though it was MI5 who had requested the surveillance operation in the first place.

Furthermore, was it necessary for WYP Special Branch to explicitly choose to share this information with MI5? The gist says that McDaid had been known to both MI5 and WYP since at least 1998, i.e. he was a joint target for both agencies. Operation Warlock, looking into the 'training camp' in the Lake District, was a joint operation. The photographs taken, i.e. the material produced by the surveillance, were shown to both WYP and MI5 sources to try to identify the attendees. Honeysuckle is explicitly described as 'a joint operation with SyS' (the Security Service, i.e. MI5), suggesting that McDaid was still a joint intelligence target and that the fruits of surveillance were going to both agencies.

The coroner to the inquests Lady Justice Dame Heather Hallett accepted the story that the information was not shared with MI5 though her final report suggests that she wasn't wholly convinced. It says, 'Despite the surveillance being carried out under a joint investigation between WYP and the Security Service, *it seems* that neither the surveillance report nor the record of the BMW was passed by WYP to the Security Service. Given the reference to Sidique Khan, Witness G accepted that, in hindsight, this had been unfortunate.'[9] (my emphasis)

Though WYP may have not shared their identification of a 'Sidique Khan' with MI5 in April 2003, and indeed though MI5 might not have needed them to share it, what the police did do was follow up on McDaid's contacts. Among the locations they looked into was 49 Bude Road, Leeds – the Iqra bookshop. The WYP summary on McDaid explains that in December 2003 they conducted further inquiries into the bookshop, finding that, 'a) The Iqra Bookshop was managed by a group of individuals, including McDaid and Tafazal Mohammed' and 'b) The Iqra Bookshop was a registered charity'.

A problem arises here. In late 2002/early 2003 the Iqra bookshop had made an application for charitable status, and as part of the paperwork had to list several trustees. As noted above, among the names on that list were Sidique Khan and Shehzad Tanweer, along with their addresses.[10] Presumably it is through looking at these papers, filed with the Charities Commission, that WYP established that the Iqra bookshop was a registered charity managed by McDaid and Taf Mohammed. Whether they actually did this is not clear, because the question has never been asked. The versions of the documents that are available apparently date from police searches on the bookshop after 7/7, not as part of the WYP inquiries in December 2003.

There is also the question of when Khan (and Tanweer) ceased their involvement in the bookshop. According to the third statement submitted by MI5's corporate spook Witness G, Khan and others 'were no longer involved in the Iqra bookshop from early 2003. This is supported by the records of the Charities Commission, obtained post 7/7, which indicate that MSK and ST were recorded as trustees of the Iqra bookshop in 2002-2003. However, when the charity updated its trustee records in December 2004, MSK and ST were no longer listed as trustees. Moreover, in relation to MSK, financial investigations after 7/7 indicated that Iqra was a membership organisation, members paid subscriptions, and that MSK cancelled his monthly subscription to Iqra in February 2003.'[11]

The problem here is that if Khan did cancel his monthly subscription to Iqra in February 2003, he could of course have still paid a subscription in cash. Alternatively, he could have 'paid' his subscription by volunteering at Iqra, which was after all a charity. The fact that his car, and in all likelihood Khan himself, gave a lift to McDaid in April 2003 suggests that whatever his formal connection to Iqra, he was still involved with that circle of people months later. That it took until December 2004 for his trustee status to be revoked corroborates this. December 2004 is also the time when Khan quit his job and travelled to Pakistan. This makes his obligations in Pakistan a far more likely explanation for the revocation of his trustee status at Iqra than the explanation offered by MI5 - that he had actually ended his association with Iqra nearly two years earlier.

The argument the security services are trying to make is that when WYP made inquiries into the bookshop in December 2003, Khan and Tanweer were no longer associated with Iqra. Witness G argued this explicitly at the inquests. The fact that it was MI5's Witness G who was talking about this shows once again that this was a joint WYP-MI5 series of operations:

Q. When was the bookshop linked to that address, do you know that date?

A. I think that's either November or December 2003.

Q. By which stage, it appears from paragraph 7 of your third statement, if that is right, he was no longer associated with Iqra bookshop?

A. That's correct.

Q. Is there anything that links MSK to Iqra bookshop thereafter?

A. No.

Q. The fact is that we didn't know, you didn't know, the Security Service didn't know -- is this right -- of the MSK/Iqra link, even the historic one at the time?

A. That's correct.

What MI5 are saying is that the additional inquiries into the Iqra bookshop in December 2003 could not have produced any information on Khan and Tanweer because by that point they were no longer involved there. As such, these inquiries could not have led WYP to finding out more about Khan and Tanweer, and so this cannot represent any kind of failure on the part of the security services. This explanation is misleading for the reasons explained   above, and also because whatever Khan's association with Iqra in April or December 2003, his name was still on the paperwork as a trustee. A basic examination of the paperwork filed for the organisation would have yielded this information, and thus provided a connection to the car seen during the Honeysuckle surveillance.

Strangely, the question as to whether the security services looked at this paperwork in December 2003 was never asked at the inquests. The WYP summary of the McDaid-Iqra story says that among the information gleaned from the December investigations was the fact that Iqra was a registered charity. We can only assume therefore that the security services did look at the paperwork for the charity, and therefore did know about Khan's connection to it. If they did not look at the paperwork then from where did they get the additional information gained in December 2003?

Ranting and Raving

None of the questions above have been raised by the mainstream media. They have focused instead on the simpler story of whether McDaid played a role in radicalising Khan and possibly Tanweer, and therefore whether these earlier surveillance operations were missed opportunities to interdict the 7/7 plot. Of course, all this presumes that Khan and Tanweer were actually responsible for the 7/7 bombings. Nonetheless there is some evidence suggesting that McDaid played the role of a radicaliser, though it may have been a 'role' in the theatrical rather than criminal sense of the word.

Two men involved in Iqra and its activities have testified that through this period some of the people at Iqra, including McDaid, were distributing extremist literature and films. Strangely, when the bookshop was raided just eight days after 7/7 no such material was found. The first witness, Mark Hargreaves, got involved with Iqra in 2001-2. He testified at the inquests via videolink, and his identity was disguised in an interview with *Newsnight*. Hargreaves was a mountain climber and youth worker, and was apparently asked by Mohammad Sidique Khan to run courses for local teenagers at the Leeds climbing wall. He also went on some of the camping trips that were monitored by the security services.

Hargreaves described Khan as 'very friendly, outgoing, passionate about working with people in the area.'[12] This chimes with most of the reports about Khan, that he was liked, well respected and involved in his community. By contrast Hargreaves described McDaid as 'ok, initially' but that he appeared more radical over time. He told the inquests that, 'you could see he had a fervour about him, a religious fervour. That became more apparent as I got to know him.'[13] Hargreaves suggested that McDaid was 'grooming' vulnerable young men.

He told the BBC about how McDaid had shown him a DVD of people training in Afghanistan, and 'anti-semitic, anti-Zionist, anti-American' leaflets. McDaid was apparently very adamant about converting people to Islam, and spoke aggressively. Though he said that Khan spoke about Islam a lot, when asked about whether Khan expressed his views in an extremist or inflammatory way, Hargreaves commented that Khan, 'was the most reasonable of all those people that I worked with in that establishment.'[14]

Hargreaves ended his involvement with Iqra because of concerns about McDaid's radicalism, but his story is somewhat corroborated by another witness. Martin Gilbertson is a self-trained IT guru who did work for Iqra and several associated organisations, helping them with their computer systems. Gilbertson gave numerous interviews after 7/7 about how the group involved at Iqra were Islamic radicals, how they showed him material that was 'anti-Western, anti-Iraq, anti-everything', how he had burned extremist films onto discs for them, even how he had helped re-assemble McDaid's computer after it had been temporarily seized by the police.

He spoke of how 'everyone' at Iqra blamed the world's problems on Jews, and that 'it came to a head one day when I pointed out that my wife was a quarter Jew.'[15] Gilbertson also claims to have been so worried about the views he was hearing and the material that he made copies of some of the material at the bookshop and wrote out a list of names of people involved there. He claims that when he approached his local police station he was told to post the information in, which he then did. Gilbertson says that he never heard anything back, and that he never followed up on his concerns.

This has been presented as another missed opportunity on the road to 7/7, though the story ended rather differently to the examples above. Gilbertson was called to testify at the inquests, the last witness before MI5's Witness G took the stand. Gilbertson stumbled through his story of how he tried to warn the police and how it seemed that they did nothing in response. He was then subjected to a barrage of humiliating cross-examination that culminated in him being accused of having made up most of his story.

Gilbertson was a terrible witness and may well have fabricated much if not all of what he has said about 7/7. His story has varied from interview to interview about when he first got involved with these organisations, whether and when he first approached the police, and when he sent in his information. The police have no record of receiving any package of information from him, and their investigation into whether such a package was ever sent appears to have been very thorough. More so than the investigation into McDaid's connection to Khan, in any case. On the witness stand Gilbertson was made to look foolish and was forced to contradict himself on multiple occasions. He was also embarrassed to have entered as evidence some of an unpublished draft manuscript of a book that he had written titled 'Why did it happen'.

In a bizarre episode, Gilbertson was pushed for his source of information for a passage in the book that said that others in the Beeston community had also warned the police about what was going on in the area. He had clearly just invented the claim but, floundering, he attributed it to a website:

Q. Who told you?

A. It was on the internet.

Q. Where?

A. On one of the -- that website, the 7 July coalition website.

Q. I don't think we're familiar with that website, Mr Gilbertson.

A. Not the coalition, the one that claimed the Government set it up.

Q. I suspect that's, then, a rather suspect source of information.[16]

It was pure theatre. Conveniently, this exposure of Gilbertson as a fabricator not only debunked one accusation of an intelligence failure but also came with an association between the fabricator and those websites suggesting that the government 'set up' 7/7. Ultimately, this led to a rhetorical question from one of the lawyers asking whether Gilbertson was 'an egocentric self-publicist, a fantasist, exaggerator, speculator, irresponsible individual?'

The whole episode provided a timely undermining of the whole notion of 'intelligence failures' and government complicity in the attacks, just before MI5's corporate spook was called to testify. MI5 had tried to avoid putting up even the single, anonymous witness that they did provide, and stringent limits were imposed to protect Witness G's identity. In this context, it would not be surprising if the whole point of calling Gilbertson to the stand was to personally humiliate him as a means of downplaying the whole idea of 'intelligence failures'. Along these lines, there was one particularly telling aspect of his testimony that was not questioned or contradicted in any way by the lawyers.

In interviews and again in his inquest testimony Gilbertson said that he was employed at a Learn Direct centre run by people in the Beeston Muslim community. He claimed that he was there on the day of 9/11, and that he saw the Muslims at the centre cheering and laughing at the attacks. He elaborated on this story by describing a party thrown the following day, apparently celebrating the attacks. Gilbertson says that either at the party or shortly afterwards was when he first met Martin McDaid and Taf Mohammed.

None of this is true. The July 7th Truth Campaign has shown that the Learn Direct centre where these celebrations are supposed to have taken place was not there at the time of 9/11. The lease was not signed until May the following year.[17] Gilbertson could not have been there to witness those events happening. That this repeatedly published but untrue story was allowed to enter the official record without contradiction illustrates the extent to which Gilbertson was being used and abused for political purposes.   The whole tale about celebrating 9/11 helps to reinforce a picture of Beeston as a locus of terrorist sympathisers and a cradle for future suicide bombers.   As a politically useful myth it was allowed to stand, even amongst the testimony of a perjurer and fantasist.

Who was McDaid?

In light of the theatricality around the idea of intelligence failures we need an answer to the question: who or what was Martin McDaid? He had been 'known to' the security services since 1998 and was still being actively investigated five years later.   At no stage was he arrested, at least as far as we know.   In the aftermath of 9/11 hundreds of British Muslims were rounded up by the authorities, most of whom were wholly innocent.   That McDaid wasn't subjected to this but was simply monitored and checked from time to time suggests that he may have been in some way working for the security services.

Just as John Joe Magee, the head of the IRA's internal security, was a former Special Boat Service soldier so too, apparently, was McDaid. It would be a truly strange, though possible, transformation for him to go from being a counter-terrorism commando to a terrorist sympathiser who ranted and raved to anyone who would listen.   That this went on during long-term but sporadic surveillance that just so happened to stop short of a supposedly far more important target is unconvincing at best.

Was McDaid for real? Did he truly convert from being a Special Forces soldier to a radical Muslim who insisted that people call him Abdullah? Was he an informant or provocateur? If the alleged bombers were actually responsible for 7/7 then did McDaid play a role in motivating them? Or was he just playing the role of an Islamist, to help generate useful background stories like Gilbertson's 9/11 party myth?

That so much of his story has been put out through the BBC rather than through the security services suggests an element of theatre or propaganda.   After all, if the alleged bombers were not responsible then it would have been necessary for the real culprits to create background legends for them, to make them look like suicide terrorists. The whole story of being involved a radical bookshop in an area supposedly populated by Muslims sympathetic to terrorism has lent unofficial credibility to the official version.

There are such things as pseudo-operations, run in various forms by the British and other security services since at least World War

Two. The aim of the pseudo-operation is to recreate the appearance of a target gang or group. This is ideally done through recruiting from the target group but can involve disguising established agents. The pseudogang or countergang then infiltrates the target group and uses their cover to carry out operations. These operations range from the assassination of significant figures to the provoking of elements of the target group into a situation where they will be ambushed, and either killed or handed over to the authorities.[18]

So it is a distinct possibility that McDaid was a pseudo-Islamist working for the security services in some way. It may be significant that Taf Mohammed, who was alongside McDaid at Iqra, was hired by the police in the years after 7/7 to consult on how to engage Muslim communities. This was portrayed in the popular press as a dangerous Muslim who had been under MI5 surveillance accidentally being given £80,000 by the police.

Similarly, McDaid's name was leaked by the security services to the Times newspaper in early 2002. The paper carried out investigations in Leeds but turned up nothing significant. Despite this apparent concern, McDaid was never arrested, either as part of the 7/7 investigation or any other investigation. Did the security services leak his name to try to give him credibility as an Islamic radical?

By contrast, the two ISC reports after 7/7 go to great pains to avoiding identifying McDaid as a figure of any significance. The first ISC report in 2006 simply did not mention him, or the MI5-WYP surveillance on him that connected him to Iqra and Sidique Khan. The second ISC report in 2009 did discuss the McDaid story to some extent, but did not even name him.

McDaid himself has since disappeared. He was last seen at the Sohar College in Oman, where he was apparently teaching English. A website was set up in 2010 describing McDaid as holding 'fundamentalist Islamist, quasi-fascist beliefs' and calling him 'the friend of the July 7 London Underground bombers'. The site implores anyone who has seen McDaid to get in touch with them, and the guestbook is littered with comments from apparent ex-students of his.[19] It is a truly bizarre legacy for a man about whom we know so little, but who could potentially tell us so much.

Khalid Khaliq

The legacy of the Iqra bookshop was that it was raided in the days after 7/7, as were various properties in Beeston, causing a disruption to the entire area. It has since been stigmatised with the accusation of having had terrorists in their midst as though the people of Beeston somehow let this terrible attack happen. The same is true to a similar extent of the whole Muslim population in the Yorkshire area, and nationwide.

As is so commonly the case with these useful myths, the reality is very different. The community in Beeston and the wider British Muslim population were not to blame for these events. The only people that the authorities could find were three men who were sometimes at the bookshop and knew the alleged bombers. Mohammed Shakil, Sadeer Saleem and Waheed Ali were wrongly accused of having carried out 'hostile reconnaissance' as part of the 7/7 conspiracy, and were eventually acquitted. They had nothing to do with the attacks, but the police had to arrest somebody (see chapter 2).

The other person the authorities managed to find was single father of three children Khalid Khaliq. He had also been involved for a time at the bookshop and knew some of the alleged bombers, and had voluntarily come forward in 2005 to assist with the 7/7 investigation. In 2007, when his house was raided the police found a box in his attic that contained a CD with the 'Al Qaeda Training Manual' on it. There was no evidence that Khaliq had downloaded the manual, or burnt it onto the disc, or was planning to use it for anything. Khaliq himself said that someone else had given him the box to store in his attic.

The CD may well have been one of those made by Martin Gilbertson in his work for the Iqra bookshop, but even aside from implications for the 7/7 investigation, this is surely a gross miscarriage of justice. The case for Khaliq's innocence is overwhelming for two key reasons. First of all, a very similar case had ruled in favour of the defendants, who had initially been convicted of the same offence. Secondly the manual was written by a notorious triple agent, and is widely available both online and in bookshops and libraries.

The similar case involved five young men from the Bradford area - Awaab Iqbal, Aitzaz Zafar, Usman Malik, Mohammed Irfan Raja and Akbar Butt. They were convicted in 2007 for having downloaded jihadi material from the internet. There was no evidence that any of them had planned an act of violence as a result of viewing this material, and they posed no threat to the public. In February 2008 they won their appeal, with the court ruling that, 'Literature may be stored in a book on a bookshelf, or on a computer drive, without any intention on the part of the possessor to make any future use of it at all.'[20] Despite this, Khaliq pleaded guilty only weeks later, and was sentenced to sixteen months in prison.

There is an even more unreasonable aspect to this prosecution, and other similar ones. The manual in question, which was widely published online by research organizations and the US Department of Justice, was written by Ali Mohamed. You wouldn't know this if you found a copy in a library or a bookshop as it is published anonymously. It was used as evidence in the *US vs Bin Laden et al* trial in 2001, and entered the public domain as a trial exhibit. As mentioned in the introduction to this book, Ali Mohamed was Al Qaeda's principal trainer, the man who turned them from an offshoot of the mujahideen guerrilla network into a transnational urban terrorist group. He ran training camps in half a dozen countries, trained Bin Laden's own bodyguards, was involved with the group in New York who bombed the World Trade Center in 1993 and he carried out surveillance for the 1998 African embassy bombings. He did all this while serving in the US Special Forces, working as a spy for the CIA, and as an informant for the FBI.[21]

Exactly whose side Ali Mohamed was on and what truly motivated him is a matter of some speculation. He pleaded guilty to a range of terrorist charges in late 2000 but was never sentenced, at least not on the public record. He, like McDaid, has now vanished. Whatever the truth about his motives, the manual was produced as part of the process of the West sponsoring radical Islam. This goes back decades and has taken various forms with the mujahideen in Afghanistan and then in the Balkans and more recently in Libya and Syria being only one strand in the history. So while Ali did not necessarily write the manual as part of his work for US intelligence, it was nonetheless a product of that collusion and sponsorship.

The fact that the Department of Justice published this document on their website suggests that they are rather proud of it. Shortly after 7/7 it was reported that a group of British politicians had written to them demanding that they remove it from their website. According to the BBC, a Department of Justice spokesman said, 'We have no intention of taking it down.'[22] How can it be illegal to simply own this document? It was in effect produced and published by the US government, but once again, someone had to be seen to be paying for 7/7. Khalid Khaliq knew the people allegedly responsible and because they could pin something to him, they did. It was a disgraceful case, and his conviction should be quashed and he and his family compensated for the hurt this has caused.

Outstanding Questions

The explanations for the 'intelligence failures' in the earlier surveillance operations are unacceptable. The failure to initially identify Khan from the 2001 photograph during Operation Warlock would be excusable, if not for the risible way that the ISC have explained what happened. It says that in the weeks after 7/7 when WYP finally identified Khan in the 2001 photograph that they didn't bother to tell MI5 about it. Warlock was a joint operation, and attempts had been made by both agencies to identify the people in the surveillance images. Despite this WYP apparently just didn't bother to tell MI5 only weeks after a major terrorist attack that they'd identified Khan. Even though the targets were considered of mutual interest back in 2001-3 and that the man they'd just identified was now thought to have masterminded four suicide bombings that killed 56 people, they just didn't bother. Even if this were plausible, it is certainly unacceptable, yet no one has been held accountable for this.

The image itself perhaps tells us a little more of the story. It is not actually a photograph but is a still from a video camera. There are therefore some additional questions that none of the investigations have asked. If this is a still from a set of frames then where are the other images of Khan from this video? Did they show his face in a way that was easier to identify? Were any of the other images of Khan shown to sources or otherwise identified?

Surveillance video still of Sidique Khan, January 2001

Newsnight's report on the eve of the inquests verdict said that the image came from a secret camera installed in the barn at Dalehead farm. Installing a camera to carry out surveillance of suspects requires access to the location in advance, and therefore advance knowledge that the suspects are going to be there. This shows that in fact MI5 and possibly WYP knew far more even back in January 2001 than they are letting on.

Two years later during Operation Honeysuckle, when WYP saw joint MI5-WYP target Martin McDaid get a lift in a car registered to Sidique Khan, they supposedly didn't tell MI5 about this. Given that they were sufficiently worried about McDaid and his associates to carry out additional surveillance this is also unacceptable. It is also likely to be untrue, because the operations on McDaid were all joint operations and he was as a joint target. Therefore his associates, particularly those who could actually be traced to a name and vehicle must logically have been joint persons of interest. Instead, at the inquests the WYP witness claimed that in fact sharing such information wasn't relevant to the purpose of the operation, leaving open the question of what was the purpose of the operation?

Both before and after 7/7 WYP Special Branch allegedly did not share critical information with MI5. Whatever the truth about the failure to identify Khan before 7/7, it is ridiculous to believe that WYP continued to not recognise his importance in the weeks after 7/7. This calls the whole story about failing to share information into question, and it appears that as the junior agency that WYP are being made to take the blame.

When further inquiries were made into McDaid's association with the Iqra bookshop in late 2003 it was discovered that Iqra was a registered charity. The WYP gist of these operations strongly suggests that the security services pulled copies of the paperwork for the organisation. The logical thing to do when finding out that a target is involved in an organisation is, after all, to find out more about the organisation. Had they done so then the paperwork would have shown Sidique Khan's name as a trustee of the Iqra charity. According to MI5 this is irrelevant because Khan was no longer involved at the bookshop in late 2003. Regardless of his involvement or non-involvement, his name was still on the paperwork in late 2003, making this diversionary story unacceptable.

The only prosecution to have come out of the post-7/7 investigations into Iqra was that of Khalid Khaliq, a man who had done nothing wrong. Being in possession of material that was produced as a result of Western sponsorship of terrorists is punished but the West's sponsorship of terrorists goes unpunished. This is also so stupid as to be an 'intelligence failure' in the most literal sense of the term.

The tale of Martin Gilbertson is laden with politically useful theatre and utter irrelevance given all the information that the security services already had before he claims to have contacted them. It suggests that some people in this story are playing at their roles, whether they realise it or not. That Martin McDaid was actually a spy of some sort cannot be proven or disproven at this stage. If he was, then the failures make a lot more sense as a means of controlling who knew about whatever it was that McDaid was up to. If he was there to create a useful backstory about Khan being an extremist then the 'failures' make so much more sense that it would be more accurate to call them 'successes'.

Chapter 7 will examine an MI5 document that puts the McDaid and Iqra story, and the 7/7 'intelligence failures' as a whole, in a new light. The document proves that the whole timeline of what MI5 knew and when is untrue, and exacerbates the deeply worrying nature of the failures outlined in this chapter. It will detail the role of two other probable spies with similar profiles to McDaid and examine the most ridiculous excuse offered so far in the 7/7 story.

Chapter 7: The Crevice

The second major set of 'intelligence failures' in the lead up to 7/7 is based around Operation Crevice, a huge counter-terrorism operation in 2003 and 2004. These 'failures' have been covered in the mainstream far more than the earlier operations discussed in the previous chapter. Crevice was an MI5 and Metropolitan Police Service (MPS) Special Branch investigation into what has been dubbed the 'fertiliser bomb plot'. From early 2003 through to the end of March 2004 the investigation identified, bugged and surveyed several men in Britain and a co-conspirator in Canada.

The group were apparently putting together a large-scale fertiliser bomb to be detonated by remote control. They were so closely monitored that as soon as they actually bought some fertiliser and stored it in a lock-up, Special Branch officers snuck in that night and replaced the fertiliser with a substitute 'inert compound'. At the end of March 2004, only weeks after the Madrid train bombings, the authorities arrested several men in Britain and one in Canada. Seven men were put on trial in the UK in 2007, resulting in five convictions. Another man, Momin Khawaja, was later convicted in a trial in Canada.

In the course of the trials it emerged that during the Crevice investigation the security services had encountered Mohammad Sidique Khan, Shehzad Tanweer, Waheed Ali and Mohammed Shakil during surveillance in early 2004. Khan and Tanweer were two of the alleged 7/7 suicide bombers, and Ali and Shakil were two of the three men who were prosecuted and acquitted of being involved in the 7/7 conspiracy. All four men, Khan in particular, were seen on multiple occasions and even followed for 200 miles to their homes in Leeds.

Thousands of miles away a man called Mohammed Junaid Babar provided terrorism training in a camp in Malakand, Pakistan. Omar Khyam and several of the other Crevice 'plotters' received training at this camp in mid-2003, as did Mohammad Sidique Khan. Babar later became an FBI supergrass and was the key witness in the Crevice trials, but it is widely suspected (if not a proven fact) that he was working for the intelligence services all along. When this information became widely known, it led one bereaved parent, Graham Foulkes, to suggest that the US authorities were complicit in the 7/7 bombings.[1] This was such a dramatic departure from the original 'clean skins' tag that it has become a focal point for the bereaved, truth campaigners, and the mainstream and alternative media.

The official reports either glossed over these issues, or took roundabout routes to avoid the serious questions. The first ISC report in May 2006 was written in a cryptic way but it does say that, 'prior to the 7 July attacks, the Security Service had come across Siddeque Khan and Shazad Tanweer on the peripheries of other surveillance and investigative operations. At that time their identities were unknown to the Security Service and there was no appreciation of their subsequent significance.'[2]

What is now abundantly clear is that this is simply untrue. MI5 had identified Khan on several occasions and as we will see in this chapter they even requested further information on him from WYP and took other steps to find out more about him. This shows that he was an investigative target, so there must have been at least some appreciation of his significance. The second ISC report elaborated, saying that they had no reason to suspect that Khan was involved in planning a terrorist attack and thus exonerated the security services.

The report describes the Crevice surveillance that encountered Khan and Tanweer, and then concludes that, 'We cannot criticise the judgments made by MI5 and the police based on the information that they had and their priorities at the time. Even considering material that was discovered after 7/7, and that which arose from the CREVICE trial, we believe that the decisions made in 2004 and 2005 were understandable and reasonable.'[3]

The evidence submitted at the inquests casts doubt on this story in terms of what was known, when, by whom, and what they did about it. The evidence also poses several important questions, particularly in conjunction with the 'failures' examined in chapter 6. The precise nature of the 'fertiliser bomb plot' suggests a theatre of terrorism similar to that seen in the story of the Iqra bookshop.

Mohammed Qayyum Khan

The first key figure in the Crevice story is Mohammed Qayyum Khan. He was the reason why the operation was started, as the second ISC report makes clear, 'In early 2003, MI5 obtained intelligence indicating that an individual called Mohammed Qayum KHAN, from Luton, was the leader of an Al-Qaida facilitation network in the UK... As a result of this intelligence, MI5 made Mohammed Qayum KHAN a "desirable" target and began an investigation into the facilitation network. This operation was given the codename CREVICE.'[4]

At the 2007 Crevice trial (*R. vs Khyam et al*), Mohammed Qayyum Khan was referred to as 'Q'. Q was a Luton taxi driver and, at least according to MI5, was suspected of facilitating terrorism. According to testimony at the Crevice trial it was Q who sent Mohammad Sidique Khan and Omar Khyam to Pakistan for terrorism training in mid-2003. This allegation has never been confirmed, because Q was never arrested. He was also never called as a witness for either the defence or the prosecution in the Crevice trial.

If he was facilitating the plot then why was he never arrested? The question came up in an episode of *Panorama* broadcast on the evening of the guilty verdict in the Crevice trial. BBC journalist Peter Taylor asked the question of Peter Clarke, then National Coordinator for Terrorist Investigations in the Metropolitan Police.

TAYLOR : Who was or is 'Q'?

CLARKE: There are a lot of people connected to this investigation. Some of them I know their identity, some of them I don't.

TAYLOR: But you know who 'Q' is.

CLARKE: I know who 'Q' is but I'm not going to discuss who he is or what he is or what he does during this interview.

And then, later in the same programme:

TAYLOR: Why was 'Q' never arrested?

CLARKE: Decisions are made during the course of investigation based upon the evidence that's available, and the decision as to who should be arrested is based entirely upon what evidence is available at the time.

TAYLOR: Was 'Q' not arrested possibly because he was working for you or MI5?

CLARKE: I'm not prepared to comment on any speculation like that. It's pure speculation.

TAYLOR: Where is 'Q' now?

CLARKE: I said I'm not prepared to talk about 'Q'.[5]

Clearly, the notion that Q might have been an agent working for MI5 or Special Branch is not a ridiculous conspiracy theory. If anything, the fact that the BBC asked the question and provoked such an obvious non-denial denial is a reason to doubt this theory. Nonetheless, 'Q' fits a profile in the same way McDaid fits a profile.

Q was the target of sporadic surveillance that mysteriously failed to uncover Sidique Khan, as was McDaid. He played an apparently central role in the fertiliser bomb plot, inasmuch as there was a plot, just as McDaid played a central role in whatever was going on at the Iqra bookshop. Q has never been arrested or called before a court to testify, either as part of the Crevice investigation or the 7/7 investigation, and nor has McDaid. McDaid has now disappeared, Q has now disappeared. McDaid claimed in a national newspaper to be a former SBS soldier, 'Q' is the nickname of the MI5 gadgets boffin (or facilitator) in the James Bond films.

There is also a comparable element of theatricality in the Q story because it was the BBC raising the question of whether he was working for the security services. The BBC were also the only media outlet to track down Q and try to interview him, in one of Richard Watson's regular British Jihadi Network reports for *Newsnight*. They found Q in a small cafe and walked in and introduced themselves. Q confronted them and told them to leave him alone and stop taping him, before he and others in the cafe shoved the camera crew out the door. It was an amusing and possibly staged scene.[6]

The new evidence made available at the inquests forces us to once again fundamentally revise what MI5 have told us through the ISC reports on 7/7. In the second ISC report we were told that mobile phones apparently used by Sidique Khan received calls from 'Q' in July and August 2003, several months into Operation Crevice. In a paragraph dated July 13th 2003 it says, 'Checks reveal that the telephone number in question is registered to "Siddique KHAN" of 49a Bude Road, Leeds (the address of a bookshop selling extremist literature). MI5 cannot match the name "Siddique KHAN" with any in their databases, and the contact is not investigated further since there is nothing to suggest involvement in any terrorist-related activity.'[7] The report goes on to details further calls in July and August, some using a different, unregistered pay-as-you-go phone.

All of these calls are presumed to have involved Sidique Khan. One of the phones was registered to him, but this assumes that it was actually being used by Khan, in the same way I assumed that when Khan's car was seen giving a lift to McDaid that Khan was driving it. MI5 produced a summary of the connections between the 'Stepford bombers' and the Crevice suspects for the inquests but it doesn't clarify much. It simply attributes calls between Q and the number

07904186076 explicitly to Khan, and says that calls on the unregistered number 07792261882 were 'probably Khan'.[8]

Were MI5 bugging these conversations or simply monitoring which numbers were called and when? Given that under the Regulation of Investigatory Powers Act phone tap evidence cannot be presented in court, we can only assume that MI5 were bugging the conversations because it makes no sense for them not to have done so. If that is true then they had much more information on who the calls were to and what they were about. According to a *Newsnight* report on Khan's links to Q, MI5 were recording the conversations between the two, and the conversations were not about terrorism.[9]

There is considerable evidence that MI5 did know more than they told the ISC. An MI5 document entered into evidence at the inquests details the subscriber check on the phone that had been called by Q. The check found that the phone, number 07904186076 (the first phone mentioned above), was registered to a 'Sidique Khan' and the given address was the Iqra bookshop. Perhaps most important is the date – 11th March 2003, not July.[10] Witness G explained this as a mistake in MI5's information to the ISC. He said that the subscriber check did take place in March but that calls were placed in July and August between Q's phone and the two phones presumed to be Khan's.[11] However, the dates in July and August given in the second ISC report are apparently also incorrect, according to Witness G.

When this document emerged during the inquests the July 7th Truth Campaign wrote to the proceedings asking several questions, some of which were then put to Witness G:

> **Q.** You told us that one of the other investigative links to the man called Sidique Khan was the subscriber check on 11 March 2003 which showed that a phone was registered to his name and the address at 49A Bude Road, we know subsequently to have been the Iqra bookshop, and you, therefore, would have been able to assess that one of the calls made in July and August by Mohammed Qayum Khan, one of the participants in Crevice in the early days, was to that name and address?
>
> **A.** (Witness nods).
>
> **Q.** Why was a subscriber check being done in March if the calls from Mohammed Qayum Khan were not until July and August?

A. Because, at that point, we were reviewing earlier billing on Mohammed Qayum Khan on which that number came up.

Q. Oh, I see, so the Crevice operation, having started earlier in the year, had meant that there were checks from the very beginning going on in relation to calls made by the participants –

A. That's correct.

Q. -- which is why a check was made in March?

A. That's correct.

Q. So Crevice started long before July and August, towards the early part of 2003, in fact.

A. In the early part of 2003, yes.

Q. Before 11 March, presumably?

A. Yes, I can't remember the exact date, but certainly before then.

Q. But logically, it must have been before.

A. It was, it was.[12]

This is an almost entirely new story, telling us that Operation Crevice began before the time of 'late March 2003' given by MI5 to the ISC for their second report. It was during this early phase of Crevice that Q was first linked to a 'Sidique Khan' at the Iqra bookshop, not midway through the operation resulting in Khan being assessed as a miscellaneous and insignificant contact. The entire story about when Operation Crevice began is untrue, as is the story of what MI5 knew about Khan and when they knew it. MI5 had Sidique Khan's name, phone number and association with the bookshop on their records from March 11th 2003. This has several important consequences.

It means that the question of whether WYP told MI5 about seeing McDaid get a lift in Khan's car in April 2003 is less relevant, because MI5 already had information on Khan tying him to the bookshop and therefore to McDaid. It also appears that the March 11th 2003 subscriber check was not shared with WYP, otherwise presumably their observation of McDaid in Khan's car would have been seen as more significant. Likewise the December 2003 investigations into the Iqra bookshop and the question of whether they looked at the organisation's paperwork that had Khan's name on it become less important. MI5 already had his name and connection to the bookshop many months earlier.

Looked at another way, if MI5 did do checks in their database due to the calls in July and August 2003, then that should have flagged up the earlier March subscriber check, so why didn't it? Did they really monitor or even bug calls from Q to Khan in July and August? If they did, did they really check their databases on the 13th July for information about Sidique Khan? Can we trust anything that MI5 told the ISC, when this document proves that the whole narrative about Khan's connection to Q told up until 2011 is false? If Q was the mastermind or provocateur behind the Crevice plot then what was his relationship with Khan?

The single page subscriber check undermines not only MI5's defence for the 'intelligence failures' during Operation Crevice, but also their defence for the 'intelligence failures' during Operation Honeysuckle and after. This document is therefore a potential smoking gun. It means that the whole timeline presented not just in the ISC reports but also at the inquests is wrong. It proves that MI5 were not honest and accurate in their presentations to the ISC, or to the inquests, and that both the ISC and the inquests failed in their duty to find out what actually happened. It casts doubt on the whole story of the Crevice investigation. As we will see below, the story only gets worse.

The document in some ways fits in with the theory that Q was working for the security services as it shows that MI5 knew far more, and far earlier, than they have explained. It raises the question of whether Q was playing a similar role to McDaid. Just as with McDaid, the 'intelligence failures' in the operation around Q had the effect of shielding Khan from further investigation. They also substantiated the backstory of Khan as a potential terrorist. That said, the question is extremely difficult to answer without finding Q and putting him on a witness stand, so at this point the document is only one piece of an incomplete puzzle.

Omar Khyam

The next major figure in this story is Omar Khyam. He was the apparent ringleader of the fertiliser plot, involved in travelling to Pakistan for training, liaising with the other conspirators, and obtaining the ingredients for the bomb. It is Khyam's story even more than Q's that poses some of the most serious questions about what was actually going on in Operation Crevice.

Khyam was a young British Pakistani Muslim who grew up in a largely secular household. He apparently became religious during his teens and became increasingly interested in the fight for control of Kashmir. He got involved with Al Muhajiroun and then, in January 2000, he ran away from home and travelled to Pakistan. While there, he attended a mujahideen training camp being run by the Pakistani Inter-Services Intelligence (ISI). After several weeks his relatives in Pakistan, including one former member of the ISI, tracked him down and sent him home.[13]

Khyam continued to travel to the subcontinent and after the March 2003 invasion of Iraq apparently became determined to do something about what he saw as a war on Muslims. In July 2003 he and others involved in the plot attended a training camp in Malakand, Pakistan. This is where the man running the camp, Mohammed Junaid Babar, discussed in detail below, provided recipes for explosives. Among these recipes was one for a mixture of ammonium nitrate fertiliser and aluminium powder. According to Babar's testimony at the Crevice trial, at the same time as Khyam was visiting his camp he also got a visit from Mohammad Sidique Khan and Mohammed Shakil. They had all apparently been sent out to Pakistan by Q.

When Khyam returned to Britain he set about formalising the plot. He developed contact with Momin Khawaja, a Canadian Muslim student who he had met at the Malakand camp. Khyam tasked Khawaja with developing a remotely controlled detonator for the bomb. He also maintained contact with Salahuddin Amin, who was still in Pakistan. Via a webchat that was monitored by the National Security Agency, Khyam asked Amin about the explosive recipe.

The BBC's reconstruction of Amin's account of the webchat sheds some light on what was going on. According to Amin, 'He asked me.. he told me that he has 600 kilogram of ammonium nitrate on him. So he asked me: 'What does he mix with that to make explosive'. So I told him: 'You've been, you've learnt it. Why are you asking me if you've already learnt it, and why are you trying to ask me about it?' And I thought he would have known about it, what he needs to mix up. And it was... 'I forgot already' you know. Basically that training that he done was no good for him.'[14]

This highly incriminating conversation was instigated by Khyam, as were most of the incriminating conversations in some way intercepted or recorded by the security services. He was prosecuted as the ringleader of the conspiracy, but there is another possibility. Was Khyam a provocateur? He was the most closely connected to Q and was the one driving the plot forward to the position where it could be interdicted and the conspirators prosecuted. He arranged for the buying of fertiliser and storing it in the lock-up. He dragged others into the conspiracy.

One hint at this possibility comes from the minutes of a meeting of the Executive Lialson Group, or ELG. The ELG for Operation Crevice was set up on February 11th 2004, and was an inter-agency set of meetings where the latest intelligence and surveillance was shared. At these meetings MI5 and the MPS decided 'how best to gather evidence and prosecute the suspects in court.'[15]

At the meeting of the ELG on February 21st the minutes record, 'We still have no indication of target or timing for any attack, though mid March appears to feature as a significant time period. We should seek to develop the evidence and intelligence, and consider drawing other targets into the conspiracy.'[16] How could they actively 'draw other targets into the conspiracy' unless they had someone within the conspiracy acting as a provocateur? Was this Khyam? Was it Q? Were Khyam's provocative acts done at Q's instigation?

Khyam also made no significant efforts to evade investigation. He left easily traceable records of his exchanges with others. He rented the truck used to pick up the fertiliser on his own credit card. His car was bugged, as were locations he frequented. The publicly available versions of these bugged conversations, just like his webchat with Amin, show Khyam driving the talk towards terrorism, discussing outlandish schemes for possible attacks. Despite this, the 'cell' never chose a specific target for attack, having discussed the Ministry of Sound nightclub and the Bluewater shopping centre, among other places.

Of course, Khyam is now serving a lengthy prison sentence, having been found guilty at the trial in 2007. If he was in some way working for the security services as part of a sting operation then they have clearly hung him out to dry. Nonetheless, this sort of disposable asset is not a radical idea. One only has to look at how the Watergate burglars, including CIA veterans, were promised money and protection only to end up broke and in prison to see this idea in action.

What happened at the trial when Khyam testified in his defence only increases the suspicion that he was, whether he knew it or not, a pawn in a bigger game. He explained his personal history, and how he had trained in the ISI camp in Pakistan and how the ISI worked with Islamic groups in the area. When he returned to the stand after the weekend he refused to answer any further questions, saying that the ISI had 'had words with' his family.

Khyam said, 'I think they are worried I might reveal more about them, so right now, as much as I want to clarify matters, the priority for me has to be the safety of my family so I am going to stop... I am not going to discuss anything related to the ISI any more or the evidence.' It was explained to Khyam that the jury could draw inferences from his refusal to answer questions, which Khyam accepted.[17]   He was consequently found guilty.

Khyam and Khan

In early 2004 Khyam had returned from the Malakand camp and was setting about formalising the 'fertiliser bomb plot'. He became the subject of intense surveillance by MI5 and during this surveillance he was seen with Mohammad Sidique Khan on five separate occasions. Their conversations were bugged as they talked about carrying out financial fraud and travelling to Pakistan, possibly to fight there. As is the case in most of the bugged conversations during Operation Crevice, there was no discussion of solid plans to carry out terrorist attacks.

According to an MI5 summary of the Operative Crevice links, on January 28th 2004, Omar Khyam received phone calls from Sidique Khan. On February 2nd 2004, surveillance teams followed Khyam and saw him in Crawley along with his brother, Shujah Mahmood. Mahmood was prosecuted in the Crevice trial and found not guilty. The two drove to Langley Parade, where they were joined by three men in a green Honda Civic. MI5 say they did not know the three men and only found out later that they were Sidique Khan, Shehzad Tanweer and Waheed Ali (then known as Shipon Ullah).

The summary explains that, 'Khyam joined MSK in the Honda Civic and they drove around for approximately 25 minutes... Khyam handed MSK a piece of paper (nfd) and all six individuals then returned to their respective vehicles.'[18] Six individuals? The document only lists five – Khyam, Mahmood, Khan, Tanweer and Ullah/Ali. In any case, the surveillance team clearly thought that the three then-unidentified men in the Honda Civic were important, because they followed them up the M1.

The car stopped at Toddington services where photographs were taken of Khan, Tanweer and Ali. These photos play a significant role in the Babar story, explained below. The car was then followed as it made its way up to Leeds and the spies noted down the addresses where Tanweer and Ali were dropped off. They also followed Khan all the way to his home in Thornhill Park Avenue in Dewsbury. Checks on the car's registration and the address yielded the name of Khan's wife, Hasina Patel, which meant nothing to the security services.

According the second ISC report, two weeks after this surveillance MI5 asked WYP to check the name 'Hasina Patel' and the address in Thornhill Park Avenue against their databases in order 'to enable us to fully identify any potential associates of Khyam'. The report says that WYP did the checks but that 'nothing significant was found and, with no evidence to justify further action, none was taken.' The report then departs from this claim, saying not just that the checks brought up 'nothing significant' but that, 'No information was discovered.' Later, in the summary timeline in the same report it reiterates that MI5 requested to WYP that they check their databases with regard to Hasina Patel and Thornhill Park Avenue, but that, 'There is no record of a written response to this request.'[19]

This makes no sense whatsoever. MI5 clearly told the ISC three different stories about these checks: that the checks found nothing significant, that the checks found nothing at all, and that WYP never actually responded to the request. Each different story contradicts the other two stories, yet the ISC saw fit to publish all three without question. This is not a matter of policy, or resources, or tactics or decision-making, but of what actually happened. Once again, the absurd nature of the ISC's failings points to an ongoing cover-up.

Unsurprisingly, the evidence at the inquests contradicted the latter two of MI5's stories, and the serious questions about why they told three different stories in the first place were never asked. Documents provided by WYP include the request from MI5 on 16th February 2004 to check databases for information on Hasina Patel and the address 10 Thornhill Park Avenue. They also include the WYP response to MI5 on the following day, detailing Hasina Patel's date of birth, her residency in Thornhill Park Avenue, and her police record of a caution in 1997 for obstructing or resisting a police officer.[20]

Also listed in the response were other people who lived at 10 Thornhill Park Avenue, though their names are redacted. Was Khan's name among those hidden behind the redactions? The WYP response does say that 'None of the subjects named or their addresses have previously come to the notice of this office.' Khan, of course, had come to the attention of WYP in April the previous year as the owner of the car that gave a lift to McDaid. So while it is now clear that the story of there being no record of a response to MI5's request is untrue, it is debatable as to how significant the information provided by WYP really was.

Though the inquests did essentially admit that the ISC's report was 'erroneous', they did not probe further. They did not ask, for example, why it was that MI5 presented three different stories to the ISC. They did not ask why MI5 falsely claimed that they received no response from WYP, once again blaming the junior agency. MI5 clearly lied to the ISC about WYP's failure to provide information in February 2004, so were they lying about other instances where WYP allegedly failed to share information? MI5 followed these three men for 200 miles yet (officially) did very little to actually follow up and find out who they were and what they were doing. Why? If they had the resources to follow them so far then they had the resources to do a bit more digging into their backgrounds.

Weeks later, on the evening of February 21st the Crevice surveillance team came across Khan once again, and a bizarre conversation between him and Khyam was recorded by MI5. A bug planted in Khyam's car picked up the conversation, though MI5 maintain that they did not realise at the time that one of the men speaking was Khan. The MI5 summary of the Crevice-7/7 links says that the surveillance only noted two men – Khyam and Shujah Mahmood – getting into Khyam's Suzuki Vitara, but the ISC report suggests that as many as five men were in the vehicle at that time. The five are Omar Khyam, Shujah Mahmood, Sidique Khan, Shipon Ullah/Waheed Ali and (possibly) Shehzad Tanweer. All the official sources agree that the conversation took place at around 9 p.m. but a BBC *Panorama* episode shows it happening during the daytime.

These discrepancies aside, it is the content of the bugged conversation that is most strange and significant. The BBC published a transcript, one of several different versions of the conversation, on their website. At one point, Khan asked Khyam if he was really a terrorist:

MSK: Are you really a terrorist eh?

KHYAM: They're working with us.

MSK: You're serious, you are basically...

KHYAM: No I'm not a terrorist but they are working through us.

MSK: Who are, there's no one higher than you?

Who were the 'they' who were 'working through' Khyam and the other Crevice conspirators? A further comment suggests that the hypothesis outlined above – that Khyam was an agent provocateur – might well be true. When discussing travelling to Pakistan, Khan brought up the issue of saying goodbye to his daughter:

MSK: With regards to the babe, I'm debating whether or not to say goodbye and so forth.

KHYAM: You know what my advice is right, these are the brothers I know yeah, very rarely, just know one or two each, very rarely do I meet them now, *I don't even live in Crawley anymore I moved out, yeah because in the next month they're going to start raiding big time all the over UK* and insh'allah when the times comes for me to leave (unclear) at the end of the day by telling them of course you love them bruv, you love them for nadeem? It's because we love nadeem this much that we stay away from them coz I know it's better for me and better for them and that's what my advice is.[21]

Khyam's prediction that 'in the next month they're going to start raiding big time' was spookily accurate. At the end of the following month Operation Crevice reached its climax with the arrests of Khyam and several others in police raids. This substantiates the suggestion that Khyam was some sort of spy or agent for the security services. This would make the whole story about not realising that Khan was speaking in this conversation a smokescreen, which might help explain the abject discrepancies in the official version.

A week later on the 28th February 2004 Khan was once again seen with Khyam and Shujah Mahmood, as was Shipon Ullah/Waheed Ali and Shehzad Tanweer. Khan, Tanweer and Ullah/Ali travelled in the same Honda Civic seen on February 2nd, Khyam and Mahmood were in Khyam's Suzuki Vitara. The men met up and travelled around Slough and Crawley, visiting several builders' merchants. They also visited a mosque, Khyam's flat and a restaurant.

All five men then bundled into the Honda Civic and headed north via the M25 and then the M1 motorway. At Junction 11 (Luton) of the M1 they stopped and had a brief meeting with Q, who was waiting for them there. The MI5 summary says that, 'this meeting is assessed to have lasted for only 10 minutes as (redacted) showed MQK entering his home address in Luton a short time after the meeting took place.'[22] Clearly they were still following Q closely at this time, yet again begging the question as to what Q was doing and why he was never arrested.

After visiting a mobile phone shop in Wellingbrough, the car then returned to Slough and dropped off Khyam and Mahmood. The three remaining men then returned to Leeds as on February 2nd, and were followed there by MPS Special Branch. The MI5 summary along with minutes from meetings of the ELG make it clear that the security services knew that the car was the same Honda Civic and that the three men were the same three men seen a few weeks earlier.

The MI5 summary states that they believed at the time that the purpose of the 28th February activities was financial fraud, a topic repeatedly discussed during the bugged Crevice conversations. The plan, to MI5's mind, was that the men would open credit accounts at the builders' merchants, purchase valuable equipment, default on the repayments and fence the equipment via third parties. The money would then be transferred to Pakistan 'for the benefit of senior Al Qaeda commanders'.

Further meetings between Khyam and Khan took place in Crawley on March 20th and 23rd, only days before the Crevice arrests. Though a bugged conversation from the 23rd once again contained discussion about travelling to Pakistan to engage with the struggle, this was assessed as unimportant and so no further action was taken. The argument here is that because there was no evidence that Khan (and Tanweer and Ullah/Ali) were involved in the fertiliser bomb plot that only minimal resources were devoted to finding out who they were and what they were doing.

The fundamental problem with this 'defence' is that raising money for Al Qaeda was still a very serious matter, so while it might not have put Khan et al at the top of the priority list, they logically would still have been relatively high priority targets. Of course, MI5 and the ISC systematically lied about the way MI5 prioritised targets at that time, as outlined in the introduction, so their whole argument is unconvincing.

The MPS carried out an additional check on the Honda Civic's registration on February 28th, despite having checked it only weeks earlier. Why? What did they expect to find that they did not already know? As it turns out the registration of the car had been switched from Hasina Patel (of Thornhill Park Avenue) to Sidique Khan (of 11 Gregory Street, Batley) earlier that month.[23]

What this later check on the Honda Civic also means is that the question of whether Khan was one of the occupants at Thornhill Park Avenue detailed in WYP's response to MI5 on February 17th becomes less relevant. MPS, and presumably therefore also MI5, knew he was the registered driver of the Honda Civic seen in the Crevice surveillance only eleven days after WYP's response that apparently said nothing about Khan.

This second check on the Honda Civic is perhaps the only time in the official story of pre-7/7 investigations into Khan where an apparently spontaneous inquiry turned up useful information. On all the other occasions it is as though the security services did not want Khan to be investigated. So how did they follow up on this information?

Operation Scraw

On the day of the Crevice arrests at the end of March 2004, MI5 initiated Operation Scraw, aimed at finding out more about some of the people they had encountered during the Crevice surveillance. Among those targeted in this operation were Sidique Khan and Shehzad Tanweer.

The second ISC report refers obliquely to this followup investigation, saying that, 'In early 2004, MI5 launched Operation SC*** to investigate individuals ***. There were *** key targets in this operation (including ***). Some remain the subject of current investigation.'[24] The full codename of the operation, its aim, the number of key targets and who they included were all redacted, preventing us from realizing the true significance at that time.

The inquest testimony and evidence did not clarify much. For one thing, Witness G referred to the operation by the codename 'Scrawl', not 'Scraw'. Though in all likelihood this was an honest mistake, it does illustrate the extent to which Witness G was not in a position to discuss these operations in any detail or from first-hand experience. As such, he was not in a position of authority to discuss the 'preventability' issues of 'intelligence failures', let alone the question of infiltrators, informants and double agents.

We were told when he first took the stand that he was not directly involved in any of the relevant pre-7/7 operations, had no expertise on the subject of Islamist terrorism, and that at the time of the inquests he was Chief of Staff to the Director of MI5, Jonathan Evans. Chief of Staff is of course a political and administrative role, not an operational one. None of the actual surveillance or desk officers involved in the operations were called to testify. Instead we were given an anonymous 'face of MI5' who wasn't in a position to discuss anything beyond the summaries and statements prepared by the Security Service.

Graham Foulkes, the father of one of those killed at Edgware Road, made his objections clear in a BBC interview, saying, 'He admitted that he wasn't in post in 2005 and he's not an Islamic anti-terrorist expert, and that he was relying on other people telling him information and him reading notes, so effectively hearsay evidence, which is not normally allowed in the judicial process.'[25] Indeed, aside from MI5 and perhaps its sister agencies, can you imagine any organization being allowed by the courts to put up an anonymous witness, reliant on hearsay?

What we did learn from Witness G was that Operation Scraw was the work of only one desk officer, with some assistance from others. They had a dozen key targets, a list which did not include Khan or Tanweer, though both were the subject of inquiries as part of the operation. Exactly how the huge number of people encountered during Crevice were whittled down to a dozen key targets and a few others was not fully explained, though Witness G did say that, 'There were a variety of reasons. Some to do with their nearness to the plot. Some to do with their ability to open up other avenues of intelligence for us.'[26] This is truly bizarre. If MI5 did not know what these people were up to then how could they possibly assess 'their ability to open up other avenues of intelligence'? Clairvoyance? Tea leaves? Guesswork?

Regardless, on 8th June 2004 MI5 sent a message to the North East Regional Intelligence Cell (NERIC) and WYP asking about the men from the Leeds area encountered during the Crevice surveillance. They outlined the cars they had seen, the registration details and addresses connected to them and said, 'We would be grateful for any details you may have in your records (including photographs) of the individuals and addresses mentioned above.'[27]

Several weeks later, on 14th July, MI5 received a response. Regarding the Honda Civic it said that, 'North East RIC, West Yorkshire Special Branch and local systems have been checked with a negative result.' It went on to explain that there had been 22 previous checks on the car's registration, 21 of which were believed to be part of Operation Crevice. On Khan the response positively identified him, his date of birth, his previous addresses and his 1992 caution for assault. It then said that there was 'No trace of Khan on NERIC/West Yorkshire Special Branch systems.'[28]

Why was there no trace of Khan? This request came in June 2004, over a year after WYP had seen Khan's car giving a lift to McDaid during Operation Honeysuckle. This information should have come up as a result of the search during Operation Scraw, and would have connected Khan to McDaid and therefore presumably alerted MI5 to Khan's possible significance. Unlike many of the important questions, this one was asked at the inquests. Lawyer Patrick O'Connor, who was representing some of the bereaved families, asked it of Assistant Chief Constable John Parkinson of the West Yorkshire Police.

> **Q.** So this is the question. You've explained very well
> what happens with vehicle records, but the name
> "Sidique Khan" is on both NERIC and West Yorkshire
> Special Branch systems, and, indeed, it's spelt exactly
> the same, so why is there no trace?

A. This is an area that we've examined very, very closely, and exhaustive enquiries have reconstructed the search at that time, and I can't give you an explanation as to exactly why that name of Sidique Khan did not respond to a search against Sidique Khan. Those enquiries include speaking to the individuals concerned that would have conducted those searches. They assure me that they conducted them properly. But we've reconstructed that and put Sidique Khan into that old Legacy system in the way that it's described there, it returns the result that we talked about earlier, the --

Q. The 2001 result?

A. -- report from 2003.

Q. I'm very sorry, the 2003 result. So it works now, it works now?

A. Yes.

Q. You could do it today --

A. Yes.

Q. -- and you'd come up with the 2003 BMW link --

A. That's correct.

Q. -- under the name?

A. Yes.

Q. Forgive me, the reason perhaps why I'm asking this is I don't think you deal with this in your witness statement.

A. There's no technical reason that we can find. In fact, those exhaustive enquiries have included examinations of the computer system to see -- or to offer some kind of explanation why that would show as a "no trace" on that West Yorkshire Police Special Branch system.[29]

According to Parkinson they tried and failed to find out why the search for 'Sidique Khan' from Leeds in June 2004 did not turn up the name 'Sidique Khan' as the owner of a car in Leeds that they had connected to McDaid in April 2003. He said that when they tried to do the search again it worked fine and the information came up. In effect, this testimony is a long-winded way of saying 'we have no idea why it didn't work, but don't worry because it is working again now.'

This is unacceptable. If there was a technical fault and the post-7/7 explorations failed to find that technical fault then it could still exist. Saying that the system has magically sorted itself out now and is no longer failing to find the 2003 information is not reassuring. Being able to find the information now doesn't matter because Khan has allegedly blown himself up. The question is why it wasn't found in June 2004 when it should have been.

Looked at another way, did someone sabotage the WYP systems to prevent the Khan-McDaid connection being passed to MI5? The fault was only temporary, encompassing the period when the search was done but then righted by the time when WYP checked the system post-7/7. If it was sabotaged (and then repaired) then presumably it must have been someone with access not just to the system, but to the communication from MI5 asking for more information on Khan. Thus, the only plausible suspect for a possible saboteur would have to be someone within the security services.

Junaid Babar

The final key figure in the Crevice story is Mohammed Junaid Babar, whose story encompasses many of the same themes and questions as McDaid's, Q's and Khyam's. Babar was born in Pakistan in 1975 but moved to the US a couple of years later. He grew up in Queens, New York and attended the boys-only La Salle military school.

He enrolled at St John's University but soon dropped out. He worked several low-level jobs including as a parking valet, where he sometimes overcharged the customers. Sometime in 2000 he joined the New York chapter of Al Muhajiroun, which had been established in the 1990s and was closely monitored by US security services. On September 11th 2001, Babar was in New York and witnessed the 9/11 terrorist attacks. His mother was actually working on, and escaped from, the 9th floor of one of the World Trade Center towers.

Far from being angry towards the terrorists who had nearly killed his mother, Babar apparently decided to join them. Within a week of the 9/11 attacks he was planning to go to Pakistan to join the jihad. By November 2001 he had arrived in Pakistan and he gave two interviews to Western journalists proclaiming that, 'When the American troops enter, we will kill them in Afghanistan. There is no negotiation... I will kill every American that I see in Afghanistan and while I am in Pakistan, if I see them in Pakistan, I will kill every American soldier I can in Pakistan.'[30]

Why did Babar trumpet his intentions so loudly? In the immediate post-9/11 period anyone and everyone who was associated with militant Islam, and many completely innocent Muslims, were targeted as being responsible for the attacks. If he was truly intending to fight and kill Americans then he would, presumably, have kept quiet.

Through most of 2002 he worked for the Al Muhajiroun office in Lahore, and for the Pakistani Software Export Board, an agency of the Pakistan government. Keeping with the security service tradition of allowing Al Muhajiroun to operate, Babar was never picked up or questioned about his involvement with the organisation. The long list of terrorist crimes that he later confessed to did not include his membership of Al Muhajiroun, which continues to operate in several countries with impunity.

Towards the end of 2002 Babar apparently became disillusioned with his work for Al Muhajiroun, and sought out contact with Al Qaeda. He became a terrorist facilitator, providing money and equipment (such as night-vision goggles), and setting up and running the training camp in Malakand. Among the attendees at the camp were Omar Khyam, Salahuddin Amin and Jawad Akbar, three of the convicted Operation Crevice conspirators. Others included alleged 7/7 ringleader Mohammad Sidique Khan and Mohammed Shakil, who was prosecuted but found innocent of involvement in the 7/7 conspiracy (see chapter 2). It has also been reported that alleged 7/7 bomber Shehzad Tanweer visited the Malakand camp at the same time as Khan, in July 2003.

Through this period Babar also visited Britain on multiple occasions, meeting with Khan and others in the Leeds area, as well as some of the Crevice plotters. In his later statements to the FBI he claimed that Khan, Khyam and the others were sent out to Pakistan in mid-2003 by Q. Babar flew in and out of Britain without restriction, and was never stopped by the authorities in either Pakistan or Britain. Given his very public interviews in 2001 why was he not at least detained and questioned?

Babar finally returned to the US in early March 2004, according to an unsealed court document. This is in contrast to most media reports that have him arriving in the US in early April. The significance of this is that, contrary to the media reports, Babar was back in the US before Crevice reached its climax and the suspects in the UK were arrested, rather than after the arrests.[31]

He was not arrested when he landed, and weeks later in early April he was approached by FBI agents on the street outside his home. He co-operated immediately and for the next few days he was holed up in a hotel, telling the FBI everything he knew. He admitted to his role as an Al Qaeda facilitator and to his involvement in the Crevice plot. A transcript of a hearing where he pleaded guilty to various terrorism charges details how he even bought the aluminium powder to be used with the ammonium nitrate in the Crevice bomb.[32] Some of this powder was later found behind the shed in Omar Khyam's garden, and this became one of the key points of evidence against Khyam at the trial.

The Al Qaeda Supergrass

Babar became the Al Qaeda supergrass, not just co-operating with the FBI in intelligence terms but also as a key prosecution witness. He testified against Khyam et al in the 2007 UK Crevice trial, and against Momin Khawaja in the later Crevice trial in Canada. He was also the key witness against Mohammed Shakil, Waheed Ali and Sadeer Saleem when they were put on trial, twice, for alleged involvement in the 7/7 conspiracy. Though Shakil, Ali and Saleem were ultimately found innocent in connection to the 7/7 bombings, Khyam and four of his co-defendants were found guilty, as was Momin Khawaja. Shakil and Ali were found guilty of conspiring to visit a terrorism training camp, largely on the basis of Babar's testimony that Shakil had visited his Malakand camp (see chapter 2). Indeed, almost everyone who passed through Babar's camp later ended up in court on terrorism charges with Babar testifying against them.

Babar's testimony, particularly at the UK Crevice trial in 2007, was pure theatre. He was delivered to the Old Bailey in an armoured van, guarded by a large police escort. Despite this show of force, there has never been a single word from Al Muhajiroun denouncing Babar for being a turncoat, a grass or a traitor. No attempt has been made on his life even though he has been living in the open for several years since leaving prison in 2008.

His testimony was, however, subject to challenges from the accused at trial. In the Crevice trial he was accused of 'creating elaborate lies to make himself a valuable witness.' While it is not clear how much of his testimony Babar fabricated, he certainly told some lies. He didn't look at the defendants once in his five days of testifying against them, and tried to claim that Jon Gilbert, one of the journalists who had interviewed him back in 2001, had paid him $500 to 'sex up' the interview. When pressed, he admitted that he had made this up.[33]

The authorities extended incredible leniency to Babar during his time in Pakistan. As far as we know he was never detained by the Pakistani authorities, or the Americans, or the British. Though it has never officially been recognised as such, this should constitute another massive 'intelligence failure' on the road to 7/7. This leniency continued after Babar's arrest in 2004, as he was granted immunity from prosecution for his crimes in exchange for providing intelligence and testimony against numerous 'terror suspects'.

The people that Babar testified against received combined sentences of over 100 years in prison, but Babar himself served far less time despite pleading guilty to equally if not even more serious charges. In December 2010, in the middle of the July 7 Inquests, Babar was finally sentenced. Before the hearing the US government sent a letter to the judge arguing the case for leniency. This is a standard practice with co-operators, but the letter went way beyond the norm.

It described Babar's provision of information and willingness to testify in the most glowing terms. It said that, 'the level of assistance provided by Babar to both the US Government and foreign governments has been more than substantial; it has been extraordinary.' This was then echoed in Babar's sentencing hearing where it was stated that his 'extraordinary co-operation' began even before he was arrested.[34]

The question, of course, is for how long before his arrest was Babar co-operating? Was Babar an informant the whole time he was in Pakistan? As with Q, this question has been posed by the mainstream media. An article in the Times during the Crevice trial in May 2007 said that, 'Some suggest that he may have already been an FBI agent' at the time of his highly incriminating 2001 interviews. Weeks later, at the end of the Crevice trial an episode of *Panorama* recounted the Babar story as it stood in 2007 and stated that, 'Inevitably there were suspicions that he'd been an FBI agent all along.'[35]

His sentence was extremely light. Babar pleaded guilty to several counts of facilitating and supporting terrorism, and has always maintained his beliefs that it is justified to kill Americans who occupy Muslim countries. Despite this, he was released from prison in 2008, having served around four and a half years. He was sentenced to time served in late 2010, after a couple of years of 'supervised release'. He was also fined $500.

Perhaps more significantly, it has recently come to light that throughout the Crevice investigation the British authorities were sharing information with the FBI. According to the BBC, 'The FBI's senior agent in charge of the American end of Operation Crevice, Art Cummings, was communicating three times a day with his MI5 opposite number at the British Embassy in Washington, so he knew everything that was going on in real time.'[36]

Why were MI5 sharing information with the FBI? There was absolutely nothing in the Crevice plot to indicate an attack on the US so what business was it of theirs? When MI5 followed Khan, Tanweer and Ali to Leeds they didn't bother to tell the local Special Branch until months later, so why were they exchanging information with the FBI 'in real time'? The only FBI connection to the Crevice plot was Mohammed Junaid Babar. The only reason for the FBI and MI5 to be sharing information before the Feds approached Babar in early April 2004 is if they were at the least tracking Babar's movements and activities.

Another BBC documentary in early 2012 all but confirmed that Babar was a spy all along, rather than being 'turned' into a co-operator. In the first part of *Modern Spies*, Peter Taylor, who presents all of *Panorama*'s episodes on the security services, referred to Babar as, 'One of the most important sources in the war on terror' and 'a human source that intelligence services dream of'. Mark Giuliano, head of the National Security Branch of the FBI, said of Babar, 'He was critical. He is an individual who had both the access and the capability to get into groups that simply would not have existed without him.'

If Babar was not in contact with the FBI until they approached him in early April 2004, then he did not have 'access' or any 'capability to get into groups', because he was in custody the whole time until his release in 2008. These comments only make sense if Babar was a spy for at least some portion of his time in Pakistan. Despite this, and in an incredible show of doublethink, the BBC maintained the 'just a co-operator' story in this documentary.[37]

PISCES

Khan's trips to Pakistan, and particularly to Babar's Malakand training camp, have been used as part of the background story to support the idea that he was a suicidal terrorist. A major problem is that the story is largely sourced from Babar's suspicious testimony, and so it may not even be true. There are also a series of 'intelligence failures' around this aspect of the official 7/7 legend that once again indicate that the security services actually knew far more than they say.

The main 'failures' are based around a system called PISCES – the Personal Identification, Secure Comparison and Evaluation System. It was launched in the late 1990s by the US Department of State's Terrorist Interdiction Program. In essence, it is a border control system specifically designed to help national governments track the movement of suspected terrorists in and out of their countries. It records passport information, pictures of passengers arriving and leaving and flight numbers. All of this information is stored not only on local systems but also on CIA and FBI servers back in the US. The PISCES system was in place in Pakistan at the time of Operation Crevice.

During Babar's interrogation by the FBI in April/May 2004 he explained how several of the Crevice suspects arrived at Islamabad airport in July 2003. The three men – Jawad Akbar, Ahmed Ali Khan and Waseem Gulzar – arrived on the same day at two other men from the UK, who Babar knew as Ibrahim and Zubair. The men were all introduced to one another and had breakfast together. They then joined the other Crevice plotters at the Malakand training camp.[38]

The significance of this is that the two men using the aliases Ibrahim and Zubair were actually Mohammad Sidique Khan and Mohammed Shakil. Apparently Babar did not know this, and so he couldn't tell the FBI and so they couldn't tell MI5. According to MI5 documents from the inquests, Babar did not say exactly when these two groups of people arrived. He initially did not explain that he knew that Ibrahim and Zubair were from the North of England, or that they had attended the Malakand camp.[39]

However, by the time MI5 got Babar's information about Ibrahim and Zubair, the Crevice suspects were in custody. The authorities had Jawad Akbar and his passport, and could have found out exactly when he travelled to Pakistan in mid-2003. They could, of course, have interrogated Akbar, or Khyam or Amin and asked them for more information on the men with them in Islamabad. It is not currently known whether they did this or not, nor whether it elicited any useful information. There was another possible avenue of investigation – PISCES.

MI5 knew that Ibrahim and Zubair had arrived in Islamabad on the same day as Jawad Akbar. It was even claimed at the inquests that they arrived on the same flight. In March 2005 Babar provided further information about Ibrahim and Zubair, namely that they were from the Bradford area and that they had attended the Malakand camp. MI5 subsequently launched the curiously-named Operation Downtempo, to try to identify Ibrahim and Zubair.

They eventually filed a request with the Pakistan authorities to check PISCES for information about Akbar's travel in and out of the country in 2003. This request was not made until June 2005, only weeks before the 7/7 bombings. The reply did not come back until nearly four months later, in September 2005. As such, MI5 sat on the information about Akbar's travel for over a year before using it to try to find out more about Ibrahim and Zubair. By then it was too late to find out that the men were in fact Khan and Shakil, the alleged 7/7 ringleader and one of his friends who was wrongly prosecuted for involvement in the attacks.

That said, there are two strong indications that MI5 did in fact know more about Ibrahim and Zubair than merely what they gleaned from Babar through the FBI. Operation Scraw – the attempt to find out more about Sidique Khan and others who were seen during the Crevice surveillance – saw MI5 request further information on Khan and others from WYP and NERIC. The request includes information on Ibrahim and Zubair that Babar did not provide until the following year.

The MI5 message says, 'reporting has indicated that two individuals from Leeds, known as IBRAHIM and ZUBAIR (nfd) were also historical contacts of Mohammed Qayoum Khan MQK in the UK. IBRAHIM and ZUBAIR are reported to have travelled from the UK to Islamabad in June 2003, in order to become involved in possible extremist activities. Nothing further is known about these individuals.'[40]

If Babar did not tell the FBI that Ibrahim and Zubair were from Bradford until March 2005 then how did MI5 know they were from Leeds in June 2004? Likewise, if Babar didn't tell the FBI until March 2005 about the two attending his Malakand camp then how did MI5 know in June 2004 they had gone to Pakistan for 'possible extremist activities'? The timeline makes no sense, unless either Babar did tell the FBI more at an earlier date or MI5 had another source of information - possibly Q or Khyam.

We were also told at the inquests that in May 2005, only two months before the bombings, an MI5 desk officer made the same connection. He suggested that the three Northern men seen during the Crevice surveillance were possible candidates for Ibrahim and Zubair. Apparently no further action was taken on the basis of this intuition.[41]

The other problem for this part of the official story is the speed at which the PISCES information on Khan (and Tanweer) appeared in the mainstream media following the 7/7 bombings. On July 18th 2005, only eleven days after the attacks and only two days after the formal identification of Khan and Tanweer, both the Times and the BBC ran reports on their trips to Pakistan. The reports contained images taken at Pakistani airports, flight numbers and other data from the PISCES system.[42]

The reports were not perfect, as they did contain claims that Hasib Hussain, the alleged bus-bomber, had also visited Pakistan in 2004. It quickly emerged that this was a different Hasib Hussain, who didn't even look particularly similar. The fundamental question is how did the mainstream media get this information so quickly? Who gave it to them? The obvious answer is that they got it from the security services. The problem there is that according to testimony and documents from the inquests, the MPS did not even request this information from Pakistan until August 1st 2005. They didn't receive an answer until August 22nd and so they couldn't have given it to the press a month earlier.[43]

That leaves a distinct possibility, that MI5 knew all along about Khan and Tanweer's trips to Pakistan and did not tell the police. It took MI5 four months to get PISCES information on Jawad Akbar, and three weeks for the MPS to get PISCES information on Khan and Tanweer, even after 7/7. Therefore, unless MI5 had the information before 7/7 then there is no realistic way they could have obtained it and given it to the press only ten or eleven days after 7/7.

What was Crevice?

In this chapter we have seen many of the same themes, issues and questions as we saw in chapter 6. Just like the 'failures' around Martin McDaid and the Iqra bookshop, the explanations for the 'failures' around Operation Crevice are unacceptable. The story about how and why Operation Crevice started makes little sense in light of the smoking gun MI5 document that linked Sidique Khan to both Q and to the Iqra bookshop in March 2003. It also means that all the subsequent identifications of Sidique Khan during Crevice should have flagged up this initial document, but there is no subsequent reference to it. This fundamentally undermines the story that MI5 told to the ISC.

In chapter 6 we saw how the Operation Honeysuckle surveillance linking McDaid to Sidique Khan's car was, at least officially, not passed on to MI5 by WYP. Similarly, when it came to a request from MI5 to WYP to check on Hasina Patel, the registered owner of a car seen during Crevice surveillance, MI5 told the ISC three different stories. They simultaneously claimed that the WYP checks found nothing significant, that they found nothing at all, and that WYP never actually responded to the request. Even more so than the allegation about WYP failing to share the Honeysuckle information with MI5, this story is not acceptable. The documentation proves that in fact WYP did respond, and that their checks did turn up some information.

A later request from MI5 to WYP and NERIC for more information on Sidique Khan yielded nothing of significance, when it should have turned up Khan's connection to McDaid from the Honeysuckle surveillance. The explanation offered for this – that they could find no technical reason for the information not turning up – should not be accepted by anyone. As far as excuses go, it is from the bargain bin where we can also find 'I did not have sexual relations with that woman' and 'I have no recollection of those events'.

We can see the same pattern from the story of the Iqra bookshop in the tale of Operation Crevice. Investigations failed to find information when they should, and 'intelligence failures' protected probable agents or informants. The three major figures in the plot all appear to have been either working for or at least protected by the security services. Q, like McDaid, was never even arrested, Junaid Babar got an incredibly lenient sentence, but Omar Khyam was hung out to dry.

What does this suggest about the nature of the fertiliser bomb plot? The plot was piecemeal and vague, as the conspirators had not determined a specific target or method of delivering a bomb. They had discussed various possible acts of terrorism in a speculative way, and Khyam did acquire some of the materials necessary for a bomb. So was the whole thing an elaborate provocation or sting operation? Was Khyam led to believe he would be protected like Q and Babar, only to be double-crossed?

Perhaps regardless of Khyam's role and status, the image that emerges is deeply worrying. Inasmuch as the alleged 7/7 bombers did things that could later be used to make them look like fanatical suicide terrorists, they did those things in connection with one of these probable secret agents. The vast majority of the intelligence failures, and all of the ones for which the excuses are risible, had the consequence of protecting not just the alleged bombers and the double agents, but specifically the relationship between them.

It is significant that much of this has played out in the mainstream media. Babar's story in particular has garnered a reasonable amount of press attention, and it was the BBC who most explicitly suggested that Q was an agent of some kind. Much of what we know about McDaid and the Iqra bookshop we know through the coverage by Richard Watson on *Newsnight*. Much of what we know about Crevice we know through the Watson's *Newsnight* reports, and through the BBC's trial coverage and the *Panorama* episode.

It is as though we are being incrementally told a pre-established story. Each question of 'intelligence failures' has come with a little bit more information about the alleged bombers that makes them look more like they might actually be bombers. The whole public narrative about 7/7 has been dominated by this notion of intelligence and 'preventability'. After nearly 7 years this whole process looks more and more like an attempt to establish a legend of the four as suicide bombers.

It is in this light that we should consider two more intelligence failures. During Operation Scraw – the attempt to learn more about targets encountered during the Crevice surveillance – the database failure was not the only problem. With Babar in custody and fully co-operating, he was frequently given photographs of various terror suspects to see if he could identify them and provide information about them. According to the handful of pages available of the FBI summary of his interrogation he routinely identified people correctly from surveillance photographs.[44]

Yet when photographs of Sidique Khan and Shehzad Tanweer were sent over to the US in April 2004, he couldn't identify either man. When you look at the photos it is easy to see why. The first image is the original surveillance photograph of Khan and Tanweer, taken at Toddington services. The second is the version sent by MI5 to the FBI.

The cropped image of Khan, on the right, was so poor that it was not even shown to Babar by the FBI. The image of Tanweer was almost as bad, and it is unsurprising that Babar did not know who he was. Witness G was confronted during the inquests with this comparison, with Hugo Keith QC commenting that, 'G, I am bound to observe, if you will forgive me, I think one of my children could have done a better job of cropping out that photograph.'

MI5's excuse for such a horrendous editing job was that, 'the cropping is all to do with not revealing the techniques by which the photograph was collected.' The ability of security services to covertly film and photograph people is not a secret, so this makes no sense whatsoever. Witness G also referred to the need for speed in sending the pictures to be seen by Babar, but this is also highly dubious. If the purpose was to have the men in the picture identified then quickly sending a poorly-cropped image to Babar that he did not identify should have resulted in sending a better version to make sure.[45]

This story did attract some media attention, and MI5's apparent incompetence was roundly criticised. The most important questions were not asked. Look again at the second image, the cropped version of Khan and Tanweer. Ask yourself these questions: is this an honest version of the original? Is this image the product of a sincere attempt to have these men identified? Or is the most obvious explanation that, in fact, MI5 wanted to prevent Babar from identifying these two men? Shortly after 7/7 Babar was shown a press photograph of Khan, who he easily identified as the man he knew as Ibrahim.

One final strand of intelligence that was never properly exploited by MI5 is information they received on two men known as 'Saddique ***' and 'Imran'. According to MI5, they received information in the period January to March 2005 about two men. The men, 'Saddique *** (surname not Khan)' and 'Imran' were from Batley in West Yorkshire, and had apparently trained at a mujahideen camp in Afghanistan in the late 1990s/early 2000s. An MI5 document at the inquests says that, 'Imran reportedly visited a mosque in Bradford and WYP provided the Security Service with the telephone number for him. This number was a contract mobile registered to Imran.'[46] WYP also told MI5 that both men were associated with a 'Taf', though to be Tafazal Mohammed, from the Iqra bookshop.

We have never been told who 'Imran' is, though it appears they identified him in early 2005. 'Saddique ***' on the other hand is apparently Sidique Khan. The ISC's second report says that on 11th July 2005, 'Before it became clear that Mohammed Siddique KHAN had died in the attacks, but when he was the prime suspect for the bombings, new intelligence indicated that "Saddique ***" (see 17 January and 1 March 2005) was Mohammed Siddique KHAN.'[47] The MI5 document from the inquests elaborates, saying the information received said that 'MSK would be prepared to use a baseball bat on someone's legs if required and MSK was capable of carrying out a martyrdom operation.'[48]

Though Imran appears to have been identified, we are told that on 1st March both WYP and MI5 checked their databases for further information on 'Saddique ***' and found nothing. No further action was taken for, in the words of Witness G, 'Good operational reasons'. These reasons cannot, of course, be disclosed but MI5 did offer a supplementary gist explaining that 'operational reasons justified the decision not to investigate the intelligence strand further.'[49]

This non-explanation is utterly meaningless, leaving open the question of why we're even being told about this. The whole purpose of this 'Saddique *** (surname not Khan)' story seems to be to establish, ultimately, that 'MSK was capable of carrying out a martyrdom operation.' Once again, the 'intelligence failure' serves to establish a legend of the alleged bombers, Khan in particular, that has been used to make them look like suicide terrorists.

Of course, the whole concept of 'intelligence failures' as it has been explored in the mainstream takes for granted the guilt of the four men. The second ISC report is titled 'Could 7/7 have been prevented?', a question that leaves no room for the possibility that the accused are innocent. In framing the questions in this way, the ISC and the mainstream media have succeeded only in asking the old question about security services of 'what did they know and when did they know it?' The more important question, to my mind, is 'what were they doing and why were they doing it?'

By asking MI5 what they knew about four people they maintain were suicide bombers it is no surprise that MI5 responded with information that made them look like suicide bombers. When asked again for more information, MI5 have invariably responded with more information that makes the four look like suicide bombers. The theatre goes on, people are convinced that we are somehow learning more about how the security services really operate and the reasons why 7/7 happened. In reality, the important questions are systematically avoided – those that stem from the possibility that the four alleged bombers are innocent.

MI5, with the collusion of the ISC, have taken part in a cover-up not just of what happened before 7/7 but also after it. In the next chapter we will see that the purpose of the ongoing cover-up appears to be to not only exonerate the security services, but also to enable them to use these 'failures' to consolidate their secret and powerful status.

Chapter 8: Fixed Around the Policy

The security services and in particular MI5 have made consistently untrue statements about what they knew, when they knew it and what they did with the information. The story of the alleged bombers has also changed over time. On the day of 7/7 and the days after it was widely reported that the attack 'bore the hallmarks of Al Qaeda', with fingers pointing at that shadowy international network. Then, a few days later, Charles Clarke said that the culprits were terrorists who were previously unknown to the security services. The four men were then publicly identified, and the story became one of homegrown suicide bombers.

The first ISC report described the four as appearing on the fringe of another surveillance operation. The second ISC report gave a timeline and outline of events that is now demonstrably untrue in most of its key aspects. The inquest testimony and the documents made available have filled in many gaps but have provoked even more questions. They give a picture of 'intelligence failures' that wilfully prevented investigation of the relationships between the alleged bombers and several probable agents of the security services in the years before 7/7.

Chillingly, the ultimate conclusion of MI5's offerings at the inquests was that there was, in fact, no intelligence failure when it came to the London bombings. This explanation was accepted by the coroner Lady Justice Hallett, by the major media, and by the ISC. This does open the door to a terrible but very real possibility – that MI5 don't see any of this as failure, that they in fact see it as success.

The ISC do not see it that way. In their annual 2010-2011 report they reiterated the same conclusion as before, that 'the Security Service and the police could not reasonably have prevented the attacks.' They did raise the question of the timeline of events published in their second 7/7 report being inaccurate, citing a letter of explanation from the Director General (DG) of MI5. They accepted the DG's explanation that, 'I am certain that there was no deliberate intent to withhold information from the Committee, particularly in light of the unprecedented amount of operational detail that was shared.'

They did consider three issues more seriously. The first is that when MI5 explained to the ISC how they categorized and prioritised targets, their explanation used terms that actually came from funding applications to the Treasury. They were not operational terms, and hence did not explain how MI5 responded to the information they had prior to 7/7. Again, the ISC cited a letter from the DG that said, 'There was no attempt to mislead the Committee on this point but, on review of the relevant evidence, I believe that we should more clearly have emphasised to the Committee how the prioritisation system operated in practice.'

The second is that during Operation Downtempo, the attempt to find out more about 'Ibrahim' and 'Zubair', an MI5 desk officer intuitively guessed that they were the same people seen during Operation Crevice. This guess turned out to be right, but nothing was done about it at the time, and as they note, 'The ISC was not provided with this information during its investigations into the 7 July bombings.' This is a textbook case of no one being blamed.

MI5 failed to give the ISC a true account during the second investigation into 7/7, but the ISC cannot come down hard on MI5 for this because if they do then the question might rebound to them. MI5 only answered the questions that the ISC asked them, so we should be asking about the questions that the ISC did not ask, and why they didn't ask them. As an aside, what was the purpose of Operation Downtempo? Why was it codenamed Downtempo? It's almost like calling it 'Operation Slowdown the investigation into these guys who we need to look like suicide bombers'.

The third issue that concerned the ISC was that MI5 had told them that when they asked WYP for information on Hasina Patel in February 2004 that there was 'no record of a written response'. This is now proven to be untrue, WYP did respond. However, the ISC wrote this off as problems in 'record keeping and information management'. They overlooked the fact that their own report on 7/7 contained three different versions of what happened in response to MI5's request to WYP.[1]

What this conclusively demonstrates is that the intelligence and security institutions in this country are not fit for purpose. In particular, the oversight supposedly provided by the ISC is disgracefully inadequate. When MI5 told them that the alleged bombers turned up on the periphery of another investigation, they accepted it. It turned out that MI5 had followed two of the men on multiple occasions, had Sidique Khan's name on several occasions, and had made further inquiries about him and others around him. MI5 then presented a timeline of what they knew and when, which the ISC accepted.

That timeline is now in pieces, with no explanation for why investigations that either were done or should have been done did not turn up information that the security services had in their systems. Once again, the ISC have accepted this, chastising MI5 for poor record keeping and ignoring the bigger questions. The fact that the ISC are so compliant makes it all the more important that we do not just accept this.

The most important question of why the security services behaved in the way that they did has never been answered. Time after time they failed to follow up leads or share information or find information that they already had. These are not isolated failures of a huge bureaucracy, but a pattern of behaviour. In trying to understand the 'intelligence failures' we need to appreciate that they did not take place in a vacuum. Rather, they took place in the context of aggressive foreign and domestic policies adopted in the name of security coupled with deceptive claims of imminent threats.

Iraq's Known Unknowns

The main event that occurred between 9/11 and 7/7 in terms of the British security services was the build-up to the invasion of Iraq in March 2003. The argument for the invasion was made by the government through the publishing of two dossiers of evidence, one in September 2002 and one in February 2003. The fundamental argument was that the intelligence showed that Saddam was developing Weapons of Mass Destruction (WMDs) and that he was colluding with terrorists. This ludicrous conspiracy theory helped inspire visions in the minds of opinion-makers of all stripes of the 'armageddon scenario' - of a terrorist attack using Chemical, Biological, Radiological or Nuclear (CBRN) weapons.

The intelligence services knew all along that the case made for war was untrue. In December 2001, a letter from the Private Secretary to Sir Richard Dearlove, the head of MI6, was written to Sir David Manning, Tony Blair's main foreign policy advisor. It included several Top Secret papers on Iraq that outlined MI6's assessment. The first paper noted that 'Action against Iraq will be seen as a change of agenda from the war against terror (which most Arab regimes support). This would undermine today's unity of purpose. There is no convincing intelligence (or common sense) case that Iraq supports Sunni extremism.'

The second paper outlined several of the reasons for seeking to remove Saddam's government from power in Iraq. Top of the list: 'The removal of Saddam remains a prize because it could give new security to oil supplies.'[2] This has long been suspected to be the true motive behind the Iraq war, and it clearly outranked sponsorship of terrorism or

WMDs in MI6's view. Ironically, Tony Blair responded to the allegation that Iraq was a war for oil by decrying it as a 'conspiracy theory'.

In March 2002 the deputy Director General of MI5 Eliza Manningham-Buller wrote to the Permanent Secretary at the Home Office Sir John Gieve. The letter is titled 'Iraq: Possible Terrorist Response to a US attack' and considers Saddam's possible use of terrorism against the West if the US and UK moved to topple his regime.

The letter explains that in MI5's assessment that the 'current period of heightened tension' between Iraq and the US was 'unlikely to prompt Saddam to order terrorist strikes against Coalition interests.' It goes on to say that 'Even limited military action is unlikely to prompt such a response.' The letter concluded that, 'Saddam is only likely to order terrorist attacks if he perceives that the survival of his regime is threatened.'[3]

So much for Iraq being one of the major state sponsors of terrorism. That leaves the question of WMD. Above MI5 and MI6 in the institutional pecking-ordering is the Joint Intelligence Committee (JIC). The JIC is responsible for co-ordinating the security services and for producing intelligence assessments for the Cabinet Office and the Prime Minister. According to the JIC's assessment in March 2002, 'Intelligence on Iraq's weapons of mass destruction (WMD) and ballistic missile programmes is sporadic and patchy.'[4] Yet the dossier presented to Parliament and to the public in September 2002 contained no such caveats, few signs of doubt. How did an assessment built on uncertain, secret intelligence turn into a certain and publicly digestible argument in favour of war?

Drafting the September Dossier

The dossier in its final form was produced by the chairman of the (JIC), John Scarlett, but his version was the culmination of months of drafting and redrafting. Documents made available by the Chilcot Inquiry and through the Freedom of Information Act show that the process was not plain sailing. The months of drafting work was not done by John Scarlett, or indeed by anyone with an intelligence background. A major draft that was kept secret until 2008 despite freedom of information requests was written by John Williams, the Press Secretary at the Foreign Office.

Williams was working as part of the Coalition Information Centre, a unit within the Foreign Office being run by Tony Blair's Director of Communications Alistair Campbell. The Coalition Information Centre oversaw the drafting process and it was Williams' draft of the dossier that Sir John Scarlett used to produce his own version. Far from being the result of intelligence analysis, the dossier was the product of spin-doctors.[5]

This is where the infamous Downing Street Memo comes into the story. The memo detailed a meeting on July 23rd 2002 between senior defence and intelligence officials and members of the Labour government. It says that, 'C reported on his recent talks in Washington. There was a perceptible shift in attitude. Military action was now seen as inevitable. Bush wanted to remove Saddam, through military action, justified by the conjunction of terrorism and WMD. But the intelligence and facts were being fixed around the policy. The NSC had no patience with the UN route, and no enthusiasm for publishing material on the Iraqi regime's record.'[6]

The phrase 'the intelligence and facts were being fixed around the policy' has drawn a lot of attention from critics of the Iraq war. The memo has been cited as a smoking gun that proves that the intelligence over Iraq's ties to terrorists and development of WMD was fabricated, the result of political pressure. The memo was made public by The Times newspaper on May 1st 2005, only days before the general election, and only two months before 7/7. The 'intelligence failure' of the threat posed by Iraq was largely blamed on the government rather than the security services. One consequence of this was that Labour lost a lot of votes at the election.

During the weeks after the meeting recorded in the Downing Street Memo, the dossier was written and re-written. This became a more and more intense process in September 2002, around the first anniversary of 9/11. John Williams, the spin doctor at the Foreign Office, did not just write a key draft of the dossier, he also wrote the media strategy to be used around it. That these two tasks were carried out by the same person illustrates the extent to which the dossier was written with public perception in mind.

The media strategy document that Williams wrote on September 4th 2002 says that, 'The evidence dossier is unlikely to be enough by itself to win the argument: it will convince persuadable opinion only in launched in the right environment, framed by a broad case that establishes Iraq as a threat to international peace and stability. There is no 'killer fact' in the dossier which 'proves' that Saddam must be taken on now, or this or that weapons will be used against us.' Even the author of the dossier was not convinced.

The media strategy report goes on to say that, 'But it does make a convincing case that Iraq has been trying to recruit people for a nuclear weapons programme and to acquire materials usable in such a programme.'[7]   While Williams might think so, certain people in the Cabinet Office clearly disagreed. An email written on September 16th by an unnamed Cabinet Office official commenting on the draft dossier said that, 'Page 4 bullet 4, "[Iraq] has assembled specialists to work on its nuclear programme" – Dr Frankenstein, I presume? Sorry, It's getting late...'[8]

It was not just the Cabinet Office who dared to doubt that Iraq posed an imminent threat. Documents made available by the Chilcot Inquiry show that staff from the Defence Intelligence Staff (DIS), i.e. British military intelligence, were shown copies of the draft dossier in September 2002. Their feedback shows that there was at least some resistance from the British intelligence 'community' to the political pressure being imposed.

In the assessment of the DIS at the time it would take Saddam at least two years to assemble a crude nuclear weapon, assuming he obtained the nuclear material from foreign sources. This view met with some resistance, leading to one DIS official writing an email saying, 'We refuse to budge on time-lines - two years min unless the IISS has information we are unsighted on pertaining to the Iraqi's capabilities, facilities, and expertise to handle, cast and machine weapons grade material.' Another email from the same batch asks, 'Why around two years to have a bomb if fissile material were procured from outside? Haven't we said that terrorists could produce a nuclear weapon in shorter timescales?'[9]

Other emails explicitly suggested changes to the proposed draft of the dossier that they were reviewing. One official commented that, 'The judgement "has continued to produce chemical and biological agents;" is too strong with respect to CW. "has probably" would be as far as I would go. And "continued to produce BW agents". This is quite strong considering what the int actually says.'

The email goes on to say that, 'The judgement "has military plans for the use of chemical and biological weapons, some of which could be ready within 45 minutes of an order to use them". Is also rather strong since it is based on a single source. "Could say intelligence suggests..."'[10] These recommendations were not taken up. The final version of the dossier claimed that, 'military planning allows for some of the WMD to be ready within 45 minutes of an order to use them.'[11]

In all likelihood, Sir John Scarlett did not know about the DIS objections to the draft dossier that bore his name. The advice he was getting was quite the opposite, as shown by a minute from Desmond Bowen, Director-General of Operational Policy in the Ministry of Defence. On the first anniversary of 9/11 he wrote to Scarlett saying, 'In looking at the WMD sections, you clearly want to be as firm and authoritative as you can be. You will need to judge the extent to which you need to hedge your judgements with, for example, "it is almost certain" and similar caveats. I appreciate this can increase the authenticity of the documents in terms of it being a proper assessment, but that needs to be weighed against the use that will be made by the opponents of actions who will add up the number of judgements on which we do not have absolute clarity.'[12] It is this document perhaps more than any other that shows how the uncertainty was being systematically downplayed and removed from the dossier and hence from the case for war.

Fundamentally, it was not just the dossier itself that was the result of a propaganda exercise rather than intelligence analysis. It was the entire process by which the dossier had been produced. The dossier may have had Sir John Scarlett's name on it, but it was, in effect, written by a Press Secretary. The claims in the dossier contradicted the documented assessments of MI5 and MI6, and removed the uncertainty from the JIC's own assessment.

Nonetheless, it was presented as an intelligence analysis, free from political bias, persuasion or considerations. An email from Tony Blair's Chief of Staff Jonathan Powell, to Alistair Campbell and David Manning explained the thinking behind this, saying, 'I think it is worth explicitly stating what TB keeps saying this is the advice to him from the JIC On the basis of this advice what other action could he as PM take Something like "I am today taking the exceptional step of publishing the JIC's advice to me because I want MPs and the British public to see the advice on which I am acting[.] When you have read this I ask you to consider what else a responsible PM could do than follow the course we have in the face of this advice?"[13] Indeed, this is essentially what 'TB' said when he presented the dossier to the House of Commons on September 24th 2002. This pretence of the government feeling compelled to publish secret intelligence granted the dossier the appearance of something more substantial than a propaganda exercise.

Normalising 'Intelligence Failures'

The 'intelligence failures' over Iraq's non-existent WMD programmes and sponsorship of terrorism should have caused tremendous scepticism towards the security services. This is particularly true at a time when we are being told of unprecedented threats to our safety. Likewise, the 7/7 'intelligence failures' detailed in the previous two chapters should have caused a lot of criticism of the security services.

In reality, both have been used by the secret, or at least covert, agencies to consolidate their position. They have bigger budgets than ever before. They are more widely accepted as being necessary than ever before. The practices of torture, indefinite imprisonment, extra-judicial assassination are becoming normalised in the name of maintaining freedom and security. The James Bond films are back in the box office and are making huge sums of money.

How has this happened? Why has this happened? Was there some kind of deal, spoken or unspoken, that if the intelligence services played along over Iraq that they would be immune from blame in the event of a terrorist attack? What we can be sure of is that there was political pressure on the intelligence services and that they colluded with the government to bring about the deception. One MI6 officer known only as SIS2 who was called to the Chilcot Inquiry alluded to this in his testimony:

> **SIS2:** I think there were discussions going on at Number 10 which, I mentioned earlier, were taking place in a very quick moving situation, but -- yes, I think perhaps SIS was at that point guilty of flying a bit too close to the sun.

> **SIR RODERIC LYNE:** In effect it crossed a line between its traditional roles of providing information and carrying out instructions that you have talked about earlier, and it actually got sucked into the process of policy making?

> **SIS2:** Not exactly policy making as such, but perilously close to it, I would say. I think a fair criticism would be that we were probably too eager to please.

> **SIR RODERIC LYNE:** And how would you counteract that? Do you think steps have since been taken that make this less likely to happen in the future?

> **SIS2:** I don't think you can ever entirely inoculate yourself against this particular virus, but yes, certainly, as things

stand at the moment, I think it would be more difficult for this kind of situation to arise.[14]

'Too eager to please' indeed. What this dialogue shows is how the British security services have successfully avoided blame for the Iraq war 'intelligence failures'. By admitting that they caved in to political pressure, by playing the mea culpa card, they have put all the blame back onto Number 10 and the Cabinet for applying that political pressure. It is a clever manoeuvre that exonerates the security services.

It also helps to normalise what they've done. No one from the security services has been sacked over their role in the Iraq intelligence deception. After putting his name to the September 2002 dossier, John Scarlett was appointed head of MI6 in 2004, an agency he had retired from back in 2001 when he held the post of Director of Security and Public Affairs. He was also awarded a knighthood, becoming Sir John Scarlett. It is now well established that the security services can submit to political pressure, deceive the public, justify a war that has killed hundreds of thousands of people, and when everyone finds out they can just get away with it.

If anything, the whole episode has strengthened the position of the secret state. The tactics of deception by propaganda and fabricating pretexts for wars are nothing new. The difference is that now they have been laid out in public with the excuse that the security services were 'too eager to please', and this has been accepted. The fact that there has been no accountability for anyone in the security services effectively sends them a signal that they can do what they like, and if anyone finds out they can just blame politicians and get away free and clear.

The security services have not only exonerated themselves over Iraq, they have helped shape the discussion for the future. SIS2's comment that we cannot ever expect the intelligence services to be entirely inoculated against the virus of political pressure should be seen in this light – as a pre-emptive excuse for the next time something like this happens. The justified outrage of the British people at being deceived was largely directed towards the Blair/Labour government. They paid for it by eventually being voted out, but the security services are, of course, still there.

What has this got to do with 7/7?

What this has to do with 7/7 is that the Iraq war intelligence was part of the context in which the 7/7 'intelligence failures' happened, and vice versa. The two stories are rather similar, particularly inasmuch as no one within the security services has been held responsible in any way. There is also the question of the rather tenuous and secondary accusation against Saddam – that he was colluding with terrorists. This was part of a wider political narrative that the greatest threat is that of international terrorism, imposed during the wake of 9/11 and used as the primary justification for the invasion of Afghanistan. Indeed, the propaganda efforts of the US went even further. They tried to draw specific connections between Iraq and potential terrorist attacks in the West.

In early February 2003, US Secretary of State Colin Powell addressed the United Nations Security Council in the hope of obtaining a new resolution that would back the war. In his efforts to present a case that would justify the invasion he made references to a supposed Al Qaeda poison and explosive training camp in Northern Iraq. He said, 'When our coalition ousted the Taliban, the Zarqawi network helped establish another poison and explosive training center camp, and this camp is located in North-Eastern Iraq...The network is teaching its operatives how to produce ricin and other poisons... Less than a pinch of ricin, eating just this amount in your food, would cause shock, followed by circulatory failure. Death comes within 72 hours.'

He went on to make a spurious connection between this camp and a supposed terrorist network in Europe, 'Members of this network have been apprehended in France, Britain, Spain and Italy...We know about this European network and we know about its links to Zarqawi...When the British unearthed the cell there just last month, one British police officer was murdered during the destruction of the cell.'[15]

Almost everything about this story was untrue. The alleged training camp was nothing more than a few poorly maintained buildings, as both journalists and UN inspectors found when they went there. There was no evidence of ricin production, nor any evidence of Iraqi government involvement in the training of terrorists. In particular the part about there being a 'cell' in Britain was utter nonsense. In January 2003 police raids across the UK had resulted in the arrests of two-dozen people for their alleged involvement in a terrorist plot using ricin.

The British press had a field day, the Mirror announcing 'It's Here', the headline superimposed over a skull and crossbones poison symbol, itself superimposed over a yellow outline of Britain. Other papers described the discovery of a 'factory of death', claimed that there was a 'Poison Gang On The Loose', and that '250,000 Of Us Could Have Died'. In Crumpsall, Manchester, the police burst in on a flat where a homeless Algerian named Kamel Bourgass was staying. As they attempted to arrest him he stabbed a police officer who later died, and Bourgass was ultimately convicted of the officer's murder.

However, Bourgass was arrested purely by chance, as officials did not know where he was. He had arrived in the UK on the back of a lorry in January 2000 and applied for asylum. His application was rejected, and in September 2001 he was sent a notice of appeal but he didn't turn up to a hearing a couple of months later. Bourgass then lived in Britain as an illegal immigrant until his arrest in early 2003. After being convicted of the murder of police officer Steven Oake, Bourgass and four others were put on trial for the supposed 'ricin plot'. Of the total 24 arrested, only Bourgass was convicted. Even then it wasn't under terrorism legislation, but of 'conspiracy to cause a public nuisance by the use of poisons and/or explosives to cause disruption, fear or injury.'

Though initial examination by experts from Porton Down found traces of ricin at the flat, this was due to highly sensitive equipment registering a false positive. A few days later the team in the lab found that there was no ricin, though this was kept from the public for over two years until the conclusion of Bourgass' trial in April 2005. A few castor beans, one of the ingredients for ricin, were found, along with recipes for making the poison. Though the government insisted these recipes proved a connection to both Iraq and Afghanistan, in reality Bourgass had obtained them from the website of an American right-wing survivalist named Kurt Saxon.

After Guardian journalist Duncan Campbell pointed out that the recipes cited at the trial had come from a website based in Palo Alto rather than from documents found in Kabul, the prosecution dropped the alleged Al Qaeda connections from their case. A fortnight later then Home Secretary David Blunket still hadn't got the message, saying that, 'Al-Qaida and the international network is seen to be, and will be demonstrated through the courts over months to come, actually on our doorstep and threatening our lives.'[16]

Even the method of delivery described by Colin Powell at the UN was wrong, as Bourgass had planned to smear the ricin on door handles of cars in the Holloway Road area of London. This method, unlike ingesting ricin, is non-fatal. Perhaps most importantly, no connection has ever been found between Bourgass and Abu Musab Al Zarqawi.

Powell himself claimed that he had been misled by US intelligence services before giving his speech before the UN. He said that 'burn notices' – indications that a source was untrustworthy – 'never rose to the right level'. He went on to say that 'the nights we were out there until midnight every night putting this presentation together, trying to make it airtight, there were people in the room who knew that burn notices had gone out on some of these sources and that was not raised to me.'[17]   Once again, intelligence information was misrepresented, exaggerating the threat in favour of a desired policy and mentality.

What this demonstrates is that just as the security services were subject to political pressure over Iraq's WMD and ties to terrorism, they were also subject to pressure over the threat from terrorism in general. Just as they colluded in presenting a false argument in favour of war we must recognise that they collude in imposing the false narrative of the great threat from international terrorism.

Operation Rhyme

What is clear is that the Bourgass case was not the only one where the authorities perceived a threat that wasn't really there. Between 9/11 and the end of 2004 there were 701 arrests under the Terrorism Act. This yielded only seventeen convictions under the Act, of which only three were Islamist-affiliated. Even then, the men convicted were not involved in planning terrorist attacks.[18]

Indeed, prior to Operation Crevice the biggest post-9/11 'terror bust' in the UK was the one involving Kamel Bourgass. Crevice appears to have been a sting operation, i.e. a situation where the people posed no threat until they were provoked into taking action. The other major counter-terrorism action before 7/7 was Operation Rhyme, based around the 'terrorist mastermind' Dhiren Barot.

Barot, a.k.a. Bilal, Abu Musa al-Hindi, Abu Eissa al-Hindi, and Issa al-Britani was born in India in 1971 to a Hindu family. His family moved to Britain when he was only 2, and he grew up in London. He converted to Islam in the early 1990s and apparently went to Pakistan and fought in Kashmir in the mid-1990s. The second ISC report picks up the story:

> In early 2003 a young British extremist known as Abu Issa AL HINDI was reported *** *** ***. He had been tutored by *** in *** skills and identified by *** as having *** ***.

> In mid-2004, reporting confirmed that AL HINDI was in fact Dhiren BAROT. The investigation into AL HINDI/BAROT and his UK-based associates (which was given the codename RHYME in mid-June 2004) intensified still further, involving the deployment of a significant amount of

covert investigative resource. Resource allocations for RHYME were in the order of:

- six weeks of 24-hour coverage;

- up to 15 surveillance teams deployed at any one time;

- 20 CCTV cameras installed and monitored (8,000 hours of product);

- 25,000 man-hours devoted to monitoring and transcription;

- *** covert searches;

- ***;

- 60 property searches; and

- analysis of seized hard drives amounting to 2.5 terabytes of data (roughly 12 times the height of Everest if printed out and stacked)

This led to the arrest of Barot and 13 alleged co-conspirators, of which eight ultimately went to trial.

Just as with the 'fertiliser bomb plot', the conspiracy involving Barot and the others was thin and piecemeal. Barot was apparently planning to attack the IMF, the World Bank, the New York Stock Exchange and the Citigroup headquarters. This became known as the 'financial buildings plot', particularly in the US. Another idea, the 'gas limos project' sought to use limousines filled them with gas cylinders, and detonate them in underground car parks.

A further 'plot' involved detonating a dirty bomb, the dreaded CBRN attack implied in the false intelligence over Iraq's weapons and collusion with terrorists. Barot was apparently inspired by reports of an accident in France involving a truck carrying hundreds of smoke detectors. There was concern at the possible exposure to small quantities of radioactive material. Barot apparently planned to buy 10,000 smoke detectors – calculating £5 per detector, apparently allowing for no discount for bulk purchase – and somehow extract the radioactive material from all of them. This would then be either burnt or blown up somehow.

The whole plan was ridiculous. Barot had no money, vehicles, weapons, explosives or equipment to carry out these ideas. He was reportedly sent to New York in early 2001 by Khalid Sheikh Mohammed, the alleged mastermind of the 9/11 attacks. He made poor-quality 'surveillance' videos of a number of buildings that look no different to millions of tourist tapes. They show nothing about the security in the buildings and hence are useless for attack planning of the type outlined.

Furthermore, using gas cylinders, which aren't proper explosives, inside limousines, which are pretty conspicuous vehicles, is an idiotic and ineffective plan for a terrorist attack. The notion of using 10,000 smoke detectors to build a dirty bomb was the most absurd of all. Even if Barot could have bought that many smoke alarms without drawing attention to himself, and then extracted the material or just set the whole pile on fire then it still probably wouldn't have killed even a single person.

Despite this, Barot pleaded guilty and in November 2006 was sentenced to 40 years imprisonment. At the time Peter Clarke, head of the counter-terrorism unit of the Metropolitan police, admitted to the BBC that, 'when we arrested, we had a wealth of intelligence but we didn't have a huge amount of admissible evidence.'[19] The following day an anonymous 'counter-terrorism source' told the Guardian that, 'It is no exaggeration to say that, at the time of the arrest, there was little or no admissible evidence against Barot.'[20] It appears this anonymous source was Clarke, as he used the exact same phrase in a speech in 2007.

Mohammad Naeem Noor Khan

The person missing from this story is a man named Mohammad Naeem Noor Khan. Noor Khan was born in 1979 in Pakistan and was arrested on July 13th 2004 in Lahore after weeks of surveillance by Pakistani and US intelligence. He has been described as 'Al Qaeda's computer expert' and his laptop contained a 'treasure trove' of information, including the alleged Dhiren Barot plans for terrorist attacks.

At some point around the 25th July 2004 Noor Khan was 'turned' and became a double agent working for Pakistani and US intelligence. Presumably his information was also being supplied to the British and formed some of the 'wealth of intelligence' against Barot referred to by Peter Clarke. He sent out emails to all his Al Qaeda contacts urging them to get in touch with him, to provide up-to-date and traceable information on their whereabouts. This trapping operation went well, and one of those who was quickly arrested was Ahmed Khalfan Ghailani, wanted in connection with the 1998 East African Embassy bombings.

The announcement of Ghailani's arrest was delayed for several days. It was finally delivered just before John Kerry announced that he would be running as the Democratic party presidential candidate, on July 29th. On August 1st the Department of Homeland Security raised the terrorist threat level and issued a warning about possible attacks on US financial buildings. This was based on the videos Dhiren Barot had filmed years earlier, that had been found on Noor Khan's laptop.

Indeed, the Bush administration even leaked Noor Khan's name to the press as the source of the information about the threat. This shows that having a potentially very useful intelligence source with good cover was a secondary consideration to hyping the threat to help Bush win the 2004 election. This created a problem – with Noor Khan's targets now aware that he was working for US intelligence, they might get jumpy and either carry out a rush attack or try to disappear.

So, the British authorities had to act, quickly arresting Barot and his accomplices before they realised what was going on. This is one of the reasons why the police had so little physical evidence, and why they needed the information on Noor Khan's laptop to use against Barot. The operation was ultimately a huge success, with both Barot and several of his co-conspirators pleading guilty.

Barot's sentence was reduced on appeal from 40 to 30 years, on the grounds that his attack plans were either ineffective or physically impossible. Nonetheless, he and the others never acted on the ideas, making his offence essentially a thought-crime. That the US authorities were happy to compromise their double agent shows that they didn't take the threat from Barot seriously, but that they wanted us (the public) to take it seriously.

Likewise, the ISC treated this a major terrorist plot and a big intelligence success that justifiably diverted resources away from potentially investigating the alleged 7/7 bombers. The statistics cited above from their second report might seem impressive but ultimately Barot was mostly harmless, however frightening his ideas might be to some.

This raises a different kind of question with regards to 7/7 – were the security services too busy trying to prove the 'war on terror' narrative that they, tragically and ironically, failed to stop a real terrorist attack? Were the authorities more concerned with creating and disrupting 'terror cells' than with actually stopping potential attacks?

The Noor Khan story does suggest this in some ways. For one thing, the speed at which he was turned and the casual way his identity was made public suggests that in fact he had already served his purpose and had been a spy or double agent for long before his arrest. Like Q in Operation Crevice, Noor Khan was never called to testify against Barot in any way. He was released without charge due to lack of evidence in mid-2007 and has, of course, disappeared.

Was Noor Khan an agent all along? Thus, was Operation Rhyme merely the British end of another international sting operation? Worthy questions, but ones studiously avoided by the ISC. Noor Khan's name, the issue of his identity being made public and the impact that had on the British investigation into Barot was not mentioned by in their second report. They did not explore the possibility that the security services were so busy fitting people up to look like terrorists that they missed some real ones. Well, not quite.

7/7: Fundraising for the National Security State?

The ISC were formed in 1994 as a result of the Intelligence Services Act of that year. The Church Committee in the 1970s in the US and several court cases in Europe in the 1980s had led to greater suspicion and demands for scrutiny of the security services. MI5 was first, put on a statutory basis in 1989. In 1992 John Major publicly admitted that MI6 existed, and the ISC was then established to provide oversight.

However, the policy remains not to discuss MI6 operations in public so the ISC says nothing about them. MI5 are treated somewhat differently, but still hide behind anonymity and operational secrecy. Though the ISC's second report into 7/7 was heralded (by the ISC themselves, and then by the major media) as providing an 'unprecedented level of detail' about MI5, the reality is quite different.

As we have seen, the entire timeline of what MI5 knew and when, and therefore what they should have done about it, is either doubtful or demonstrably untrue. The statistics provided in the report are an attempt to gloss over the fact that the ISC failed to provide meaningful oversight. MI5 simply did not tell them the truth and even when the ISC realised this they just let MI5 get away with it.

The argument presented by MI5 to the ISC for their second report is that they were busy jumping limited resources from plot to plot and couldn't follow up on their limited knowledge of the alleged 7/7 bombers. This argument was accepted by the ISC and subsequently by the major media. They say that throughout 2003 they were primarily concerned with Operation Crevice, and shortly after Crevice finished in 2004 they had to move on to Dhiren Barot and Operation Rhyme.

As we have seen though, neither plot posed a serious threat, and in both cases it appears the security services had agents or informants in the middle of the action. By cutting these two points out of the discussion, the ISC succeeded in portraying the terrorist threat as real and avoiding the question of state provocation. They did not ask if these cases were plausible. They did not ask why MI5 devoted limited resources to pointless targets who posed no significant threat.

They did not ask whether MI5 was subject to pressure (akin to the pressure over Iraq) to find and interdict the great terrorist menace. Instead, the question they asked became 'were MI5 just too busy chasing all these terrorists that they missed a few?' Naturally, MI5 said yes, and were rewarded with a larger budget and a huge intake of staff.

We do not know by how much the budget has grown, because MI5's funding is a state secret. Nonetheless, the ISC produced a meaninglessly reassuring graph showing that MI5 have a lot more resources than they used to.

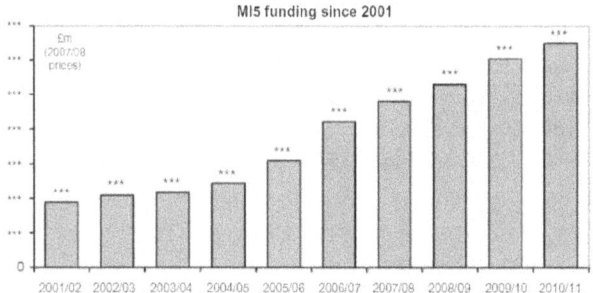

So, we return to a question posed in the introduction: Were MI5 treating the whole ISC process as a fundraising exercise? When they explained to the ISC why they never made Sidique Khan a priority target, MI5 used terms not from operational assessments, but from funding applications to the Treasury. The result of the process was that 'blame' for 7/7 was largely put down to inadequate resources and MI5's budget was drastically increased.

In considering this question it is worth reminding ourselves that Operation Theseus – the £100 million police investigation into 7/7, produced no convictions in connection with the attacks. By contrast, several police officers have stood trial for using the investigation as a means to make large sums of money. Detective Constable Darren Pooley and his wife Nicola were found guilty in 2010.

As part of the same scam – based around fiddling accommodation costs for investigating officers – Pooley's brother in law Stephen pleaded guilty. The trio had managed to fraudulently obtain nearly £100,000 due to officers being allowed to withdraw money on AmEx cards to pay for living costs. One other officer, Detective

Sergeant Peter Allbut, was found innocent despite depositing over £9,000 into his personal bank account. Another Detective Sergeant, Nevill Caldecourt, was also found innocent of involvement in the scam.

This whole discussion omits an even more devastating possibility. It may be this scenario that the ISC is ultimately seeking to avoid talking about by sidestepping even the more conventional questions outlined above. With a mandate to convince the public of the terrorist threat did the security services either allowed an attack to happen, or make it happen? Were the 'intelligence failures' deliberate?

The pattern outlined in the previous two chapters shows that the consequences of the 'failures' were not just that the alleged bombers were never arrested, but that their connections to Q, Babar and McDaid were obscured. WYP supposedly did not tell MI5 that Khan's car had given a lift to McDaid in April 2003. Investigations in December failed to discover Khan and Tanweer's involved in the Iqra bookshop. The picture of Khan and Tanweer sent to Babar could not be identified because it was so poor. MI5 Operations Scraw and Downtempo failed to identify that the men from Leeds connected to Q and Omar Khyam were also the men who visited Babar's Malakand training camp.

We see a similar story in the Dhiren Barot investigation. According to some media reports Sidique Khan was in contact with Barot's 'cell' in the UK, possibly via Noor Khan. The 'cell' were based in Luton, which was also Q's stomping ground. Nothing solid has been presented that connects Sidique Khan with Barot or with Noor Khan but it does present another possibility. The leak of Noor Khan's name meant that the British had to shut down Barot and his supposed accomplices very quickly. Had they continued their surveillance on him they might have found his connection to Sidique Khan, if there was such a connection.

As with most of the previous 'intelligence failures', the failure that was leaking the name of Noor Khan had the consequence of protecting the relationship between a double agent and the alleged 7/7 bombers. That said, without stronger information on what, if anything, was the connection between Sidique Khan and either Dhiren Barot or Noor Khan we cannot develop this line of questioning further. This is perhaps a minor consideration in light of all the other information the security services had on Sidique Khan but it does present us with a distinct question.

Was Sidique Khan a Spy?

This question has been raised by a lot of different people in the years after 7/7. As Martin Gilbertson's story started to gain significant media coverage just before the first anniversary of the attacks, one former detective suggested this scenario to the BBC's *Newshour* programme. Charles Shoebridge, a former counterterrorism detective with the Metropolitan Police said, 'The amount of information coming out and the quality of information coming out. The fact that that has been so consistently overlooked it would appear by the security service MI5, to me suggests really only one of two options. Either, a) we've got a level of incompetence that would be unusual even for the security services. But b) possibly, and this is a possibility, that this man Khan may even have been working as an informant for the security service. It is difficult otherwise to see how it can be that they've so covered his tracks in the interim.'[21]

Shoebridge raises some fair points, but there is another, perhaps even more important angle to consider. Khan was under repeated surveillance of varying kinds, connecting him to various 'terror suspects' over a period of several years. As we have examined in this chapter, the perception at the time (that largely continues today) was one of a widespread threat of terrorism from Muslims at home and abroad. This was even woven into a false argument for a full-scale war of aggression against Iraq.

So let us consider this from Sidique Khan's perspective. In March 2004 several men that he knew were arrested at the culmination of Operation Crevice. These were men that Khan had apparently been sent to Pakistan with in mid-2003, men that he had many contacts with, including conversations about criminal activity and fighting overseas in Pakistan/Afghanistan. Men who were arrested in a fanfare of publicity and who were said to have been part of the British jihadi terrorist network.

Why wouldn't Khan have thought that he too was under surveillance or the subject of security service investigations? The same question applies to Shehzad Tanweer, but even more so to Khan, especially if he was actually in contact with Dhiren Barot or Noor Khan, who were both arrested only a few months after the Operation Crevice suspects. Why wouldn't Khan assume that he was being watched? One answer is that he had some other channel of information or reason to believe that he was being left alone.

The dialogues between Khan and Khyam that were bugged by MI5 do suggest that Khan was some kind of spy. Through the transcripts, the recurring theme is that Khan asked the questions, such as 'are you a terrorist?' and then wanting to know who are the people that Khyam said were 'working through' him. Khyam often answers the questions in an assured, authoritative manner, as though he is trying to prove his credentials, where Khan gives up very little information about himself.

Indeed, the whole notion of Khan being an informant makes a lot more sense than him being a suicide bomber. For one thing, he had no reason to want to die. He had a wife, a young girl and an additional baby on the way. He had every reason to live, and to want to live. The same is true of the other three alleged bombers.

Khan's transition from a mild-mannered school mentor who worked with children with learning difficulties and occasionally helped the police deal with local gang problems, into a fanatical, suicidal terrorist has never been explained. As one of his former co-workers put it, 'It's a huge moral paradox, the more you think about it the more the whole thing is totally paradoxical.'[22]

The particular part of Khan's story that has most often been exploited to portray this transition is from the autumn of 2004 onwards. Khan was a contract teaching mentor at Hillside Primary School from March 2001. In December 2004, Khan quit his job at the school and travelled to Pakistan, not returning until February 2005. The key elements of this story – his increasing absence from work and eventual resignation, the trip to Pakistan and a video he made for his baby daughter before he left – all warrant serious scrutiny.

Under the heading 'Early signs of extremism?' the Home Office narrative says of Sidique Khan that, 'More problematic was his increasingly poor attendance record. This culminated in a period of sick leave from 20 September to 19 November 2004. The school administration had reason to believe that the absences were not genuine and dismissed him. At the same time, he had in any case, written to say he would not be returning to work.'[23]

As with so much of the official narrative there are problems with this part of the story. The school's personnel records on Sidique Khan were released in response to a FOIA request by J7 and they contradict the narrative in several respects. For one thing, there is no record of Khan being dismissed by the school. For another, the long period of absence towards the end of 2004 apparently ran up to at least November 30th.

The reason the narrative contains the date of the 19th November appears to be because that is the date they have Sidique Khan flying out to Pakistan with Shehzad Tanweer. However, the FOIA disclosure letter says that among Khan's periods of absence was '1 December 2004 – 7 December 2004 – Unauthorised absence resulting in Mr Khan handing in his resignation on 7 December 2004.'[24] How could Khan hand in his resignation more than two weeks after he had left for Pakistan?

Khan's resignation letter and his leaver's form only make the question harder to answer. The form is dated 17th December, and his resignation letter says that 'we are departing next week'. The letter has some information redacted, including the logical place where the date would be so quite how the letter and the form relate is unclear. On the leaver's form the reason indicated is 'Resig, Family Commit'. This not only raises the question of when Khan left for Pakistan (after 19th November, at any rate) but also why he went there.

When his wife, Hasina Patel, was interviewed by Sky News after being arrested and held for several days under the Terrorism Act, she explained that, 'He has family in Pakistan and for people who come from those countries it is normal to travel back, you have family there, you have property, land, there are plenty of reasons you could be going there.' Like others who knew Khan, she struggled to believe he was a suicide bomber, saying, 'It is like two different people, I can't link the two things together at all.'[25]

What is clear is that Khan did not know when he would be coming back. Despite the redactions, his resignation letter clearly refers to his intention to travel somewhere, saying, 'there is no definite time frame as to when I will return.' Likewise he made a home video of his talking to his daughter, saying goodbye to her and explaining how he was going away and would miss her.

References in the video to not getting to see her growing up have been interpreted by some as evidence that Khan did not intend to come back from Pakistan, indeed that he may have been on a martyrdom mission. Another view is that the video simply suggests that he was going to miss out on seeing his child during a very rapid stage in her development and that he wasn't sure when he would return.

A potential explanation for this uncertainty is implied by the fact that Khan and Tanweer returned from Pakistan on February 8th 2005. This is the exact same day that Crevice suspect Salahuddin Amin was sent to Britain by the Pakistani authorities, who had arrested him nearly a year earlier and, according to Amin, tortured him in custody. Were Khan and Tanweer in Pakistan to aid with the Pakistani's interrogation of Amin? It would explain why they came back to Britain on the same day, albeit on different flights.

In any case, Khan's home video with his daughter is difficult to reconcile with the notion of him carrying out mass murder. A common response to the video is that it does not come across like the confession of a suicidal fanatic. Even one of the relatives of victims of the 7/7 bombings commented on this. Julie Nicholson, whose daughter Jenny was killed at Edgware Road, said, 'I could not measure up this person, that seemed to be loving and compassionate. This person on the video looked ordinary, normal, trustworthy, decent. And that filled me with a fear.'[26]

The Home Office narrative comments sought to describe the motivation for these alleged suicide bombings saying, 'The best indications of the group's motivation are set out in Khan's video statement, first aired on the Arabic television channel, Al Jazeera on 1 September and in his last Will and Testament, discovered by the police after the bombings.'[27] According to the official narrative all the conspirators in the 7/7 attack died in the explosions, so who held on to the video and released it to the media? Though some have cast doubt on its authenticity, it appears to show Khan in a typical jihadist video setting.

The speech made by Khan contained various clichés of such videos, including the phrase 'we are at war and I am a soldier', and vague threats such as 'Now you too will taste the reality of this situation'. There is no clear indication of suicidal intent. The video does bear a resemblance to one that Junaid Babar described making with Khan for propaganda purposes in Malakand, though Babar said Khan's face was obscured in that video.

A similar video of Tanweer emerged on the eve of the first anniversary of the attacks. These tapes have been used by advocates of the official story as proof of the four men's guilt. The major problem is that we have no idea when these videos were made, by whom, for what purpose. There are no equivalent tapes for Hussain and Lindsay, and there is no explanation for why this 'self-radicalizing cell' would not have recorded such videos together. It is not a difficult thing to do, and clearly Khan had a camcorder because he recorded other entirely innocuous tapes like the one to his daughter.

Khan's will is also a matter of some contention. It is cited in the narrative as one of seven key points of evidence proving these were co-ordinated suicide bombings, as is the Khan 'confession' tape. For many years it was not made publicly available despite being referred to in the Home Office narrative and a lot of mainstream media reporting. One page was made available at the inquests, but it poses more questions than it provides answers.

The will is undated, and addressing Khan's daughter it says 'As a father the best gift I can give to you is the promise that I will intercede for you on the day of judgment and take you to paradise, if Allah (SWT) accepts me as a shaheed.' This word 'shaheed' can be use to mean 'martyr' as has been portrayed as evidence of Khan's intent to kill himself. But to be accepted as a shaheed can mean simply to die as a good Muslim and thus be accepted into paradise, like being accepted into heaven after a life as a good Christian.

In context it looks even less like a confession of intent to commit suicide, coming as it does after two sentences that say, 'I even found changing your nappy so cool and by the way you always enjoyed it as well. I'm proud to say that I was the first to bath you, feed you ice cream, give you spending money and get you eid presents.'[28] These are clearly the words of doting father, not a violent fanatic seeking martyrdom.

So, if he wasn't a suicide bomber then what was Sidique Khan up to? Not only do we have to wonder why he went to Pakistan but also why did he come back? If he believed that he was under surveillance and fled to Pakistan then he wouldn't return only weeks later. However, if he was an informant of some kind and was either going to Pakistan on a mission, or for a completely mundane reason, then it makes sense that he would return to the UK.

The story of Sidique Khan is the one that we know the most about but it is extremely difficult to ascertain exactly what was going on at any stage. What is clear is that the official narrative's attempts to paint him as a suicidal fanatic are weak, inaccurate and misleading. In combination with the 'intelligence failures' in the context of a hostile domestic and foreign security policy it is possible that Khan, like others, was somehow an actor in a much bigger theatre.

The Policy?

The 7/7 'intelligence failures' took place in the context of a hostile and paranoid war on terror foreign and domestic security policy. In particular, the fixing of intelligence around the policy of the Iraq war provokes the question of 'intelligence failures' being fixed around the policy of the overall war on terror. Indeed, the 7/7 attacks took place in this same context, and not just the 'intelligence failures' but also the attacks themselves may have been 'fixed around the policy'.

Almost everyone in this story of what the four were up to in the years before 7/7 wound up being charged with terrorism offences.

Almost everyone involved at the Iqra bookshop was arrested and prosecuted after 7/7. Almost everyone who passed through Babar's Malakand training camp ended up prison. Everyone in Dhiren Barot's 'cell' that was linked to Noor Khan and possibly to Q likewise found themselves on the wrong side of the Terrorism Act.

There are some notable exceptions, of course. McDaid and Q were never arrested. Babar and Noor Khan were arrested, but were 'turned' into co-operators and got laughably short sentences. That only leaves the four alleged bombers themselves, who ended up dead and being blamed for a terrorist atrocity. They were never arrested despite turning up numerous times as part of surveillance operations and investigations into those around them.

Was this the plan all along? Were the Iqra bookshop and Babar's camp in Malakand carefully spun traps designed by the security services to ensnare whoever went near them? If so, that would explain the 'intelligence failures' far better than any of the various stories told to us by MI5, the ISC and the major media.

If McDaid, Q and Babar were spies acting as part of a complex covert operation or set of operations then it would be important to obscure their connections to the four people who were designated to become 'suicide bombers'. Every time the alleged bombers did something that could later be used to make them look like suicide bombers, they did it through or via one of the probable spies. Every time, the connections between the four and the probable spy or spies was obscured by security service intelligence failures.

There were several direct and predictable consequences of this pattern of behaviour. At the time, in the run-up to 7/7, it meant that the alleged bombers were never seriously investigated. Because certain connections were never made, they were never designated as high priority targets for surveillance. This meant that after 7/7 there wasn't a huge paper trail on the four men that made MI5 look corrupt or incompetent.

It also meant that when MI5 looked back, after 7/7, having been asked what they knew about these four men, they could point to various suspicious facts that to the untrained eye made the men look like terrorists. Their involvement in a radical bookshop, their contacts with men who would later be arrested on terrorism charges, their visits to Pakistan – all of this has been used as evidence of their guilt.

However, because the relationships between the four and the probable spies were obscured before 7/7, those relationships remained obscure after 7/7. There isn't a vast paper trail connecting the alleged bombers to McDaid, Q and Babar when there should be because those connections were consistent and lengthy.

The pattern of the four men only acting like potential terrorists when they came into contact with a probable spy, and of the security services obscuring these contacts both before and after 7/7, is quite simple. However, it has taken considerable time and effort to reconstruct the story and isolate this pattern because of the extent to which MI5 have avoided questions and given obtuse and often misleading answers. This pattern very much suggests a deliberate policy on the part of MI5 to manipulate the alleged bombers before 7/7 into doing things that could be used as evidence against them after 7/7.

Naturally, you will not find any mention of this in the statements of political institutions, particularly those who are responsible for oversight of the security services. Whatever malevolent attitudes and malfeasance existed in this collusive relationship between politicians and permanent security institutions in 2002-3 still exist today. The extent of the ISC's failed efforts to hold MI5 to account for what they knew and when they knew it resulted in the security services getting away with their roles in both the Iraq war and in 7/7. If anything, their position is strengthened because much of this struggle has played out in public, with little outcry and objection. It is becoming an established norm that the security services can lie, even about mass murder (whether a war or a terrorist attack), and nothing will be done about it. The oversight is so poor that the security services have no reason to change.

It is perhaps no coincidence that there have been attempts to link the 7/7 bombings to the Iraq war. The mainstream Left media talk of 'blowback', of how we provoked anger in 'the Muslim world' and that 7/7 are just the predictable lashing out of an assaulted people. The problem with this, besides there being little evidence to support it with regards to the 7/7 attacks, is that it associates opposition to war with suicidal violence.

Like millions of others I marched in the name of peace, against the invasion of Iraq, and was ignored by the policy makers. I have not for one moment thought of killing ordinary members of the public as a means of expressing my anger. The allegation that 7/7 was payback for the Iraq war is a casual and lazy slur against Pacifism that continues to blame Muslims for this act of mass murder. Just as the story of Sidique Khan's increasing radicalisation dissolves under scrutiny, so does the notion that he was somehow taking revenge for Muslims killed in Iraq.

It is in this context that we should consider one further line from the Home Office narrative. In their description of what motivated the four alleged bombers the Home Office note that, 'Conspiracy theories also abounded, at least some of the bombers seem to have expressed the view that the 9/11 attacks were a plot by the US.'[29] Thus, it is not only pacifists opposed to the Iraq war who are potential suicide bombers, it is also conspiracy theorists.

It is these conspiracy theories, how the themes explored in the last three chapters are subject to speculation and imagination, that we turn to in the final section of the book. There are many conspiracy theories that have sprung up about 7/7 and the next two chapters show that much of that process began even before the attacks happened. The fixed intelligence over the Iraq war is only one dimension of the context for the 7/7 'intelligence failures'.

Chapter 9: Predictive Programming

Aside from the question of 'intelligence failures', the other main context in which 7/7 happened was one of a media obsessed with Islamic terrorists. The previous chapters looked at how much the security services knew, when they knew it and what they did about regarding the alleged 7/7 bombers. The picture that emerges is one of paranoid institutions, committed to a hostile security policy both at home and abroad. This paranoia was unleashed on hundreds of innocents, primarily young Muslim males, in the period between 9/11 and 7/7 (and since). Yet despite MI5 having mobile phone numbers, car registration numbers and addresses for Sidique Khan on multiple occasions, he was apparently never arrested, or even questioned.

As Charles Shoebridge noted, this does suggest that Khan was some sort of agent or informant for the security services. What a wider analysis shows is that the 'intelligence failures' had the consequence of protecting the connections between the alleged 7/7 bombers and several probable agents, whether informants, provocateurs or otherwise. We are presented with questions and disturbing possibilities. Was 7/7 the result of gross negligence and/or the mishandling of covert agents? Was it done on purpose in the name of the war on terror?

This sort of idea is typically filed under 'conspiracy theories' but polls indicate that somewhere between 15% and 25% of people believe in this sort of scenario. That is not a tiny fringe, but the sort of proportion that second-tier political parties all over the world achieve in general elections. Indeed, most of the remaining people also believe a conspiracy theory – the government's own theory that four British Muslim suicide bombers conspired to carry out the attacks.

The official investigation has essentially been abandoned, and though unofficial investigations continue they receive little attention from the public at large. The space left by the failed official investigation is largely filled with conflicting conspiracy theories about the event and the context in which it happened. Why? Why have most people reached the position that they either accept the official conspiracy theory or accept one of the alternative conspiracy theories?

One part of the answer to this very broad question is the prevalence of conspiracy theories in popular media. For decades spy novels and films have been bestsellers and blockbusters, glorifying the work of secret agents and lacing popular culture with suspicion and intrigue. This is particular true of the years before 7/7, when a large number of television shows, all involving the BBC, in some way predicted what would happen on 7/7. The same memes, the same key details that would form part of either the official or alternative conspiracy theories about 7/7, occurred and recurred in these programmes.

Many, but not all, of the relevant programmes are from the BBC spy thriller action series *Spooks*, broadcast in the US as *MI-5*. *Spooks* ran from mid-2002 to late 2011, generally attaining UK audiences of between five and seven million people. The show featured stories inspired by almost every conspiracy theory imaginable, from UFOs to the death of Princess Diana, with frequent references in the dialogue to potent phrases like 'New World Order'. The building used as the external shot of MI5 HQ is Freemason's Hall, home to the United Grand Lodge of England.

As such, *Spooks* was the premier conspiracy-themed entertainment (or conspiratainment) show on British television during the 9/11 to 7/7 period, and during the immediate post-7/7 period. It is therefore the main channel or route for information, however wrapped up in fiction, for conspiracy theories about the 7/7 attacks. More people regularly watched *Spooks* than have read the Home Office narrative or watched any of the alternative documentaries on 7/7. It is probably fair to conclude that even without the other relevant TV shows, *Spooks* has had a bigger influence on what people think about 7/7 than any other single source of information.

Spooks Season One

What is immediately striking when reviewing the first season of *Spooks* is how white the show is. Aside from one black MI5 officer (Danny, played by David Oyelowo) the permanent characters are exclusively white for almost the entire first three seasons. By contrast, the only references to Muslims in the dialogue in the opening two episodes of the show are to terrorists.

In the third episode we encounter the first Muslim characters in the show who, unsurprisingly, are terrorists. A group of Kurdish militants, led by well-known *Eastenders* actor Ray Panthaki, take over the Turkish embassy in London and demand the release of political prisoners. As it happens, MI5 have an agent undercover in the embassy at the time of the attack who quickly alerts them to the danger.

What soon emerges is that the hostage-taking in the embassy is just a distraction, being used by mercenaries commanded by a former MI5 agent. His real target is getting into the secret bank that MI5 use to pay their agents and he uses the Kurdish terrorists as a diversion. His mercenaries are provided with a means of escaping the embassy after successfully hacking into the bank, but the Kurds are left to fend for themselves. This ultimately leads to one of the Kurdish terrorists being shot dead by Special Forces.[1]

What the public saw in this episode was the use of several key memes that would recur with alarming frequency in the years between it being broadcast in May 2002 and the 7/7 attacks in 2005. The absence of any Muslims who aren't terrorists in the first season of *Spooks* clearly helped to establish the enemy image of Al Qaeda and militant Islamism. The use of a familiar terrorist scenario – the seizing of an embassy – helped reinforce this notion. Indeed, the whole episode is based on the Iranian embassy siege of 1980.

Forming an even closer connection to the official version of the 7/7 the MI5 crew in the episode even discuss at one point the possibility of the Kurds carrying out suicide bombings, though this is left hanging, unresolved. Somewhat bizarrely, the rogue ex-MI5 officer behind the whole plot is described as having worked in Middle East, 'recruiting clean skins'.

This episode did not just employ certain memes of the official 7/7 conspiracy theory (Islamic terrorists, suicide bombers), it also employed one of the main memes of the alternative conspiracy theory. The notion that the four alleged 7/7 bombers were somehow set up by the security services, or at least someone who used to work for the security services, is widely believed in the 'truth movement'. Muslims terrorists being manipulated as a cover for the actions of Western power players is a relatively common phenomenon in the real world, and it is an idea returned to repeatedly in later series of *Spooks*.

We find a similar set-up in the final episode of season one. The episode opens with a former IRA terrorist walking into an MI5 safehouse holding a hand grenade and demanding to speak to 'the landlord', i.e. MI5. The Irish terrorist offers to make a deal with the security service, saying that if they turn a blind eye to his group for a couple of days that he will provide them with information on 'Asabiyah'. This is a fictional Middle Eastern terrorist group described as 'a fragment from the Al Qaeda fallout'. Once again, the only role for Muslims in this episodes is as terrorists. That said, the character of the Irish terrorist, unoriginally named Patrick McCann, is also extremely stereotyped.

Initially, the spooks discuss assassinating McCann, though this plan is dropped, not because of the moral or legal issues but just because it is thought to be a strategically bad idea. When they meet with McCann MI5 learn that Asabiyah are planning an attack on a British nuclear power station. McCann offers to provide them with information in return for being left alone to do 'a bit of business'.

The spook supervisor, Harry Pierce, rules against turning a blind eye to McCann in order to obtain information, so his underlings go over his head to the Director-General of MI5. It then becomes clear that McCann's group are planning to bomb Broad Street railway station while MI5 are deliberately looking elsewhere. In order to fool both their own boss and McCann, the spooks stage a dummy attack at the station that kills no one, intercepting and stopping the real bomb. Ultimately, McCann is convinced that his attack has been successful, and gives up the information on Asabiyeh. This enables Special Forces to stop the terrorists from attacking the nuclear facility, with only seconds to spare. The terrorists, who unlike McCann are not given any words with which to explain their actions, are shot dead.[2]

So we again have Muslim terrorists, who are effectively suicide terrorists because they are attempting to use a short-range missile to blow up a nuclear facility. We have no idea of their motives, no context in which to place their actions, they are simply a horrifying, terrifying threat. They don't even have character names in the credits. The attack on a London train station pre-empted 7/7. In particular, Broad Street station has been disused since the 1980s, it's functions taken over by Liverpool Street, one of the real targets in 2005. The notion of MI5 staging an attack for reasons of psychological manipulation is, of course, one of the major suspicions and alternative conspiracy theories about the 7/7 bombings.

Spooks Season Two

Only two episodes into the second season of *Spooks* we encountered another example of predictive programming. The episode opens with an MI5 informer being uncovered in an extremist mosque in Birmingham. He is tortured and nearly killed, thrown out of a window and onto the roof of the van where the spooks are listening in. It soon emerges that an extremist Afghan mullah at the mosque is trying to brainwash young men to become suicide bombers.

With their original asset slowly losing his mind in a hospital, MI5 luck into a new recruit. An Algerian illegal immigrant volunteers his services as a spy, is signed up and successfully infiltrates the mosque. He tells the mullah there that he is working for MI5, but that he is actually loyal to the extremist cause. In reality, he is still loyal to MI5 and is trying to stop the suicide bombing that is being planned. This technique of going to covert organisation A and admitting that you're are working for covert organisation B as a means of gaining A's trust is known as the 'dangled mole'. It has actually been used by security services since at least World War Two.

The Algerian agent discovers that a teenage Muslim boy has been convinced to carry out the suicide bombing in the centre of Birmingham. Though he makes valiant attempts to stop the bombing he fails, and the boy kills himself and the Algerian agent. Meanwhile, the mullah is arrested. Perhaps critically, this is one of very few episodes of *Spooks* where MI5 are unsuccessful, where they fail to stop the impending attack. This episode broadcast in June 2003, just as the real-life Operation Crevice was gathering steam.[3]

In this episode the role for Muslims in the show was expanded to include not just terrorists, but also agents working for MI5. There was still no room for ordinary Muslims who aren't up to anything suspicious. The Muslim suicide bombing in the show was the first time that such an event had been portrayed on British television – years before it (officially) happened for real. It no doubt helped to encourage people to believe the official 7/7 conspiracy theory, and the addition of Muslim MI5 agents no doubt helped to provoke some of the alternatives theories.

Three episodes later another *Spooks* show again pre-empted the 7/7 attacks. The fifth episode of the second season featured a surprise training drill – an 'EERIE' (Extreme Emergency Response Initiative Exercise). When it is suggested that this is 'just a glorified fire drill', spook overlord Harry Pierce responds, 'It's more than that – terrorist attack, how prepared are we? Bali, Kenya, the Moscow theatre, at any minute it will happen here.' Note, not just that it could happen here, but that it *will* happen here. As the exercise develops it becomes apparent that there has actually been a real terrorist attack on London – a truck bombing in Parliament Square using VX gas.

Though there is no mention of Muslims, suicide bombers or bus or tube train bombings, this show did anticipate 7/7 in one crucial aspect. On the morning of the 7/7 attacks a private management consultancy firm was running some kind of training exercise based on a very similar scenario to the real attacks. Eerie indeed. In conjunction with the fact that on the morning of the 9/11 attacks there were various training exercises that in some ways replicated the real attacks, the 7/7 exercise has spawned many alternative conspiracy theories. In the *Spooks* episode it all turns out to be just part of the exercise, there wasn't actually a real attack.[4]

As such, these two episodes in season two of *Spooks* did not just anticipate the 7/7 attacks, they helped condition people to believe both the official conspiracy theory and some of the major alternative conspiracy theories.   The second episode of the season featured a brainwashed suicide bomber and a double agent. Both of these are ripe ground for conspiracy theories. The fifth episode of the season featured a training exercise that appeared to coincide with a real attack. This is also a fertile ground for conspiracy theories.

In understanding how and why these episodes were produced we can turn to comments made by the cast and crew. When the second series was released on DVD the suicide bomber episode had an additional feature with comments from people who worked on the show. This was in response to the BBC receiving over 1000 complaints (none of which were upheld) about the potentially Islamophobic content of the show.

The director of the suicide bomber episode, Bharat Nalluri, took a strange line. He directed the first two episodes in each of the first two seasons of *Spooks* and he said, 'I think it would be very strange for us to do a show about MI5, which is about internal security in Britain and we dealt with the Irish problem in terms of the IRA, we dealt with Chechens, we've dealt with just about every terrorist faction you can go, and we hadn't dealt with the fundamentalist Muslim problem, or the idea that there was a problem.'

This is all demonstrably untrue.   The only references to and appearances of Muslims in the whole of the first series were as terrorists. The only mention of suicide bombers was in association with Muslims. The 'idea that there was a problem' had not just been 'dealt with' already, it had been catapulted into the minds of the audience in the most crude and obvious way.   Furthermore, by the time of the suicide bomber episode in season two there had been only seven prior episodes of *Spooks* – hardly enough to deal with 'just about every terrorist faction'. Indeed, if we look at those seven episodes we find that Nalluri is simply not telling the truth:

Episode	Major target/subject
1	Pro-life anti-abortion fundamentalists
2	Racist right-wingers (non-terrorism episode)
3	Kurdish liberationists
4	Anarchists
5	Disgraced former MP (non-terrorism episode)
6	Irish Republicans/Islamic militants
7	Serbian militants

So in fact the 'fundamentalist Muslim problem' was 'dealt with' in *Spooks*. The idea had already been somewhat explored twice but clearly the makers of the show, Nalluri included, decided that twice in seven episodes wasn't enough. Furthermore, there is no mention of Chechen terrorists in any of the early seasons of *Spooks*, and of course many of the Chechen terrorists are Muslims. All in all, Nalluri's explanation is outright untrue and positively deceptive in attempting to excuse the suicide bomber episode that he directed. This does, of course, suggest that there was a quite different reason why that particular episode was made.

For part of the answer we should look at comments made by Howard Brenton, the man who conceived of and wrote the script for the suicide bomber episode (and the exercise episode). In a DVD production feature about the episode, Brenton said, 'I wanted to do a story about a good Muslim, that was the idea. A Muslim hero. And to put it into the dangerous world of Al Qaeda-like militant Islamic activity. And to broach the terrifying subject of suicide bombing, because it's obsessing our security services.'

This DVD box set was made available in 2004, well before 7/7. Brenton's remarks suggest that the story was inspired by conversations and contacts he had within the security services, because otherwise how could he know which scenarios were obsessing them? It isn't as though we can just ask the security services which scenarios they think are likely to happen. If we did they would not tell us, not just for fear of giving ideas to possible terrorists but also due to the general secrecy of these organisations.

Indeed, it is through shows like *Spooks*, and some of the other programmes that are discussed below, that our impressions of likely future terrorist attacks (and other events) are formed. The daily reality in

Britain is that there are virtually no terrorist attacks, and yet we are fed a constant stream of claims about the terrorist threat. As fiction, as simulations, shows like *Spooks* fill the gap between the reality and the nightmares inflicted on us. As Brenton noted, 'It's almost become a hallmark of the series, that a lot of the stories are nearer reality than some other series are... a lot of the material is quite hot.'

An actor from the series, Rory McGregor, commented that, 'It was just an exploration of something that might happen, and that's what *Spooks* is about. When you start to make it you don't really realise if these things are actually going to happen, you read the script and you think well, is that going to happen? It's like the VX episode as well, could that happen? Well, yes, it could but you don't find that out until we've started shooting the episode and suddenly it comes out in the papers and it's there, and yes this is real threat.'

Actor David Oyelowo was also interviewed for this feature and said, 'When I first read the suicide bomber episode I thought ooh, my goodness, this is a hot potato. Primarily because the thought of suicide bombings taking place in this country was terrifying and real. And I personally thought goodness, don't let us put, y'know, ideas in people's heads.'[5] There are of course two ways in interpret this. The first, what Oyelowo probably meant was that the show could help inspire real suicide bombings, copycats. The second is that one of the ideas being put in people's heads is the notion of Muslims carrying out suicide bombings in Britain, i.e. the idea at the centre of the official 7/7 narrative.

Beyond *Spooks*

These first two series of *Spooks* were broadcast in 2002 and 2003. In 2004 the predictive programming went into overdrive, with several further shows employing the same memes. In early 2004 the pilot episode of a new BBC show called *Crisis Command* was aired. The show took a small panel of members of the public and presented them with a crisis scenario, which they then had to manage. They were fed information through mocked-up news broadcasts, they were presented with several moments where they had to make key decisions and in the end their decisions were assessed. Among the experts presenting the show and providing them with advice was Charles Shoebridge.

The pilot episode was based around a series of terrorist attacks that bore a striking resemblance to the 7/7 attacks. Initially a series of power surges and power cuts were detected, just as on the morning of 7/7. Then there were two bombings on the London train network around Waterloo station, which left a tube train stranded in the tunnel while water began leaking in from the Thames. Not content with that, a plane was hijacked by terrorists and directed towards London.

The *Crisis Command* team had to decide whether to try to rescue the stranded passengers or close the floodgates and protect the rest of the underground network. They also had to decide whether or not to shoot down the plane headed for London. Unsurprisingly they dithered and catastrophe struck. The floodgates weren't closed, leading to a crippling of the tube network. The plane was allowed to stay in the air and was ultimately crashed into the Houses of Parliament.[6]

The series was commissioned for several episodes, each dealing with a different kind of crisis but it is the pilot episode that most warrants scrutiny. The same memes from critical *Spooks* episodes – attacks on the underground, suicidal terrorists – can be seen in *Crisis Command*. Of particular interest is the scenario of bombing the underground to try to use the Thames to flood the entire network.

The same idea turned up in two other places. Firstly, when Dhiren Barot and the 'financial buildings plot' was busted up in August 2004, the laptop apparently containing his plans did note this same idea for an attack. As with the rest of the 'plot', it was one of several outlandish schemes for which Barot had no equipment or personnel. As with the *Spooks* suicide bomber episode we are bound to ask, was the idea jotted down on the laptop in response to the BBC broadcast of *Crisis Command*?

The other place this notion appeared was in a British National Party (BNP) online newsletter shortly after 7/7. In an 'exclusive' the BNP claimed that in fact there was a much larger plot around 7/7, and that 'A team of terrorists with a fifth bomb – intended to explode in the tube network directly under the River Thames – was arrested the night before.' The newsletter claims there was a huge cover-up, which conveniently accounts for why no one has ever found the slightest bit of corroborative evidence for this story.

This bomb under the Thames idea was almost certainly political propaganda, scare tactics from the same people who issued a post-7/7 election leaflet with a picture of the bombed bus and the tagline 'Maybe now it's time to start listening to the BNP'. Did the BNP simply lift this tube-flooding bomb scenario from the reports of the laptop being used by Dhiren Barot/Noor Khan? Did they simply lift it from the pilot episode of *Crisis Command*?

In May 2004, not long after the *Crisis Command* pilot episode was broadcast, BBC's flagship factual programme *Panorama* produced a special episode. The special, titled *London Under Attack*, was not just similar to 7/7 but also to *Crisis Command*. Again, a panel was fed a crisis scenario through mocked-up news broadcasts. This time the panel were not members of the public, they were expert talking heads from various fields (politics, emergency services, security services). Also, they did not make decisions on how to manage the crisis so much as comment on the decisions that other people should make in response to such an event.

The crisis scenario portrayed by *Panorama* was remarkably similar to 7/7. Three explosions on underground trains early in the morning were followed by an explosion on a large road vehicle, albeit a chlorine tanker and not a bus. Indeed, the chlorine tanker even explodes near Liverpool Street station, which is seen in much of the faked footage of a huge gas cloud enveloping part of central London.

As the voice over says at the opening of the programme, 'This is the kind of terrorist attack the government repeatedly says is going to happen.' The programme defined itself as 'a mock exercise which exposes failings in official planning for such an attack.' The show did highlight some serious issues, such as radios not working on the underground, that then affected the emergency service response on 7/7.

There was even a designated enemy. Periodically during the show real-life BBC News 24 presenter Kirsty Lang presented highly convincing mock news clips that updated the panel and the watching TV audience. Amongst these faux-updates she reported that 'the Home Secretary has said the attacks bear the hallmarks of Al Qaeda'. On the evening of 7/7 former Home Secretary (and then Foreign Secretary) Jack Straw used the exact same phrase, 'hallmarks of Al Qaeda' to describe the real attacks. Perhaps coincidentally, Kirsty Lang was also on duty on the day of 7/7, and had to report on nearly-identical events for real, both in terms of the attacks and the 'hallmarks' phrase.[7]

Though it is not made clear in the *Panorama* episode, the tube bombings in the conceived scenario were the result of suicide bombings. At the time the show was being made the BBC tried to elicit the co-operation of the Home Office. The Home Office said that their involvement was contingent on a change of scenario to something more conventional, such as car bombings or hostage taking. The BBC stuck to their tube train scenario and the Home Office refused to take part in the show, branding the whole exercise 'alarmist and irresponsible'.[8]

Just in case some people missed the *Panorama* episode the BBC joined up with US producer/broadcaster HBO to produce yet another programme with a very similar storyline. *Dirty War* was a high budget made-for-TV thriller film that broadcast on BBC One on

September 24th 2004. This was just after the third anniversary of 9/11 and only months after the *Panorama London Under Attack* episode. The film centred around the same tropes and themes.

The film begins with a full-scale terrorism training exercise clearly inspired by the 2003 Operation Osiris II exercise run on the London underground. The issue of training exercises is covered in detail in the following chapter. The audience are then shown the journey of some radioactive material, all the way from Turkey to the UK, where it is made into a dirty bomb. The climax of the film is dirty bomb attack in London along very similar lines to the scenario for the training exercise that opens the film. The culprits? Muslim terrorists, of course, even though there wasn't and still isn't a single recorded attack in history where Muslim terrorists used such weapons.

Even more spooky is the fact that when the bombs are ready one of them is used in a suicide bombing attack on Liverpool Street underground station. Though the precise scenario is a truck bomb on the street by the entrance, rather than a backpack bomb on a tube train leaving the station, the film showed remarkable foresight of the 7/7 attacks.

The film was not finished there – in fact the attack plan involved four Muslim suicide bombers, even closer to the official 7/7 narrative. Though two of the bombers successfully attack Liverpool Street, the other two are (like Jean Charles de Menezes and numerous terrorists portrayed in *Spooks*) shot dead by Special Forces. In the closing sequence of the film we are briefly shown a shot of the outside of Aldgate East underground station, which was among those affected by the 7/7 attacks.

Spooks Season Three

The BBC weren't done there. Not content with predicting the 7/7 attacks with uncanny accuracy in a range of shows throughout 2004, the third season of *Spooks* followed in the footsteps of the first two series. The third episode of the season shows the chairman of the JIC making a secret deal with an Islamic terrorist behind the back of MI5. When MI5 find out the JIC chairman is confronted by spook section head Harry Pierce, and he responds, 'If you're asking me is there at present anything we shouldn't do to achieve our ends then frankly I don't know. Post 9/11 we made a decision that nothing and nobody was to be off limits anymore.'[9]

In this episode in particular we see a developing trait in *Spooks* that goes beyond uncannily accurate predictions of future terrorist attacks. From the mouths of major characters we hear the excuses and justifications for the advancement of the National Security State. The logic of 'we must behave worse than them in order to defeat them' is explicitly put forward in a later episode in season three where MI5 torture a terrorist suspect to try to prevent an atrocity being committed.

Similarly, in *Dirty War* the mastermind behind the suicide bombings is partially drowned as the security services attempt to find out the plan of attack. In *Spooks*, one character raises objections to the use of sleep deprivation, minor poisoning and other 'enhanced interrogation techniques', but he is largely ignored and his character is killed off in the following episode. In *Dirty War* no one raises any objections.

This role of the mainstream media in, as Edward Herman called it, 'normalising the unthinkable' is well documented when it comes to factual media. Politicians' speeches, thinktank reports and news coverage are all relatively well recognised channels for making the horrendous seem necessary because of the threats we supposedly face. What is less well recognised is the role that fictional entertainment plays in accomplishing the exact same thing. In fact, when a handsome young actor playing a glamorous role such as a spy excuses torture, assassination and so on it probably has even more impact then when a tired, boring, ugly politician excuses it.

The tenth and final episode of *Spooks* season three returned to what was clearly a favourite storyline of the BBC. A counter-terrorism raid turns up a map of the London underground with three locations (one of them King's Cross) circled in marker pen. The raid also finds information on Sarin gas – the poison used to attack the Tokyo subway in the 1990s.

In a scene that was scripted but didn't make the final cut of the show, while examining this evidence the MI5 agents discuss how 'people are very scared' of the terrorist threat. They watch CCTV footage from a tube station showing an Asian man being set upon and beaten up by other passengers. One of the spooks mentions how 'He was reading the Koran but a group of passengers became convinced that he was about to launch some kind of suicide attack.' She then explains that, 'The "suicide bomb" turned out to be a bag with some birthday presents for his kid.'

Aside from the repetition of the notion of Muslim suicide bombers, what this un-broadcast scene shows is that the makers of *Spooks* were well aware of the effects of the terror hype and fear-mongering. The fact that this scene was not included in the broadcast episode perhaps demonstrates that the show's makers realised that they too were involved in provoking such responses.

As the episode progresses the Sarin attack on the tube turns out to be a ruse that enables a terrorist cell to capture two MI5 officers. The kidnapping is used by the terrorists as a means to blackmail one of the spooks into helping them gain access to the building that is hosting a speech by the Prime Minister. The spook, Adam, manages to get a female member of the terrorist cell past security, and she reveals that she has had a bomb and chemical poison surgically implanted in her abdomen. The bomb is set up to be detonated remotely be the terrorist mastermind holding the two MI5 agents hostage.[10]

Once again we were presented with a Muslim suicide bomber, though the exact nature of the tactic is perhaps more akin to the IRA's 'human bombs'. Typically, Republican terrorists would kidnap a family, telling the father that his wife and children would be killed if he did not drive a car-bomb into a target in a suicide attack. This type of 'unwilling suicide bomber' was seen several times in the 1990s before the IRA abandoned the tactic due to public outcry against it. The notion of Al Qaeda masterminds convincing women to have bombs surgically implanted – even in their breasts – was seriously floated in early 2010. The mainstream press lapped up this lurid story but there is no known case of this actually happening.

The idea of Muslim human bombs, explored in *Spooks* long before it was picked up by the mainstream news media, does illustrate a significant point about 7/7. Even if it could be established that the four men died at the scenes through explosives that they manually detonated then that would not necessarily be the sum total of the plot. It is always possible that someone could be forced or manipulated into doing such a thing without being a 'suicide bomber' in the typically understood sense of the term.

In the *Spooks* Muslim human bomb episode the woman changes her mind at the last minute and disaster is averted. The terrorist mastermind's hideout is stormed by Special Forces and he is, inevitably, shot dead. Unlike the suicide bomber show from season two, this episode did not provoke widespread complaints from the British public. Part of the reason for this is that the major dramatic event in the show is the killing of the character Danny, one of the original cast of the show. The death of a popular character distracted from what was in reality one in a long line of predictive programmes.

The episode also saw the introduction of Danny's replacement character, Zaf. As they got rid of the one non-white face in the show they replaced him with a Muslim MI5 officer. Clearly there are strict ratios that only allow the BBC to show MI5 as having one ethnic minority agent at a time. Ironically, the actor playing the new character, Raza Jaffrey, played the terrorist mastermind in *Dirty War*. Terrorist, MI5 agent. MI5 agent, terrorist. It must get confusing.

Spooks Season Four

Though the fourth season of *Spooks* was broadcast in the autumn after 7/7, several of its episodes were filmed before the attacks. In particular, the opening two episodes of the series are a two-part story based around terrorists motivated by the idea that the world is overpopulated. They carry out a bombing campaign, once again targeting a London train station.

Among those caught up in the drama is ex-*Eastenders* favourite Martine McCutcheon, who is roped into helping MI5 stop the bombers. At one stage she asks, 'that bomb this morning, was it the Muslims?', perfectly illustrating the prejudices sown into the minds of the British public by programmes like *Spooks*. As seems to be obligatory in these predictive programmes, the show also features one of the terrorists being shot dead by Special Forces.

The two-part show included a discussion between two senior spooks about an 'Operation Omega', in what are obviously references to the very real Operation Gladio. Harry Pierce expresses with some reservation, 'The principle of Omega, to stage terrorist provocations in Europe to justify a government crackdown...' His counterpart responds, 'I think we did rather well.' This two-part episode was sent out, in what was presumably a deliberate bit of scheduling, on September 12th and 13th 2005, just after the fourth anniversary of 9/11 and only weeks after 7/7.[11]

An article in the Independent several years later titled 'Spooks: A drama that sees the future', reflected on this particular double episode as an example of how the show consistently predicted real life events. An interview with Peter Firth, the actor who plays Harry, revealed that, 'The obvious example is 7/7. In June 2005, we filmed a train station being bombed by terrorists – a month before the same terrible event happened in real life. At one point, the episode wasn't going to be shown because it was too near the mark. In the end, the episode went out in a very heavily edited version.'

Curiously, even though the sequence where the train station is bombed was 'heavily edited', the sequence where Special Forces shoot dead a female terrorist remained intact. The sensitivity shown towards victims of 7/7 was not shown towards the family of Jean Charles de Menezes, gunned down only weeks before this episode was broadcast. The Independent article went on to interview Richard Armitage, another actor from the show, who said, 'I was reading episodes of *Spooks* and at the same time ripping out press cuttings to create parallels between fiction and reality. You could have filleted the headlines and woven them straight into the drama. Are the *Spooks* team writing the newspapers as well?'

The Independent also interviewed Chris Fry, the producer of the show, who said, 'The ideal thing is when an episode goes out and the following morning viewers open their newspapers and say, "my God, I saw that story last night in Spooks."'[12] Going beyond all these comments, and in a statement that is downright suspicious, the managing director of Kudos, the production company behind *Spooks*, said in a DVD bonus feature for series 3 that, 'Spooks is really well researched and sometimes we look like we're ahead of the game. It's just *we know stuff that's happening*, and it'll come out in the news a bit later on.'[13] (my emphasis)

Further comments in other DVD extras explain that when producing *Spooks* they made use of advisors from the security services.[14] If the show was a channel for propaganda by the security services then it would not be the first time this sort of thing has happened. At the beginning of World War Two the British War Cabinet formed a Committee on the Issue of Warnings against Discussion of Confidential Matters in Public Places. Their major concern was state secrecy. The involvement of the mass population in the war effort meant that most people in Britain knew something that could compromise that effort.

The Committee tasked the Ministry of Information with encouraging people to keep quiet about what they knew. Posters with 'rhyming admonitions' such as *Loose Lips Sink Ships* were distributed in their hundreds of thousands. Warnings flashed up in cinema theatres across the country before the main feature was shown. Beyond this overt, white propaganda they also made use of covert, grey and black propaganda.

One of the more covert means was the use of popular writers to write on the virtues of secrecy. One report by the Minister of Information to the War Cabinet in March 1940 notes that, 'Various well-known writers, including Somerset Maugham, Agatha Christie and E.M.

Delafield are being asked to supply articles or stories on the results of careless talk.'[15] Somerset Maugham is of particular interest because he worked for MI6 during World War One as an agent in both Switzerland and Russia. Maugham subsequently published a fictionalised version of his experiences working for the Secret Service called *Ashenden*.

Several other writers including Arthur Ransome and Compton McKenzie also worked as British spies and published books inspired by their experiences. While the security services had no problem with the fiction, such as *Ashenden* or *Swallows and Amazons*, they clearly did have a problem with MacKenzie's detailed memoir *Greek Memories*. It exposed in literal detail some of the workings of MI6, and it was banned from publication and MacKenzie was prosecuted under the Official Secrets Act.

By contrast, another report from the Minister of Information lists a record of propaganda broadcasts from in March 1940. Among them was an adaptation of 'Miss King', one of the *Ashenden* spy stories.[16] 'Ban the fact, use the fiction' appears to be the underlying logic. Thus, the notion of using stories, spy stories in particular, to promote a certain attitude in the public is not alien to the British state. Like then we are now in a state of war, indeed, the War on Terror has lasted longer than WW2 and it shows little sign of stopping. So we are left to consider a bizarre but very real possibility: that *Spooks*, like *Ashenden*, was used by the security services as a means of predictive propaganda.

Predictive Conspiracy Theories

To many people this will seem like a strange idea – using a popular TV show to promote attitudes in the public about an event before it even happens. Indeed, it is a strange idea, but it is in keeping with the wartime propaganda. In the early part of the war the aim was to alert the public to the imminent German invasion and to give them confidence that the invasion could and would be repelled.[17] That invasion never actually happened, but nonetheless the propaganda was predictive, aimed at programming or conditioning a certain response in the public.

Fast forwarding to more recent times, an MI6 operation codenamed Mass Appeal was set up in the late 1990s to help turn public opinion in favour of war in Iraq. This involved the Secret Intelligence Service planting stories in the mass media about Iraqi WMD.[18] The invasion of Iraq did not take place until March 2003, showing that for several years prior to the event MI6 were engaged in conditioning people to accept it when it did happen. Though it is a strange idea, it is also a distinct reality.

If it were a case of only one or two shows, in particular programmes that explicitly worked with hypothetical scenarios, then one could easily argue that it was simple coincidence. Given the number of TV shows being made, at least some of them will depict events that then go on to happen for real. That is not the case with 7/7. For the makers of *Spooks* it is clear that Muslim suicide bombings were a continual preoccupation in the years running up to the attacks. Several other shows also centred around this scenario.

The sheer number of shows means that the counterargument of it being mere coincidence is much harder to accept. What may be particularly telling is that the BBC, the state broadcaster, produced all of these shows. There was no equivalent predictive programming regarding 7/7 from the other major or minor broadcasters in the UK. If this was somehow a deliberate process by the state then it would account for why only the BBC were involved.

So, did the logic of 'ban the fact, use the fiction' continue after World War Two? It appears so, for while the existence of MI6 was not formally admitted until 1992 there were over a dozen James Bond films glorifying the security services. It should be noted that it was not made explicitly clear in the Bond films that he works for MI6 until after the agency's avowal by John Major in the early 1990s.

In the middle of the period (1945-1992) where MI6's existence was officially denied we find another political battle that shows that this logic was still in operation. In the early 1980s the Thatcher government engaged in a struggle with the BBC over an episode of *Panorama* on the British security services. Recently released files from the National Archives show that Thatcher was even prepared to use the government veto to block transmission of the programme, though in the end this did not happen.

Instead, pressure was brought to bear on BBC Director General Sir Ian Trethowan who then showed an early edit of the documentary to MI6 legal advisor Bernard Sheldon. Sheldon then 'recommended' a number of cuts, resulting in the broadcast show being an insipid and butchered version. Even this didn't satisfy the office of the Prime Minister, but as Cabinet Secretary Sir Robert Armstrong put it, 'short of using the veto (which Ministers have decided not to do) there is little more we can do.'[19]

In the pre-7/7 period we see the same logic being employed. As noted above, the Home Office refused to participate in the 2004 *Panorama: London Under Attack* episode, accusing it of being 'alarmist and irresponsible'. Yet they appeared to raise no objection to the nightmare scenarios regularly depicted in *Spooks* or in *Dirty War*. Though they did not actually ban the *Panorama* episode we can once again see the logic of 'ban the fact, use the fiction'. They had no problem with depictions of suicide bombings and CBRN terrorism in fictional programming, only in its more factual equivalent.

What is the result of all this? What emerges from this overview of predictive programmes is that they frequently anticipated 7/7 and conditioned people to accept the official conspiracy theory. In each story where there were suicide terrorists, those terrorists were Muslims. Some programmes went beyond this, depicting Muslim suicide terrorist attacks against the London underground, even getting one of the stations right.

However, the conditioning of the public was not limited to encouraging acceptance of the official conspiracy theory. The conditioning also predicted some of the major alternative conspiracy theories, particularly those involving a simultaneous training exercise. We were also presented with the notions of MI5 staging an attack, of them employing double agents within terrorist groups, and of them colluding with one kind of terrorist group to get information on another. All of this no doubt encouraged not just the official conspiracy theory of 7/7, but also many of the alternative conspiracy theories.

Suspicious Broadcasts

In the years between 9/11 and 7/7 the BBC aired a large number of shows that pre-empted and predicted the 7/7 attacks. These shows established the idea of Muslim suicide bombings taking place in Britain. In particular, they established this idea alongside or in conjunction with the more conventional idea of attacks on the London underground system. In effect, they predicted the entire official version of what happened on 7/7. Was this deliberate? We cannot be certain with the evidence currently available to us. We can be sure of is that the reasons given by the director of the suicide bomber episode of *Spooks* in season two are simply untrue. The makers of *Spooks* were clearly preoccupied with Muslim suicide bombers, and Muslim terrorists in general, to the point of being accused of racism.

We can also be sure that in World War Two the British state made use of predictive programming as part of their propaganda efforts. The military Chiefs of Staff made this clear in a paper they wrote on Propaganda Policy in November 1940, saying, 'Propaganda as an arm in war has two main functions - To wage psychological warfare - (a) with the simultaneous object of destroying the moral force of the enemy's cause and of sustaining and eventually enforcing conviction of the moral force of our own cause; (b) by co-operating with the other arms to prepare the way for and to exploit the effects of the military and economic offensive.'[20]

If one of the main purposes in World War Two was to 'wage psychological warfare' in order to 'prepare the way for' forthcoming actions then the notion that this could be going on in the 'War on Terror' is not so strange and radical as it might immediately appear. We can also be certain that as part of this wartime predictive programming that the state made use of spy stories written by one of their own ex-spies. The potential and real parallels with *Spooks*, who used former security service personnel as advisors, are obvious.

However, the process may have become subtler than that. Not only did these shows anticipate and condition people to believe the official 7/7 conspiracy theory of Muslim suicide bombers, these shows did the same with some of the alternative conspiracy theories. In particular the *Spooks* episode where a training exercise coincides with a real attack conditioned people to focus on Peter Power's exercise on the morning of 7/7 that to some extent replicated the real attacks. It may be significant that the episode that predicted this alternative conspiracy theory broadcast on July 7th 2003 – exactly two years before 7/7.

Indeed, the process appears to be even more complex. These predictive programmes did not just condition people to accept the official conspiracy and some of the alternative conspiracy theories. It helped to normalise the National Security State, in particular its response to terrorism. In several of these shows terrorists are shot dead by Special Forces, and this is invariably portrayed as justice being meted out against evil people. In other episodes torture is portrayed as a 'necessary evil', which either goes unquestioned, or is questioned only by a character who is killed off in the following episode. The message is clear: these things must be done, no matter what you might feel about them. If you oppose them then you make it more likely that you will be killed by terrorists.

The *Spooks* suicide bomber episode is also one of very few where MI5 substantively fail to prevent or interdict the attack. Despite them having a double agent within the terrorist group, the young suicide bomber blows himself up, though he only kills himself and the double agent. The show did not just pre-empt the official version of the 7/7 attacks, but also the official excuse that MI5 can't prevent every attempted attack. Almost the entire dialogue that has emerged in the aftermath of 7/7 was predicted years before it happened.

Extending this theme a little further, in the third season of *Spooks* there is an episode where one of the main characters is put on trial for her role in a spree killing. The character, Zoe, is not named in court, but is known only as 'officer X', just like 'Witness G'. Unlike G, Zoe appears in person but of course we (the audience) already know who she is so there is nothing to be gained dramatically from hiding her. For G, things were somewhat different.

Nonetheless, the theme of the security services not being held to account for their role in very serious crimes was explored in *Spooks* in a way that was accurate enough to be called predictive of G's appearance at the 7/7 inquests. In the episode when Zoe is found guilty, MI5 find a way to swap her for another prisoner, and she escapes to South America. Fundamentally, the security services are shown to be above the law, helping to normalise the total lack of accountability discussed in the previous three chapters.

Despite all this, very few critics of the official 7/7 narrative have discussed the question of predictive programming. The lone *Panorama London Under Attack* show is relatively notorious but it was not until my 2011 film *7/7: Crime and Prejudice* that people within the online and alternative communities began discussing the other broadcasts. The next chapter will look at similar examples of 7/7 being predicted in several training exercises, the other kind of terrorism 'simulation' aside from TV shows. It will consider the training exercise being run on the morning of 7/7 itself and the conspiracy theories that have sprung up around it, in the context of predictive programming.

Chapter 10: Simulated Terror

Films and TV shows were not the only fictions that predicted 7/7. Running alongside the timeline of the predictive programmes, there is also a timeline of training exercises that foresaw different elements of the attacks. There was also an exercise running on the very morning of 7/7 that to some extent replicated the scenario of the real bombings.

The exercise on 7/7 has become a focal point for many of those questioning the official conspiracy theory, and for almost all of those advancing alternative conspiracy theories. The majority of people consider it in isolation, rather than as part of a pattern of comparable simulations of terrorism. These simulations take the form of both TV shows, fictional portrayals in that sense, but also training drills, desktop exercises and the like.

The predictive TV programming explicitly sought to make guesses about what might happen in the future. Their demonstrable effect of conditioning people's beliefs about and responses to certain scenarios, including terrorist attacks, is essentially implicit. It is a key part of what they do, but not one that is discussed openly.

At the end of *Panorama*'s *London Under Attack* while the credits rolled the editors included a few last snippets from the expert panel responding to the fictional attack. Former Defence Secretary Michael Portillo commented that, 'I am wondering about the purpose and effect of this very programme. It will alarm people but may lead decision makers to think again.'[1] Thus, the notion that such shows would have a psychological impact on the public and politicians was brought up by one of the show's participants.

Training simulations are of course much more explicit in seeking to prepare people for attacks. That is their overt aim. Such simulations are at least as old as World War Two. From children being trained to put on their gas masks to full-scale Civil Defence Corps rescue drills with hundreds of mock victims they have long been a part of British life.

The key issue explored in this chapter is how these simulations also have a somewhat more covert role that is akin, or even identical, to predictive TV programming. Just as TV shows, books and so on have been used since World War Two to help shape people's understanding and expectations of potential threats, so have training simulations. Regardless of whether the projected threat is Nazi mustard gas attacks, Communist invasion or Islamist terrorism, we have been conditioned, taught, and prepped.

Exercises on the Tube

On September 7th 2003 a full scale, suited and booted training drill codenamed Osiris II was run at Bank underground station. This was just before the second anniversary of 9/11 and exactly two months after the *Spooks* episode based around a training exercise. The scenario for the drill, just as in the *Spooks* episode, was a CBRN terrorist attack. It involved around 500 emergency service personnel rescuing people from an underground train caught up in the attack. Mock victims were brought out and decontaminated.

Osiris II was criticised for its lack of realism. It was held on a Sunday in closely controlled conditions but it still took 30 minutes to rescue the first 'victims'. Communications systems did not work, and the emergency service personnel could not talk to each other through their gas masks. Perhaps crucially, ordinary underground staff were not part of the drill. In particular the Fire Brigades Union raised serious concerns, including that, 'the decontamination tents may have been put in the wrong place because not enough attention was paid to the wind direction.'[2]

Months later, in early 2004 the pilot episode of *Crisis Command* – featuring an attack on the tube, was broadcast. Like the *Panorama London Under Attack* show in May 2004 this was a different sort of exercise, a different sort of simulation. Nonetheless they employed very similar scenarios to Osiris II, so any allegation the TV shows were fear-mongering could equally be levelled at the Osiris exercise.

Meanwhile, across the pond the US authorities were also running drills based on the scenario of terrorist attacks on underground train networks. Curiously, on the same day that the *London Under Attack* programme was shown, a training exercise was run in New York called Operation Transit Safe. Simulated bombs went off on underground trains and real people played the roles of dead and injured passengers. New York's 24 hour news service NY1 interviewed NYC Transit President Lawrence Reuter who said, 'There was two bombs gone off on both the northbound and the southbound trains in this incident, and you had 300, over 300 people who were injured and/or killed because of those bombs that went off.'[3]

This particular comment illustrates a truth of much of the media coverage of these crisis management simulations. The watching audience, particularly those who are channel hopping, might well mistake an exercise for a real attack. At the very least, even if they realise that it is just a drill then they would still have an increased sense of the threat of such incidents happening for real. Ultimately, not just the exercises themselves but also the media coverage of them have very similar if not identical consequences to the predictive programming discussed in the previous chapter.

In July 2004 a follow up to the Osiris II exercise was held in Birmingham. It was codenamed Horizon and was based on the scenario of suicide terrorists spraying the public with a chemical poison. As with the predictive TV programming, the notion of suicidal terrorists came up in the other kind of terror simulation. The exercise, which involved around 450 volunteer 'victims' and 2000 emergency service personnel, was the biggest ever held in Britain at the time.

The Osiris exercise was not the only physical, on the ground type of drill held on the London underground. There were others at Southgate station in 2003 and Lambeth station in 2004. A BBC article on the Lambeth drill doesn't provide much clarification but quotes Penny Hazell, general manager of the Bakerloo line saying , 'With a real incident, there would be no advance warning. That is why details are not revealed, enabling London Underground and the emergency services to treat the exercise as if it were actually happening.'[4]

A further simulation codenamed Dartboard was run at Tower Hill in June 2005. It was featured in an episode of popular TV series *The Tube* titled 'Special Operations'. Broadcast immediately after two special episodes of *The Tube* devoted to 7/7, the show outlined in some detail the role of the Emergency Response Unit, who took part in the exercise. The scenario for Dartboard was an incapacitated driver crashing his train into a buffer, and, particularly prescient of 7/7, a passenger falling underneath the train.

The *London Under Attack* show included footage of the Osiris drill and raised some of the criticisms mentioned above. One member of the 'expert panel', former Commander of the Metropolitan Police David Gilbertson, said, 'I've heard Osiris described as a very expensive photo opportunity. Now I'm not so cynical as to say that's the case.'[5]

Since Gilbertson has brought up the question of the role these exercises play in terms of public perception we ought to consider whether these drills have the same effect as the predictive TV programming. They have essentially the same origin – to predict particular scenarios based on a broad and general perception of a threat. They have the same ultimate aim in terms of the public reception – to be alert to the perceived threat but at the same time be reassured that the authorities are taking steps, and taking the right steps. They help to normalise the 'fear therefore security' politics of our time.

Indeed, given that the Osiris exercise was so bad, we must wonder whether its PR role was the greatest consideration. Despite its failings, the simulation found that emergency service radios either don't work on the underground, or work very poorly. This was also highlighted in the *Panorama* programme, but what they didn't mention is that this had been known since at least the King's Cross fire in 1987.

Indeed, Sir Desmond Fennell's 1988 report into the fire devoted an entire chapter to communications systems. Some of its recommendations were apparently taken up, such, 'improvements to the standard and coverage of CCTV equipment in station.' However, Fennell's view that, 'I believe it to be essential that radios used by London Underground and each of the emergency services must be compatible' appears to have been ignored.[6]

On 7/7 the radio systems were not compatible, leading to considerable delays and much confusion. As we saw in chapter 3 the CCTV was not up to much either. This very much suggests that as real preparation for real disasters the exercises on the tube were not particularly effective. In establishing memes that would later coalesce into the official version of the 7/7 attacks they were rather more successful.

Atlantic Blue

A different kind of drill was run in April 2005, only weeks before 7/7. It was codenamed 'Atlantic Blue' in the UK but it was coordinated with US and Canadian exercises. The Canadians called theirs 'Triple Play', and the US codename was 'TOPOFF3' (the 'Top Officials' drill is held annually, and the 2005 one was the third in the series). In Britain Atlantic Blue was a CPX, or Command Post Exercise, where emergency services are not physically deployed but instead it is the management structure that are responding to the mock-up emergency.

According to an article in The Job, the Metropolitan Police's bi-monthly magazine, Atlantic Blue was run 24 hours a day for five days, 'The UK Command scenario, based in Hendon, involved 2,000 people from the Met, City of London and British Transport police services, Ministry of Defence and 14 government departments and agencies, two London Borough councils, the fire and ambulance services and the NHS.'

The Job also explained that American arm, TOPOFF3, was 'A full-scale scenario... including 8,000 volunteers.'[7] A Department of Homeland Security (DHS) fact sheet explains that the Canadian side,

Triple Play, was actually running for several months, involving 'a series of training sessions, seminars and tabletop exercises of increasing complexity.' This then culminated in, 'Canada's first Large Scale Game', an on the ground type drill.[8]

So what was the scenario for the UK-based Command Post Exercise? According to an article in The Observer, it 'included 'bombs' being placed on buses and explosives left on the London underground.'[9] Even more prescient of 7/7, the attack in the scenario 'coincided with a major international summit.'[10] Atlantic Blue did also involve other attacks, including the world leaders at the summit being attacked with a biological weapon (hurrah!). Nonetheless, the simulated scenario was close enough to 7/7 to be picked up by newspapers within days of the attacks.

What is perhaps most interesting about Atlantic Blue is the extent to which media, and media management, was a focus of the drills. According to The Job, the British arm included 'pseudo-media coverage of the event', i.e. it 'used mocked-up news reporting covering the events as they happened in the exercise. Ch Supt Webb said it played an important role in making the scenario real to the players in Hendon, and they were able to make it relate to a real event.'[11] So the crisis managers in Hendon were just like the contestants in *Crisis Command* or the expert panel in *London Under Attack*. They were sitting in a room, receiving fake news updates on a simulated crisis that they then tried to manage.

Fake news broadcasts were also used in the TOPOFF3 part of the exercise in America produced by VNN – the Virtual News Network. They featured interviews with fake witnesses and real rescue crews talking about a simulated attack as though it were real. Some of the video from these broadcasts is available online and is classified 'For Official Use Only', 'UK Restricted, Protected Other Government'. What this shows is that the fake news broadcasts were not just being fed to US crisis managers, but also to British crisis managers involved in the simulation.

It also ties Atlantic Blue and similar Command Post or tabletop exercises more closely to terror simulations like *Panorama*'s *London Under Attack*. Just as in the BBC show a news update informed the panel that 'the attacks bear the hallmarks of Al Qaeda', the TOPOFF3 fake news also featured terrorist suspects. They were, of course, Muslims with very Muslim-sounding names. The host of the virtual news even held up pictures and asked the watching audience to contact the FBI if they saw either of the two men.[12]

So just like the predictive TV programming for the masses in the form of *Spooks* and so on, this VNN broadcast was effectively predictive programming for the very people who would respond to 7/7. Just as the public were being prepped for an attack on the London underground system by Muslim terrorists, so were the officials who would then be in charge of responding to and investigating the attacks. According to the DHS webpage on their National Exercise Program, TOPOFF3 'marked the launch of a new simulated media tool – the interactive web site VNN.com.'

Indeed, both the US and UK planners were concerned with media as one of the principal aspects that they focused on in Atlantic Blue/TOPOFF3. The DHS fact sheet notes that, 'The United States, Canada, and the UK have worked together throughout a two-year planning process to achieve shared objectives in four key areas.' One of those key areas was 'Public information', with the DHS saying the objective was, 'To practice strategic coordination of media relations and public information issues in response to linked terrorist incidents'.[13] The Cabinet Office webpage on Atlantic Blue is no longer available via their website but backup versions can be found via the National Archives. It also lists objectives, among them 'Public information.' It says that the aim was, 'To practice the joint response of the UK, US and Canadian governments to media handling and public information.'[14]

A Home Office publication that goes by the delightful name of CBRN News sheds some light on this issue. It detailed Atlantic Blue in its June 2005 issue and explained how just like the Americans, the British had a 'pseudo media' team dedicated to producing coverage to be fed to the exercise participants. Just as the Americans had VNN.com, we had VBCNews.com. One 'pseudo journalist' who 'normally works in a policy team' was interviewed for CBRN News and explained how they had worked on the website, updating it as the exercise progressed. They commented that, 'In terms of the exercise, the online tool was also very helpful in reflecting the perceived media and public response to how the incidents were being handled, and *in consultation with Exercise Control we were able to drive player action accordingly.*'[15] (my emphasis)

The 7/7 Exercise

Numerous training exercises pre-empted or predicted 7/7. The meme of Muslim suicide bombers is not as common in this type of terrorist simulation than in the TV shows, but the notion of attacks on the London underground was well established. Even more explicitly than the predictive TV programming, the exercises sought to condition and prepare people mentally for when a real attack occurred. Through real news coverage the exercises influenced the public, through fake news they influenced their own participants.

It is in this context that we need to consider one of the more bizarre and controversial events on July 7th 2005. On the morning of 7/7 a crisis management response exercise was being run based on the scenario of simultaneous bombings at some of the same stations affected by the real attacks. Perhaps unsurprisingly this has spawned a lot of speculation and indeed many alternative conspiracy theories that the exercise was somehow the means by which the bombings were carried out.

The CEO of Visor Consultants, former Metropolitan Police officer turned management consultant Peter Power, appeared on BBC Radio Five on the afternoon of 7/7 to talk about the simulation. He said, 'at half-past nine this morning we were actually running an exercise for a company of over a thousand people in London based on simultaneous bombs going off precisely at the railway stations where it happened this morning, so I still have the hairs on the back of my neck standing upright!' He was asked by presenter Peter Allen, 'To get this quite straight, you were running an exercise to see how you would cope with this and it happened while you were running the exercise?' to which Power responded, 'precisely.'

A few hours later Peter Power also appeared on ITV news at 20:20 on the evening of 7/7. He explained, 'Today we were running an exercise for a company - bearing in mind I'm now in the private sector - and we sat everybody down, in the city - 1,000 people involved in the whole organisation - but the crisis team. And the most peculiar thing was, we based our scenario on the simultaneous attacks on an underground and mainline station. So we had to suddenly switch an exercise from fictional to real.' He was asked by the presenter, 'Just to get this right, you were actually working today on an exercise that envisioned virtually this scenario?' to which Power replied, 'Er, almost precisely.' Power also gave interviews to Canadian TV in the days after 7/7 where he essentially repeated the same story.

These interviews have since been reproduced online and been seen by hundreds of thousands if not millions of people. They have been used, in one way or another, in every documentary on 7/7 that explores or advances alternative conspiracy theories. The exercise Power was running is by some distance the most-discussed issue about 7/7. From my own work making films, writing and giving presentations and interviews about 7/7 I can firmly say it is the topic I get asked about more than any other.

Despite this, in broad terms the arguments in favour of these exercise-based alternative conspiracy theories are as weak, poorly sourced and self-contradictory as the official conspiracy theory of Muslim suicide bombers. They almost invariably rely on misleading statistical arguments, crude misinterpretations of Power's interviews, and baseless speculation. Given the popularity of these theories this assessment will not be easily received by many, so we need to qualify it with evidence.

The arguments that the Peter Power exercise was somehow the secret means by which the 7/7 attacks were carried out typically begins with one of two premises. First, that there were also exercises running on 9/11 that in some ways replicated the attacks and second that the chances of the Peter Power exercise being a coincidence are so low as to be impossible. We will deal with the 9/11 comparison first.

On the morning of the 9/11 attacks several agencies were running disaster management drills or wargames based around very similar scenarios to the real attacks. The National Reconnaissance Office (NRO) were running a drill to see how they would respond to an airplane hitting their building. The Federal Emergency Management Agency (FEMA) were running a bio-terrorism drill at the World Trade Center. The North American Aerospace Defense Command (NORAD) were running a series of overlapping wargames based around hijacked commercial airliners.

So the comparison, to those in the know about these simulations, is obvious. Or is it? Are the two situations where exercises coincided with real terrorist attacks really so similar? On closer examination they are not. There were several exercises on 9/11 and only one on 7/7. The 9/11 exercises coincided with an attack that despite being highly unusual could have been intercepted and prevented. There was a period of time in between when the Federal Aviation Administration (FAA) realised that the planes were hijacked and when the planes hit their targets for which there is no equivalent in the 7/7 attacks. It isn't as though the alleged bombers gave half an hour's warning to the police to provide them with opportunity to hunt them down.

Perhaps most importantly, the 7/7 exercise was being run by a small private management consultancy rather a major government defence or crisis management agency like NORAD, the NRO or FEMA. Visor Consultants had no responsibility whatsoever for stopping terrorist attacks, let alone the specific kind of terrorist attack that struck London on 7/7. By contrast, NORAD is responsible for intercepting airborne threats over the US and as such was the agency right in the middle of trying to stop the 9/11 attacks. The roles of the relevant organisations on the two days are as vastly different as the manner of the attacks.

Lies, Damn Lies and Statistics

So, we look to the statistical argument. It is most simply expressed in the independent film *Terrorstorm*, probably the most-viewed internet release on 7/7, which says, 'On the morning of 7/7 in London there was a simultaneous exercise targeting the exact same trains, the exact same bus, at the exact same locations, at the very same time... If we use a standard actuary employed by major insurance companies to calculate the probability of these events coinciding in a ten year mean we learn that the probability of this happening is greater than one in three hundred trectragillion.'[16]

There are several problems with this argument. There is no such number as a 'trectragillion'. A standard actuary employed by an insurance company is actually a person, rather than a multiplication method as the film's visuals imply. As such, it is very difficult to understand how the makers of *Terrorstorm* came to this conclusion. For the numbers we can turn instead a webpage on the Infowars site produced by the same people who made the film. According to the calculations there the probability of the exercise and the attack coinciding is 'One chance in 3,715,592,613,265,750,000,000,000, 000,000,000,000,000'.[17] This is, to be sure, one chance in over three duodecillion, which is a real number.

Nonetheless, as you might expect this number has been exaggerated. For one thing, it is calculating across a period of ten years, when both terrorist attacks and particularly training exercises occur a lot more often than once per decade. The calculation also presumes that all 274 tube stations in London are equally likely to be chosen as terrorist targets, when in reality King's Cross and Liverpool Street are much more likely targets than, say, Oakwood, Ruislip or Epping. Despite these problems with the calculation, this statistic has been uncritically and unquestioningly repeated by those advancing an alternative 7/7 conspiracy theory based around the exercise. This was no doubt helped by the same number being used by the makers of *7/7 Ripple Effect*, another popular film about the attacks.

Different calculations and resultant probabilities have been proffered by others involved with the 7/7 case. Journalist Tony Gosling has offered two different numbers: 6 billion to one, and 7.6 billion to one. During a PressTV debate on 7/7, self-styled conspiracy debunker David Aaronovitch challenged Gosling over his claim of probability. Gosling replied, 'I sat and worked it out. 275 tube stations times three multiplied by 365 days of the year.'[18]

Unfortunately for Gosling, even if this were an appropriate method to calculate probability, it doesn't produce anything close to 6 billion to one odds. 275 x 3 x 365 = 301,125. Gosling was also making the assumption that every station is an equally likely target, and that every day is equally likely to see an attack. He also assumed, incorrectly, that there is at most one attack and one exercise per year.

We find much the same problem with the calculations of another writer on 7/7, Nick Kollerstrom. In an article on his website titled 'Just a Coincidence...' Kollerstrom wrote:

> If we surmise that a false-flag terror act has to happen between 8-10 am to get into the news that day, and not say in the afternoon or evening, then let's estimate a figure of 1 in 100 for having the time of day exact to a minute. You could put it much higher if you wish. Then let's say there were two such anti-terror drills per year (again one could make this figure higher or lower) and we get a probability of 2/260 as there are 260 working days in the year, assuming no-one would do it on a holiday.

> Finally, if there are 275 tube stations and they are equally likely to be chosen, the likelihood of Peter Power's Visor terror-drill choosing the exact same three – as he stressed more than once – would be 3/275 x 2/274 x 1/273. One could say that the outer-London tube stations were not likely to be chosen, and so divide that by eg a factor of 3; or, you may say that Edgware Road and Aldgate have very high Muslim populations, so it was highly unlikely that Muslim terrorists would choose them, which would greatly increase the improbability. But, let's just omit these two counterbalancing factors.

> Then, the likelihood of Peter Power's terror drill synchronising by chance with what happened on 7/7 is: 1/100 x 2/260 x 3/275 x 2/274 x 1/273 = 1 in 44,569,525,000[19]

There is so much wrong with this calculation that it is difficult to know where to begin. First, Kollerstrom took Peter Power's statement that, 'at half-past nine this morning we were actually running an exercise' and turned this into a down-to-the-minute coincidence of the exercise and the bombings. In fact, there was approximately 40 minutes between the tube bombings and 9:30, at least by the commonly accepted timeline of events. Kollerstrom gives this a 1/100 chance of happening, even though there's no evidence that it happened.

He then assumes that there are only two such exercises per year but this isn't true. Alongside Atlantic Blue and the Tower Hill drill there was also a desktop exercise run by the Metropolitan codenamed Hanover based on the scenario of multiple tube bombings. A similar exercise was also run by Deutsche bank a short time before 7/7, though it is unclear exactly when that took place. Added to the Peter Power exercise that makes five exercises just between April and July 2005, i.e. more than one a month. The irony is that Kollerstrom reported on these additional drills in another article on the same website, making his assumption of only two per year extremely dishonest.

Though he acknowledges that not all the tube stations are equally likely to be terrorist targets Kollerstrom counters this by pointing out that two of the stations hit on 7/7 are in areas with large Muslim populations. This is bizarre because though it might make those places less likely to be targeted by Muslim terrorists, Kollerstrom maintains that Muslims were not to blame, so the question of the targets having Muslim populations should be irrelevant. It is a strange and illogical equivocation to only employ the notion of Muslims being responsible in order to try to build a statistical argument that concludes that Muslims were not responsible.

What we find in these statistical arguments is a combination of hideously poor mathematics, logical equivocations, self-contradiction and outrageously misleading representations. In trying to prove that it could not be a coincidence that Peter Power was running a simulation on the morning of 7/7 that so closely mirrored the real attacks the commentators above, and many others, have only succeeded in muddying the waters of the investigation. That is not to say that the coinciding of the simulation and the real attack necessarily was a coincidence, just that those who have argued that it wasn't have exaggerated to a ridiculous and self-defeating extent.

On-the-Ground or on-the-Desk?

In the immediate aftermath of Peter Power's interviews the website of his company, Visor Consultants, received a large number of emails asking about connections between his exercise and the real attacks. Many people interpreted his comment about 'a company of a thousand people' to mean that a thousand people were involved in the drill. They therefore assumed that it was a full-scale on-the-ground type exercise rather than a CPX or other office based simulation.

Power responded a few days after 7/7 by issuing a stock email saying, 'It is confirmed that a short number of 'walk through' scenarios planned well in advance had commenced that morning for a private company in London (as part of a wider project that remains confidential) and that two scenarios related directly to terrorist bombs at the same time as the ones that actually detonated with such tragic results. One scenario in particular, was very similar to real time events.'

The email went on to explain that, 'In short, our exercise (which involved just a few people as crisis managers actually responding to a simulated series of activities involving, on paper, 1000 staff) quickly became the real thing and the players that morning responded very well indeed to the sudden reality of events.' Though this email did not explicitly contradict the interviews Power had given on 7/7 and immediately afterwards, it was seen as a backtrack or climb-down.

Peter Power was also interviewed for the BBC's *Conspiracy Files* show, dealt with in detail in chapter 5. This show was due to be shown in 2008 but was delayed due to the retrial of the three alleged 7/7 co-conspirators. As a result, Power made a post on a blog about disaster management that provided the same details he had given to the BBC. The post said that the client who were paying for the exercise was Reed Elsevier, the publishing company. They chose the time and date, 9:00 a.m. on July 7th 2005.

Power went on to explain that, 'The test was planned as a table-top walk through for about six people (the CM team) in a lecture room with all injects simulated. Everything was on MS PowerPoint.' He outlined the similarity with 7/7 saying that, 'Of just eight nearby tube stations that fell within possible exercise's scope, three were chosen that, by coincidence, were involved in the awful drama that actually took place on 7 July 2005. A level of scenario validation that on this occasion, we could have done without.'

This is essentially the same story that Peter Power told the BBC, and the broadcast included clips from his PowerPoint presentation. The scenario for his exercise was incendiary bombs on three tube trains around King's Cross, Russell Square and Liverpool Street underground stations. This was then followed by 'an above ground fictitious bomb' near the headquarters of the Jewish Chronicle magazine. This scenario was said to have affected eight stations, mostly in East and Central London.

As such, if we are to believe Power's clarifying statements then his scenario was only about half right. There was nothing in his exercise about a train in or near Edgware Road, and no bus bombing or anything to do with Tavistock Square. The notion that the exercise reproduced the 7/7 attack exactly, at the exact same time and locations, is simply untrue. Perhaps most importantly, Power said that his scenario was inspired by an IRA attack on the tube in 1992 using incendiary bombs i.e. there was no mention of suicide bombers.

Should we believe Peter Power? There is nothing factually inconsistent between Power's earlier statements and his later ones. They are very different in tone, from 'the hairs on the back of my neck are still standing upright' to 'choosing the London Underground was logical rather than just prescient.' Ultimately, it is up to the reader to make his or her own decision on whether to believe him, though there is one important implication. Power is the only source of information we have that there even was an exercise on 7/7, so if we disbelieve him then we should logically be sceptical that such an exercise actually took place.

There is one brief comment from his 7/7 interviews that bears some scrutiny. Power told ITV news that, 'I was up to 2 o clock this morning' preparing for the exercise. If this was just a PowerPoint presentation, the like of which he had given throughout his career, then would Power have been up until two o clock in the morning the day before running a simulation at 9 a.m.? Was he just very disorganised? This strains credulity given his position as a respected crisis management consultant and terrorism pundit. So was he lying?

If he was lying then we are faced with something of a paradox. Either he wasn't running a small-scale simulation for half a dozen crisis managers, or he wasn't actually up until two o clock in the morning the night before. Curiously, this point has been overlooked by the alternative conspiracy theorists in favour of misleading statistical calculations. The possible reason for this is that if Power was exaggerating about being up so late the night before then his obvious motive was self-promotion. This then presents the possibility that Power's motive for appearing on national news on the day of 7/7 was to promote his work and his company.

If this is true then it makes far more sense than if he was secretly involved in a dastardly and horrific false flag terrorist attack. After all, if he were involved then why would he have told everyone? If he were complicit in this horrible crime then why would he appear on national TV giving people a reason to think that he was complicit?

Peter Power: A Patsy?

There is another way of looking at the Peter Power drill in the context of the predictive programming discussed in the previous chapter. The TV shows that predicted 7/7 did so in a way that encouraged belief in the official conspiracy theory and the official culprits before the attack even happened. If this was done deliberately then we might wonder if it was not just the official conspiracy theory that was 'seeded' before the event. What if, part of the same process, they also seeded an alternative conspiracy theory?

So we might well ask, was Peter Power a victim of predictive programming? He participated in a 2004 TV show where he was presented with a hypothetical terrorist attack involving suicide bombings on three tube trains and a bomb on a large road vehicle. Around a year later he was hired to run an exercise on the same day as a real terrorist attack that involved bombings on three tube trains and a large road vehicle, blamed on suicide bombers. If I were Peter Power then in that situation the hairs on the back of my neck would be standing upright.

Indeed, we should wonder if Peter Power was set up as a patsy. If it is true that his exercise was just a PowerPoint presentation with no on-the-ground element then the drill could not, as many have claimed, have had anything to do with physically carrying out the attacks. However, that does leave us with the psychological dimension of the attacks. What kind of role could Power's exercise, and specifically his public interviews about his exercise, have played in that aspect of the bombings?

With the alleged terrorists dead, they gained precisely no propaganda value from the attacks. Indeed, the whole notion of four people acting alone to carry out an attack in which they all die, without anyone else left over to make statements or demands, makes little sense. Rather, it was the state who gained from the attacks. It was the National Security State agenda of consolidating secret power that was the one most served by the attacks. The 2006 Terrorism Act, control orders, and above all a heightened sense in the minds of the public of a need for greater security were the predictable result of 7/7.

As discussed in the previous chapter, much of this was predicted and prepared by television programming produced by the BBC. In this chapter we have seen how some saw these training exercises as a 'photo opportunity', i.e. more about public perception than serious preparation of responses to crises. So was Peter Power a victim of predictive programming in another sense? Was he a patsy?

Just as the official conspiracy theory of Muslim suicide bombers was predicted by *Spooks*, so was the alternative conspiracy theory of an attack coinciding with a training exercise. Indeed, the episode that predicted an exercise that turns into a real event was broadcast on 7/7/03, the sort of numerological significance many conspiracy theorists focus on. So, is the connection between the real 7/7 attacks and Power's simulation not a physical one, in terms of making the attacks happen, but a psychological one, in terms of producing a suspect for those members of the public who would be prone to not believing the official conspiracy theory?

After all, it was not just Power's exercise that predicted 7/7, but a whole range of exercises and a significant number of TV shows. Only days before 7/7 the Metropolitan Police ran an annual drill codenamed Hanover that was also based around triple tube bombings. The stations were Waterloo, Embankment and St James's Park, none of those attacked on 7/7, and it was a Command Post or tabletop drill. Likewise, the BBC reported that on the day of 7/7, 'there had actually been a security drill with armed officers entering the New York subway.'[20] All this establishes that this sort of attack scenario was one that the authorities were most keenly anticipating. With Power's connections to people in government, and his experience of being on the *London Under Attack* show, it is perhaps not that surprising that he chose the same kind of scenario for his own exercise. Was he simply a copycat, and thus an accidental patsy?

In the context of the predictive programming and the other pre-7/7 exercises, Power's exercise does not particularly stand out as being incredibly close to the official version of the real attacks, except that it took place on the very same day. According to Power, that was the choice of the client, Reed Elsevier, not himself. The frequency with which such drills were taking place does beg the question of how likely that is to happen, and the answer is certainly that they are more likely than the calculations of alternative conspiracy theorists have claimed.

So was Power the prepared, predicted, programmed suspect for the alternative conspiracy theorists in the same way as the four alleged Muslim suicide bombers were the prepared, predicted, programmed suspects for the official conspiracy theorists? If this is the case then several pieces of information do make more sense.

Power admitted to his involvement in the 7/7 exercise of his own accord, talking to both the BBC and ITV in live, unedited broadcasts that were seen and heard by hundreds of thousands if not millions of people. If he was involved in the attacks then this makes no sense, but if he suspected that he was being set up then it makes perfect sense. He would want the story out there in a way he could control rather than leave it to whoever one might suspect could have set him up to 'blow the whistle' on him.

Power has a curious past. In his time with the Metropolitan Police he turned up at a number of major events. He was the deputy forward controller at the Libyan embassy during the siege when WPC Yvonne Fletcher was shot in 1984. According to a 1996 edition of *Dispatches*, she was murdered not by Libyans, but by British and American intelligence agencies. A few months later, during a fire at Oxford Circus tube station, Peter Power just happened to be on the train at the time. He took control of the train, got on the tannoy and lied to the passengers saying that everything was fine, and then confronted the train's driver in an incident that resulted in the driver being knocked out. He eventually helped lead passengers to safety, resulting in him being labelled by the BBC 'the Pied Piper of the underground.'

Three years later and Power was involved in another major fire on the underground, this time at King's Cross. He was sent there to coordinate the emergency services and ran the forward command post for most of the evening. When he arrived at King's Cross a detective inspector, one Ian Blair, said to him, 'Peter, I think we've had a bomb explosion here. At least one of the casualties has metal deep inside him... but we're not going to go public on it.'[21] Ian Blair would of course later become Sir Ian Blair, and was Commissioner of the Met Police on 7/7.

Unsurprisingly, the BBC mentioned none of this when he appeared on *London Under Attack*. The details they provided were simply that he worked for the MPS from 1971-1992, was director of BET Group Security from 1992-94 and has worked for Visor Consultants from 1995-present. One of the many problems with this presentation of Power is that between 1990 and 1993 he was actually working for Dorset Police. He was suspended and became the subject of an internal inquiry, which did result in a file being submitted to the Director of Public Prosecutions. We do not know if charges were ever filed against Power and he left the Dorset force in the autumn of 1993.[22]

So we are presented with a question. Is this the profile of a man who would be recruited to play a central role in a false flag terrorist attack? He is a man with a questionable past and a curious habit of turning up in the middle of a crisis. He is a man who had been on a TV show that to a large extent predicted the 7/7 attacks over a year before they happened. By contrast, is it the profile of a man employed as a patsy, who wouldn't be trusted by inquiring minds because of the questions emerging from his past activities? It is not a question that we can answer easily.

Between Fact and Fantasy

What we can be sure of is how the exercises play much the same role as the predictive programming. Both forms of 'simulated terror' fill the space between the real, the fact that daily life in Britain is non-violent, and the virtual, the possibility of massive and horrifying violence. They bridge the gap between fact and fantasy, between reality and nightmares, they shape our expectations of what could happen, what will happen, and who will be responsible when something does happen.

The use of mock broadcasts – fake news – as part of these substantiates this interpretation. The *Panorama: London Under Attack* show, along with *Crisis Command*, made copious use of mocked-up news to lend credence to their simulations. Even the *Spooks* episode that featured a training drill included fake news reports being fed to the MI5 agents as part of the exercise.

Power's exercise on 7/7 also used fake news. In an interview in the Manchester Evening News the day after 7/7, Power commented that, 'Yesterday, we were actually in the City working on an exercise involving mock broadcasts when it happened for real. When the news bulletins started coming on, people began to say how realistic our exercise was – not realising that there really was an attack. We then became involved in a real crisis which we had to manage for the company.'[23]

In his 2008 statement Power revealed that the mock broadcasts used in his 7/7 exercise were taken from the *London Under Attack* programme. He wrote, 'The scenario developed for our client even started by using fictitious news items from the *Panorama* programme.' This explicitly ties the *London Under Attack* show to the exercise on the morning of 7/7, suggesting that Power himself may have been inspired by appearing on the show to choose the tube for the attack scenario for his 7/7 drill.

Further blurring the lines, the Atlantic Blue 'pseudo journalists' mixed both fictional and real news in order 'to drive player action accordingly.' CBRN News notes that, 'While the exercise took place, VBCNews made regular pseudo news updates on screens situated around the site, with real news being shown between pseudo broadcasts. This provided the feeling of round-the-clock coverage.'

In the American 'pseudo media' produced for Atlantic Blue/TOPOFF3 they did not just mix clips of fake news with clips of real news. In their 'pseudo news' coverage they included interviews with real-life officials and experts responding to the simulated attack. This included Vice Admiral David P. Pekoske of the US Coast Guard, intelligence analyst and terrorism expert Jeff Cozzens, and New Jersey Attorney General Peter Harvey. The fake news was presented by Forrest Sawyer, an anchorman for ABC and then NBC/MSNBC.

Two post-7/7 incidents demonstrate some of the problems caused by the use of simulated events and crisis management exercises in general. In December 2005 Clare Bowker was taking her daughter to appointment at Good Hope Hospital in Sutton Coldfield. She was stopped by security staff and made to prove her identity, and was told that a baby had been kidnapped from the hospital. It turned out to just be part of a security exercise but she was so upset and perturbed by being falsely told about a kidnapped baby that she suffered PTSD and eventually quit her job. In 2008 she was awarded a 'five figure sum' in compensation by the NHS trust.

In 2009, on the eighth anniversary of the 9/11 attacks, the US Coast Guard ran a counter-terrorism training exercise on the Potomac river in Washington DC. It was a live exercise, involving real boats and personnel, but was reported by CNN and other media outlets as a real attempted attack. They reported gunshots and played radio messages of the Coast Guard demanding that a suspicious boat leave a restricted area of the river. This caused immediate panic as people believed what they were seeing, leading to flights out of the nearby Reagan National Airport being suspended.

When it emerged that it was just an exercise and that the radio messages has been intercepted from a 'training frequency', CNN defended their reporting. White House Press Secretary Robert Gibbs said, 'before we report things like this, checking would be good.' CNN responded by admitting they had called the Coast Guard twice and received no confirmation of the incident. However, they claimed that, 'it would have been irresponsible not to report on what we were hearing and seeing.'[24]

The Potomac river incident shows how in filling the gap between the real and the virtual, simulated crises and in particular simulated terrorism blurs the lines between the real and the virtual. The importance of this is that this is one way that the public is kept in a near-perpetual state of fear, because they can get caught up in these simulations and think they are real terrifying events. Even for those that know that the drills are a fiction the simulations serve as reminders of the threats we supposedly face in this modern world of globalised terrorism.

It is clear, therefore, that the exercises have psychological impact similar in scale, scope and nature to the predictive programming of TV shows, films, books and other popular culture. The two phenomena occupy an almost identical psychological space, stem from similar aims and have essentially the same results. They do prepare us for possible future crises, but not in terms of physically dealing with them and knowing what action to take. Rather, they condition our mental states, our emotional and political responses to such events.

In this context the notion that the 7/7 exercise was a piece of psychological warfare or propaganda, designed to create a fake patsy for alternative conspiracy theorists, is not so outrageous. It is in keeping with the well-known and sometimes intended impact of such exercises on the minds of the public. The confusion caused by this blurring of the line between fact and fiction means that those who reject the official conspiracy theory are often looking for something that explains the event in a simple way. The 7/7 exercise has provides them with that, along with its concomitant alternative conspiracy theories. Amongst all the ridiculous statistics, historical comparisons, programming and predictions we should ask: was that the true aim of the 7/7 exercise?

Alert and not Alarmed

What we find in the training exercises run prior to 7/7, and the simulation run on the day of 7/7 itself, bears direct comparison with the predictive programming we examined in chapter 9. Just as the predictive programming firmly established the notion of Muslim suicide bombers staging an attack in Britain the training drills firmly established the notion of attacks on the London public transport network. In particular, the exact scenario of triple bombings on the tube came up repeatedly in these simulations.

Even more so than TV shows and films, the exercises explicitly seek to prepare people so that when disasters or terrorist atrocities happen that people respond and react in the desired way. The drills failed to adequately prepare the emergency service response to the real attacks on 7/7. They failed to identify and fix the long-running problem with radio communication systems. As such, we are left in the position of wondering what they purpose of these exercises really was.

The notion of these drills being a 'photo opportunity' was explored in *London Under Attack*, one of the TV shows that sit between fictional drama like *Spooks* and boots-on-the-ground drills like Osiris II or TOPOFF3. In these simulations there is an element of what computer security specialist and author Bruce Schneier called 'security theatre'. Indeed, the simulations do serve as a show of force, reinforcing the ideas that there is a huge threat from terrorists and that the state is ready to respond to whatever the terrorists might do. As such, they play the same role and have the same effect as the predictive programming and the 'intelligence failures' in consolidating the power of the National Security State.

This simulated terror occupies much the same psychological space as predictive programmes. It fills the gap between real life and apocalyptic nightmares about terrorist attacks. In occupying this space the programmes and simulations blur the line between the non-violent reality of life in the UK and the terrifying possibilities described by our political and institutional leaders.

One of the outcomes of this process is that it creates an artificial tension between the government and the mainstream media. The media predicts events and conditions people to respond in the desired way via predictive programming. The government predicts events and conditions people to respond in the desired way through the training exercises.

Perhaps ironically, both then blame the other for scaring the public. When the BBC made *London Under Attack* they sought the cooperation of the Home Office, but the government did not comply. They accused the BBC of making a show that was 'alarmist and irresponsible.' In turn, when the authorities carried out Exercise Horizon, the suicide bomber-poison gas simulation in Birmingham, they were criticised by the media for scaring the public.

It took three hours to begin decontaminating the 400 members of the public that were playing the victims of the mock attacks. According to the BBC, a press photographer covering the drill commented that, 'the coffee and cream cakes arrived before the emergency services.' As one of the public participants in the exercise put it, 'We felt we would have died while we waited for the emergency services.'[25]

There is an aspect of doublethink in this crisis management philosophy. Both the state and the mainstream media blame each other for fear mongering, for scaring the public witless with predictions of horrific scenarios. As we saw with the interaction between the BBC and the government in 2004 over *London Under Attack* and Exercise Horizon, they both made justifiable accusations against one another. Of course, the reality is that both are involved, to the extent of collusion and complicity with one another, in hyping the terrorist threat.

This is most clearly evidenced in the mock broadcasts used as part of these simulations. In the US real journalists and officials participated in the production of fake news as part of the TOPOFF3 exercise. In the British side of the same drill, Atlantic Blue, we see an even more complex mixing of fact and fantasy. The 'pseudo journalists' working for the government mixed mocked up news with real news, and fed this to exercise participants. As such, the mutual accusations of fear-mongering create a false or illusory tension between the two sets of institutions. This is perhaps a different kind of 'security theatre'.

There is also a tension, and an element of doublethink, in how the public are told we should react to the supposed great terrorist threat. Clearly we are supposed to be scared, otherwise the predictions of attacks would not be so frequent and the scenarios so apocalyptic. That said, they do want us to carry on going to work, paying taxes, buying products. As Helen Braithwaite, deputy director of the regional resilience team who planned Exercise Horizon, put it, 'Everyone is aware that the threat from international terrorism remains real and serious. But the public should remain alert and not alarmed.'[26]

This doublethink philosophy, where a contradiction is maintained at the heart of how we conceive of the terrorist threat and thus how we respond to it, is only further evidence that the established view of the exercise on 7/7 is questionable. Most commentators have accused Peter Power of somehow being involved in carrying out the attacks, and have tried to support this contention through recourse to ridiculous statistical arguments. The whole philosophy behind these preparatory exercises engages a kind of doublethink that causes tensions in the minds of the public.

Thus, it is not a huge leap to speculate that the purpose of the 7/7 exercise was likewise to generate a tension, a tension between rival conspiracy theories. For several years the focus of the alternative media and most researchers and activists has been trying to find ways to express their suspicion or beliefs about Power's possible involvement in the attacks. All that energy could have been spent backing the state into a corner over the untruths it has told about the attacks, the context in which they happened, and the terrorist threat. Maybe that was the point all along.

Chapter 11: Conspiracy Theories

Today, almost everyone is a conspiracy theorist. One of the more commonly believed conspiracy theories is that the majority of terrorist attacks are carried out covertly by the security services of different nations. This is what US Air Force commander David Beecroft called 'the conspiracy theory of terrorism' in his 1986 Masters thesis.

Beecroft explained that at that time there were two views of 'the conspiracy theory of terrorism': 'Viewpoint "A" of the conspiracy theory of terrorism is the viewpoint which espouses the involvement of the American government, the Central Intelligence Agency, and elite business interests in sponsoring and supporting terrorism throughout the world.' By contrast, 'Viewpoint "B" of the conspiracy theory of terrorism is the viewpoint which espouses the involvement of the Soviet Union, the KGB, and the Communist surrogates in sponsoring and supporting terrorism.'

In his thesis, Beecroft concluded that, 'Evidence exists supporting both the Viewpoint "A" and Viewpoint "B" of the conspiracy theory of terrorism.' But in our modern monopolar world system there is no Soviet Union and Warsaw Pact that 'balances' the US government and NATO. If we take the Soviets out of the equation because the Cold War has ended (or so they say), then what is left? Without the simple dualism of the Cold War how has this idea progressed into the 21st century?

Beecroft notes how, 'The proponents of the opposite views of conspiracy theory of terrorism are commonly thought to be at opposite ends of a terrorism continuum' but that, 'the opposite ends have several things in common.' In effect, he argues, the two viewpoints are very similar except that they identify different 'allies and enemies'.[1] Today, there are still two opposing viewpoints of terrorism, though the ground has shifted somewhat.

One group believes that the terrorist threat is real, that there are tens of thousands of highly organised political extremists just biding their time before they slaughter large numbers of random, innocent citizens. This is, of course, a conspiracy theory, where the conspirators are men like Ayman Zawahiri and previously Osama Bin Laden, inspiring and directing 'cells' of fanatics to carry out acts of murder. This group rarely acknowledges the reality of state sponsorship of terrorism, and when they do it is only Middle Eastern governments such as Iran, Saudi Arabia and Pakistan who are said to be involved in such dirty work.

Another group of people believe that the terrorist threat is essentially fictional, an excuse for imperialistic foreign wars and the advancement of the National Security State. This is also a conspiracy theory, at least for most of the people who believe it, but the conspirators are Western states, or at least their security services, and their allies within the Middle East and beyond. Just as during the Cold War, the two viewpoints are actually very similar except for the fact that they have opposing beliefs about who the conspirators behind terrorism really are.

The way this has impacted on the debates, discussions and investigations around 7/7 is critical to understanding how we can progress from where we are now to some kind of resolution. Most people believe one of two basic conspiracy theories about what happened that day. The first group, the majority, believe that the attacks were premeditated, intentional suicide bombings carried out by fanatical Muslims. The second group, a considerable minority, believe that the four Muslims were patsies and that the real perpetrators were some combination of security services.

There are other theories about what happened on 7/7, but all of them involve some kind of conspiracy. Almost no one believes that what happened that day happened by accident or by chance. Almost everyone believes that it happened as a result of deliberate, premeditated actions by one or another group of conspirators. Anyone who claims that their beliefs about 7/7 do not constitute a conspiracy theory either has a highly unusual take on the events, or is not being honest about the nature of their beliefs.

So, it is not just unemployed internet addicts who believe in conspiracy theories, it is practically everyone who has any firm opinion on such topics as terrorism. It is also anyone who has suspected their friend or neighbour of having an affair and anyone who believes that governments and corporations lie for private gain. We have to be honest with ourselves – we love the intrigue, and we embrace our capacity for suspicion and speculation in order to fill in the gaps in our knowledge. If this were not the case then the films of Alfred Hitchcock would not have been so popular, and no one would have cared about Watergate.

As the previous two chapters illustrated, our perceptions of the terrorist threat were shaped in the years immediately before 7/7 by two kinds of simulated terror: predictive TV programming, and crisis management training exercises. The conspiracy theories about 7/7, both official and alternative, did not spring from a vacuum.

Instead, they sprung from a context in which the notions of psychotic, suicidal Muslim terrorists, double agents, and exercises that turn into the real thing were being openly portrayed on the most popular conspiracy-oriented show on British television. They sprung from a context in which the scenario of the attacks had been repeatedly predicted and trained for by the people and agencies who then had to respond when the real attacks happened. This process, whereby simulated terrorism influenced the public discourse about real terrorism, did not stop when 7/7 happened. It continued for years afterwards.

Northstar V

On Sunday January 8th 2006, five months after 7/7, there was a full-scale multi-agency civil emergency training exercise in Singapore called Northstar V. This drill is run annually and involved around 2000 emergency service personnel, 500 mock victims and around 3400 ordinary commuters caught up in the action. The scenario chosen for the simulation was based on the real 7/7 attacks.

Northstar V was run between 6:25 and 9:30 a.m. and involved, 'thunderflashes, smoke and fire simulators', to give the appearance of simultaneous bombings on trains at four underground stations. Some time later an explosion blew up a double decker bus on its way into Toa Payoh Bus Interchange. There was also some kind of chemical attack at Raffles Place station, one of those that had been bombed earlier. They even used raw meat deposited near the mock victims to add a 'stench' of realism.

What was particularly concerning about this exercise is the way in which the public were involved whether they liked it or not. Posters were put up at stations in the days before, warning of a forthcoming drill. However, 'To further invoke a sense of realism, the date, time and exact details of the exercise were not released until 15 minutes before the exercise, after which announcements on the exercise were carried by local broadcast media. This was a deliberate move to better gauge and test the exercise participants, including the train commuters who were either in the trains or MRT stations when the exercise started.'[2]

As Channel News Asia reported, this meant that thousands of commuters 'were told of the exercise only minutes before it started.' In an interview Singapore Prime Minister Lee Hsien Loong spoke of, 'The public, which must be psychologically prepared, remain calm, take instructions, react rationally, go about their business.' Footage of the fake bombed out bus in the Channel News Asia reports bears a startling resemblance to the bus blown up on 7/7.

There was even a mocked-up arrest of a 'suicide bomber' at Raffles Place station. Watching the news footage it becomes obvious that this was a purely psychological, theatrical element of the drill. The 'suicide bomber' in question was just an ordinary Singaporean presumably hired as part of the simulation. They were not wearing a fake bomb, a suicide vest, a bag or backpack of any kind. The police simply wrestled them to the ground and handcuffed them, which is not how they would really handle a suicide bomber.

This links the Northstar V exercise to the Atlantic Blue/TOPOFF3 drill, and in a slightly tangential way to *Spooks* and *Dirty War* and their portrayal of suicide bombers. It serves no physical training purpose to have the police arrest someone playing the role of a suicide bomber in such an unrealistic way. The only thing it does is to reinforce the notion that these sorts of attack on public transport systems are done by suicide bombers. That the 'arrest' was shown on the nightly news illustrates how the target and aim of that part of the exercise was public perception.

One of the commuters caught up in the drill was a hotel worker named Hari Chandra. He told Channel News Asia that his first reaction was, 'I think it's real.'[3] Another commuter interviewed by Straits Times TV said, 'I thought something happened, I mean it's a bit... I feel scared at first so I don't know what happened because I read the newspaper that today they were having some exercise but I do not know where.'[4]

So we see the same process, whereby reality and simulation are blurred together as a means of psychologically influencing the public, after 7/7 as we did before 7/7. In another interview with Channel News Asia Prime Minister Lee said, 'In a real incident, there is of course the public response and the political response. The government will have to come out, the PM and the ministers will have to come out and explain what has happened and calm people and re-assure people that everything is under control and what can be done is being done.'[5]

This comment illustrates the same tension, the same doublethink that was discussed in the previous chapter. The officials in Singapore used the exercise to remind people of the terrorist threat, and to reinforce the notion that Singapore could, like London, suffer an attack from 'suicide bombers'. At the same time though they want people to be reassured that the National Security State is ultimately in control, that 'what can be done is being done.'

It is perhaps significant that Northstar V included observers not just from the 22 participating local agencies, but also Chief Constable Ian Johnston from the British Metropolitan Police. Johnston told

Channel News Asia, 'What is interesting about yours is that you have actually involved the commuters on the line. It is a really interesting initiative and that is something we did not use and will give you some insights into how people actually feel during these events.'[6]

Shooting *Spooks*

Back in Britain the makers of *Spooks* were clearly inspired by the 7/7 attacks. Having predicted the attacks, and helped encourage both the official and alternative conspiracy theories about the attacks, they featured aspects of these conspiracy theories in their post-7/7 shows. The fourth season was still in production when 7/7 happened and aside from the opening two episodes, discussed in the previous chapters, there is some tangentially relevant material.

The sixth episode of series four focuses on a Muslim man who MI5 suspect is a terrorist coordinator, and who has been imprisoned without charge for a number of years. They have him released from prison so they can monitor him more closely, and send in a spy to pose as PR agent pretending to be motivated by the injustice he has suffered. It turns out that he is in fact completely innocent and that another man with the same name has been shot dead by French Special Forces.

The man MI5 have been watching turns out to be an Algerian illegal immigrant who is terrified that he and his family will be tortured or killed if he returns home. Terrorists kidnap the man's family and blackmail him to carry out an assassination, but at the last moment MI5 rescue the family and prevent him from shooting the target. The family are reunited and sent off to make a new life in Ireland.[7]

As such, while this is one of few episodes where the apparatus of the National Security State is shown to be at fault, ultimately the story is resolved satisfactorily, unlike in the real world. The message appears to be that even though occasionally the state gets it wrong, it only does so in the name of protecting us from all these dastardly Muslims who want to murder us. Indeed, the real terrorists in the show are, of course, Muslims, and their motives are never explored or explained. They are simply Muslims who want to kill us.

As such, when they are shot dead at the climax of the show they have been completely dehumanised, we feel nothing for them and don't care that they've been killed. To be sure they were guilty of kidnap, blackmail and attempted murder but that is hardly a justification for their brutal summary executions. Again, the message appears to be that the state has to meet force with greater force.

Two memes in combination in this episode bear closer consideration. An innocent man is mistakenly thought to be a terrorist and this leads to a summary execution. This is basically the story of Jean Charles de Menezes, who was supposedly mistaken for Hussain Osman, one of the men involved in the 21/7 incidents. Even though Menezes did not look much like Osman, he was followed by security service personnel into Stockwell underground station and shot dead on a train.

That afternoon several eyewitnesses, including one highly suspicious man going by the name Mark Whitby, appeared on news broadcasts giving demonstrably false testimony about Menezes' behaviour in the minutes before his death. Even a *Panorama* reconstruction of the shooting got basic facts wrong, such as showing Menezes running through the station and onto the tube train. The police doctored photos to try to make Menezes look more like Hussain Osman, and lies were told about the CCTV footage from the station.

Ultimately, at Menezes' inquest the jury were told they could not return a verdict of unlawful killing, they either had to say the killing was lawful, or record an open verdict. To their credit they refused to conclude that the killing was lawful, but an open verdict does not do justice to what happened. If it is not unlawful for the authorities to shoot dead an innocent man, and then lie about the circumstances in which it happened, then our security services can literally get away with murder. It makes no difference, at least morally, if they intended to kill that particular man or intended to kill someone else.

It is unclear whether the *Spooks* episode that reflected the story of Menezes' murder was written before or after his killing, so we cannot know whether they predicted the event or were inspired by it. Nonetheless, there was a repetitive use of the same trope of a Muslim terrorist being shot dead in other episodes that were definitely prior to the Menezes killing. Thus, *Spooks* helped normalise the idea of summary executions being carried out by the security services years well before the events of July 22nd 2005.

It is also interesting to note that the other great British conspiracy theory of recent years – that Princess Diana was assassinated by the security services – was also woven into the fourth season of *Spooks*. In the final episode of the season a former MI5 officer of some renown is traumatised when her lover commits suicide. He was a former Royal protection officer who was driven to killing himself by the belief that Diana was murdered in Paris in 1997.

The former MI5 officer bluffs her way into Thames House and using a pretend bomb in a handbag blackmails the spooks into reinvestigating Diana's death. She demands to know how Diana was assassinated. The spooks then patch together a conspiracy theory and feed it to her, before discovering that there never was a real bomb. In a very tacked-on twist at the end of the episode it turns out that the whole stunt was a bluff to enable the ex-MI5 officer to attempt an assassination attempt on the Royal family, which is then foiled.[8]

The message of this episode appears to be that Diana was not assassinated and that the real danger is that a nutty conspiracy theorist might have a pop at the Royal family out of some sense of revenge. The show's makers employed a very popular conspiracy theory only in order to try to debunk it and to portray people who believe in it as lunatics. This rather naked and obvious method of exploiting the Princess Diana conspiracy theory was paralleled in the way *Spooks* exploited 7/7 conspiracy theories in the aftermath of the attacks.

Spooks Season Five

While Season Four only dealt with the events of July 2005 in a comparatively tangential way to previous seasons, the fifth series went into fifth gear in its exploration of 7/7 conspiracy theories. Just like season four, season five began with a two-part special, broadcast just after the anniversary of 9/11. Clearly that is the preferred time of year to run a series that is so clearly inspired by the conspiracy culture.

The two-part special featured an attempted coup d'etat in Britain using false flag terrorism. The coup attempt is carried out by the head of MI6, the Cabinet Secretary, a tabloid newspaper mogul and an oil company executive. A terror campaign begins with the bombing of an oil depot, closely followed by the apparent outbreak of a plague that makes people weep blood before they die.

These attacks are blamed on Al Qaeda but in reality it is the coup faction who are behind them. They are used as a pretext to try to get the Prime Minister to sign emergency legislation that would effectively turn Britain into a dictatorship. A third major attack in planned by the conspirators that involves hacking the air traffic control system and causing a mid-air collision over London.

MI5 avert the plane crash at the last moment and by the end of the second episode in the special they manage to dismantle the entire coup plot. Nonetheless, the notion of a coup faction carrying out false flag terrorism and blaming it on Al Qaeda in order to strengthen the

National Security State was presented in all its glory. Aside from those who focus on the Peter Power exercise, this conspiracy theory is perhaps the most popular alternative view of 7/7.[9]

The first episode after the two-part season opener also explored ideas that make up elements of alternative 7/7 conspiracy theories. An Al Qaeda mastermind is running a cell of terrorists in London, one member of which is the Muslim MI5 officer. The episode opens with the terrorist mastermind shooting an innocent man dead in front of the cell in an attempt to flush out infiltrators. The MI5 officer makes a brief attempt to prevent the killing, but ultimately lets the man die.

It emerges that the Al Qaeda cell is trying to obtain a thermobaric bomb, for use in an attack on London. MI5 decide to try to buy the bomb themselves before Al Qaeda can get their hands on it, because, as one spook puts it, 'You don't make a thermobaric bomb with nail polish remover and a rucksack, there's only one or two of them floating around out there, and just a couple of dealers who are big enough to shift one.'[10] This is an obvious reference to the official version of 7/7, which involves rucksack bombs made using organic peroxide.

In the episode we are shown the bomb in transit from Uzbekistan to the UK, in much the same way as the dirty bomb material is shown in *Dirty War*. In *Spooks*, MI5 fail to acquire the bomb but succeed in turning and recruiting a member of the terrorist cell. He and the undercover MI5 officer are given the job of driving the bomb to its target in central London. They are told that the bomb is on a timer to enable them to get away, but this is a lie, and it emerges that the bomb is to be detonated by remote.

As such, the two drivers are unwilling suicide bombers, who know they are carrying a bomb but not that they will be killed when it goes off. This does not just suggest a particular theory of the 7/7 attacks, it also plays on the notion of the IRA 'human bombs' as discussed in chapter 9. In *Spooks* the terrorist in control of the remote detonator is shot dead by Special Forces, even though they are unsure if they have targeted the right man.

What we can take from this is that in their first episodes of *Spooks* written after 7/7, the show's makers suggested that the attack were either sponsored by the state in some form of a coup, and that the alleged bombers were betrayed by an Al Qaeda mastermind. You might have thought that this was enough 7/7-related conspiracy theorising for one season of one show, but they didn't stop then.

The fifth season also included another two-part special in episodes six and seven. The storyline is that Britain is negotiating a deal to sell nuclear energy technology to Saudi Arabia. Meanwhile, a group of highly-trained terrorists get into the UK by murdering a guard at a port. MI5 assume they are Muslim suicide bombers looking to cause an atrocity and scupper the nuclear technology deal.

The story then undertakes a lengthy diversion where the Saudi princes negotiating the deal are shown according to the full racist stereotype of oil-soaked and sex-obsessed Arabs. Parallel with this we are shown a meeting between the senior member of the terrorists and a mole, an MI6 agent who is involved with the MI5 operation to stop the terrorists. The mole hands over a copy of the terrorist watchlist to the senior terrorist and tells him to use people who are close to MI5 informants for a distraction operation, so that MI5 will find out about it but not realise that it is a distraction.

The senior terrorist then meets with one of the targets on the watchlist, who goes by the name Hasan Khan. They have a conversation where many of the phrases are lifted directly from the 'martyrdom video' of alleged 7/7 ringleader Sidique Khan. These lines include, 'our words are dead until we give them life with our blood', and 'we are at war, and I am a soldier'. It emerges that the distraction operation involves four Muslim suicide bombers, though they are given fake explosives. MI5 find out about the operation but think it is a real attack, leading them to shoot dead one of the fake suicide bombers before realising the 'explosives' are just putty.

This serves as a diversion, enabling the real terrorists to take over the Saudi 'trade centre', taking the negotiators and their guests hostage. In a repeat of the embassy-hostage story in series one, MI5 just happen to have a female officer inside the 'trade centre' at the time. The terrorists send out a transmission identifying themselves as Al Qaeda, and demanding the release of prisoners.

In a dramatic twist it emerges that the terrorists are not Al Qaeda, but in fact are Israelis working for the Mossad pretending to be Al Qaeda, who are trying to disrupt the nuclear deal for their own purposes. MI5 discover the mole within their ranks, though he kills himself just as they realise who he is. Special Forces break into the trade center and shoot most of the terrorists, but the truth about who was responsible for the attack is covered up. So, not content with blaming an internal British coup faction and an Al Qaeda mastermind for 7/7, *Spooks* quickly moved on to blaming the Mossad.[11]

Spooks Season Six

This process of exploring alternative conspiracy theories about 7/7 continued into season six, which also began with a two-part special. The entire series was focused on the possibility of war with Iran, which in 2007 was, as now, a major topic of foreign policy discussions. In the first episode of the new series MI5 are tricked into thinking that an Iranian intelligence agent is on his way to London to carry out an attack. They decide to try to assassinate him before he even leaves Iran.

The sole Muslim MI5 officer is given a bomb which he plants under the train that the Iranian agent is due to catch the following morning. He then detonates it by remote, killing dozens of innocent people. That afternoon he discusses his reservations about the bombing with his spook supervisor, who tells him, 'I know it was a difficult call, *the point of the operation was to fabricate an inside job*, make it look like Iranian spies killing Iranian spies.'[12]

A couple of episodes later the same extremist from the 'unwilling suicide bomber' episode has become a fully-fledged MI5 informant. He once again accepts a mission to be a driver for an Al Qaeda terrorist mastermind, having obviously failed to learn from his previous appearance in the show. This time he doesn't even realise that the car is carrying a bomb, making him an 'unwitting suicide bomber'. The target is the Iranian Special Consul, but at the last moment MI5 save the day and no one is killed when the bomb goes off.[13]

This episode broadcast on October 30th 2007. Only days later, on November 5th an online film called *7/7 Ripple Effect* was released. It did not discuss any of the evidence analysed in the latter two sections of this book, though much of it was available at the time. Instead the film tried to construct an alternative narrative of 7/7 based purely on media reports of the events of the day itself.

This is an extremely problematic approach because it overlooks vast quantities of high quality evidence. Almost all of the information available from the day itself has come to us through the mainstream media and as detailed in chapter 1 their reporting was contradictory to say the least. *7/7 Ripple Effect* simply cherry-picked and quote-mined its way to an alternative narrative, ignoring all media reports and other evidence to the contrary of its desired conspiracy theory. In that respect it is very similar to the Home Office narrative.

7/7 Ripple Effect's story was that the four alleged bombers were recruited as part of Peter Power's training exercise, and thought they were just playing the role of terrorists. There is no evidence that any of the four alleged bombers met with Power or had any connection with the exercise, but despite this a lot of people simply took this theory as the truth. The film goes on to claim that the bombs on the tube were planted under the train, a possibility raised by certain witness statements. It concludes that MI5 and/or the Mossad were actually to blame, citing a report of an apparent warning sent to Benjamin Netanyahu on the morning of the attacks.

Netanyahu was in London for a conference on the morning of 7/7 and his hotel was not far from Liverpool Street station. This story of a warning was initially reported by the Associated Press, though they pulled their report only hours after posting it. WTQV, a local ABC affiliate, reported that, 'Just before the first blast, Netanyahu got a call from the Israeli Embassy telling him to stay in his hotel room. The hotel is located next to the subway station where the first attack occurred and he did stay put and shortly after that, there was the explosion.'[14]

Israeli newspaper Arutz Sheva also reported on the story, saying that, 'Scotland Yard had intelligence warnings of the attacks a short time before they occurred. The Israeli Embassy in London was notified in advance, resulting in Finance Minister Binyamin Netanyahu remaining in his hotel room.'[15] Ynet News likewise said that, 'the Mossad office in London received advance notice about the attacks, but only six minutes before the first blast.'[16]

An article by private intelligence firm Stratfor posted on the evening of the attacks contradicts these stories in two key aspects. First, it says that it was the Israelis who warned the British authorities, not the other way around, and second it says that the warning came days before 7/7, not on the morning of the attacks. The article says, 'Contrary to original claims that Israel was warned "minutes before" the first attack, unconfirmed rumors in intelligence circles indicate that the Israeli government actually warned London of the attacks "a couple of days" previous.'[17]

Whether or not there even was a warning is not certain, let alone when it was sent, by which agency and to which agency. Nonetheless, *7/7 Ripple Effect* assumes that there was a warning sent to Netanyahu on the morning of 7/7 and asks, 'Was the London bombing a covert MI5 operation, or an Israeli Mossad operation, or a joint operation by both of them?'[18] This was not just an example of cherry-picking news sources to try to establish a culprit, but it also picks up on the very theories explored in episodes of *Spooks*. The fundamental ideas that make up the alternative conspiracy theory provided by *7/7 Ripple Effect* had all appeared in episodes of *Spooks* prior to the release of the film. Exercises coinciding with real attacks, fake suicide bombers,

MI5 planting a bomb under a train, Israel taking part in a false flag attack – all were the subject of storylines put out by the BBC.

Spooks Season Seven and 21/7

Almost exactly a year later the show returned to a 7/7-inspired storyline. A member of Pakistani military intelligence warns MI5 of a forthcoming attack that will begin with a 'waterfall' of internet chatter about an attack. He says that this will be followed by one team of practice suicide bombers doing a dry run, and then a second team will come in and carry out the actual attack.

Once again, MI5 have an agent within the 'dry run' team, played by Alex Lanipekun, the third actor to take on the token ethnic minority MI5 agent role in the show. He is chosen as one of the practice bombers and the four are given sports bags. The agent realises that he is carrying a live bomb, and that it is not a dry run but the real attack. The bombs are actually set up to be detonated by remote, in a repeat of the 'unwitting suicide bomber' scenario.

This causes chaos on the streets of London as MI5 track the bombers and try to stop them. Two bombs are defused, and one of the bombers is shot dead by armed police, before one bomb goes off, killing two policemen. The man MI5 thought was the mastermind of the operation turns out to be a decoy, with the actual mastermind being the Pakistani intelligence officer. His family had been kidnapped by terrorists who blackmailed him into double-crossing MI5.[19]

This particular episode, where there are supposedly two teams of suicide bombers, one a practice cell and then the real thing, is probably an allusion to the incidents of 21/7. On that day, exactly two weeks after 7/7, four men set off devices in rucksacks on three underground trains and a bus in London. A fifth man dumped his rucksack device in a park.

That evening, the Abu Hafs Al-Masri brigade posted a claim of responsibility for the 'attempted bombings' on the internet. The same group had also claimed responsibility for 7/7, the 3/11 bombings in Madrid, the 2003 electricity blackouts in North America, and the 2003 bombings in Istanbul. The group doesn't actually exist, except as an entity that claims responsibility for things, but this fuelled the suspicion that there was some link between 7/7 and 21/7.

The four 'attempted suicide bombers' Muktar Said Ibrahim, Yassin Omar, Ramzi Mohammed and Hussein Osman were quickly rounded up and arrested. The fifth man who dumped his rucksack in the park, Manfo Asiedu and a sixth supposed co-conspirator, Adel Yahya, were also arrested. All of them except Asiedu were from East Africa. The authorities did not stop there. They also arrested dozens of other people who knew the six alleged conspirators, several of which are now serving lengthy prison sentences for sheltering fugitives or failing to come forward with information.

The five main 'bombing' suspects went on trial in 2007. They were prosecuted for conspiracy to cause explosions and conspiracy to murder, rather than under terrorism legislation. A further charge of conspiracy to cause explosions likely to endanger life was left off the indictment. The men's defence was that their actions were never intended as real bombings, but were some kind of protest or stunt in opposition to the Iraq war. Muktar Ibrahim, who constructed the devices, said that he carried out tests to make sure they would only making popping noises and not actually explode. Indeed, that is exactly what the devices did, suggesting that either Ibrahim is telling the truth or that he is a very poor bomb-maker.

The prosecution team showed videos of mock-ups of the devices made by explosives experts at Porton Down. To be sure, the devices in the videos exploded, but an explosives expert for the defence explained that the devices used on 21/7 were not capable of exploding. A presentation by Professor Hans Michels said that, 'Is there any conclusive scientific or technical evidence related to an intentional major explosive objective? None that I have been able to identify.'[20] Indeed the mixture of the 'main explosive charge' was hydrogen peroxide and chapatti flour, a unique recipe in the history of bomb-making. If it had been Ibrahim's intention to make a viable explosive device then why did he not use a more conventional, tried and tested recipe?

The 'hoax' defence was undermined by two of the suspects. Manfo Asiedu, who had dumped his backpack in a park, maintained at trial that he thought that it was supposed to be a stunt but that he found out on the morning of 21/7 that they were to be real suicide bombers. This 'cut throat' defence led to him being separated from the other suspects in the dock. Another defendant, Hussein Osman, maintained the 'hoax' defence until very late on the trial, but shortly before the jury were sent out he apparently reversed his testimony. He was reportedly taken ill overnight while in custody, and made a confession to a prison guard. However, this confession was never subject to any kind of cross-examination in the court.

Perhaps unsurprisingly, four of the six defendants were found guilty. Muktar Ibrahim, Yassin Omar, Hussein Osman and Ramzi Mohammed were given 40-year prison sentences. Regarding Manfo

Asiedu the jury could not come to a verdict. Shortly before his retrial was due to begin Asiedu pleaded guilty to conspiracy to cause explosions, in return for the conspiracy to murder charge being dropped. Adel Yahya, who wasn't even in London at the time of 21/7, was accused of sourcing the ingredients for the devices. He pleaded guilty to the lesser charge of collecting information useful to a person committing or preparing an act of terrorism.

At the sentencing of the four main suspects the judge Mr Justice Fulford said, 'What happened on July 7th in 2005 is of considerable relevance, These were not truly isolated events. On the contrary, they were to an extent co-ordinated and connected. I have no doubt that they were both part of an Al Qaeda-controlled and inspired sequence of incidents.' On what basis did Fulford make this claim?

There is no evidence of any direct connection between the two sets of events. That is not to say that lawyers at the trial and the mainstream media did not try to make a connection. Indeed, Asiedu's lawyer Stephen Kamlish QC said that he had documents proving that Muktar Ibrahim was in Pakistan at the same time as Shehzad Tanweer and Mohammad Sidique Khan. Kamlish asked Ibrahim, 'Has there been any discussion between you and them on how to make effective bombs to start a bombing campaign in this country, the first of which was 7/7, the second of which was going to be 21/7?' Ibrahim replied, 'No.'[21]

Indeed, it is only if one accepts the official version of 7/7 and the official culprits, i.e. Muslim suicide bombers, and assume that 21/7 was intended to be a suicide bombing attack that there is a parallel to be drawn between the two. That said, two figures in the 21/7 plot do raise similar questions to certain figures in the 7/7 story.

Manfo Asiedu offered the cut-throat defence that the plot was intended to be a real attack but that he backed out once he realised this. This defence helped to convict his co-defendants. However, Manfo Asiedu is apparently not his real name, as he came from Ghana to the UK in 2003 on a passport bearing the name 'George Nanak Marquaye'. Prosecutors at the trial claimed that in fact he is 'Sumaila Abubakari'. Exactly who the man was who stood trial and claimed that 21/7 was supposed to be a real coordinated suicide bombings attack is not clear.

'Asiedu' apparently gave himself up to the police voluntarily, though the exact circumstances of his arrest are subject to much contradictory reporting. If this is true, then we should wonder if there is an element of Junaid Babar about him. It may be significant that after coming to the UK he tried to join the British Army, but, at least officially, was turned down because he was an illegal immigrant. The Army apparently made no attempt to tell the relevant authorities and have him deported, they just turned him down.

Even after he was found guilty, officials were still accusing him of having woven a web of deceit. Adding to the suspicion that all is not quite right with this story, a Ghanaian news article that apparently interviewed his parents described how they had been invited to London by the British security services. His father said that he went to the UK and was told by the security services to try to get his son to confess to his role in the plot.[22]

The other somewhat spooky character in this story is Siraj Yassin Abdullah Ali. He was convicted in 2008 of having helped the 21/7 suspects evade capture and of having prior knowledge of the plot but not telling the authorities. He was given a sentence of twelve years but like Junaid Babar only served four and a half before being let out of jail. Was he some kind of informant, or just one of several people jailed for getting swept up in this bizarre and unresolved event?

It does raise the possibility that these were in fact mock bombings, orchestrated to help sell the official conspiracy theory of 7/7. Almost immediately after 21/7, CCTV footage was released of the 21/7 suspects on the trains and bus, and a manhunt ensued. By contrast, very little CCTV has been made available of the 7/7 bombings, and most of it took years to be released. Many people believe they have seen CCTV from 7/7 that officially does not exist, and cannot exist due to supposed technical failures. The most likely explanation for that they are mistaking the 21/7 CCTV footage for 7/7 CCTV footage.

The *Spooks* episode in which they are supposedly two teams, one a practice cell and one a real suicide bomber cell, reinforced the connection between the two events. It is clear from Justice Fulford's statements that the authorities want us to see a connection, and it is only because of Asiedu's strange cut-throat defence that a connection was made at the 21/7 trial. Is this all an attempt to make out that both sets of events were part of the same conspiracy? Are we looking at an attempt to amalgamate two official conspiracy theories into one?

Just Fiction?

The conventional discussion in the mainstream media about conspiracy theories is that they are just wacky beliefs held by a fringe minority mostly composed of bored people without enough to do with their lives. What this discussion carefully ignores is that conspiracy theories are a common part of politics and everyday life. Indeed, the state is the biggest conspiracy theorist of all.

It is the state that tells us that four suicidal Muslim fanatics conspired to carry out 7/7. It is the state that told us that nineteen suicidal Muslim fanatics conspired with Khalid Sheikh Mohammed and Osama Bin Laden to carry out 9/11. It is the state that tells us that there is, or was, a global network of suicidal Muslim fanatics called Al Qaeda who are hell bent on trying to kill as many people as possible. It is the state that told us that Al Qaeda were collaborating with Saddam Hussain's government in devilish pact to deliver a CBRN-WMD attack on a major Western city.

Likewise, the mainstream media are the biggest propagators of these official conspiracy theories. The state has published a handful of reports on 7/7, 9/11 and Iraq's WMD but the mainstream media ensure that millions of people hear or read the salient points of the official conspiracy theories over and over again. Herein lies a key lesson from the previous two chapters, in particular chapter 9 on predictive programming: conspiracy theories are a part of mainstream politics and mainstream culture.

It is not just official conspiracy theories that the mainstream media shows an obvious willingness to help propagate. It is also unofficial conspiracy theories. The boundaries of the entire discussion about 7/7, official and alternative, have been delineated by the mainstream media. Nowhere else have the possibilities of unwitting or unwilling suicide bombers been given so much exposure. Nowhere else has the possibility of MI5 appearing to have an agent inside every Muslim terrorist cell in Britain been explored so thoroughly. Perhaps crucially, nowhere else have these theories been seen by so many people. Whatever the accomplishments of those in the alternative media in obtaining and distributing important information about 7/7, the simple fact is that more people watched *Spooks* and similar programmes.

Despite this, there are those who will say that the security services don't really do these sorts of things, that they don't have a license to kill like James Bond, in short, that these shows are *just fiction*. In turn, this means that the sorts of conspiracy theories portrayed and advanced by such shows must also be just fiction. The fact of it being fictional entertainment helps to reinforce the divide into two opposing camps, those that believe the official conspiracy theory and those who believe an alternative conspiracy theory.

For those prone to believing that the state would never be involved in terrorism against its own citizens they will see these ideas as fantasies, the stuff of television entertainment programmes. For those prone to thinking that the state was involved in 7/7 these television programmes provide a validation of their suspicions without providing any additional evidence about the attacks. Thus, both the official and unofficial conspiracy theories are advanced by such shows, as is the forming of the dialogue into one where opposing conspiracy theories battle for supremacy.

Indeed, the argument that the Bond films and *Spooks* are just fiction was made, repeatedly, in a 2012 BBC documentary called *Modern Spies*. It was the first ever show to feature interviews with currently serving members of MI5 and MI6, though their identities were obscured. The slow reveal, the striptease of information about the security services, is clearly a BBC specialty.

Modern Spies broached the topic of whether the British security services are involved in assassinations and torture, but not whether they are involved in terrorism. 7/7 was only briefly mentioned as being a possible 'intelligence failure'. Far more often the show referred to *Spooks* and the James Bond films as mere fiction, in contrast to the much more staid and boring activities of the security services in reality. The very argument provoked by *Spooks* was reinforced in a documentary by the same broadcaster only months after the last episode of *Spooks* was broadcast.

DEMOScracy

There is, perhaps, an even more overt way in which this dissection of the public into two opposing camps has been deliberately provoked and encouraged. In 2010 the thinktank DEMOS published a report called *The Power of Unreason*. It followed on from several essays and a book by an American author called Cass Sunstein, who is now an advisor to President Obama. DEMOS, for their part, had a lot of influence over the New Labour government in the UK.

The thesis running through the work of DEMOS and Sunstein is that conspiracy theories are powerful but irrational beliefs that inspire political radicalism, extremism and even terrorism. In 2008 Sunstein wrote that, 'The point about quasi-beliefs suggests that many do not in fact take any action on the basis of their mistaken beliefs. However, this does not at all entail that conspiracy theories are inconsequential. Even if only a small fraction of adherents to a particular conspiracy theory act on the basis of their beliefs, that small fraction may be enough to cause serious harms. Consider the Oklahoma City bombing, whose perpetrators shared a complex of conspiratorial beliefs about the federal government. Many who shared their beliefs did not act on them, but a few actors did, with terrifying consequences.'[23]

The argument here is both circular and self-contradictory. It is self-contradictory because it sidesteps the question of the official story of the OKC bombing being a conspiracy theory, just like the official stories of 7/7, 9/11 and other similar events. It assumes that the official conspiracy theory about the OKC bombing is true in order to claim that the official perpetrators carried out the atrocity because they believed in conspiracy theories. Thus, it advances a conspiracy theory in order to decry belief in conspiracy theories, a straightforward and utter contradiction.

The argument is circular because it presumes the perpetrators of the OKC bombing were actually Timothy McVeigh and Terry Nichols. It is only if this is true, i.e. only if the official conspiracy theory is true, that the argument that might have been inspired by belief in conspiracy theories has any relevance. After all, if McVeigh and Nichols were not the perpetrators, or there were additional perpetrators, i.e. if there was a larger conspiracy than the official theory says, then the conclusion not only doesn't follow from the premises, it actually contradicts them. One cannot legitimately criticise alternative conspiracy theorists as potential terrorists and use as your example a terrorist attack where the alternative conspiracy theory might actually be true.

The 2010 DEMOS report elaborated on the same hypothesis, employing the same logical fallacies in making much the same argument. Its authors, Jamie Bartlett and Carl Miller, wrote, 'Our analysis shows that conspiracy theories are widely prevalent across this extremist spectrum, despite the vast differences in the extremist ideologies themselves... The frequency of conspiracy theories within all these groups suggests that they play an important social and functional role within extremism itself.'[24]

The argument in both papers is that conspiracy theories are a dangerous threat because they might inspire terrorists. This is basically the same argument that the Home Office narrative of 7/7 implies, listing in a section about the alleged bombers' motives, 'Conspiracy theories also abounded, at least some of the bombers seem to have expressed the view that the 9/11 attacks were a plot by the US.'[25] The authors of all three reports use the same circular and contradictory reasoning that doesn't call official conspiracy theories 'conspiracy theories', and assumes that official conspiracy theories are always true.

The DEMOS report in particular is almost unbelievably bad. It says, as a qualifying remark for its overall argument, 'This does not mean that conspiracy theories are the proximate cause of extremism or violence. There are many extremist groups that do not believe conspiracy theories as far as we can tell, such as the Real IRA or the Unabomber.' The Real IRA was formed because it saw the Good Friday Agreement as nothing more than a repeat of the 1921 treaty that partitioned Ireland in the first place.

In a 2003 statement they said that, 'the Agreement was falsely presented to the people as 'the only show in town'...We regard the implementation of the Belfast Agreement and the full participation of the Provisional Movement in that process as a classic example of a successful counter-insurgency strategy practiced on the part of the British and Dublin Governments.' The statement goes on to say that, 'We believe that the Unionist community are also the victims of British imperial and colonial history. It has to be borne in mind that they were used by the British in the past, armed and financed by them, to play the role of the colonial garrison. We hold the British Government to be the guilty party in this manipulative scenario.'[26]

This notion that the British government was manipulative, that the Good Friday Agreement was a deliberate deceit as part of a counter-insurgency strategy, that the Unionists were just British proxies in a dirty war – is this not a conspiracy theory? Is this not citing a specific group or body, the British government, as a lying, manipulative force for evil? Is this not the interpretation of specific events as being part of an overarching, disguised agenda? This suggestion that the Real IRA did not believe in conspiracy theories is a weak argument, based on an equivocating definition of what qualifies as a conspiracy theory.

Demonstrating a similar lack of consistency in their research and analysis, they discussed what they saw as extremist groups who were 'not quite' conspiracy theorists. DEMOS discussed the case of Philadelphia-based black liberation organization MOVE, writing that, 'There are other examples of ideas that revolve around accusations, half-truths and myths but are not quite conspiracy theories. For example, MOVE – an anarcho-primitivist group involved in a police shooting in 1985 in the United States – spoke of government corruption and blamed all the world's ills on technology.'[27]

This presentation of the MOVE story is astoundingly inaccurate. Several members of the commune were involved in a shootout where a police officer was killed, but that was in 1978, not 1985. Entirely omitted from the DEMOS version is the fact that the MOVE commune was subjected to a horrific siege by Philadelphia police in 1985. Tear gas canisters were hurled in, the house was drenched with water cannons, thousands of rounds were fired at the building and then a helicopter dropped a C-4 bomb on top of them. This killed eleven people including five children, and caused fire and destruction that ultimately consumed 65 houses.

So, rather than see MOVE's talk about government corruption as the predictable result of the police violence against them, DEMOS described them as extremists and 'not quite' conspiracy theorists. According to Bartlett and Lewis, being suspicious of the government after a government agency has committed a vicious attack against you is a 'half truth' or 'myth', and you are an extremist.

Infiltration and Dogma

Having defined belief in (alternative) conspiracy theories as a threat both Sunstein and DEMOS had the same answer to the question of what should be done about this threat. Sunstein wrote,

> 'What can government do about conspiracy theories? Among the things it can do, what should it do? We can readily imagine a series of possible responses. (1) Government might ban conspiracy theorizing. (2) Government might impose some kind of tax, financial or otherwise, on those who disseminate such theories. (3) Government might itself engage in counterspeech, marshaling arguments to discredit conspiracy theories. (4) Government might formally hire credible private parties to engage in counterspeech. (5) Government might engage in informal communication with such parties, encouraging them to help. Each instrument has a distinctive set of potential effects, or costs and benefits, and each will have a place under imaginable conditions. However, our main policy idea is that government should engage in cognitive infiltration of the groups that produce conspiracy theories, which involves a mix of (3), (4) and (5).'

Sunstein described this 'cognitive infiltration' in some detail, saying that:

> 'How might this tactic work? Recall that extremist networks and groups, including the groups that purvey conspiracy theories, typically suffer from a kind of crippled epistemology. Hearing only conspiratorial accounts of government behavior, their members become ever more prone to believe and generate such accounts. Informational

and reputational cascades, group polarization, and selection effects suggest that the generation of ever-more-extreme views within these groups can be dampened or reversed by the introduction of cognitive diversity. We suggest a role for government efforts, and agents, in introducing such diversity. Government agents (and their allies) might enter chat rooms, online social networks, or even real-space groups and attempt to undermine percolating conspiracy theories by raising doubts about their factual premises, causal logic or implications for political action.'[28]

In short, the purpose of this cognitive infiltration is to spread uncertainty about alternative conspiracy theories. In identifying such theories as being the result of closed communications circles and confirmation bias, this 'solution' follows logically from that. The same basic argument was made by DEMOS in their paper, which says that, 'Government agents or their allies should openly infiltrate the Internet sites or spaces to plant doubts about conspiracy theories, introducing alternative information.'

There are many problems with this strategy, from whether it is moral to seek to change people's opinions, to the hypocrisy of only identifying some conspiracy theories as conspiracy theories. From the point of view of covert operations there is one other overriding issue. Conventionally, an infiltration strategy is more successful if the target group do not know they are being targeted for infiltration. They might suspect it, but they cannot be sure.

However, in the case of Sunstein's and DEMOS's 'solution' they are openly announcing the use of infiltrators, and even the specific purpose of the infiltration strategy. These papers are publicly available, and have drawn a lot of attention from the very groups targeted for infiltration. As such, we must wonder what the real purpose of these essays is. If the purpose was simply to advance a particular policy (that in reality was probably already in operation) then why not limit the paper's readership to policymakers? The whole point of secret agents is that they are meant to be secret, not easily identifiable because they look just like those described in a policy paper on secret agents.

So, is the cognitive infiltration strategy, or at least the announcement of the strategy, a double bluff? Was publishing it in such a way that it would inevitably draw attention from the very people targeted by such a strategy precisely the point of publishing it? Was the announcement of the strategy of cognitive infiltration itself a form of cognitive infiltration?

After all, what is the effect on the target group of announcing you are seeking to infiltrate them in order to cast doubt on what they believe? The obvious effect is to make them suspicious of people within their number who are raising doubts. Those who fervently preach dogmatic conspiracy theories are left alone, but those adopting a more compromising position of not presuming absolute, dogmatic knowledge will be viewed as possible infiltrators.

This is the dynamic at play in the current 7/7 truth movement. Those who don't advance a particular theory of events are seen as possible infiltrators by the dogmatists who insist that 7/7 was an 'inside job', somehow perpetrated by a private crisis management consultancy. Almost whenever someone raises questions with those advancing a concrete alternative theory, they are accused of working for MI5. Anyone who does not endorse the dogma is seen as a heretic, and hence dismissed as probably working for the other side. I have experienced this personally over a long period of time.

So, the result of DEMOS's and Sunstein's public announcements about using infiltrators has had the opposite effect to the one they publicly identified. Rather than causing alternative conspiracy theory groups to become more self-critical, more questioning of their own ideas, less dogmatic about their beliefs (and therefore supposedly less prone to extremism), the opposite has happened. Dogma is rife amongst alternative conspiracy theorists, and those adopting a more sceptical and inquisitive approach are often marginalized and attacked as probable infiltrators working on behalf of DEMOS and Sunstein.

The question all this poses for us is whether that was the aim all along, to make these groups ever more insular, suspicious and dogmatic? After all, those who believe they already have the truth about 7/7 focus their efforts on 'getting the truth out' and trying to 'wake up the sheeple' who don't believe what they believe. Very few of those advancing an alternative theory have continued to investigate the crime or the new evidence made available at the inquests.

The consequence of this is that much of the 7/7 truth movement has isolated itself with only those people who agree with the proposed alternative conspiracy theory (or theories). They put no pressure on the authorities, are uninterested in acquiring or accumulating new evidence, and do not reach out to people beyond their existing circles. They do not apply their scepticism and criticism of the official narrative to their own narratives, and as such do not refine their alternative narratives as time goes on. They are, in short, guilty of the exact same failings as those they claim to oppose.

Seeding a Debate

When 7/7 happened there were essentially two different reactions to the attacks. The majority of people believed the official story, in some ways before that official story had even been formed. A significant minority believed that the official story was not true, and that those who had put out the official story were the real culprits behind the attacks.

The debate tends to go back and forth between the two positions, each side distrustful of the other, both sides throwing casual insults and lazy rhetoric at the other. This debate, this battle of rival conspiracy theories, has been encouraged by the mainstream media. They have explored possible alternative conspiracy theories of 7/7 through the same means of simulated terror that helped condition people before 7/7.

As this dialogue has been playing out over the years since 7/7 the murder of Jean Charles de Menezes has gone largely unanswered. Neither the people who shot him nor the people who gave the order to shoot him have faced serious charges in court. The process of killing suspected terrorists has been glorified and normalised by the same show that has exploited conspiracy theories.

The events of 21/7 have been tied to 7/7 as part of a wider conspiracy both officially, by the judge in the main 21/7 trial, and unofficially, through yet another episode of *Spooks*. The defence that the 21/7 'bombers' were just carrying out a stunt was not accepted at the trial, and yet the possibility of mock, fake, unwilling or unwitting suicide bombers has been repeatedly woven into fictional storylines.

There is, to be sure, another way to interpret the notion of 21/7 being a stunt. It could also be classed as a sort of simulated terror, something that has the appearance of terrorism without the reality of death and destruction. If we do interpret the men's actions in this way then what does it suggest about the ultimate purpose of those actions? Were they, like *Spooks* and exercises such as Northstar V, ultimately intended to be a reinforcement of the official 7/7 narrative?

It was not just the official narrative that was being reinforced. The notions of unwitting or unwilling suicide bombers, human bombs, inside jobs, state-sponsored false flags and coup d'etats have been explored through the same medium that predicted and prepped the public for the attacks. With curious synchronicity, the very same ideas and storylines put out through the mainstream fiction of *Spooks* have been propagated by the alternative media as fact.

Thus, we have been corralled into a simple dialectic, fighting over which bunch of cherry-picked nonsense is more likely to be true. Each side uses arguments that are largely circular and reek of confirmation bias. Both sides go through the charade of ongoing investigation, but only present evidence in ways that they think supports and substantiates their favoured theory.

While all this was happening, opportunities for significant advances in the investigation have been lost. Time and energy that could have been devoted to putting pressure on the institutions of power or to bringing new evidence into the public domain has been spent bickering over conspiracy theories. Accusations and counter-accusations are fired over the ramparts, with few taking the time to step up and see what the battlefield actually looks like.

As such, when the policy of cognitive infiltration was advanced first by Cass Sunstein and then by DEMOS, it caused a predictable and perhaps intentional result. Those who are sceptical of the official narrative but crucially do not advance an alternative narrative are seen as possible spies. This in turn feeds into the dogmatism with which alternative theories are advanced, as though doubt is somehow undermining the effort to get to the truth.

This is, of course, because many of those advancing alternative narratives believe that they have already got to the truth. As such, they see no point to continue investigating 7/7. Where they have continued to investigate, they have only sought to draw people's attention to the evidence that they feel supports their desired theory. In this respect, they have mirrored the ISC's investigations almost perfectly.

The only way to avoid these pitfalls and traps, if indeed that is what they are, is to be aware that they are there, and to carefully distinguish between the evidence we have and the suspicions that the evidence engenders. Ultimately, without rival theories of what happened on 7/7 we would have no way to frame our questions and prioritise our investigations, and nothing to test against the available evidence.

The problem is not with alternative conspiracy theories per se, but with dogmatic conspiracy theories, in particular those propagated through state programming. The dogmatism can provide an obstacle to investigation and analysis, and encourages the simple oppositional dialectic that plays into the hands of those seeking to continue covering up the truth. Just as with the 'intelligence failures', the only resolution to this situation is to press on with the investigation.

Conclusion: How to Solve 7/7

First and foremost, 7/7 was a crime. It was the worst mass murder in London's history since World War Two and despite all the rhetoric from officials, the vast amount of money and work devoted to the case, to date not even a single person has been held responsible. We have been told, over and over, that Muslim suicide bombers were to blame, conveniently ensuring that the case against the primary alleged culprits will never have to face judicial standards of evidence.

Things might have been very different if one of two things had happened. During the trials of the three alleged 7/7 co-conspirators who were eventually acquitted their lawyers opted against contesting the official version of the bombings. They did not attempt to argue that there was any doubt that Sidique Khan and the others had carried out the attacks, when at that time (as now) there were abundant reasons for people to doubt that. Instead they argued that there was no evidence of their clients being involved in the conspiracy, and were ultimately successful. Perhaps they felt that arguing against the official 7/7 story, however logically correct, would have alienated the jury.

The other thing that could have happened is there could, and under the law most definitely should, have been inquests into the deaths of the alleged bombers. If that had happened then the case against them would have been subject to at least some kind of scrutiny by the legal representatives of their families. Instead, when the inquests into the deaths of the 52 were separated from the inquests into the deaths of the four alleged culprits, the inquests into the 52 were held first and the relatives of the alleged culprits were denied legal aid, preventing them from challenging the evidence at the inquests.

In the end, those running the investigations opted to not even hold inquests into the deaths of the four alleged culprits. This is not only unjust, it is almost certainly illegal. Under the Coroners and Justice Act 2009 coroners are obliged to carry out an investigation, including an inquest, where 'the deceased died a violent or unnatural death' and/or 'the cause of death is unknown'. Given that all four men are officially claimed to have died in suicide bombings, these surely qualify as 'violent or unnatural' deaths.

Likewise, the cause of death is unknown. Taking Sidique Khan's case, the sections of the post mortem report read into evidence at the inquests did not include a cause of death, only saying that, 'The nature and extent of damage is consistent with the deceased being in the immediate proximity of the explosive device.'[1]   When forensic anthropologist Julie Ann Roberts, who reconstructed the bodies of the alleged bombers, took the stand she admitted that she was 'not qualified' to 'distinguish between degrees of explosive damage to parts of the body'. Nonetheless she summarized the damage to Khan's body, saying it 'suggest[ed] that the blast came from ground level and the suspect was bending over the device at the time.'[2]

Neither description is a conclusive account of the cause of death, and yet in the absence of inquests into the deaths of Sidique Khan and the others this is all that we have been offered. The only submission received by Lady Justice Hallett arguing that inquests into the deaths of the four should be held came from the July 7th Truth Campaign. It appears that by that stage, nearly 6 years on from the attacks, even the bereaved relatives of the four alleged culprits just wanted it to all be over. Despite J7 including a range of legal and political arguments in favour of holding inquests, Hallett ruled that, 'I consider they have not provided any sufficient reason to resume the inquests into the four bombers... I can find no cause whatsoever to resume the inquests into the deaths of the four men.'[3]

So, the 7/7 crime remains unsolved. The very people and institutions that should be most interested in demonstrating that they've found the true culprits have shied away from releasing or examining the evidence for that conclusion at every opportunity available to them. Even sceptics of the official story, let alone those who believe in an alternative story, are treated with hostility and encouraged to engage in futile exercises such as the *Conspiracy Roadtrip*. Meanwhile, much of the alternative media have simply filed the case under 'false flags' and failed to do their duty in promoting independent investigations.

There are some notable exceptions. I attribute much of the success of my films to the research assistance provided to me by the July 7th Truth Campaign, and to the promotional assistance provided by James Corbett of the Corbett Report, Keelan Balderson of WideShut UK and the pseudonymous Brit of ResistanceRadio. While I am thankful to others who have also provided avenues and opportunities to me these are the core people without which I would have found it much harder, if not impossible, to achieve what I have in both investigating 7/7 and making the public aware of my findings.

While the scale of these accomplishments may not fundamentally change the world it is nonetheless important to recognize their symbolic value. A handful of people with virtually no money, no legal authority and no professional training have provided a better criminal investigation of the bombings themselves and a more thoughtful, thorough and balanced presentation of their findings than the government and mass corporate media put together. If nothing else, this shows what can be done by sincere, intelligent people who are motivated by nothing more complex than a desire for truth and justice.

Lies about Spies

This small group have also provided a better investigation of the security services, what they knew and when and what they were doing about it in the years before 7/7. Reconstructing that timeline is not a simple task, but it was nowhere near as difficult a task as the ISC made it. Throughout the process the ISC simply accepted MI5's constant revisionism and failed to even broach the topic of human intelligence sources (spies) in the close proximity of the alleged bombers, let alone ask what the spies were doing.

In the years prior to 7/7 the four alleged bombers only did things that made them look like possible bombers through contact with these likely spies, or in the case of Junaid Babar, through contact with a known American spy. At each point that they connected to something that might be called Al Qaeda, they connected through likely spies and at each point that this happened there were significant and inexplicable 'intelligence failures'. Information wasn't found, wasn't shared, or wasn't explored or exploited with any degree of haste or sense of urgency.

Officially, these 'failures' had the effect of concealing the identity of the alleged bombers from the security services in the years before 7/7. However, they still had half a dozen instances where they had Mohammad Sidique Khan identified via his name, phone numbers, vehicles and addresses. Nonetheless, MI5 maintain that they never had any idea that he was going to become a suicide bomber.

This is a fine example of doublethink, because in excusing themselves for failing to stop Sidique Khan before 7/7 they are also admitting that they have no evidence that he actually was a suicide bomber. Despite their many hours of surveillance of Khan they never came across anything suggesting he was preparing to kill himself or anyone else. Thus, in slowly revealing tidbit-by-tidbit what information they did have on Khan from before 7/7 it is only if you believe that he was a suicide bomber that any of it looks incriminating. Khan's visits to Pakistan, his contact with subsequently convicted 'terror suspects', his involvement at a radical bookshop are all presented by MI5 as reasons why they didn't find Khan suspicious, all the while telling us that these are reasons why we should find him suspicious.

In reality, these failures not only allowed Khan to carry on doing whatever he was doing up until 7/7, they also obscured his and the other alleged bombers' contact with Babar and the other likely spies. So were these 'failures' really failures, or were they the result of compartmentalizing intelligence to facilitate secret operations? In particular, were they the result of compartmentalizing intelligence to facilitate a black, false flag operation? The pattern suggests that this is true, but the available information is partial in the extreme. It is always possible that this too is mere smoke and mirrors, though it would be in keeping with the model implied by the Finucane assassination discussed in the introduction.

Adding more weight to this interpretation is a central aspect of Germaine Lindsay's backstory. While Khan, Tanweer and Hussain were all linked to a greater or lesser extent to the Iqra bookshop and the Operation Crevice plot, Lindsay lived in a different area and did not turn up in any of the pre-7/7 surveillance operations. However, his widow Samantha Lewthwaite is the daughter of a British soldier who served in Northern Ireland during the previous 'War on Terror'. Very little was heard from her since 7/7 until she hit the headlines repeatedly throughout 2012, with the stories saying she was travelling around East Africa and was involved with local Islamist group Al Shabaab.

It was a very vague story that seems to have now been dropped, brought up only to give the papers something new to say around the 7th anniversary of the bombings. Aside from the tale of Samantha Lewthwaite in East Africa the inevitable flurry of news stories at that time simply re-iterated the official narrative. To someone who believes that narrative the Lewthwaite story would appear to add weight to the idea that Lindsay was a suicide bomber. To someone who thinks otherwise, the whole tale sounds like more spook theatre.

While the mainstream media has fed off MI5's drip-drip of information and have occasionally asked questions about, for example, the role of Q - Mohammed Qayyum Khan – or Junaid Babar, they have singularly failed to follow up on the implications of such questioning. In particular they seem to be ignoring the obvious when it comes to Martin McDaid. They have never sincerely re-assembled the scattered information to try to make sense of it, they have simply gone along with MI5's doublethink and theatrics. Instead, it has been ordinary people who have taken on that task.

Perhaps even more importantly, the ISC have played a crucial role as a compartmentalized go-between for MI5 and the mainstream media. Virtually all of the information that has entered into the mainstream discussion of 7/7 'intelligence failures' has come through the blurry filter of the ISC. They let MI5 tell them at least three different stories, all of which are demonstrably untrue, and presented those stories in such a way as to obscure the most significant connections and decisions. While the Home Office narrative was clearly designed to be easy to read, it appears the authors of the ISC report took the opposite approach.

Once again, this is an issue where the alternative media and citizen investigators have done a much better job. While both of my films contain sections on the questions provoked by the 'intelligence failures' and the connections with Q, McDaid and Babar they have also been outlined in Keelan Balderson's film *7/7 What Did They Know?* Many of the discoveries about the McDaid story were not made by Richard Watson in any of his various *Newsnight* reports, but by J7. The ISC is clearly not fit for purpose when a handful of volunteers can do a better job.

Suppressed Evidence

So what evidence could resolve some of the key questions about 7/7? With regards to the explosions themselves and whether or not the alleged bombers were even at those locations, while much of the physical evidence has been destroyed there must be hundreds of crime scene photos and hours of video. There may also be a great number of exhibits from the scene that might still yield some chemical data on the composition of the explosives.

In particular there is no reason for the authorities to continue to suppress or refuse to release the full explosives laboratory reports on the bombings. Despite FOIA requests, and promises to publish the report after the inquests, this is still secret. Likewise the full post mortem reports from the pathologists who examined the alleged bombers, and the report of the forensic anthropologist as well as the photographic or other records from these processes is still being withheld. While it would be needlessly graphic to simply broadcast such images on the TV news they could be of tremendous use to a real investigation.

Some of the questions about the movements of different people at Luton station could be answered through the release of the full CCTV record from that morning. In particular, whether the alleged bombers really did move through the station in such a short time, around three times faster than they did only days earlier. The precise movements of the mystery Jaguar could also be determined if the sequences that have been edited out of the releases were restored. The question as to who moved the cameras at Luton in the days before 7/7 may be somewhat harder to answer.

To resolve the question of warnings on the day of 7/7 or possibly beforehand the most likely source of confirmation would be diplomatic cables in and out of London in the period. These were not amongst those released by the Wikileaks cabledump otherwise they would have been discussed in this book. While such cables are not sources of gospel truth they could at least provide additional details on this very murky and controversial question.

The wider and longer story of MI5 'intelligence failures' would require an investigation with legal authority but without the normal political limits that come with that, i.e. outside of the confines of the Inquiries Act or the normal judicial process. To find out whether Q and McDaid were spies, and what they were doing, and what really happened in the operations Warlock, Honeysuckle and Crevice would require access to people and the ability to compel statements from them. While Babar's whereabouts are known the other two men would be much harder to find, and the likelihood of getting MI5 officers from those operations to testify is very slim.

However, a starting point would be the members of the ISC during its 7/7 investigations as they may be able to provide additional information on what was redacted, why, and the dynamic at play between public officials and the secret services. Also, as noted in chapter 8, the Iraq War inquiry saw intelligence officials testify (albeit anonymously) and numerous relevant communications from within defence and intelligence institutions have been published. If the same process were carried out for 7/7, even if it were compromised in the way the Chilcot inquiry has been, we would at least get a subtler picture of what was going on in the years between 9/11 and 7/7.

Similarly, the question of predictive programming, the extent to which the pre-conditioning of the public to accept one of several prefabricated was deliberate and knowing, could be determined by interrogating those who wrote and produced the TV shows. The kicker to the story about *Panorama*, *Spooks*, *Dirty War* and so on is that in 2004, a year before 7/7, a book called *At Risk* also featured an unwilling suicide bomber/MI5 double agent blowback storyline. It was written by former head of MI5 Stella Rimington.

The extent to which the training exercises and simulations assisted or augment the predictive programming, and how deliberate that process was, could likely be established by simply talking to the participants. The importance or otherwise of the Peter Power exercise on the morning of 7/7 could only be determined in that context, as Power himself is not particularly reliable nor at all willing to revisit the events.

Overcoming Apathy

The only way to gain access to this information, short of hacking or stealing it (which would morally compromise any investigation resulting from it, and is therefore totally counterproductive) would be a fresh investigation. Public inquiries have become a disgrace, though some of the inquiries into Gladio and collusion in Northern Ireland have yielded powerful admissions of state-sponsored terrorism. One alternative is a truth and justice commission, whereby state agents and others could be offered immunity for testifying truthfully.

The other option, though it would lack the necessary legal authority required to compel and subpoena evidence, is a well-funded citizens inquiry. In bypassing the state it would be able to ask the questions no official investigation has even considered, and potentially provide truthful answers. While the work of J7, the only 7/7 citizens inquiry worth mentioning, has been admirable in its persistence, its breadth, depth and rigour they do not have the funds or access to, for example, carry out their own explosives tests and analysis. No doubt if they had such resources then we would all be a lot closer to the truth.

One of the major challenges to a well-resourced independent investigation is the general apathy of the British and wider public towards this issue. We are fed a steady stream of political and corporate controversies, some worthy of our attention, some total distractions. In each case we are pummelled with an overload of information about the issue in a short timeframe before the story dies and is replaced by the next scandal. This results in people becoming jaded towards questions of serious criminality within the state or beyond it.

The easiest defences against a culture of constant but largely meaningless controversy are to be cynical or to be passive and apathetic. Thus, it becomes very difficult to simply make people care about the question of whether people within our government killed 56 people and then blamed four of those victims. It is perhaps even harder to get people to discuss the issue of why they might have done this, and what we can or should do about it.

It is not a matter of numbers. As detailed throughout this book there is a proportion somewhere between 15 and 25% of the British public who believe that this was an act of state-sponsored terrorism.

The real problem is illustrated well by comments made at the press conference at the end of the July 7 Inquests, when the bereaved got an opportunity to make their feelings known.

Some, such as Marie-Fatayi Williams maintained their calls for a public inquiry. She said, 'The security services don't want to have any blame, they don't want to say, if they made an apology, it meant that they were guilty of something, and if they are guilty of something then it meant that somebody is to blame, and nobody wants to be blamed, and so 7/7 is to be forgotten.'

Others, like Grahame Russell recognized that there were many outstanding questions, but said that it was too painful to continue fighting the government for answers. He said, 'I mean everybody's got issue with various areas. I think there are people with issues with the intelligence services, there are people with issues with the emergency services, my own particular issue with Transport for London, so I think there are still issues. The problem we have, no, the problem I have is that if I continue to hold concerns about issues that went on, my life would become very bitter.'

While members of the wider public obviously do not have to endure the pain of those who lost loved ones in this crime there is a similar dynamic at play. What motive do ordinary people have to either press for further investigation or do it themselves? It is a grim topic, in many respects a depressing topic that contains little by way of resolution let alone a happy ending (at least so far). Set against that there is the fact that in our world, where serious corruption is becoming widely recognized, there is a growing realisation that the simple virtues of truth and justice are the answer to so many of our problems. History, or at least future history, will prove whether that is enough.

Documents

This appendix comprises around 50 pages of select material from the 7/7 papertrail. Much of this was previously sealed or classified but all is now in the public domain, much of it published on the website for the July 7 Inquests, which can be found at: http://7julyinquests.independent.gov.uk/

Documents 1-3 were published by the central government, the first two by the Home Office and the third by the ISC. Documents 4-7 on the MI5-WYP investigations into Martin McDaid and the Iqra bookshop were all published on the July 7 inquests website. Documents 8-11 all come from Operation Crevice and likewise were published on the inquests website.

Document 12 is a record from the US court system that I obtained on the Scribd website. Document 13 was part of a batch of records from Hillside Primary School in Beeston where Khan worked from 2001-2004 released to the July 7th Truth Campaign in response to a FOIA request. I downloaded a copy from their website's profile of Khan at: http://www.julyseventh.co.uk/7-7-profile-mohammad-sidique-khan.html. Document 14 was published on the inquests website.

As with all the images used in this book, the original PDF versions of these documents are all available to download via my website at www.investigatingtheterror.com.

Document 1: Amendment to the Home Office Narrative. This is the only officially acknowledged change to the Home Office's story about 7/7, as a result of the original train time at Luton being wrong. This is no longer available on the Home Office website, but the original narrativewith the wrong train time is still accessible.

Report of the Official Account of the Bombings in London on 7th July 2005

HC 1087 Session 2005-2006

ISBN 0 10 293774 5

CORRECTIONS

1. Page 4. The time of 07.15 should be changed to 07:14 and the text should read "Lindsay walks through the entrance foyer of the station, walks to the ticket hall and appears to check the departure board. Lindsay then walks back out of the station to rejoin Tanweer, Khan and Hussain at the rear of their vehicles. The 4 then put on their rucksacks and walk towards the station. They enter Luton station and go through the ticket barriers together. It is not known where they bought their tickets or what sort of tickets they possessed, but they must have had some to get on to the platform."

2. Page 4. The time of 07.40 on the left side of the page immediately preceding the paragraph that commences, "The London King's Cross train leaves Luton station". The time of 07.40 is incorrect and should be replaced by 07.25 which is the correct time.

August 2007
LONDON: THE STATIONERY OFFICE

Document 2: Extract from CBRN News, Issue 3, June 2005. This page describes the use of 'pseudo media' as part of the April 2005 Atlantic Blue training exercise that predicted and pre-empted the 7/7 attacks.

The pseudo media effect

In any large emergency or major incident the media plays a vital role in determining what information the public receives and when, as well as providing a running commentary on how the incident is being handled both politically and on the ground.

In order to convey some of this pressure within an exercise scenario, a 'pseudo media' team was brought together tasked with producing in-exercise broadcast coverage of the events as they unfolded.

This is nothing new, but for the first time an online news site (VBCNews.com) was also produced by the Home Office in order to provide an alternative pseudo media news source, and designed to add further pressure to players, while providing greater accessibility of international news coverage to all involved in the exercise.

Roles reversed – a pseudo journalist's account...

"As someone who normally works in a policy team, the experience of working as part of the VBCNews.com team on Atlantic Blue really highlighted how important it is for the media to be kept fully informed of the situation in an emergency.

"Working alongside the web-team, we were able to upload articles onto the website within a short time of an 'incident' occurring; this meant that any shortcomings in information or the length of time it took to receive responses were quickly apparent not only to us, but to anyone using the site as a news source.

"It was also clear how important accuracy in the reports and the briefing from the various key players is in providing information and reassurance to the 'public'.

"In terms of the exercise, the online tool was also very helpful in reflecting the perceived media and public response to how the incidents were being handled, and in consultation with Exercise Control we were able to drive player action accordingly."

News updates

While the exercise took place, VBCNews made regular pseudo news updates on screens situated around the site, with real news being shown between pseudo broadcasts. This provided the feeling of round-the-clock coverage.

The VBC website – as with real news websites – allowed a varied spread of stories and points of view, but had to be deliberately accessed and logged into. This also allowed records to be kept of how the site was used. Over the week the site was visited 2,200 times, with 47,070 page views and an average length of visit of 26 minutes. This reliance on technology during the exercise showed the need for strong IT and information systems during exercises and in the event of a real incident.

The exercise took place over 5 days. On the VBC website 152 articles were written that covered subjects as wide ranging as the weather forecasts to latest updates on the 'terrorist' events.

International coverage

To reflect the international focus of the exercise, our pseudo media team linked up daily with the US and Canada in live 'down the line' interviews and news clips.

The strong co-operation between the UK and the US on the pseudo media allowed information to be fully shared, and website articles to be jointly used encouraging the international perspective of the exercise to be conveyed to players on both sides of the Atlantic.

Document 3: ISC Annex A to second report. A detailed timeline of what information MI5 had on the alleged bombers, particularly Sidique Khan, in the years prior to 7/7. At least, a detailed timeline of what information MI5 *told the ISC they had* during the ISC's 2007-8 inquiry.

ANNEX A: DETAILED TIMELINE

**Detailed timeline of MI5 and police contact with
Mohammed Siddique KHAN and Shazad TANWEER**

3 February 1993
A man named "Sidique KHAN" (gives his date of birth as 20/10/1974 and place of birth as Leeds) is arrested and cautioned for a Section 47 assault (medium level) committed on 26 December 1992. As is normal procedure, a police record is created and his photograph is taken. Previous addresses shown on West Yorkshire Police records are given as 30 Runswick Place, Holbeck, Leeds (as at 2001) and 99 Stratford Street, Leeds (as at 1993). This incident is not related to national security and so the information is not passed by West Yorkshire Police to MI5.

1995
Shazad TANWEER is arrested by West Yorkshire Police for an alleged burglary. His personal details are recorded, but are not added to the Police National Computer (PNC) as the charges are dropped.

January 2001
As part of West Yorkshire Police's Operation WARLOCK, a number of unidentified men are photographed taking part in an "outward bound" expedition organised by two known Islamist sympathisers and attended by approximately 40 men. Efforts are made by MI5 and police to identify them, and 9 of the 40 individuals are identified.

Late March 2003
MI5 initiate Operation CREVICE to investigate a network providing support to overseas jihadi activity.

14 April 2003
West Yorkshire Police "pattern of life" surveillance (unconnected to CREVICE) of a known extremist, as part of an investigation with MI5, sees the extremist leaving a mosque in Beeston, Leeds, with four or five others, getting into a BMW and being given a lift for three minutes towards the city centre before being dropped off. On 16 April 2003, West Yorkshire Police checks on the PNC reveal that the keeper of the BMW is "Sidique KHAN" of 11 Gregory Street, Batley (near Leeds). The contact lasted only three minutes, and it was assessed not to have any national security significance or be relevant to the subject of the investigation.

Detailed timeline *(continued)*

13 July 2003

Data from a mobile phone associated with Mohammed Qayum KHAN (see paragraph 18) shows a number of calls with a telephone number MI5 had not seen before. Checks reveal that the telephone number in question is registered to "Siddique KHAN" of 49a Bude Road, Leeds (the address of a bookshop selling extremist literature).[72] MI5 cannot match the name "Siddique KHAN" with any in their databases, and the contact is not investigated further since there is nothing to suggest involvement in any terrorist-related activity. ***. Information on this call is recorded, as a matter of routine, on Mohammed Qayum KHAN's file as follows: *"INFO: Several calls to and from an [untraced individual] on [telephone number] *** ***. Calls are made *** and ***."*

19 July 2003

The mobile phone associated with Mohammed Qayum KHAN is used to call an untraced phone number ***. Checks on this pre-pay mobile phone do not reveal a registered keeper. There is no intelligence to suggest that this telephone contact is linked to the facilitation network and so no further action is taken.

24 July 2003

The same pre-pay mobile phone number as that used on 19 July 2003 is used again to call the mobile phone associated with Mohammed Qayum KHAN and ***. There is still nothing to suggest that this telephone contact is linked to Al-Qaida or extremism. No further action is taken.

17 August 2003

The mobile phone associated with Mohammed Qayum KHAN is used to call another untraced telephone number ***. There is no further intelligence regarding *** and no action is taken to investigate it.

Late January 2004

Omar KHYAM is formally identified (in MI5's terms) as a member of the CREVICE facilitation network and is placed under limited surveillance as part of MI5's attempts to learn more about the network.

Detailed timeline *(continued)*

2 February 2004
Surveillance of Omar KHYAM sees him parking his car in Crawley (with another occupant) and then sees a green Honda Civic (registration R480 CCA) with three occupants parking alongside. After two minutes the Honda (with two occupants later described by surveillance as KHYAM and an unidentified man) drives up and down the A23 while the other three individuals remain in KHYAM's parked car. ***, but surveillance believes that KHYAM and the UDM are driving around for the purpose of a meeting (although it is not known what is discussed). The men return to their original cars and both cars drive off. The Honda is followed to try and obtain some further information on the UDMs in case, at a later date, they are thought to be of interest and followed up on. At Toddington Service Station on the M1, the MI5 surveillance team secretly photograph the three unidentified males in the Honda car and classify them as UDMs C, D and E. The Honda continues its journey and two men alight at Lodge Lane and Tempest Road, Leeds. The car then drives towards Dewsbury and is seen to park outside 10 Thornhill Park Avenue.

Early February 2004
MI5 receive intelligence to suggest that there was a bomb plot probably aimed at the UK (***). Surveillance on KHYAM is increased.

11 February 2004
The CREVICE Executive Liaison Group is formed to manage the operation. They set out their aims to ensure public safety and to investigate the bomb plot (with a view to arresting and prosecuting those involved).

16 February 2004
MI5 runs checks on the green Honda Civic (seen on 2 February), which is shown to be registered to a "Hasina PATEL" at 10 Thornhill Park Avenue, Dewsbury. MI5 ask West Yorkshire Police for any details they have on "Hasina PATEL" in order *"to enable us to fully identify any potential associates of KHYAM"*. There is no record of a written response to this request.

20 February 2004
A call to the Metropolitan Police Service (MPS) Special Branch anti-terrorist hotline reveals that KHYAM is connected to a storage facility where a suspicious quantity of fertiliser is being held. MI5 realise that the CREVICE group now have both the intention and capability to mount an attack in the UK – this triggers consistent intensive surveillance coverage on KHYAM. The core CREVICE group are monitored discussing bomb making.

Detailed timeline *(continued)*

20–22 February 2004
An electronics expert arrives from Canada to advise KHYAM and some of the other bomb plotters on the construction and operation of remote-controlled detonation devices.

21 February 2004
Surveillance shows KHYAM and Shujah MAHMOOD (a man assessed at the time to be part of the CREVICE group but later acquitted of CREVICE-related charges) driving to pick up food in KHYAM's car.[73] Surveillance reports that *"At 21:05 the Silver Suzuki arrived back in the area [and] (KHYAM) and (MAHMOOD) remained in the vehicle chatting until approximately 21:34"*. The note made during the live monitoring of eavesdropping devices says *"operation, indistinct speech/do something"*. The MI5 surveillance team report that they saw two people in the car. Taking this information together, the assessment was that the meeting was between KHYAM and Shujah MAHMOOD.

28 February 2004
Intelligence coverage of KHYAM *** an unidentified individual. MI5 surveillance then observe the Honda Civic seen on 2 February (R480 CCA) with UDMs C, D and E meeting KHYAM and MAHMOOD in a car park in Crawley at 08:56. They make a series of visits to builders' merchants, travel to a mosque in Slough, and then stop at KHYAM's address in Hencroft Street (***). They then travel to Wellingborough (near Northampton), via Toddington Service Station near Luton (where they meet Mohammed Qayum KHAN at 17:30 hours), before returning to Slough to drop off KHYAM and MAHMOOD at 23:35 (nothing of significance was heard discussed in KHYAM's car during the day). The MI5 surveillance team stay with KHYAM, but the MPS surveillance team follow the remaining unidentified men back to West Yorkshire – again with the aim of finding something as a reference point should it be assessed that these men were suspicious and needed following up later. They stop again at Toddington Service Station, and at Castle Donington Service Station (near Derby), Tempest Road (Leeds), outside a church in Lodge Lane (Leeds), and finally park in Pickles Field, Batley (near Leeds). CCTV stills from Toddington Service Station are initially requested by the police (but later cancelled).

29 February 2004
The MPS check on the Honda Civic and find it is registered to "Sidique KHAN", who lives at 11 Gregory Street, Batley, West Yorkshire. (The vehicle registration document for the Honda Civic shows ownership was transferred to "Sidique KHAN" on 1 February 2004.) His date of birth (obtained from his insurance policy, the details of which are supplied by the customer and not verified) is given as 20 October 1974. The car is linked to two previous addresses: 10 Thornhill Park Avenue, Dewsbury, and 99 Stratford Street, Leeds.

Detailed timeline *(continued)*

2 March 2004

MI5 ask West Yorkshire Police about a storage facility at 99 Stratford Street that may be linked to KHYAM. The MPS's investigation of the address names three individuals, including a "Mohammed Sadique KHAN" with a date of birth of 20 October 1974. The name on his driving licence is spelt "Sidique". The MPS note in their records (CREVICE Action 990) that *"due to a lack of significant traces of Sidique KHAN, consideration might be given to the [possibility] that this name is an alias"*.

21 March 2004

A green Vauxhall Corsa (registration YB52 LUF), driven by a then unidentified person, arrives at an address in Crawley and picks up KHYAM and MAHMOOD, and they drive around for 40 minutes before returning to the same address.

22 March 2004

Intelligence coverage of KHYAM *** a man called "Millie" (the assessment now is that this refers to the meeting with Siddique KHAN on 23 March).

23 March 2004

Further surveillance on KHYAM observes him and four UDMs travelling from Crawley to Slough. The individuals travel in KHYAM's car and a green Vauxhall Corsa (YB52 LUF) with the words "Car Clinic" and a telephone number on the side. The surveillance team believe that the driver of the Corsa is identical to the driver of the Honda Civic on 28 February (UDM E). Another of the individuals is described as being identical to one of the passengers in the Honda Civic on 28 February (UDM D). During the afternoon, in KHYAM's car, KHYAM and a UDM speak briefly about the *"success of the Madrid bombings"*. KHYAM and UDM E visit an internet café before returning to KHYAM's flat (***). Eavesdropping at KHYAM's flat hears that the men are from Leeds and the conversation is largely related to financial fraud. Video stills are produced from surveillance. The police later find that the Vauxhall Corsa is registered to Lombard Vehicle Management Ltd.

30 March 2004

The men alleged to be involved with the fertiliser bomb plot are arrested.

March 2004 onwards

Out of the several thousand contacts monitored during Operation CREVICE, MI5 are unable to identify 150. Of these unidentified individuals, based on the threat that they are thought to pose to national security, 15 are categorised as "essential" targets and 9 new MI5 operations are launched. UDMs D and E are among a group of 40 of the 150 unidentified contacts categorised as "desirable" targets.

MI5 are then diverted from the follow-up work by an even bigger and more sophisticated operation – Operation RHYME – which absorbs their resources.

Detailed timeline *(continued)*

4 April 2004

Shazad TANWEER is given a criminal caution by West Yorkshire Police for a public disorder/verbal harassment offence. His personal details are taken, together with a photograph, fingerprints and a DNA sample. These details are added to the West Yorkshire Crime Information System, and to the Viewdata system, and a Police National Computer (PNC) entry is created.

April–May 2004

A detainee says that two men from the UK, known as "IBRAHIM" and "ZUBAIR", had travelled to Pakistan in 2003 and that they had met those who were to become the CREVICE plotters whilst there.

*** May 2004

Another intelligence source reports that two men known as "IBRAHIM" and "ZUBAIR", from Leeds, had travelled to Pakistan in 2003. ***.
***.
***.

In connection with CREVICE more generally, ***.

25 May 2004

The MPS provide MI5 with a summary "cluster" of intelligence found on the Honda Civic (R480 CCA), which confirms "Hasina PATEL" as the registered owner in 2003.[74] Her address is given as 10 Thornhill Park Avenue, and the cluster also confirms her date of birth as 23 November 1977. It also shows that the new keeper of the car is "Sidique KHAN" of 11 Gregory Street, Batley, and provides his date of birth (20 October 1974) and previous addresses as 10 Thornhill Park Avenue and 99 Stratford Street. This cluster also shows that there was no Automatic Number Plate Recognition (ANPR) trace for the Honda Civic on 3 March 2004, but that *"the details have since been entered on Operation WEDGE"*. (The ANPR system enables police units to identify vehicles from registration plates, and is used when the vehicle is suspected of involvement in crime or where intelligence is needed on the vehicle. The details of the Honda Civic are not added to the WEDGE counter-terrorism database, contrary to the cluster message.)

Detailed timeline *(continued)*

8 June 2004

MI5 provide West Yorkshire Police with details summarising CREVICE connections to the Leeds area – this includes information on 12 individuals, 13 addresses and related data. Amongst these details is the green Honda Civic registered to "Sidique KHAN" of 11 Gregory Street, Batley (near Leeds), and previously registered to "Hasina PATEL" of 10 Thornhill Avenue, Dewsbury. Checks of publicly available records reveal that "Sidique KHAN" has links to 10 Thornhill Park Avenue, Dewsbury, and 99 Stratford Street, Leeds. The communication also notes the addresses in Tempest Road, Lodge Lane and Pickles Street where the Honda Civic was observed to be picking up and dropping off individuals during the CREVICE investigation. MI5 state that they believe the driver of the Honda Civic on 28 February was the same person as the driver of the green Vauxhall Corsa on 23 March. Separately, MI5 also ask West Yorkshire Police for any information they might have that could enable "IBRAHIM" and "ZUBAIR" (the men that the detainee and other source of information had said had trained in Pakistan) to be identified.

14 July 2004

The North East Regional Intelligence Cell (NERIC) respond to the details provided by MI5 on 8 June 2004 (this response was dated 14 July, but sent on 17 July). They find no positive results for the Honda Civic against the databases of the NERIC, West Yorkshire Special Branch, or local police systems. A check against the PNC shows 22 inquiries have been made on the car between August 2003 and July 2004, 21 of which are related to Operation CREVICE. (The 22nd was a routine check made on 20 August 2003, which did not warrant any further action.)

In the same response NERIC provide MI5 with details of "Sidique KHAN" and his various addresses and date of birth, together with the photograph from his caution in 1993. Information that the police hold on "Hasina PATEL", as well as a number of other individuals, is given. West Yorkshire Police are unable to provide any insight as to the identities of "IBRAHIM" or "ZUBAIR". No further action is taken independently and West Yorkshire Police await any further tasking.

12 August 2004

The detainee is shown black and white photocopies of fairly good quality, medium-distance group photographs and CCTV stills of unknown males (including UDMs D and E which were provided by the MPS). The detainee says that they cannot tell who UDMs D and E are from the photographs provided.

17 January 2005

West Yorkshire Police Special Branch receive information indicating that a man named "Saddique ***" and a man named "IMRAN" had undergone training in Afghanistan in the late 1990s/early 2000s. Both men are reported to live in Batley ("Saddique ***" in the Soothill area) and are committed to the extremist cause. West Yorkshire Police cross-check this information against their records with no results. This report is shared with MI5 a few weeks later and they too check their records with no result.

Detailed timeline *(continued)*

27 January 2005
In the process of gathering evidence for the CREVICE trial and completing actions relating to the operation, the MPS take a statement from the "Just Car Clinic", a collision repair company that leased the Vauxhall Corsa to an individual at the time of Operation CREVICE (see entry on 23 March 2004). From this statement the police are able to *"nominally identify the driver"* as "Mr S. KHAN".

9 February 2005
MPS Action A4076 (one of the records of actions undertaken during a police investigation) reveals one result on "Sidique KHAN" that relates to his Honda Civic (R480 CCA) being placed on the ANPR *"should the vehicle enter the confines of Heathrow Airport (re Op Crevice)"*. This is standard operating procedure for vehicles that feature in surveillance during a counter-terrorism operation. This was instigated by the Counter-Terrorism Command National Joint Unit (NJU) on 17 February 2004, and was one of 72 vehicle registrations of interest (including 39 others from CREVICE). Instructions were that *"[should] activations occur the vehicles are not to be stopped but NJU are to be notified immediately..."* The MPS Action also confirms that the Vauxhall Corsa was leased by "Just Car Clinic" to a "Mr S. KHAN" whilst his Honda Civic (R480 CCA) was being repaired. The individual had given his mobile telephone number and his address (11 Gregory Street, Batley), and asked for his car to be picked up from 10 Thornhill Park Avenue, Dewsbury, West Yorkshire. A driving licence check reveals a last known address of 99 Stratford Street, Leeds.

1 March 2005
West Yorkshire Police and MI5 receive further information about "Saddique ***" indicating that he is in his early 30s and has reportedly received some military training in a mujahaddin camp in Pakistan in early 2001. This was the total of the relevant information received and it was not possible to corroborate it or investigate to find out more.

March 2005
A detainee confirms that "IBRAHIM" and "ZUBAIR" (who he describes as coming from Bradford, West Yorkshire) had been, in 2003, at the same training camp in Pakistan as individuals who later became the CREVICE plotters, ***.
***.
***.

12 April 2005
Operation DO*** begins. The purpose of the operation is to identify "IBRAHIM" and "ZUBAIR" and to establish whether they pose a terrorist threat.

Detailed timeline *(continued)*

27 January 2005

In the process of gathering evidence for the CREVICE trial and completing actions relating to the operation, the MPS take a statement from the "Just Car Clinic", a collision repair company that leased the Vauxhall Corsa to an individual at the time of Operation CREVICE (see entry on 23 March 2004). From this statement the police are able to *"nominally identify the driver"* as "Mr S. KHAN".

9 February 2005

MPS Action A4076 (one of the records of actions undertaken during a police investigation) reveals one result on "Sidique KHAN" that relates to his Honda Civic (R480 CCA) being placed on the ANPR *"should the vehicle enter the confines of Heathrow Airport (re Op Crevice)"*. This is standard operating procedure for vehicles that feature in surveillance during a counter-terrorism operation. This was instigated by the Counter-Terrorism Command National Joint Unit (NJU) on 17 February 2004, and was one of 72 vehicle registrations of interest (including 39 others from CREVICE). Instructions were that *"[should] activations occur the vehicles are not to be stopped but NJU are to be notified immediately..."* The MPS Action also confirms that the Vauxhall Corsa was leased by "Just Car Clinic" to a "Mr S. KHAN" whilst his Honda Civic (R480 CCA) was being repaired. The individual had given his mobile telephone number and his address (11 Gregory Street, Batley), and asked for his car to be picked up from 10 Thornhill Park Avenue, Dewsbury, West Yorkshire. A driving licence check reveals a last known address of 99 Stratford Street, Leeds.

1 March 2005

West Yorkshire Police and MI5 receive further information about "Saddique ***" indicating that he is in his early 30s and has reportedly received some military training in a mujahaddin camp in Pakistan in early 2001. This was the total of the relevant information received and it was not possible to corroborate it or investigate to find out more.

March 2005

A detainee confirms that "IBRAHIM" and "ZUBAIR" (who he describes as coming from Bradford, West Yorkshire) had been, in 2003, at the same training camp in Pakistan as individuals who later became the CREVICE plotters, ***.
***.
***.

12 April 2005

Operation DO*** begins. The purpose of the operation is to identify "IBRAHIM" and "ZUBAIR" and to establish whether they pose a terrorist threat.

Detailed timeline *(continued)*

4 May 2005

MI5 provide a summary of the intelligence they have on Operation DO*** to West Yorkshire Police. They provide West Yorkshire Police Special Branch with details of two possible "ZUBAIRs" from West Yorkshire and ask if they can provide *"any trace on your records for both of these individuals"* (neither of these was Mohammed Siddique KHAN). MI5 also say that, in *"the near future"*, they hope to provide *** with photographs of the two individuals *"in the hope of positively identifying 'ZUBAIR'"*.

21 June 2005

West Yorkshire Police Special Branch telephone MI5 to state that they can find no information on "IBRAHIM" or "ZUBAIR".

21 June 2005

MI5 send a "cluster" message to West Yorkshire Police Special Branch stating that they have provided the photographs of the two potential "ZUBAIRs" to *** but have not yet heard ***. MI5 also say *"we can't move forward and deploy more intrusive investigative resources until we can be more certain we have the correct 'ZUBEIR' [sic] in our sights"*. MI5 also inform West Yorkshire Police Special Branch that, as part of Operation FL*** (created to follow up on other leads from CREVICE), they have identified "IMRAN" as Zeeshan Anis SIDDIQUI and that they *"are optimistic that continued coverage will shed light on other leads from CREVICE, including [identifying 'IBRAHIM' and 'ZUBAIR' from] DO***"*.

7 July 2005

Terrorist attacks on the London transport network kill 52 people and injure more than 700.

7–13 July 2005

The MPS begin to piece together the identities of the bombers. A detailed account of these events is included on pages 15 and 16.

9 July 2005

Following the discovery of credit cards at two of the bomb sites that are in the name "Mohammed Sidique KHAN", the police check this name against their records. They discover that the name features on intelligence records relating to Operation CREVICE. (This link was documented in Message M173 of Operation THESEUS – the 7/7 investigation – at 09:10 on 10 July 2005.)

11 July 2005

Before it became clear that Mohammed Siddique KHAN had died in the attacks, but when he was the prime suspect for the bombings, new intelligence indicated that "Saddique ***" (see 17 January and 1 March 2005) was Mohammed Siddique KHAN.

Detailed timeline *(continued)*

11 July 2005
The MPS ask West Yorkshire Police to investigate their primary suspect, and as a result West Yorkshire Police obtain authorisation to place tracking devices on four cars parked outside Mohammed Siddique KHAN's address in Leeds.

11 July 2005
Mohammed Siddique KHAN, Shazad TANWEER, Hasib HUSSAIN and (on 13 July) Jermaine LINDSAY become the police's primary suspects, and search warrants are executed on related addresses and vehicles.

13–16 July 2005
DNA checks confirm that KHAN, TANWEER, HUSSAIN and LINDSAY had died carrying out the attacks.

Mid-July 2005
A detainee identifies "IBRAHIM" from unmarked press photographs of Mohammed Siddique KHAN. MI5 investigate further and are able to ascertain *** that "ZUBAIR" is a man called Mohammed SHAKIL. ***.

Late July 2005
The assessment that "ZUBAIR" and SHAKIL are the same person is confirmed when a detainee identifies a photograph of SHAKIL as being the man he knew as "ZUBAIR".

Late July/August 2005
An intelligence officer working in West Yorkshire Special Branch reviews photographs of unidentified individuals who had attended training camps, and recognises one of the photographs taken during Operation WARLOCK in 2001 as being Mohammed Siddique KHAN. This information comes to the attention of MI5 in May 2007 in the course of this Review.

Autumn 2005
***
***. This indicates that Mohammed Siddique KHAN was also in the car, with KHYAM and Shujah MAHMOOD, on 21 February 2004.

December 2005
Two MI5 sources are shown photographs from Operation WARLOCK (the 2001 extremist training camp) and identify Mohammed Siddique KHAN as one of the attendees.

February 2008
In preparation for a terrorism-related trial, a Detective Constable from West Yorkshire Police further analyses the recording of the conversation in KHYAM's car on 21 February 2004. This new analysis confirms that Mohammed Siddique KHAN was in the car, and suggests that Shazad TANWEER may also have been present.

Document 4: West Yorkshire Police 'Gist' re: Martin McDaid and the Iqra bookshop. This summary of Martin McDaid and the security service operations and investigations around him only became available in 2011. Notice how little of this information made it into the ISC's 2008 timeline, where McDaid is not even named let alone properly identified.

Gist re: Martin McDaid

1. McDaid had been known to the SyS and WYP since at least 1998. He was suspected of being an Islamic extremist and of possible involvement in extremist activities including Jihad Training since at least 1998.

Operation Warlock - 2001

2. A 'training camp' took place at Dalehead in the Lake District between 26.10.01 and 28.01.01. This is the camp referred to at paragraphs 46 and 280-1 of the ISC Report dated May 2009.

3. WYP performed surveillance on the training camp at the time it took place. WYP and SyS were aware that McDaid was one of the organisers of the camp.

4. As a result of the surveillance operation WYP carried out a number of enquiries to identify those attending the camp. Those inquiries included:

    a) PNC checks on vehicles observed at the camp.
    b) Obtained photographs of persons linked to the vehicles and compared those with video stills taken from the surveillance of the camp.
    c) Identified a number of persons thought to have attended the camp. McDaid, McClintock and "Tafalal Mohammed" (later identified as Tafazal Mohammed) were amongst those identified.
    d) The results of the enquiries by WYP were supplied to SyS.

5. MSK attended the camp and the surveillance operation produced photographic images of attendees at the camp, including one image of MSK (see paragraphs 280-281 of the ISC Report).

6. WYP showed the photographic images from Operation Warlock, including the one depicting MSK, to one source in 2001. The source was unable to identify the individual in the image depicting MSK. Security Service records indicate that the photographic images were also shown at this time to sources in other areas of the country, also without MSK being identified.

7. After 7 July 2005 a number of WYP and SyS sources were shown the operation Warlock photographic images and identified the image of MSK. None of these sources had been recruited prior to November 2003.

8.   The Dalehead camp was one of several that occurred and which were
        subject of investigation.

9.   SyS assessment of the information obtained from the camps was that it
        was useful in having identified repeat attendees and therefore the more
        significant individuals. There had been no indication of illegal activity
        seen on any camps and no intelligence to suggest that such activity
        was a likely development. Unless the intelligence picture changed, the
        information from the camps was of diminishing return as it continued to
        identify many of the same figures plus a few others who were largely
        on the periphery of SyS interest.

Operation Honeysuckle - 2003

10.   In pursuance of a joint operation with SyS, WYP performed
        surveillance on McDaid over 14 and 15 April 2003.

11.   [..]

12.   In the course of surveillance on 14 April McDaid was seen to get into
        and be given a lift in a blue BMW car registration J 729 EUB. The lift
        lasted for 3 minutes. Subsequent checks on the car showed it was
        registered to Mr Sidique Khan of 11 Gregory Street, Batley, West
        Yorkshire, WF17 6NH. Checks on police record systems revealed a
        reference to a previous caution. There was no previous record of
        Sidique Khan on WYP Special Branch systems.

13.   As part of the operation WYP also conducted enquiries into other
        premises, addresses and vehicles seen in the course of the
        surveillance. Those enquiries included:

        a)   Research into a Renault Espace vehicle showed the registered
                keeper was Tafazal Mohammed of 5 Ladypit Lane, Beeston.
        b)   Research into 49 Bude Road, Beeston linked the address to
                Tafazal Mohammed.
        c)   Research into a Mosque in Beeston visited by McDaid identified
                previous information received by WYP from another Police
                Force. That information suggested that Imans at the Mosque
                were recruiting for Jihad. The intelligence was assessed at the
                time it had been received as from an untested source the
                reliability of which was incapable of assessment.

14.   The WYP conducted further enquiries into the Iqra Bookshop in
        December 2003. Those enquiries revealed, amongst other things, the
        following:

        a)   The Iqra Bookshop was managed by a group of individuals,
                including McDaid and Tafazal Mohammed.
        b)   The Iqra Bookshop was a registered charity.

    c)   The Iqra Bookshop was closely linked with the Rays of Truth Bookshop 44 Woodsley Road, Leeds, which was managed by the same group of individuals.

    d)   The Iqra Bookshop was located close to the Hamara Healthy Living Centre, Leeds. The Leeds Community School was linked to the Hamara Healthy Living Centre.

15.   [...].

16.   [...].

Document 5: WYP Special Branch check on Blue BMW reg number J729 EUB. A day after WYP observed this BMW giving a lift to McDaid they carried out a check to see who the car was registered to. They found that the registered owner was one Sidique Khan. This information was not passed to MI5, at least officially.

WYP00000012-043

Exhibit 8

Action

Region :	WEST YORKSHIRE POLICE
Branch :	HQ Special Branch
Operation / Job No. :	OPERATION HONEYSUCKLE ▮▮▮▮ *(Current)*

Priority :	High	Action No. :	00007

Origin :

Subject : Enquiries / research re Blue BMW Reg No J729EUB

Date Raised :	16/04/2003
State :	Allocated
Allocated To :	▮▮▮▮
Allocated By :	

Nature of Action :-

Enquiries / research re Blue BMW Reg No J729EUB

Result of Action :-

Cross References :-

Object References :-

Notes :-

Updates :- CHECKS ON VEHICLE REVEAL NO TRACE ON SYSTEMS.
(16/04/2003 @ 14:46 ▮▮▮▮
CHECKS ON KEEPER REVEAL NO TRACE ▮▮▮▮.
▮▮▮▮ N89908 - CAUTIONED 1992 for S.4-7, SIDIQUE KHAN.
▮▮▮▮ - NO TRACE

Document 6: MI5-WYP-NERIC email exchange, June-July 2004. As part of Operation Scraw, MI5 requested more information about Sidique Khan, among others, from WYP and NERIC. The response says that there is 'no trace' of Khan on WYP and NERIC systems, when the checks should have found the previous document on the car registered to Khan.

SYS00011004-001

OUT-MESSAGE

Action:	North East RIC
Info:	West Yorks SB
For the attention of:	DI ███████ at North East RIC
From:	████████
Date:	08 June 2004
File Reference:	████████████
Copied to:	████████████████
Our Reference:	██████████

SUBJECT: Op CREVICE/SCRAW: Background and links to Leeds

THE FOLLOWING INFORMATION HAS BEEN COMMUNICATED IN CONFIDENCE AND SHALL NOT BE DISSEMINATED OUTSIDE OF YOUR BRANCH WITHOUT THE AGREEMENT OF THE SERVICE. THIS INFORMATION IS EXTREMELY SENSITIVE AND MUST BE TREATED ACCORDINGLY.

Please refer to the attached ████████████ dated 30 March 2004 for background information on OP CREVICE.

2.   During OP CREVICE we identified the following possible connections between the CREVICE network and associates from the Leeds / West Yorks area.

3.   A green Honda Civic, R480 CCA was observed during OP CREVICE as an associated vehicle for Omar KHYAM. The registered keeper since 1 February 2004 is Sidique KHAN, 11 Gregory Street, Batley, West Yorkshire, WF17 6NH. The previous owner since 25 July 2003 was given as Miss Hisina PATEL, 10 Thornhill Ave, Dewsbury, West Yorks. The owner before her was a ████████████ of █ ████████████████████████████ Open source checks reveal that Sidique KHAN has links to two separate addresses within the last two years. These are as follows: 10 Thornhill Park Ave, Thornhill, Dewsbury, West Yorks and 99 Stratford Street, Leeds, West Yorks LS11 6JG. *Security Service Comment: None of these individuals or addresses had previously come to our attention.*

4.   On 28 February 2004 surveillance showed that KHYAM and his associate Javid AKHBAR, in his Suzuki Vitara, met with the green Honda Civic (three UI

males on board) in a McDonalds car park. After travelling in convoy to 56 Hencroft Street, Slough (KHYAM's home address) KHYAM and Javid AHKBAR boarded the green Honda Civic. Coverage against the green Honda Civic eventually observed KHYAM and AHKBAR being dropped of at Herschel St, Slough. The third passenger was dropped off at either ▓ or 115 Tempest Road, Leeds LS11. The fourth passenger was dropped off at Lodge Lane (nfd) and the vehicle was housed at number 12 or 14 Pickles Field off Pickles Street in Batley, West Yorkshire. *Security Service Comment:* ▓ *checks show that Mr* ▓ *is registered to the 12 Pickles Field address. A* ▓ *is registered to this address, the owner since* ▓ *is shown as* ▓ *born* ▓

5.   The driver of the green Honda Civic R480 CCA seen on 28 February 2004 is believed to identical with the driver of the green Corsa YB52LUF (nfd) seen by surveillance on 23 March 2004.

6.   ▓

7.   The users of the following telephone numbers have also been in contact with members of the CREVICE network: ▓ subscribed to Miss ▓ , and ▓ subscribed to ▓

8.   Finally, subsequent reporting has indicated that two individuals from Leeds, known as IBRAHIM and ZUBAIR (nfd) were also historical contacts of Mohammed Qayoum KHAN MQK in the UK. IBRAHIM and ZUBAIR are reported to have travelled from the UK to Islamabad in June 2003, in order to become involved in possible extremist activities. Nothing further is known about these individuals.

9.   **We would be grateful for any details you may have in your records (including photographs) of the individuals and addresses mentioned above, particularly any further information that will enable us to fully identify IBRAHIM and ZUBAIR.**

10.   Please do not hesitate to contact us if you have any further questions.

11.   Many Thanks

NNNN

For the Attention of: ███████████
From: ███████████ North East RIC

Date: 14th July 2004

Your File Ref: ███████████
Your Ref: ███████

SUBJECT: Op CREVICE / SCRAW: Background and Links to Leeds

With regards to the above subject, please read the following report in conjunction with your Cluster of the 8th June 2004.

Green Honda Civic R480CCA – Observed during OPERATION CREVICE as an associate vehicle for Omar KHYAM – Registered to Sidique KHAN

North East RIC, West Yorkshire Special Branch and local systems have been checked with a negative result.

PNC Audit on R480CCA shows 22 enquiries on PNC for this vehicle between the period 01/08/03 – 12/07/04. Of these the majority are enquiries carried out by the Metropolitan Police and 21 are believed to be related to Operation Crevice. (Operation Crevice is referred to in 3 transactions, a further 8 are ████████ activations). There are ███████████ these may be enquiries by the Security Services. Enquiries if required regarding these transactions should be directed to ███████████ In relation to West Yorkshire there is an enquiry on 20/08/03 at 04:13 which relates to a moving vehicle at Kirkstall Rd, Leeds. The enquiry was carried out by PC ███████████ Firearms Ops Support team. There is no corresponding OIS entry relating to this stop however the officer may have made a pocketbook entry.

Enquiries are in hand to liaise with PC ███████████ re circumstances of stop on 20/08/03.

Green Honda Civic R480CCA registered to Sidique KHAN of 11 Gregory Street, Batley, West Yorkshire WF17 6NH

Sidique KHAN

Sidique KHAN has been identified as born 20/10/1974 in Leeds.
He was cautioned for a S47 Assault in 1992.
Previous addresses on West Yorkshire Police Crime Information System are 30 Runswick Place, Holbeck, Leeds as at 19/10/2001 and 99 Stratford Street Beeston, Leeds as at 03/02/1993.
No Trace of KHAN on NERIC / West Yorkshire Special Branch systems.

See photograph of Sidique KHAN dated 03/02/1993.

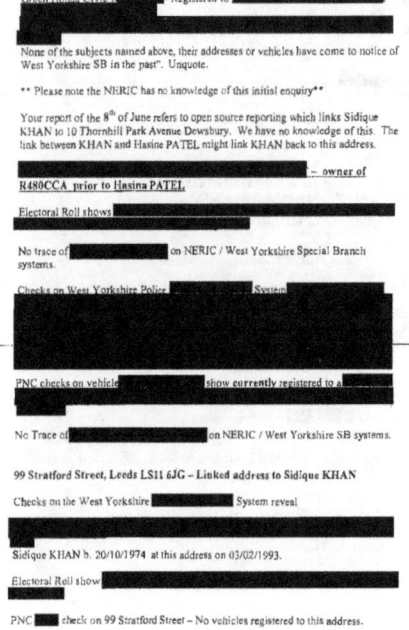

Green Honda Civic S████ - Registered to ████████████

None of the subjects named above, their addresses or vehicles have come to notice of West Yorkshire SB in the past". Unquote.

** Please note the NERIC has no knowledge of this initial enquiry**

Your report of the 8th of June refers to open source reporting which links Sidique KHAN to 10 Thornhill Park Avenue Dewsbury. We have no knowledge of this. The link between KHAN and Hasine PATEL might link KHAN back to this address.

████████████████ - owner of R480CCA prior to Hasina PATEL.

Electoral Roll shows ████████████

No trace of ████████ on NERIC / West Yorkshire Special Branch systems.

Checks on West Yorkshire Police ████████ System ████████

PNC checks on vehicle ████████ show currently registered to a ████████

No Trace of ████████ on NERIC / West Yorkshire SB systems.

99 Stratford Street, Leeds LS11 6JG – Linked address to Sidique KHAN

Checks on the West Yorkshire ████████ System reveal

Sidique KHAN b. 20/10/1974 at this address on 03/02/1993.

Electoral Roll show ████████

PNC ██ check on 99 Stratford Street – No vehicles registered to this address.

███ Tempest Road / 115 Tempest Road – Third Passenger Dropped off

Electoral Roll shows ████████

Enquiries in hand to ascertain who resides at Flat B, ███ Tempest Road, Leeds.

No Trace of ████████ or ██ Tempest Road on NERIC / West Yorkshire SB systems.

West Yorkshire Special Branch systems show a report from Dc ████████ dated 23/02/04 to Dc ████████ in response to their cluster of 17/02/04 re Operation CREVICE and 115 Tempest Road Leeds LS11 6AN as follows:-

Quote "There is no number 115 Tempest Road Leeds. The postcode given is allocated to Tempest Place and there is no number 115 in this street either. Tempest Road house numbers stop at ██ and commence again at ██. The house which one would imagine number 115 to be is the rear of number ██ Colwyn Road, Leeds LS11 6LQ. Enquiries reveal that ████████████████████

owner of a ████████████████ and there is no garage at the premises. The persons, address and vehicle mentioned have not previously come to the notice of this office nor local police indices. Enquiries with local records reveal noone from the address are registered as having an unattached lock up garage". Unquote.

** Please note – The NERIC has no knowledge of this initial enquiry**

Lodge Lane – Fourth Passenger dropped off

West Yorkshire Special Branch systems show a report from Dc ████████ dated 23/02/04 to Dc ████████ in response to their cluster of 17/02/04 re Operation CREVICE and ██ / ██ Lodge Road, Pudsey LS28 7LY as follows:-

Quote "There is a Lodge Road in Pudsey with the postcode LS28 7Ly, however there are no numbers ██ / ██. This is a small road numbering 1 to 15 and 2 to 14. There are no persons living in this road that could be described as ethnic. The location is such that it can only be described as all traditional English named families with English sounding names. None of the persons living in Lodge Road, according to local council records. Unquote

** Please note – the NERIC has no knowledge of this initial enquiry**

The only reference to Lodge Lane on West Yorkshire Special Branch systems is that the 'Iqra' Bookshop is situated there.

████ Pickles Field off Pickles Street Batley – Green Honda Civic R480CCA housed

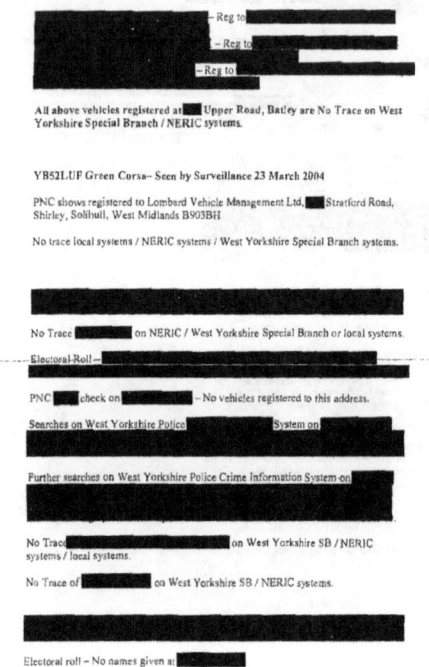

All above vehicles registered at ▓ Upper Road, Batley are No Trace on West Yorkshire Special Branch / NERIC systems.

YB52LUF *Green Corsa* – Seen by Surveillance 23 March 2004

PNC shows registered to Lombard Vehicle Management Ltd, ▓ Stratford Road, Shirley, Solihull, West Midlands B903BH

No trace local systems / NERIC systems / West Yorkshire Special Branch systems.

No Trace ▓▓▓▓ on NERIC / West Yorkshire Special Branch or local systems.

Electoral Roll – ▓▓▓▓▓▓▓▓▓▓▓

PNC ▓ check on ▓▓▓▓ – No vehicles registered to this address.

Searches on West Yorkshire Police ▓▓▓▓ System on ▓

Further searches on West Yorkshire Police Crime Information System on ▓

No Trace ▓▓▓▓▓▓▓ on West Yorkshire SB / NERIC systems / local systems.

No Trace of ▓▓▓▓ on West Yorkshire SB / NERIC systems.

Electoral roll – No names given at ▓▓▓▓

27

Document 7: Extracts from Charity Commission Declaration of Trustees for the Iqra bookshop. Though additional investigations by WYP into Iqra in late 2003 found that it was a charity run by Taf Mohamed and Martin McDaid, they supposedly did not see this paperwork showing that Khan and Tanweer were trustees.

INQ00009370-002

OP THESEUS - X22399 - JSM/54 - Book 454.0057 - Page 1 of 6
49 BUDE ROAD, BEESTON, LEEDS

Charity
COMMISSION
for England and Wales

Declaration by Charity Trustees

This form asks for the full name, address, occupation, date of birth and signature of every person who is, or it is known, will be, a charity trustee. We ask for this information so that we can identify those persons who are, or will be, the charity trustees and can contact them if necessary. Where we have agreed to consider a draft governing document we want all those who expect to be first trustees to sign this declaration.

We ask for details of occupation as it is useful when considering an organisation for registration, to establish the relevant qualifications of trustees who act in connection with certain types of charity: charities offering medical treatment for example.

We ask for the date of birth of each trustee for two reasons. We need to ensure that each trustee is over the age of eighteen. persons under the age of eighteen cannot be held legally responsible for their acts and decisions as a trustee, and do not usually have any voting rights. We also need to be able to

distinguish between trustees who have the same name and address.

The signatories are also asked to confirm whether they have read booklets CC21 and CC3 (which is included as part of the Application Pack). The reason for this is that we consider it of great importance that trustees are made aware of the duties and responsibilities of their position at the outset. We therefore ask each of the trustees to sign the declaration. We will not refuse to register an organisation simply on the grounds that this form has not been completed, but we will enquire why the trustees feel unable to sign. The people listed on this form will be sent information about trusteeship on registration, it is therefore important you let us know if the trustees change.

Further copies of the form of declaration can be obtained from us on request if necessary, or you may photocopy additional pages if you prefer.

Providing us with information which you know or suspect to be false may be a criminal offence under section 11 of the Charities Act 1993.

PLEASE COMPLETE IN BLACK INK AND CAPITAL LETTERS

Name of charity: I Q R A

Reference number (if any):

Number of charity trustees: 6

We, the undersigned, declare that:
- We are willing to act as charity trustees in respect of the above named organisation and are fully aware of the organisation's purpose as set out in form APP 1 (Application for Registration);
- We are not disqualified from acting as a charity trustee, for example, because of unspent convictions for dishonesty offences (see CC21, paragraph 32);
- We understand the responsibilities involved in running a charity and will run the charity in accordance with the guidelines set out in publication CC3;
- We are aware that further information is available to us in the Registration Information Pack (which has been read by the person(s) making the application on our behalf).

OP THESEUS - X22399 - JSM/54 - Book 454.0057 - Page 2 of 6
49 NAMES, OCCUPATIONS, USED NAMES AND ADDRESSES OF TRUSTEES OF YOUR...

Charity

1

Signature	*[signature]*
	Title: MR
Full name (IN BLOCK CAPITALS)	NAVEED KHAN
Full private address	personal information
	Postcode: personal information
Occupation	SCHOOL ACTIVITY WORKER
Date of birth	personal information

2

Signature	*[signature] Y. Mohammed*
	Title: MR
Full name (IN BLOCK CAPITALS)	TAFAZAL MOHAMMAD
Full private address	personal information
	Postcode: personal information
Occupation	Youth & community WORKER
Date of birth	personal information

3

Signature	*[signature]*
	Title: Mr
Full name (IN BLOCK CAPITALS)	SIDIQUE KHAN
Full private address	personal information
	Postcode: personal information
Occupation	Youth and Community Worker.
Date of birth	personal information

Charity

4

Signature	S. Saleem — Title MR
Full name (IN BLOCK CAPITALS)	SADEER SALEEM
Full private address	personal information
	Postcode personal information
Occupation	UNEMPLOYD
Date of birth	personal information

5

Signature	S. Ullah — Title MR
Full name (IN BLOCK CAPITALS)	SHIPON ULLAH
Full private address	personal information
	Postcode personal information
Occupation	UNIMPLOYD
Date of birth	personal information

6

Signature	[signature] — Title
Full name (IN BLOCK CAPITALS)	KHALID KHALIQ
Full private address	personal information
	Postcode personal information
Occupation	Youth WORKER
Date of birth	personal information

OP THESEUS - X22399 - JSM/54 - Book 454.0057 - Page 6 of 6
49 BUDE ROAD, BEESTON, LEEDS. \ NAMES AND ADDRESSES OF TRUSTEES OF IQRA

IQRA

49A Bude Road
Beeston Leeds LS11 6HX

Tel/Fax: [personal information]
E mail: [personal information]mail.com

1st May 2003

NAMES AND ADDRESS OF TRUSTEES

Naveed Khan
Tafazal Mohammad
Sidique Khan
Sadeer Saleem
Shipon Ullah
Khalid Khaliq
Sophina Ali
Arbab Ahmad
Saheed B. Alam
Shezad Tanweer

personal information

Tafazal Mohammad
Secretary

Document 8: MI5 subscriber check on mobile phone linked to Mohammed Qayyum Khan (Q). According to the ISC's timeline the calls between this phone and Q's did not take place until the summer of 2003, and yet the subscriber check took place in March, linking Sidique Khan to the Iqra bookshop before the Honeysuckle surveillance on McDaid that identified his car.

SYS00011076-001

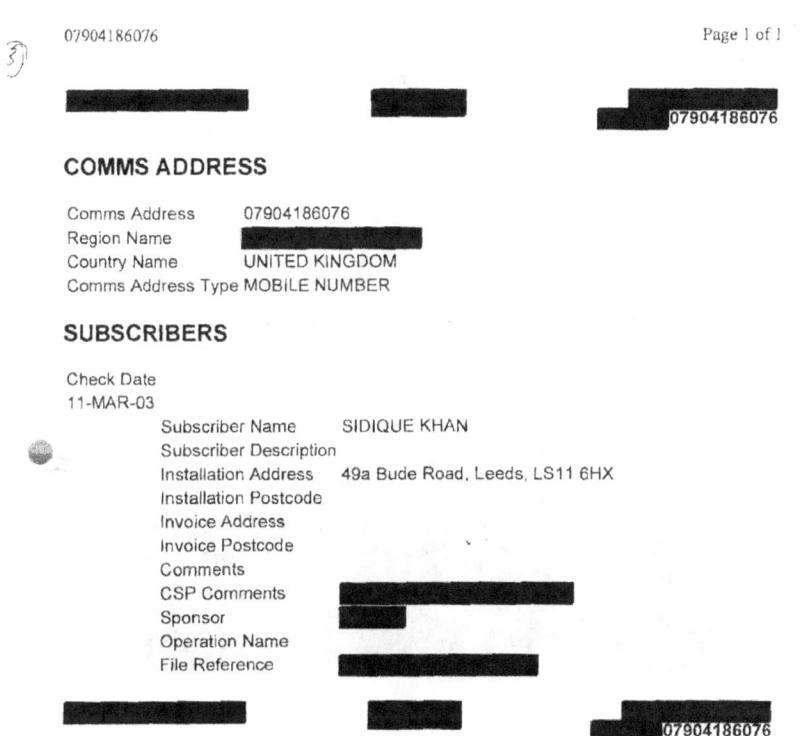

07904186076

Page 1 of 1

07904186076

COMMS ADDRESS

Comms Address   07904186076
Region Name
Country Name   UNITED KINGDOM
Comms Address Type MOBILE NUMBER

SUBSCRIBERS

Check Date
11-MAR-03

Subscriber Name   SIDIQUE KHAN
Subscriber Description
Installation Address   49a Bude Road, Leeds, LS11 6HX
Installation Postcode
Invoice Address
Invoice Postcode
Comments
CSP Comments
Sponsor
Operation Name
File Reference

07904186076

Document 9: MI5 summary of Operation Crevice-Stepford bombers links. This MI5 timeline was prepared for the inquests and records all the instances when any of the 'Stepford bombers' (i.e. the alleged 7/7 bombers) turned up during surveillance of the Operative Crevice suspects. Note that even this timeline says that the calls between Q and Sidique Khan took place in summer 2003.

SYS00011079-001

This document summarises the occasions when two of the STEPFORD bombers (MSK and Shezad TANWEER) came to our attention during the CREVICE investigation and related enquiries.

Early links to Mohammed Qayum KHAN (MQK)

1.　On 13 July 2003 ▮▮▮ the mobile phone of Mohammed Qayum KHAN (MQK) ▮▮▮ contacted the unidentified user of **07904186076** *(now known to be Mohammed Siddique KHAN)* on several occasions ▮▮▮

2.　On 19 July 2003 ▮▮▮ MQK's mobile ▮▮▮ contacted **07792261882** ▮▮▮
07792261882. MQK made three subsequent calls ▮▮▮ Incidentally, MQK contacted this individual on **07904186076** in two of their four communications that day, ▮▮▮

3.　On 24 July 2003 probably MSK using **07792261882** contacted MQK ▮▮▮ The same ▮▮▮ called MQK 45 minutes later ▮▮▮

4.　On 15 August 2003 MSK (using **07904186076**) ▮▮▮

Subscribers

07904186076: SIDDIQUE KHAN: 49a Bude Road, Leeds, West Yorks, LS1 1 6HX

07792261882: Unregistered PAYG

Assessment/Action taken when reporting received

5.　In the summer of 2003 we assessed MQK to be the co-ordinator of a Luton-based network of Al Qaida facilitators. He would use couriers to send money ▮▮▮ to, ▮▮▮ AQ operatives in Pakistan. Technical and surveillance coverage of MQK during the Spring/Summer of 2003 indicated that he was in contact with a large number of individuals. ▮▮▮

6.　In 2003 we had no intelligence to indicate that MQK's facilitation network stretched beyond the Luton area, let alone as far as Leeds. ▮▮▮ , there was no intelligence to suggest that their association was linked to AQ support activity or Islamist extremism in general. MSK was therefore regarded as one of many associates of MQK and he was not investigated further.

Malakand Training Camp - July 2003

7.   In April/May 2004 reporting from Mohammed Junaid BABAR (MJB) indicated that two individuals known as IBRAHIM (now known to be MSK) and ZUBAIR (now known to be Mohammed SHAK1L) arrived at Islamabad airport in July 2003, where they were met by ███████████████. Co-incidentally, on the same day three Operation CREVICE targets Ahmed Ali KHAN, Jawad AKBAR and Waseem GULZAR also arrived in Islamabad with the intention of attending a training camp in Malakand. They were met at the airport by KHYAM and MJB. Members of the two groups were then introduced to each other and they had breakfast together.

8.   In May 2004 ███████████████████████████ also highlighted the existence of IBRAHIM and ZUBAIR, who he described as originating from Leeds. The information ██████ provided on the two individuals effectively mirrors that gleaned from MJB in April/May 2005 (see para.7), although he provided a couple of additional snippets. ██████ stated that IBRAHIM and ZUBAIR were sent to Pakistan by MQK on a fact-finding mission about Mujahideen fighters gaining access into Afghanistan. He also mentioned that the two individuals wanted to meet senior AQ commander Abu MUNTHIR. ██████ stated that MQK had left the decision as to whether IBRAHIM and ZUBAIR should travel to the tribal areas to his discretion. ██████ maintained that he advised them not to travel there and instead they returned to the UK after two weeks. It has been confirmed, post 7/7, that MSK and SHAKIL departed Lahore for London on 7 August 2003.

9.   During an evidential interview with SO13 in March 2005, MJB provided additional information on IBRAHIM and ZUBAIR and their visit to Pakistan. He described them as originating from Bradford and confirmed information previously provided by ██████ that the two individuals had been sent to Pakistan by MQK to gain an insight into Mujahideen operations on the Pakistan/Afghanistan border. MJB also mentioned that IBRAHIM and ZUBAIR attended the Malakand training camp along with several of the CREVICE targets.

10.   MJB advised that the Malakand training camp commenced in early July 2003 with the initial attendees consisting of: Omar KHYAM, Shujah Uddin MAHMOOD, Anthony GARCIA, Shiraj Ul-ISLAM @ AYOUB, Zeeshan SIDDIQUE @ IMRAN, Rizwan SHAMIM @ RIAZ and Atif JALEEL @ Uni Boy. Later in July 2003 this group was joined by KHAN, AKBAR, GULZAR, Mohammed Momin KHAWAJA, MSK @ IBRAHIM and Mohammed SHAKIL @ ZUBAIR. The group were reported to have fired weapons and used rocket launchers at the camp as well as experimenting with explosives.

Assessment/Action taken when reporting received

11.   The FBI provided us with notes from their debriefs of MJB in April/May 2004, which included references to IBRAHIM and ZUBAIR. However, it is important to note that these were two of many individuals named by MJB. Although the information he provided showed that they had met members of the CREVICE network in Pakistan, there was no indication that they were involved in terrorist planning or even AQ support activities. It is worth noting that MJB described other individuals who appeared far more likely to be involved in terrorist planning than IBRAHIM and ZUBAIR. It is also worth noting that the FBI debriefs were received in several parts and as scanned images. It was therefore a lengthy process to manually collate all the intelligence on each target.

12.   In May 2004, the A4 surveillance photos of MSK, TANWEER and Shipon ULLAH were included in a pack of all CREVICE-related photographs sent ███████████████ ███████████████████████ for identification purposes. However, he did not positively identify any of the three individuals. The photos of TANWEER and ULLAH were also amongst a set shown to MJB during FBI debriefs in April/May 2004. MJB did not positively identify TANWEER and ULLAH, who were depicted in the surveillance photographs. The surveillance photo of MSK was omitted from the pack shown to MJB due to its poor quality.

13.   The evidential statement taken by SO 13 from MJB in March 2005 was the first time that the intelligence he provided was assembled in chronological order, which made it easier to judge the significance of each target he mentioned. In late March 2005 facts relevant to each target were collated. Recommendations were then made to ██ management that we should initiate investigations into three sets of individuals described by MJB in the statement - these included IBRAHIM and ZUBAIR. This recommendation was accepted and Operation DOWNTEMPO commenced on 12 April 2005 in order to fully identify and investigate IBRAHIM and ZUBAIR.

14.   Several possible candidates for IBRAHIM and ZUBAIR were identified, but the identification was difficult as the above bears no resemblance to their real names and the task was further complicated as MJB erroneously reported that they were from Bradford as opposed to Leeds. In May 2005 the three Leeds-based individuals who featured in the 2 February 2004 surveillance coverage of Omar KHYAM (see para. 18) were flagged up as three of several possible candidates for IBRAHIM and ZUBAIR.

15.   Despite the fact that IBRAHIM and ZUBAIR were recommended as investigative targets, the intelligence cases against them did not justify them being considered as high priority ████ targets.

Activities of 2 February 2004

16.   On 28 January 2004 ████████████ KHYAM's phone ████████ received a call from **07951364275,** ██ ██ ██ ██

17.   ██ Later in the day, ████████████████████ Omar KHYAM's mobile indicated that he was in contact ████████ with MSK, who was using **07951364275** ████████

18.   At 20:28 KHYAM and Shujah MAHMOOD in the Suzuki Vitara travelled to Langley Parade in Crawley, which is near to his home address. A few minutes later a Green Honda Civic (R840 CCA) pulled up alongside the Vitara. We now know that its three occupants were MSK, Shezad TANWEER and Shipon ULLAH. However, all three were unidentified at the time. KHYAM joined MSK in the Honda Civic and they drove around for approximately 25 minutes, possibly for the purpose of a meeting. KHYAM handed MSK a piece of paper (nfd) and all six individuals then returned to their respective vehicles. The Honda Civic proceeded north on the M1 while KHYAM and MAHMOOD probably returned to the home address.

19.   A4 Surveillance followed the vehicle to Toddington Service station where photographs of ULLAH, TANWEER and MSK were taken. They were labelled Man C, D and E respectively at the time. The Honda then carried on North to Leeds where ULLAH and TANWEER were dropped off in the vicinity of addresses (a) and (b), while MSK was housed at address (c).

a)   115 or 117 Lodge Lane, Leeds, West Yorkshire, LS1 1 6JF

b)   115 Tempest Road, Leeds, West Yorkshire, LS1 1 6AU

c)   10 Thornhill Park Avenue, Dewsbury, West Yorkshire, WF12 ODA

Assessment/Action taken when reporting received

20.   Our assessment of Omar KHYAM at the time was ▮▮▮ The 2 February meeting preceded the ▮▮ ▮▮▮▮▮▮▮ This intelligence was received ▮▮▮▮ February 2004 and triggered the major CREVICE investigation.

21.   Our initial telephone coverage of KHYAM showed that he had many associates and used his phone regularly. ▮▮▮

22.   It is important to realise that Shipon ULLAH, TANWEER and MSK were not identified at the time and were labelled Man C, D and E respectively. Furthermore, based on the intelligence available, there was no clear indication that MSK was the individual ▮▮▮▮▮ back in July 2003: MSK was not listed on the voters roll at 10 Thornhill Park Avenue, the phone he used to contact KHYAM was a pre-pay mobile and the mobile he used to contact MQK in 2003 was registered to a different address in Leeds. Incidentally, post 7/7 phone record analysis shows that MSK was actually in contact with KHYAM as early as October 2003.

23.   On 11 February 2004 a cluster was sent to MPSB which included details of the addresses and vehicles associated with the 'Leeds three' to date. A request for further details regarding the owner of the Honda Civic driven by MSK and the associated address (Hasina PATEL, 10 Thornhill Park Avenue, Dewsbury) was sent to West Yorkshire SB on 16 February 2004. Thornhill Park Avenue and the Honda Civic appear on a list of vehicles and addresses recommended for priority targeting by A1/A4 on 18 February 2004.

Activities of 21 February 2004

24.   At 18:39 KHYAM and 2 UMs were seen to exit 92 Langley Drive (this is probably 90 Langley Drive: the home address of Waheed MAHMOOD). KHYAM and one of the UMs joined Shujah Uddin MAHMOOD and Momin KHAWAJA in the Suzuki. The other UM (strongly assessed to be Waheed MAHMOOD) boarded a White Morrisons van. Both vehicles drove south. Surveillance allowed the van to proceed and the Suzuki eventually

stopped outside 2 The Hollow (the home address of Waseem GULZAR). All four individuals entered the address.

25.   Surveillance observed KHYAM and Shujah MAHMOOD leaving 2 The Hollow at 20:49. They boarded the Vitara and drove to a Kebab shop on Langley Parade. At 21:05 the Vitara returned to the area of 2 The Hollow and surveillance observed KHYAM and MAHMOOD chatting in the car until approximately 21:34, when they re-entered the address. Eavesdropping product from the device installed in the Vitara between 20:50 and 21:30 indicates the presence of a third individual in the vehicle.

26.   At approximately 00:00 seven UMs and Ahmed Ali KHAN exited 2 The Hollow and boarded four separate vehicles. Three boarded a White Morrisons transit van (ND02 HLH), one of whom is almost certainly Waheed MAHMOOD. The other vehicles observed were a Blue Toyota Avensis (VRN unknown), a Silver Vauxhall Corsa (FP53 UEM) and Ahmed Ali KHAN's Blue VW Golf.

27.   At 00:38 the Silver Corsa returned to 2 The Hollow, where a UM alighted and entered with a key (this could be Waseem GULZAR). At 04:58 a UM wearing a checked jacket boarded the Corsa and drove North on the A23 to Manor Royal Industrial Estate, and entered the carpark for Invenysis. Crews then handed over control of the Corsa to Police surveillance teams. At 06:07 the Corsa was seen parked empty outside 2 The Hollow.

28.   At 09:18 on Sunday 22 February 2004, surveillance observed KHYAM, Shujah MAHMOOD and Momin KHAWAJA leaving 2 The Hollow. They subsequently boarded the Vitara and drove to KHYAM's flat in Slough.

Assessment/Action taken when reporting received

29.   In view of the personnel who attended the meeting at 2 The Hollow, our assessment at the time was that the meeting was likely to be of significance in an Islamist extremist context and possibly relevant to the CREVICE plot. However, given that there was no audio eavesdropping device installed at the address, this is conjecture.

30.   There is no mention in the surveillance report of a third individual *(now known to be MSK)* boarding the Vitara at 20:49 with KHYAM and Shujah MAHMOOD. Furthermore, surveillance observed only two individuals (KHYAM and MAHMOOD) re-entering 2 The Hollow at 21:34. The original transcript of the 40 minute conversation, which took place in the Vitara between 20:50 and 21:30, indicates that three individuals were present, referred to as UM1, UM2 and UM3. There is no mention of any individual having a Northern accent. Also, there was no telephone contact between KHYAM and MSK prior to their meeting, unlike the other four occasions when they met It would therefore have been impossible to identify the third individual in the Vitara as MSK when the reporting was received.

31.   The original transcript of the conversation is unclear and disjointed. Also, given that all three individuals are listed as UMs it is unclear which passages of speech relate to each individual. Pakistan, the tribal areas and various fraud scams are mentioned. However, given what we knew at the time (in a pre-MJB statement era) and in view of the lack of a verbatim transcript of the conversation, it was not possible to understand its true significance. Another important factor is that there was no mention of the CREVICE plot in this particular conversation, which was the primary focus at the time. As a consequence, no further work was carried out in relation to this piece of intelligence as the investigation was moving at a fast pace, identifying separate intelligence which was relevant to the CREVICE conspiracy.

32.   On 28 February 2004 between 06:33 and 06:56 ██████████████

33.   At 08:56 KHYAM and Shujah MAHMOOD in the Suzuki Vitara arrived at Sainsburys car park in Crawley and pulled up alongside the Honda Civic (see surveillance of 2 February 2004). Three unidentified males (now known to be MSK, TANWEER and 'ULLAH') entered McDonalds with KHYAM and MAHMOOD. The Suzuki and the Honda then travelled in convoy to several builders merchants in Crawley. An individual believed to TANWEER enquired about opening accounts with the companies they visited.

34.   At 13:07 the two vehicles travelled to a Mosque in Slough where they stayed for approximately 40 minutes. All five individuals then travelled to 56 Hencroft Street, Slough. which is KHYAM's flat. CCTV coverage of the address showed that KHYAM was carrying a video camera. At 15:36 CCTV footage showed KHYAM, Shujah MAHMOOD, MSK, TANWEER and 'ULLAH' leaving 56 Hencroft Street.

35.   After visiting the New Kabana Restaurant, all five individuals boarded the Honda Civic and travelled north on the Ml via the M25. The CREVICE log indicates that at 17:30 the Honda stopped at Junction 11 of the Ml (Luton turn-off) where MQK was waiting for them. The meeting is assessed to have lasted for only 10 minutes as ████████ showed MQK entering his home address in Luton a short time after the meeting took place.

36.   The Honda Civic continued travelling north on the Ml until it reached Easytalk.com, a mobile phone shop in Wellingborough, Northants which is owned by radical Imam Bisharat ALL All five individuals entered Easytalk.com at 19:00 and left at 21:26 when the shop closed down. The group moved to Flames Restaurant in Wellingborough before returning to 56 Hencroft Street, Slough where KHYAM and Shujah MAHMOOD were dropped off. MPSB S-Squad followed the Honda back to Leeds where two individuals, probably 'ULLAH' and TANWEER were dropped off at Lodge Lane and Tempest Road. The driver, believed to be MSK, was housed at 12 or 14 Pickles Field, Batley at 03:05 on 29 February 2004.

Assessment/Action taken when reporting received

37.   We were aware at the time that the three Leeds-based individuals who featured in the surveillance on 28 February 2004 were identical with Man C, D and E. ELG minutes from 28/02/04 record that the ELG was briefed to this effect. ████████████████
████████████ Our assessment at the time was that the CREVICE targets were opening accounts with a number of building merchants with the intention of obtaining a large quantity of expensive building equipment on credit.

38.   We believe their subsequent intention would have been to default on the repayment of the money and possibly sell the equipment to third parties for cash. The CREVICE targets would therefore have fraudulently obtained large sums of money, which they are likely to have intended to transfer to Pakistan for the benefit of senior Al Qaida commanders. This is

supported by the fraud-related discussion between the above mentioned individuals on 23 March 2004 (see para.51). We assessed that most of the other activities observed by surveillance on 28 February 2004 are likely to be innocuous.

39.   The visit to Easytalk.com was interesting as it occurred after opening hours and their presence there was clearly for the purpose of having a meeting. Although it was quickly established that the shop was owned by Bisharat ALI, his significance was unknown at this time. The reporting stating that he was a radical Imam was not received by the Service from Northants SB until 6 May 2004. As a result, there was no reason to suspect that this meeting was any more suspicious than the numerous other meetings KHYAM had with various associates.

40.   At this point in the investigation the focus was very much on the fertiliser plot and the investigative resource was devoted to those individuals who were clearly linked to it: Man C, D and E were not. Although this was the second occasion the Leeds three had featured, apart from KHYAM and Shujah MAHMOOD, none of the other CREVICE principles appeared to have direct links to the Leeds three.

41.   On 20 March 2004 ██████████████████████████████████████ ██████████████████████████████ 14 Langley Walk showed a car arriving at the address at 23:20, which was subsequently identified as MSK's hired Vauxhall Corsa (YB52 LUF). Probably MSK alighted the vehicle and rang the bell of 14 Langley Walk. Two individuals, believed to be KHYAM and Shujah MAHMOOD, left the address and all three individuals boarded the Vauxhall Corsa.

42.   The Vauxhall Corsa drove around for approximately 30 minutes, returning to 14 Langley Walk at 00:51 on 21 March 2004. KHYAM, Shujah MAHMOOD and probably MSK engaged in a 10 minute conversation on the pavement outside the address. KHYAM and MAHMOOD returned to the home address at 01:00, while MSK and his unidentified passenger(s) were allowed to proceed and may have returned to Leeds.

Assessment/Action taken when reporting received

43.   Our assessment at the time was that KHYAM, MAHMOOD, MSK and his associates drove around for the purpose of a meeting, which mirrors their activities on 2 February 2004. Unfortunately, there was no eavesdropping device installed in MSK's vehicle and we were therefore unable to establish what was discussed during the meeting. We maintained our assessment that the Leeds-based individuals were unlikely to be directly related to the fertiliser plot, which was clearly our prime focus at the time given that it represented a direct and credible threat to National Security.

Activities of 23 March 2004

44.   On 22 March 2004 ████████████ KHYAM's operational mobile indicated that he contacted MSK on **07944420814** ██
██

45.

46.   MPSB S-Squad observed KHYAM leaving 36 Langley Drive, Crawley with four unidentified males (now known to be Shujah MAHMOOD, MSK, TANWEER and 'ULLAH'). They visited Nadeem ASHRAF's address in Crawley before travelling to the home address of Azhar Shezad KHAN in Slough. KHAN joined KHYAM and TANWEER in the Vitara and they proceeded in convoy with MSK, Shipon ULLAH and Shujah MAHMOOD, who were travelling in a Green Vauxhall Corsa (YB52 LUF). This vehicle was hired by MSK.

47.   At 13:25   KHYAM's operational mobile   received calls on **07745909000** and **07969723498,**

48.   At 14:45 the two vehicles travelled to Uxbridge town centre before heading to Ilford. Eavesdropping product from KHYAM's vehicle during the journey covered a lengthy conversation predominantely between KHYAM and TANWEER. Large parts of their discussion are unclear, but they did mention the importance of being physically and mentally prepared for travelling to Pakistan. A verbatim transcript of this product has not yet been produced. The six individuals mentioned in para.46 visited SS Designers, Raman Cash and Carry and the Subrung Bookshop on two separate occasions (the second visit lasted approximately 1 hour).

49.   The two vehicles returned in convoy to Hencroft Street, Slough arriving at 21:11. CCTV footage showed that KHAN, Shujah MAHMOOD, TANWEER and ULLAH entered the home address while KHYAM and MSK visited the Universal Internet Cafe.

                   KHYAM and MSK returned to Hencroft Street.

Assessment/Action taken when reporting received

50.   Our assessment of the activities of 23 March 2004 almost mirrors that of 28 February 2004. The surveillance observed them meeting up in the morning and travelling to places that had not previously featured in the investigation i.e. the Subrung bookshop, SS Designers and Raman Cash & Carry. Similar to the conversation between KHYAM and MSK on 21 February 2004, it was not possible at the time to understand the significance of the former's conversation with TANWEER. It is worth re-iterating that the focus in March 2004 was on the CREVICE conspiracy and not individuals travelling to Pakistan. This piece of audio product was therefore judged to be irrelevant to the plot and no further action was taken.

51.   The meeting later that evening was also judged not to be significant or relevant to the CREVICE plot. Although Bisharat ALI was in attendance, his significance was not known at the time. Product from the eavesdropping device indicated that the attendees mainly discussed how they could defraud various financial institutions. This appeared to tie in with their visits to the Builders Merchants on 28 February 2004. There was no direct reference to the CREVICE plot or other groups planning terrorist operations and no comments which could have been interpreted to refer to these subjects.

Document 10: MI5-WYP email exchange re: Hasina Patel. In February, after they has followed Khan and Tanweer to Leeds after a meeting with Omar Khyam, MI5 asked WYP for more information on the address where they'd seen the car stop. According to the ISC, MI5 never received a reply, but they did (overleaf).

WYP00000009-002

 THE SECURITY SERVICE

Our Ref: Operation CREVICE/SSER

Your Ref:

Date: 16 February 2004

To: HSB West Yorks

Subject: Op CREVICE – Trace request

THE FOLLOWING INFORMATION IS PASSED IN CONFIDENCE AND SHOULD NOT BE DISSEMINATED OUTSIDE OF YOUR BRANCH WITHOUT THE PRIOR AGREEMENT OF THE SECURITY SERVICE.

Op CREVICE is an investigation into an individual called  Omar KHYAM, a member of a Luton based network who we assess to be involved in the creation of an Improvised Explosive Device (IED) in the UK.

2.   We would be grateful for any details you have in your records of the following, particularly any information which would enable us to fully identify any potential associates of KHYAM:

Miss Hasina PATEL
10 Thornhill Park Avenue,
Dewsbury,
West Yorkshire,
WF12 0DA

3.   You will appreciate that the information we have concerning this matter is very sensitive. We therefore request that only routine enquiries be made as we would not wish our interest in this particular individual to be known.

4.   The Emergency room (SSER) will open from 0800 to 2200 with a limited overnight presence, as the Security Service point of contact for any queries relating to Op CREVICE. The SSER can be contacted on ▮▮▮▮▮▮▮▮▮▮▮▮▮▮▮

5.   Many thanks and regards.

West Yorkshire HQ

From:	West Yorkshire HQ ████████████ on behalf of West Yorkshire HQ
Sent:	17 February 2004 16:07
To:	Security Service ████
Subject:	Operation CREVICE

Importance: Low

AttentionOf:
ClusterID: ████
DeskBy: None
Message Classification: ████
Message Precedence: Routine
Originator: HSB & ████

1. I refer to your cluster dated 18th February 2004 a trace request in connection with the above named operation.

2. Hasina PATEL, 10 Thornhill Park Avenue, Dewsbury, West Yorkshire WF12 0DA is identical to :-

Hasina Abdul Salam PATEL
d.o.b. 23/11/1977
CRO 111047/97K
PNCID 97/211005N

This refers to her conviction at Batley/Dewsbury Magistrates Court on the 6th May 1997 when she pleaded guilty to Resist or Obstruct a Constable. She was given a Conditional Discharge for 12 months.

3. Also living at this address are :-

4. All ████ have resided at this address since 1999, prior to which they all resided at ████████████

5. None of the subjects named or their addresses have previously come to the notice of this Office.

Regards

████

Ends

1

Document 11: Minutes of 11th meeting of the Executive Liaison Group (ELG) for Operation Crevice. The ELG was set up so that the police and MI5 could exchange real-time information and make quick decisions as Operation Crevice progressed. Note how they discussed 'drawing other targets into the conspiracy' suggesting they had a spy or provocateur within the group.

ELG 11: 21/02/2004 at 10:00

Meeting chaired by DAC Peter Clarke. Other attendees include DSupt John Prunty (SIO, SO13) and representatives from SyS, SO12 and Thames Valley, Sussex and Bedfordshire SBs.

Intelligence update: SyS briefing: A call to NCS from member of public has revealed a lock up containing a 600kg bag of fertilizer. The lock up is linked to Khyam. The Canadian visitor [Mohammed Momin Khawaja] has received several calls from East London. SyS firmly assess that Khawaja is an explosives expert sent to assist Khyam. Khyam's girlfriend has arrived in the UK.

Operational update: SO13 feel they have sufficient evidence to justify executive action on the basis of conspiracy to cause explosions against Khyam, Shujahuddin Mahmood and Khawaja which relies primarily on the probe evidence from 20/2. The group agreed to establish whether the target group have purchased any further quantities of fertilizer in addition to that identified. It is a real possibility that planning for more than one device is underway. Financial investigation from NTFIU will reveal more. SyS assess that turning the fertilizer in the lock up into a viable device will be lengthy process. "We still have no indication of target or timing for any attack, though mid March appears to feature as a significant time period. We should seek to develop the evidence and intelligence, and consider drawing other targets into the conspiracy".

Aims and objectives: No change

Operational strategy: Circumstances in which immediate executive action will be undertaken were outlined. Thought will be given as to whether Khawaja should be allowed to leave the UK. Coverage of MQK should be maintained because he has re-emerged as a significant figure. Coverage of Film Crew to be kept under review. Khyam should not be allowed to travel unless for a specific purpose or to progress the investigation. Associates travelling with Khyam should also be stopped.

Technical and surveillance deployments: Surveillance has been withdrawn from Sheet Metal and Sussex resources have been deployed to the lock up. MPSB resources have been moved to Front Row. A particular address remains a priority for technical coverage. A further address of interest is being researched. There are six items on the current priority list for technical coverage.

Any other business: SyS will begin to prepare a suitable inert substance for possible substitution with the fertilizer.

Other matters, relating both to the headings above and to other headings, were discussed.

Document 12: 5K1 letter, US vs Mohammed Junaid Babar. The first 7 pages of a 12-page letter from the DOJ to the judge in Babar's case, requesting leniency when sentencing due to Babar's 'extraordinary' co-operation. Babar ended up serving only 4 ½ years out of a possible 70-year sentence.

U.S. Department of Justice

United States Attorney
Southern District of New York

The Silvio J. Mollo Building
One Saint Andrew's Plaza
New York, New York 10007

November 23, 2010

TO BE FILED UNDER SEAL
BY HAND DELIVERY

Honorable Victor Marrero
United States District Judge
Southern District of New York
United States Courthouse
500 Pearl Street, Room 660
New York, New York, 10007

Re: United States v. Mohammed Junaid Babar,
04 Cr. 528 (VM)

Dear Judge Marrero:

The Government respectfully submits this letter to advise the Court of the pertinent facts concerning the assistance that Mohammed Junaid Babar has rendered in the investigation and prosecution of other persons. In light of these facts, and assuming that Babar continues to comply with the terms of his cooperation agreement and commits no additional crimes before sentencing, the Government intends to move at sentencing, pursuant to Section 5K1.1 of the United States Sentencing Guidelines and Title 18, United States Code, Section 3553(e), that the Court sentence Babar in light of the factors set forth in Section 5K1.1(a)(1)-(5) of the Sentencing Guidelines. Babar is currently scheduled to be sentenced on December 10, 2010.

Babar's Offense Conduct

As set forth in the Probation Office's Pre-sentence Report dated October 29, 2010, Babar first became known to law enforcement through his activities with the fundamentalist group al-Muhajiroun ("ALM") in New York. ALM was founded in 1985 and supported the overthrow of Western governments and the institution of an Islamic state. In the late 1990s and early 2000s, ALM maintained offices in New York, London and Pakistan, among other places.

Babar joined ALM while a student at SUNY-Stonybrook in 2000. It was through his membership in ALM that Babar met and befriended Syed Hashmi. Babar was active in ALM from January to September 2001, and held ALM meetings in the basement of his parents' house in Queens. During this time period, Babar and Hashmi organized numerous ALM-sponsored events, including lectures and demonstrations, in and around New York City.

Honorable Victor Marrero
November 23, 2010

On September 20, 2001, following the attacks of September 11, 2001, Babar left the United States to move to Pakistan to provide support to the Afghan jihad. At the time, Babar intended to travel to the front lines in Afghanistan to fight for the establishment of an Islamic state in Afghanistan.

After Babar arrived in Pakistan in the fall of 2001, he immediately began working at the ALM office in Lahore. At the office, he participated in a video recorded television interview with a British news reporter. On November 4, 2001, the British 5 News in the United Kingdom broadcast a story describing Al-Muhajiroun as a facilitator of United Kingdom citizens' travel to Afghanistan through Pakistan to fight for the Taliban against Western forces. During this broadcast, under the caption, "Taliban New Yorker," Babar stated, "I did not feel any remorse for the Americans [who died]. . . . I am willing to kill the Americans. I will kill every American that I see in Afghanistan. And every American soldier I see in Pakistan." During initial proffers with the Government, Babar stated that he made these statements to the reporter because the reporter paid Babar $500 to do so. However, Babar later admitted that he was never paid any money by the reporter.

According to Babar, he still supports today the killing of American military service members on battlefields in Muslim countries. Babar has advised that he also supports the killing of Americans (both military and civilian) in Muslim countries "occupied" by the United States.

During his first year in Pakistan in 2001 and 2002, Babar worked at the Pakistani Software Export Board ("PSEB"), an agency within the Pakistan Government. Babar used his PSEB employment identification card to create approximately ten false identification cards for his friends and fellow jihad supporters. The false PSEB identification cards were valuable within Pakistan because they allowed the holder to claim an affiliation with the government and to travel more freely. In addition, after leaving the PSEB in early 2003, Babar stole five laptop computers from the agency, some of which he sold to friends.

Notwithstanding his jobs during his initial months in Pakistan, Babar spent the majority of his time working for ALM-Pakistan whose primary goal at the time was the overthrow of the Pakistan Government. Babar worked directly with Sajeel Shahid, the head of ALM-Pakistan, as he (Babar) continued to search for opportunities to support the Afghan jihad.

During this period, Babar participated in two different sets of discussions regarding plots to assassinate the President of Pakistan. During the first of these discussions, machine guns and grenades were obtained by others and Babar buried them for later use. Neither set of discussions advanced past the planning stage.

At this time, Babar also participated in discussions about bombing the French embassy in Pakistan, as well as an English library and cultural center in Pakistan; however, these discussions also did not advance beyond the planning stage.

Honorable Victor Marrero
November 23, 2010

As part of his efforts to raise money in support of jihadist activities in Pakistan, Babar traveled to London in December 2002. During that trip, Babar met Omar Khyam, a known U.K.-based jihad supporter, at a lecture, and asked Khyam for money for jihad; however, Khyam refused to give Babar any money at that time.

After a one-month stay in London, Babar returned to Pakistan. In early 2003, Babar attended a meeting of al Qaeda supporters in Islamabad and saw Khyam again. During that meeting, another al Qaeda supporter, Salahuddin Amin, a/k/a "Khalid," discussed the different types of training he could arrange for members of the group. Approximately one month later, Babar met with Khyam again in Pakistan, and Khyam discussed for the first time with Babar the fact that he worked for Abd al Hadi al Iraqi ("Hadi al Iraqi"). According to Babar, Khyam told him that Hadi al Iraqi was the third in command within al Qaeda behind Osama bin Laden and Ayman al Zawahri and the senior commander of al Qaeda's fighters in Afghanistan and Pakistan.

Shortly after this meeting with Khyam, Babar returned to London to meet with al Qaeda supporters based there. During this visit, he met with Khyam again at a hotel outside the city. During this meeting, Khyam introduced Babar to his brother and told Babar that he was in England to buy equipment to send back to Pakistan for a training camp he was setting up. After approximately one month in England, Babar returned to Pakistan.

In May 2003, Khyam contacted Babar in Pakistan, and asked Babar if he could live in the guest quarters of Babar's house in Lahore. Babar agreed, and in June 2003, Khyam and a friend of his, Anthony Garcia, moved in with Babar. At this time, Khyam asked Babar if he could arrange a training camp for him and his associates to conduct physical training and weapons training.

After Khyam moved into the guest quarters at Babar's residence in Pakistan, Khyam told Babar that he wanted to bomb soft targets, including trains and nightclubs, in England. Khyam also spoke in positive terms about a recent suicide bombing at a restaurant in Israel. In response, Babar said that more needed to be done. This conversation was the first of several that Khyam and Babar had about potential targets for detonating a bomb, though Babar was never aware of any specific targets identified by Khyam and the other members of the plot.

As part of the conversations about the bomb plot in England, Khyam asked Babar to transport detonators in radios from Pakistan to Khyam in Belgium who would then transport them to England. In furtherance of this plan, Khyam gave Babar several detonators. Khyam also sent Babar approximately 230,000 Pakistani rupees (approximately $2700) via a wire transfer and told Babar that some of the money was for expenses related to Babar's transport of the detonators. Babar never bought any additional aluminum powder and never brought any detonators to England. Babar and Khyam also discussed possibly targeting the U.K., Spain and France; Babar suggested hitting multiple targets either simultaneously or seriatim.

Honorable Victor Marrero
November 23, 2010

When Khyam was staying in Babar's house in Lahore, Khyam had a black grocery bag filled with what Khyam said was ricin. Ricin is a severely toxic protein that has been used as an agent of chemical and biological warfare in the past. When Khyam left Pakistan in September 2003, he left the ricin in Babar's house; Babar stated that he later disposed of it.

In July 2003, Babar arranged a three-week training camp in a remote region of Pakistan where Khyam and about ten other young men received training on various types of weapons. Babar charged Khyam 4,000 British pounds for setting up the facility. Babar also coordinated the rental of a private bus to transport the individuals to and from the camp near Peshawar. The training lasted for the entire month. At the camp, the attendees received training in basic military skills, as well as the use of explosives and weapons. Babar only attended the last few days of the camp but during that time, he saw Khyam detonate a one pound ammonium nitrate bomb. In addition, according to Babar, during the stay at the camp, Khyam was "feeling people out" regarding their interest in martyrdom for the bomb operation in England.

During the training camp, Babar provided a video camera which was used to tape the participants, who wore scarves to cover their faces, as they shot at targets and chanted about jihad. According to Babar, Khyam wanted to make the videotape to distribute to associates in the U.K.

After returning from the camp, at Khyam's suggestion, Khyam and Babar together bought different types of substances for use in making bombs, including aluminum powder, ammonium nitrate and urea. They stored the substances in a closet in Babar's residence in Lahore. Around that time, Khyam and Babar constructed a bomb using a jar from Babar's kitchen and then detonated it in the backyard of Babar's residence.

Khyam returned to London in September 2003. He brought some of the aluminum powder he and Babar had bought with him. He also asked Babar to bring additional aluminum powder with him on his next trip to England, and later sent Babar several hundred British pounds to pay for Babar's airfare and for the additional aluminum powder. Babar never brought any aluminum powder to England.

In October 2003, Khyam and Amin, a known al Qaeda supporter, asked Babar to send gear to Hadi al Iraqi that Khyam had left behind in Pakistan with Amin. Babar met with Amin to receive the gear and Amin confirmed to Babar that he also worked for Hadi al Iraqi. After receiving the gear from Amin, Babar sent it to Hadi al Iraqi who was based in North Waziristan in the border region between Afghanistan and Pakistan.

Also in October 2003, Babar traveled to Islamabad to meet with Momin Khawaja. Khawaja, a Canadian resident, was part of the group led by Khyam plotting to bomb soft targets in England. During this trip, they met with Amin. Khawaja was a computer programmer in Canada and they discussed the possible use of remote devices, i.e., devices that could detonate explosives from a distance. Khawaja also told them that he was working on creating a model

Honorable Victor Marrero
November 23, 2010

airplane that could carry explosives and could be navigated by a GPS system. During this meeting, Khawaja gave Amin 1,000 to 1,500 British pounds to give to Abu Munthir, a known al Qaeda leader.

In early January 2004, Babar arranged for another individual who knew Hadi al-Iraqi to introduce him (Babar) to the senior al Qaeda commander. During the first meeting at a mosque in North Waziristan, Pakistan, Hadi confirmed that he had received the gear that Babar had sent him a few months earlier, specifically boots, sleeping bags, and clothing, which Babar had received from Amin. In addition, Babar and another individual gave Hadi al Iraqi 10,000 Pakistani rupees to support jihad activities.

Approximately one week later, Babar traveled to meet with Hadi al Iraqi again. During this meeting, Hadi al Iraqi asked Babar to provide him with materials in support of al Qaeda's jihad activities in Afghanistan. Specifically, Hadi al Iraqi asked Babar to provide him with money and gear, namely, ponchos, shoes, socks, and sleeping bags. Babar agreed to this request.

In January 2004, Babar traveled again to London in an effort to resolve a dispute among al Qaeda supporters about who was actually working for Hadi al Iraqi. Shortly after Babar arrived in London, he and Khyam met in Khyam's car. During this meeting, Khyam asked Babar, "Are you with us?" Babar understood Khyam to be asking whether Babar planned to be part of the bomb plot. In response, Babar indicated to Khyam that he planned to work on his own.

During the same visit, Babar stayed with Syed Hashmi, his friend whom he had met through ALM-New York in 2000, and used Hashmi's cellphone to contact Khyam and other al Qaeda supporters. Babar also introduced Hashmi to Khyam and Khyam's brother. Babar and Hashmi also attended several meetings with al Qaeda supporters about the need to support Hadi al Iraqi.

During his nearly two-week stay with Hashmi in London, Babar collected two to three garbage bags full of gear from other al Qaeda supporters in London, which he stored in Hashmi's bedroom with Hashmi's knowledge. The gear included ponchos, waterproof socks and raincoats. Babar collected this gear in order to deliver it to Hadi al-Iraqi when he returned to Pakistan. When he left Hashmi's apartment in early February 2004, he took some of it, as well as additional gear he received from Tanveer Ali, another London-based al Qaeda supporter, with him on the plane back to Pakistan. Babar left the remainder of the gear from Hashmi's apartment with Ali for Ali to bring to Pakistan the following week.

In February 2004, after he returned from the U.K., Babar again traveled to meet with Hadi al-Iraqi for the third time. During this trip, Babar provided Hadi with the ponchos, waterproof socks, and raincoats that he had received from Tanveer Ali in the U.K. One of the individuals who accompanied Babar on the trip, Ansar Butt, was one of the London-based al Qaeda supporters who had asked Babar for an introduction to Hadi al-Iraqi. During the meeting, Butt gave Hadi

Honorable Victor Marrero
November 23, 2010

2,000 British pounds. Babar met alone with Hadi for 15 minutes during this trip. During this private meeting, he showed Hadi all of the gear that he had brought and also discussed activities in Afghanistan.

On or about February 21, 2004, Babar made his final trip to meet with Hadi. Babar traveled with Tanveer Ali who had arrived from England. Babar and Ali gave Hadi more ponchos, waterproof socks, sleeping bags, one set of night vision goggles and one set of binoculars with night vision capability. Babar told Hadi that he was going to the U.K. for some period of time but that he would continue to raise money and bring similar items to Hadi in the future. Ali did not return with Babar from South Waziristan; he told Babar that he intended to stay and fight jihad with Hadi for one year.

In early March 2004, Babar returned to New York to live with his parents in Queens. Babar planned to save money working as a taxi cab driver and return to Pakistan to live with his wife and daughter. There is no evidence that Babar returned to the United States in furtherance of any terrorist activity.

On March 30, 2004, as part of a English investigation known as Operation Crevice, Omar Khyam and others were arrested in England for their participation in a plot to detonate fertilizer bombs in various locations across England, including a shopping center and a nightclub. The thirteen-month trial revealed that, over the course of at least five months, the group planned to make an improvised explosive device from ammonium nitrate fertilizer, which they intended to mix with aluminum powder, the necessary fuel for the detonation of the fertilizer. They also discussed using a remotely operated detonation system to detonate the bomb. In November 2003, in furtherance of the plot, the conspirators bought 600 kilograms (approximately 1,300 pounds) of fertilizer at a wholesale agricultural company in rural England, and rented a storage unit to secure the 600 kilogram bag of fertilizer.

On April 6, 2004, FBI agents approached Babar on the street after he walked out of his parents' house in Queens. The FBI agents informed Babar that they wanted to speak to him and Babar voluntarily agreed to accompany them to a hotel room in Manhattan. Once they arrived at the hotel, Babar was advised of his *Miranda* rights. Babar waived his *Miranda* rights orally and in writing. At the conclusion of the first interview by the FBI agents on April 6, 2004, the agents informed Babar that they wanted to continue to speak with him. Babar voluntarily agreed to stay in the hotel room and continue the interview the next day. The FBI agents continued to interview Babar from April 7, 2004, through April 10, 2004.

On April 10, 2004, at the conclusion of five days of voluntary interviews, Babar was arrested on a material witness warrant and taken into custody by the FBI. On April 12, 2004, Babar was appointed counsel, presented before District Judge Leonard B. Sand, and ordered detained.

Honorable Victor Marrero
November 23, 2010

On June 3, 2004, after nearly two months of proffering, Babar pled guilty to a five-count Information before this Court, in which he was charged with four counts of providing and conspiring to provide material support to a foreign terrorist organization, namely al Qaeda, and to terrorist activity, in violation of 18 U.S.C. §§ 2339B and 2339A, and one count of making a contribution of funds, goods and services to, and for the benefit of, al Qaeda, in violation of 50 U.S.C. § 1705(b). Following his plea, Babar remained detained until December 18, 2008, when he was released on bail. Accordingly, to date, Babar has served approximately four years and eights months in prison in connection with the offenses to which he pled guilty.

Babar's Other Criminal Conduct

Aside from the terrorism-related offenses to which Babar pled guilty in this case, Babar's other documented criminal conduct is limited to a New York State conviction for driving without proof of insurance for which he was fined $75. (See PSR §§ 64-65.) Babar has also admitted that he knowingly overcharged customers while working as a parking valet in New York in the late 1990s.

Babar's Guidelines Range

The Government agrees with the Probation Office's calculation of Babar's sentencing range under the United States Sentencing Guidelines. Based on his plea to the five terrorism charges in Information 04 Cr. 528 (VM), Babar's base offense level is 26. Because the offenses involved the provision of funds and other material support or resources with the intent, knowledge or reason to believe they would be used to commit or assist in the commission of a violent act, a two-level increase is warranted. In addition, because the offenses are felonies that involved or were intended to promote a federal crime of terrorism, a twelve-level increase is warranted. After reducing the offense level three levels for acceptance of responsibility, Babar's total offense level is 37. Accordingly, given that he falls within Criminal History Category I, Babar's applicable Guidelines range is 30 years to life imprisonment. The statutory maximum sentence for Counts 1 through 5, however, is 70 years' imprisonment. Accordingly, absent cooperation, Babar would be facing a Guidelines range of 30 to 70 years' imprisonment.

Babar's Cooperation and Assistance

Over the last six and a half years, the level of assistance provided by Babar to both the U.S. Government and foreign governments has been more than substantial; it has been extraordinary. As described in more detail below, Babar testified as a government witness in four terrorism trials overseas; was prepared to testify in a fifth terrorism trial in this District earlier this year; and met with authorities from the U.S. government and foreign governments on nearly 100 occasions in total during which he provided information about organizations and individuals engaged in terrorist activities in various parts of the world.

Document 13: Sidique Khan resignation letter. A letter sent from Sidique Khan to his boss, the headteacher of Hillside Primary Sarah Balfour, resigning from his position. The date the letter was sent has been redacted, as has Khan's explanation for his trip to Pakistan, though the attached leaver's form is dated 17th December 2004 and his reason for leaving was 'Resig. Family Commit'. This contradicts the Home Office narrative in every respect.

Sidique Khan

Dear Sarah Balfour

I'm sorry I have not been in touch for a while, a lot has happened in the last few months. _____ there is no definite time frame as to when I will return. We are departing next week.

Unfortunately this letter is therefore a letter of my resignation from my post. Its been great working with you and I will be in touch when I return.

Yours Sincerely

Sidique Khan

Leeds City Council & Education Leeds   Form 000:

Notification of Leaver

Please tick the relevant box to indicate if the employee is weekly or monthly paid: WEEKLY ☐   MONTHLY 16th ☐   MONTHLY 26th ☐

PLEASE COMPLETE IN MICROSOFT WORD OR WRITE CLEARLY - SEE GUIDANCE NOTES TO ASSIST COMPLETION

PART A   To be completed by Department / School

Personnel Area (Department)   Code   **Organisational Unit**

Education   Hillside Primary

Leaver Details

Title e.g. Mrs., Mr.	Surname	Forename(s)	Personnel Number
MR	KHAN	SIDIQUE	7 9 1 7 4 2

Assignment

Position ID Number   Position Title   MENTOR

Leaving Details

Last day of employment *(dd/mm/yy)*

Reason for Leaving *(Select appropriate category)*

☐ 01 Death in Service
☐ 02 Dismissal, Capability
☐ 03 Dismissal, Conduct
☐ 04 Dismissal, Ill Health Cap
☐ 05 End of Casual Contract
☐ 06 End of Temp Contract
☐ 07 Frustration of Contract
☐ 08 Redundancy, Compulsory

☐ 09 Repudiation
☐ 10 Resign, Emigration
☐ 11 Resig, Entering Education
☐ 12 Resig, Alternative Employ
☒ 13 Resig, Family Commit
☐ 14 Resig, Follow Mat Leave
☐ 15 Resig, No Reason Given
☐ 16 Resig, Private Sector

☐ 17 Resig, Relocation
☐ 18 Resig, To Other Authority
☐ 19 Resig, To Other Auth SS
☐ 20 Retirement, Ill Health
☐ 21 Retirement, Compul Age
☐ 22 Retirement, Optional
☐ 23 TUPE Transfer
☐ 24 Unsatisfactory Probation

☐ 25 VER 85 Rule
☐ 26 VER Efficiency
☐ 27 VER Redundancy
☐ 28 Voluntary Severance
☐ 30 Change of Company

Forwarding Address

House number/street		Communications	
2nd Address Line		Telephone Number	
District/City		1st Additional Number	
Postal code		2nd Additional Number	

Items on loan

Key	Item/Equipment	Returned	Comments
		☐ Yes ☐ No	
		☐ Yes ☐ No	
		☐ Yes ☐ No	

Annual Leave

Annual Leave Entitlement		Days ☐ Hours ☐	(EAS ONLY) Entered on to 0315 Temporary Variations:	
Annual Leave Taken To Date		Days ☐ Hours ☐	Balance of Leave	Days ☐ Hours ☐
Suspended Leave		Days ☐ Hours ☐		
Lieu Time		Days ☐ Hours ☐	Outstanding ☐ Overtaken ☐	

Leeds City Council & Education Leeds

Form 0003

Notification of Leaver

Other Information (Include any action taken on Outstanding Loans)

See attached Letter.

Originator / Authorised Signatory				
Signature	Name	Position Title	Date:	Contact telephone number:
[signature]	SARAH BALFOUR	HEADTEACHER	17.12.04	2717259

PART B To be completed by Employee Administration Service

Permanent Deductions Infotype D014	Actions

Outstanding Loans Infotype D045	Actions

Tax Credits Infotype D087	Actions

Other Actions	

EAS Input				
Input by:	Date:	Authorised by:		Date:

Document 14: Extract from Last Will and Final Testament of Sidique Khan. This was finally published years after the Home Office and major media had used details from it to support the idea that Khan was a suicide bomber. In particular the use of the word 'shaheed', which can mean martyr, though the document itself shows this is in a paragraph about changing his daughter's nappy and feeding her ice-cream.

OP THESEUS - X18351 - INM/5 - Book 1520 0096 - Page 1 of 17
SPLIT FROM EXHIBIT SML/1 \ THE ISLAMIC WILL AND TESTAMENT OF SIDIQUE KHAN

The Last Will and Final Testament of Sidique Khan (Abu

May Allah bear witness to my love for you, but Islam came to give the limits to this love. Allah says:

'Say: If your fathers, your sons, your brothers, your wives, your kindred, the wealth that you have gained, the commerce in which you fear a decline, and the dwellings in which you delight...are more dearer to you than Allah and his messenger, and striving hard and fighting in his cause, then wait until Allah brings about his decision (torment). And Allah guides not the people who are Al-Fasiqun (the rebellious disobedient to Allah).' (Quran 9:24)

My Baby

Firstly I want to begin by saying that the most difficult thing in my life was to leave you. I love you so much and will always do so. Your birth was the most exciting day of my life and I remember it like yesterday. I enjoyed every moment with you, I even gave myself back ache picking you up so much and never considered putting you down as an option. I even found changing your nappy so cool and by the way you always enjoyed it as well. I'm proud to say that I was the first to bath you, feed you ice cream, give you spending money and get you eid presents. As a father the best gift I can give you is the promise that I will intercede for you on the day of judgement and take you to paradise, if Allah (SWT) accepts me as a shaheed. So I leave you to the protection of AL RAQIB the watchful, AL MUQIT the maintainer, AL WAKIL the trustee, AR RIZZAQ the provider, DHUL JALAL WAL IKRAM lord of majesty and bounty. And I ask you to forgive me for not being a part of your life in this world. You filled my heart with love and joy for every moment that I spent with you and thought about you. I thank you for that.

To My Dear Wife

I know you will take good care of our child inshallah. You have been very patient with me even though I never told you what I was doing and often lied to you. I know you trusted me and for that I thank you. Please forgive me for the deceit, lies and my absence, it was to please Allah. Be patient and have strong Emaan, raise our well and try to understand what I did. I love you and inshallah will se you in paradise.

To My Family

You must stop committing shirk and associating partners with Allah (SWT). Make Barah from the Peers, correct your aqeedah and enter into the fold of Islam. Then if Allah (SWT) blesses me with Shahada I will be able to assist you on the day of torment.

Notes

Prologue

1. Scotland Yard, Its Mysteries and Methods, The Anarchists, Reynolds Newspaper, April 7th 1895

2. Scotland Yard, Its Mysteries and Methods, The Walsall Plot and the Spy, Reynolds Newspaper, April 14th 1895

3. Letter to the editor of Reynolds Newspaper, published April 21st 1895

4. Scotland Yard, Its Mysteries and Methods, Reynolds Newspaper, April 28th 1895

5. Thirty Years at Scotland Yard, No. 3 – The True Story of the Greenwich Park bomb, Thomson's Weekly News, June 15th 1907

6. Information Tribunal ruling, March 30th 2009

7. An Accident of History? The Evolution of Counter Terrorism Methodology in the Metropolitan Police from 1829 to 1901, With Particular Reference to the Influence of Extreme Irish Nationalist Activity, doctoral thesis submitted by Lindsay Clutterbuck to the University of Portsmouth, June 2002

Introduction

1. Home Office, *Report of the official account of the bombings in London on 7th July 2005,* (Home Office Narrative) page 11

2. Intelligence and Security Committee, *Report into the London Terrorist Attacks on 7 July 2005*, May 2006, (ISC 1) page 2

3. ISC 1, page 11

4. ISC 1, page 32

5. Frank Gardner, BBC, 7/7 report reveals MI5's workings, May 19th 2009

6. Intelligence and Security Committee, *Could 7/7 Have Been Prevented*, May 2009, (ISC 2), page 27

7. ISC 2, page 27

8. July 7 Inquests, February 22nd 2011, morning session, pages 84-85

9. July 7 Inquests, February 22nd 2011, morning session, page 86

10. CIA, Clandestine Service History, "Overthrow of Premier Mossadeq of Iran, November 1952-August 1953", section 5, Mounting Pressure Against the Shah

11. Belfast Telegraph, Half of all top IRA men 'worked for security services', December 21st 2011

12. Sir John Stevens Inquiry 3, Overview and Recommendations, April 17th 2003

13. Cory Collusion Inquiry Report: Patrick Finucane, April 1st 2004, p103

14. The Guardian, Finucane widow urges judges to shun inquiry, April 14th 2005

15. Finucane Application for Judicial Review re Failure to Establish Public Inquiry, January 13th 2012,

16. Interview with Vincenzo Vinciguerra in *Gladio*, (1992, Allen Francovich, UK)

17. ibid.

18. The Guardian, Hamza set up terror camps with British ex-soldiers, February 12th 2006; see also the World Socialist Web Site, Britain: Why did it take so long to bring Abu Hamza to trial?, February 16th 2006

19. The Times, Al-Qaeda cleric exposed as an MI5 double agent, March 25th 2004; London Evening Standard, 'I spied on Abu Qatada for MI5', January 28th 2005

20. The Jamestown Foundation, Al-Muhajiroun in the UK: An Interview with Sheikh Omar Bakri Mohammed, May 25th 2005; Ron Suskind, *The Way of the World: A Story of Truth and Hope in an Age of Extremism*, 2008, p200-202

Chapter 1: The Hallmarks of Al Qaeda

1. *The Radio Factor with Bill O'Reilly*, July 6th 2005

2. Fox News, Terrorist Attack Backfires, July 7th 2005

3. The Independent, King's Cross: For hours, convoys of ambulances took away the victims, July 8th 2005

4. BBC, 'I've never seen anything like it', July 9th 2005

5. Greater London Authority, 7th July Review Committee, hearing March 1st 2006

6. The Telegraph, 'We were like sardines in there, just waiting to die', July 8th 2005

7. BBC, Reliving the London bombing horror, October 16th 2005

8. National Geographic, *7/7 Attack on London*, first broadcast October 1st 2005

9. Cambridge Evening News, 'I was in tube bomb carriage – and survived', July 25th 2005; The Mirror, 7/7: Blitz On Britain: The Survivor - 'I Close My Eyes and Can See Everything', July 11th 2005

10. BBC, I'm lucky to be here, says driver, July 11th 2005

11. Christian Broadcasting Network, The Benton Sisters: Remembering 7/7, 2007; CNN, Breaking News, July 22nd 2005

12. Jerusalem Post, Rules of conflict for a world war, July 7th 2005

13. The Independent, Aldgate East: 'Smoke poured into the carriage, but we couldn't break the windows', July 8th 2005

14. MSNBC, Bombings in London: Saira's diary, September 23rd 2005

15. CNN, July 7th 2005, available on youtube as 'Westbound Circle Line Aldgate to Liverpool Street Survivor'

16. The Guardian, Latest CCTV footage of 7/7 bomb attacks, May 1st 2008

17. Manchester Evening News, Top chef relives bomb blast horror, July 7th 2005

18. The Independent, Thursday: Minute by Minute the Horror Emerges, July 10th 2005

19. Daily Mail, Gut-wrenching insensitivity: Without warning, families of the 7/7 victims are sent horrific details of how their loved ones died, November 30th 2007

20. The Guardian, Obituary: Jenny Nicholson, July 20th 2005

21. July 7th Truth Campaign, Incident Analysis: Edgware Road/Paddington

22. Home Office Narrative, page 5

23. July 7th Truth Campaign, Incident Analysis: Number 30 bus

24. Home Office narrative, pages 6 and 12

25. CBS, *The Early Show*, July 15th 2005

26. BBC, *Real Story*: Special with Fiona Bruce: Terror Comes to London, July 11th 2005

27. Scottish Sunday Mail, 7/7 LONDON THE WITNESS: I THOUGHT BOMBER ON MY BUS WAS ONLY PLAYING WITH iPOD, July 10th 2005

28. July 7 Inquests, January 12th 2011, afternoon session, pages 10-22; Diagram of number 30 bus by Richard Jones, July 9th 2005, inquests exhibit INQ10040-3

29. July 7 Inquests, January 25th 2011, afternoon session, pages 1-10

30. London Fire Brigade, Report of Michael J Ellis, inquests exhibit LFB57-9 and LFB 57-10; MPS SO13 Explosives Officers Call Out Form, inquests exhibit INQ10245-3 and INQ10245-4

31. July 7th Truth Campaign, Tavistock Square & the second controlled explosion... of Richmal, February 11th 2011

Chapter 2: A Wider Conspiracy?

1. Home Office narrative, page 10

2. July 7 Inquests, October 13th 2010, morning session, pages 60-101

3. July 7 Inquests, October 13th 2010, afternoon session, pages 2-20

4. July 7 Inquests, October 13th 2010, afternoon session, pages 37-47

5. Home Office narrative, page 4

6. The Observer, Omar was a normal British teenager who loved his little brother and Man Utd. So why at 24 did he plan to blow up a nightclub in central London?, January 20th 2008

7. July 7 Inquests, October 13th 2010, afternoon session, pages 37-53

8. BBC, Trio cleared over 7/7 attacks, April 28th 2009

9. BBC, 7/7 accused 'joined weapons camp', April 18th, 2008

10. The Times, Top al-Qaeda Briton called Tube bombers before attack, July 21st 2005

11. Fox News interview with John Loftus, July 29th 2005

12. Home Office Narrative, page 9

13. ISC 1, page 12

14. ISC 2, page 74

15. Redacted schedule of calls to and from the 15 MSK, Tanweer, Hussain and Lindsay-attributed 'Operational' phones March-July 2005, Inquests exhibit INQ11177

16. July 7 Inquests, February 2nd 2011, morning session, pages 20-21

17. BBC, Three held over 7 July bombings, March 22nd 2007

18. BBC, Three charged over 7/7 bombings, April 5th 2007

Chapter 3: The CCTV

1. The Mirror, EXCLUSE: THE HUNT, July 9th 2005

2. New York Times, BOMBINGS IN LONDON: PHYSICAL EVIDENCE; London Bombs Seen as Crude; Death Toll Rises to 49, July 9th 2005

3. Home Office narrative, page 5

4. Home Office narrative, page 4

5. Home Office narrative, page 10

6. July 7 Inquests, October 13th, morning session, pages 1-59

7. July 7 Inquests, October 14th, afternoon session, pages 40-67

8. Nick Kollerstrom, *Terror on the Tube*, chapter 6, 2011

9. *The RichPlanet Starship*, episode 55, broadcast April 29th 2011

10. *The RichPlanet Starship*, episode 49, broadcast March 25th 2011

11. Nick Kollerstrom, *Terror on the Tube*, chapter 10

12. July 7 Inquests, October 13th 2010, morning session, pages 27-28

Chapter 4: Suicide Bombings?

1. The Mirror, Was It Suicide? July 16th 2005

2. New York Times, 'Military quality' bombs in London, July 13th 2005

3. Home Office Narrative, page 23

4. ISC 1, page 11

5. Jean Charles de Menezes Inquest, November 7th 2008

6. Jean Charles de Menezes Inquest, September 24th 2008

7. Jean Charles de Menezes Inquest, September 25th 2008

8. Jean Charles de Menezes Inquest, October 16th 2008

9. July 7 Inquests, February 1st 2011, afternoon session, pages 49-53

10. MPS, Forensic finds located in the Nissan Micra, Inquests exhibits INQ9557-4 to -7

11. MPS, Forensic Links of Note, Inquests exhibits INQ11228-1 to -4

12. Home Office Narrative, page 9

13. July 7 Inquests, November 24th 2010, morning session, page 80

14. July 7 Inquests, November 3rd 2010, afternoon session, pages 18-21

15. July 7 Inquests, October 11th 2010, morning session, page 59

16. Home Office narrative, page 11

17. Home Office narrative, page 5

18. July 7 Inquests, December 17th 2010, morning session, pages 131-135

19. Cambridge Evening News, "I was in tube bomb carriage - and survived", July 11th 2005

20. July 7 Inquests, November 22nd 2010, morning session, page 59; DC Potter's diagram inquests exhibit INQ00008708-002

21. July 7 Inquests, November 8th 2010, morning session, pages 26-34

22. July 7 Inquests, January 12th 2011, morning session, pages 70-81

23. July 7 Inquests, December 17th 2010, morning session, page 133

24. July 7 Inquests, November 24th 2010, morning session, page 64-66

25. July 7 Inquests, February 1st 2011, afternoon session, pages 77-87

26. Nafeez Ahmed, *The London Bombings: An Independent Inquiry*, page 37

27. Sky News Ireland, *7/7 Voices*, broadcast July 7th 2006

28. The Benton Sisters: Remembering 7/7, Christian Broadcasting Network, July 9th 2007

29. July 7 Inquests, October 19th 2010, afternoon session, pages 57-66

30. July 7 Inquests, December 1st 2010, morning session, page 121

31. July 7 Inquests, November 11th 2010, morning session, pages 1-10

32. July 7 Inquests, November 11th 2010, morning session, page 41

33. The Guardian, Suicide bombs breakthrough gives police vital clues, August 24th 2005

Chapter 5: Debunking 7/7 Debunking

1. The Guardian, Seeing isn't Believing, June 27th 2006

2. Channel 4, *Conspiracy: Who Really Runs the World – The Psychology of Conspiracy Theory*, broadcast January 1st 2007

3. BBC, *Conspiracy Files: 7/7*, broadcast June 30th 2009

4. Dr Rory Ridley Duff, Theorising Truth: What Happened at Canary Wharf on July 7th 2005?, October 2009

5. The Guardian, We warned MI6 of tube attacks, claim Saudis, September 4th 2005

6. July 7 Inquests, October 11th 2010, morning and afternoon sessions

7. http://www.mathematics.jhu.edu/skhan/

8. David Aaronovitch, *Voodoo Histories*, chapter 7

9. Nick Kollerstrom, *Terror on the Tube*, page 166

Chapter 6: The Iqra Bookshop

1. BBC *Newsnight*, October 25th 2005

2. ISC 1, pages 13-16

3. West Yorkshire Police document 'Gist re: McDaid', inquests exhibit WYP00000011

4. The Mirror, EXCLUSIVE: BOMBERS AND THE SPECIAL FORCES SOLDIER, July 21st 2005

5. ISC 2, page 66

6. West Yorkshire Police document 'Gist re: McDaid'

7. July 7 Inquests, February 24th 2011, morning session, pages 86-87

8. WYP check on BMW registration number J729 EUB, April 16th 2004, inquests exhibit WYP00000012-043

9. Lady Justice Hallett, Report under Rule 43 of The Coroner's Rules 1984, May 6th 2011, page 5

10. Declaration by Charity Trustees for Iqra, inquests exhibit INQ00009370

11. Third Open Witness Statement of Security Service Witness "G", inquests exhibit SYS00011082

12. BBC *Newsnight*, May 5th 2011

13. July 7 Inquests, February 16th 2011, afternoon session p3

14. July 7 Inquests, February 16th 2011, afternoon session p11

15. BBC *Newsnight*, June 23rd 2006

16. July 7 Inquests, February 16th 2011, afternoon session, pages 60 and 61

17. July 7th Truth Campaign, The Perjury of Martin Gilbertson, May 4th 2011

18. This strategy was first outlined in detail in Sir Frank Kitson's 1960 book *Gangs and countergangs*

19. http://martin-abdullah-mcdaid.webs.com/

20. Court of Appeal Ruling, February 13th 2008

21. The Ali Mohamed story is most thoroughly explored in Peter Lance's 2006 book *Triple Cross*, though I do not accept Lance's overall analysis of who and what Ali Mohamed was.

22. BBC, US under fire over al-Qaeda guide, July 27th 2005

Chapter 7: The Crevice

1. The Guardian, interview with Graham Foulkes, February 14th 2011

2. ISC 1, page 16

3. ISC 2, page 54

4. ISC 2, page 7

5. BBC, *Panorama*, *Real Spooks*, broadcast April 30th 2007

6. BBC *Newsnight* report on 'The 7/7 Connection', broadcast April 30th 2007

7. ISC 2, page 58

8. MI5 document 'Summary of occasions when two of the Stepford bombers came to our attention during the Crevice investigation', inquests exhibit SYS00011079

9. BBC *Newsnight* report on 'The 7/7 Connection', broadcast April 30th 2007

10. MI5 subscriber check on mobile phone number 07904186076, March 11th 2003, inquests exhibit SYS00011076

11. July 7 Inquests, February 21st 2011, afternoon session, pages 35 and 36

12. July 7 Inquests, February 22nd 2011, morning session, pages 14 and 15

13. BBC, Profile: Omar Khyam, April 30th 2007

14. BBC *Panorama*, *Real Spooks* transcript

15. MI5 Operation Crevice summary, inquests exhibit SYS11080

16. Minutes of the Executive Liaison Group, February 21st 2004, inquests exhibit MPS00000005-015

17. The Hindu, U.K. terror suspect alleges ISI threat, May 1st 2007

18. MI5 document 'Summary of occasions when two of the Stepford bombers came to our attention during the Crevice investigation', inquests exhibit SYS00011079

19. ISC 2, pages 20, 24 and 59

20. MI5 request to WYP re: Hasina Patel, 16th February 2004, inquests exhibit WYP0000009-002; WYP response to MI5 request re: Hasina Patel, 17th February 2004, inquests exhibit WYP0000009-003

21. BBC, Revealed: Bomber Transcript, May 1st 2007; *Panorama*, *Real Spooks* transcript, April 30th 2007

22. MI5 summary of the connections between the 'Stepford Bombers' and the Crevice suspects, inquests exhibit SYS00011079

23. Operation Crevice action form 895, inquests exhibit MPS00011009-20

24. ISC 2, page 13

25. BBC Radio 4, Today Programme interview with Graham Foulkes, February 26th 2011

26. July 7 Inquests, February 22nd 2011, morning session, page 43

27. MI5 request to NERIC and WYP re: Operation Scraw, June 8th 2004, inquests exhibit SYS00011004

28. Response to MI5 request re: Operation Scraw, June 14th 2004, inquests exhibit SYS00010994

29. July 7 Inquests, February 24th 2011, afternoon session, pages 19 and 20

30. ITN interview with Mohammed Junaid Babar, broadcast November 4th 2001

31. US vs Mohammed Junaid Babar, 5K1 letter, November 23rd 2010

32. US vs Mohammed Junaid Babar, Guilty Plea, June 3rd 2004

33. The Times, The supergrass I helped to create - Mohammed Junaid Babar, May 3rd 2007

34. US vs Mohammed Junaid Babar, 5K1 letter; Sentencing hearing, December 10th 2010

35. The Times, The supergrass I helped to create, May 3rd 2007; BBC *Panorama*, *Real Spooks* transcript

36. BBC, Could the 7/7 bombings in London have been Prevented?, February 18th 2011

37. BBC, *Panorama*, Modern Spies episode 1, broadcast April 2nd 2012

38. MI5 summary of the connections between the 'Stepford Bombers' and the Crevice suspects, inquests exhibit SYS00011079

39. MI5 manifest document, inquests exhibit manifest-24022011

40. MI5 request to NERIC and WYP re: Operation Scraw, June 8th 2004, inquests exhibit SYS00011004

41. July 7 Inquests, February 23rd 2011, morning session, pages 89-90

42. BBC, Three UK bombers visited Pakistan, July 18th 2005; The Times, Bombers travelled around Pakistan for three months, July 18th 2005

43. July 7 Inquests, February 24th 2011, afternoon session, page 12; Mohammad Sidique Khan PISCES printout, inquests exhibit INQ9398-2

44. FBI summary of interrogation of Mohammed Junaid Babar, inquests exhibit MPS00000004

45. July 7 Inquests, February 21st 2011, afternoon session, pages 50-58

46. MI5 Amended Gist re Saddique *** and Imran, inquests exhibit SYS00000053

47. ISC 2, page 65

48. MI5 Amended Gist re Saddique *** and Imran

49. MI5 Supplementary Secret Service Gist re Saddique *** and Imran, inquests exhibit supp-gist240211

Chapter 8: Fixed Around the Policy

1. ISC Annual Report 2010/2011, pages 66-73

2. Letter from PS/Sir Richard Dearlove to Sir David Manning, December 3rd 2001

3. Letter from Eliza Manningham-Buller to John Gieve, March 22nd 2002

4. JIC Assessment, The Status of Iraqi WMD Programmes, March 15th 2002

5. Chris Ames, Who really wrote the WMD dossier?, Iraq Inquiry Digest, September 17th 2010

6. Memo from Matthew Rycroft to David Manning, July 23rd 2002

7. John Williams, Iraq Media Strategy, September 4th 2002

8. Cabinet Office email, September 16th 2002, 22:00 re: Dossier – New Biotechnology Revelation

9. DIS emails sent September 9th 2002, 18:00 re: Public Dossier and 18:45 re: FW: Iraq Dossier – Further Questions

10. DIS email sent September 17th 2002, 08:45, re: 02-09-17 Comment on Final Draft (FLASH)

11. Iraq's Weapons of Mass Destruction: The Assessment of the British Government, September 24th 2002

12. Minute TO7934 from Desmond Bowen to John Scarlett re: The Iraq Dossier, September 11th 2002

13. Cabinet Office email from Jonathan Powell to Alistair Campbell and David Manning, September 17th 2002, 13:36, re: Revised dossier foreword

14. Chilcot Inquiry, Transcript of private hearing of SIS2, declassified July 14th 2011

15. Remarks to the United Nations Security Council, Colin Powell, February 5th 2003

16. The Guardian, The Ricin Ring that Never Was, April 14th 2005

17. Meet The Press, interview with Colin Powell, June 10th 2007

18. Home Office, Prevention of Terrorism Bill 2005 Background Briefing Papers

19. BBC interview with Peter Clarke, November 7th 2006

20. The Guardian, Most senior al-Qaida terrorist yet captured in Britain gets 40 years for plotting carnage, November 8th 2006

21. BBC *Newshour* interview with Charles Shoebridge, June 26th 2006

22. Interview with anonymous former colleague of Sidique Khan, BBC *Newsnight*, October 25th 2005

23. Home Office Narrative, page 15

24. Freedom of Information disclosure letter from Education Leeds, January 26th 2006

25. Sky News, interview with Hasina Patel, July 27th 2007

26. BBC, interview with Julie Nicholson, August 1st 2008

27. Home Office narrative, page 19

28. The Last Will and Final Testament of Sidique Khan, inquests exhibit INQ00009365-002

29. Home Office narrative, page 19

Chapter 9: Predictive Programming

1. *Spooks*, Season 1 Episode 3, 'One Last Dance', broadcast May 30th 2002

2. *Spooks*, Season 1 Episode 6, 'Lesser of Two Evils', broadcast June 17th 2002

3. *Spooks*, Season 2 Episode 2, 'Nest of Angels', broadcast June 9th 2003

4. *Spooks*, Season 2 Episode 5, 'I Spy Apocalypse', broadcast 7th July 2003

5. *Spooks* episode 2.2 bonus feature, Season Two DVD, disc 1

6. *Crisis Command*, pilot episode, broadcast February 3rd 2004

7. BBC, *Panorama*, London Under Attack, broadcast May 16th 2004

8. BBC, Terror programme 'irresponsible', May 15th 2004; Wall of silence over terror threat, May 16th 2004

9. *Spooks*, Season 3 Episode 3, 'Who Guards the Guards?', broadcast October 23rd 2004

10. *Spooks*, Season 3 Episode 10, 'The Suffering of Strangers', broadcast December 13th 2004

11. *Spooks*, Season 4 Episodes 1 and 2, 'The Special', broadcast September 12th and 13th 2005

12. The Independent, Spooks: A drama that sees the future, November 3rd 2009

13. *Spooks* episode 3.9 bonus feature, Season 3 DVD, disc 5

14. *Spooks* episode 3.5 commentary by Simon Crawford Collins and David Oyelowo, Season 3 DVD, disc 3

15. Report by the Minister of Information to the War Cabinet, March 13th 1940, The National Archives (hereafter TNA) CAB 67/5/29

16. Report by the Minister of Information to the War Cabinet, May 11th 1940, TNA CAB 68/6/23

17. Memo from the Minister of Information to the War Cabinet, July 20th 1940, TNA CAB 66/10/6

18. BBC, MI6 ran 'dubious' Iraq campaign, November 21st 2003

19. TNA PREM 19/587

20. Memo from the Minister of Information and the Minister of Economic Warfare to the War Cabinet with attached note by the Chiefs of Staff, TNA CAB 66/13/24

Chapter 10: Simulated Terror

1. BBC *Panorama*, London Under Attack, broadcast May 16th 2004

2. BBC News, Terror test exercise criticised, October 6th 2003

3. NY1, City Officials Call Terror Training Drill A Success, May 16th 2004

4. BBC News, Tube suspended for emergency test, October 17th 2004

5. BBC *Panorama*, London Under Attack, aired May 16th 2004

6. Sir Desmond Fennell, Investigation into the King's Cross Underground Fire, November 1988, Chapter 16: Communications Systems

7. The Job, Atlantic Blue tests international readiness, April 15th 2005

8. Department of Homeland Security, Fact Sheet: TOPOFF3 Exercising International Preparedness, March 28th 2005

9. The Observer, Anti-terror drill revealed soft targets in London, July 10th 2005

10. The Scotsman, The world stands shoulder to shoulder with British people, July 8th 2005

11. The Job, Atlantic Blue tests international readiness

12. Video from the Virtual News Network broadcast can be found on youtube under the title 'TOPOFF3 Scripted Terror Drill 2005 - Virtual News Network'

13. Department of Homeland Security, Fact Sheet: TOPOFF3 Exercising International Preparedness

14. TNA, UK Government Web Archive, Cabinet Office website, National Exercises: Case studies, Exercise Atlantic Blue

15. Home Office, CBRN News, Issue 3, June 2005

16. *Terrorstorm*, Alex Jones, 2006

17. Probability of 7/7 Drill and Attack Coinciding, www.infowars.com

18. PressTV debate on 7/7, broadcast October 17th 2007

19. Nick Kollerstrom, Just a Coincidence…, www.terroronthetube.co.uk, February 16th 2011

20. BBC, US boosts security after attacks, July 7th 2005

21. BBC, On This Day, 18th November 1987, Disaster underground

22. July 7th Truth Campaign, CV fakery: 7/7 terror rehearsal man suspended from Dorset Police. February 7th 2008

23. Manchester Evening News, King's Cross Man's Crisis Course, July 8th 2005

24. CBS News, CNN Defends Reporting Coast Guard Story, September 11th 2009

25. BBC News, 'Victims' unnerved by mock gas alert, July 18th 2004

26. BBC News, 'Largest' simulated terror attack, July 16th 2004

Chapter 11: Conspiracy Theories

1. David R Beecroft, The Conspiracy Theory of Terrorism: Analysis and Application, thesis submitted towards a Masters of Science in Criminal Justice, California State University, June 30th 1986

2. Singapore Civil Defence Force, News Release on Exercise Northstar V, January 8th 2006

3. Channel News Asia, reports on Northstar V, January 8th 2006

4. Straits Times TV, report on Northstar V, January 8th 2006

5. Channel News Asia, Major subway bomb blast drill during peak hours being considered: DPM Wong, January 8th 2006

6. Channel News Asia, British Transport Police observe Exercise NorthStar V, January 8th 2006

7. *Spooks* Season 4 Episode 6, The Innocent, broadcast October 13th 2005

8. *Spooks* Season 4 Episode 10, Diana, broadcast November 10th 2005

9. *Spooks* Season 5 Episodes 1 and 2, 'Gas and Oil', broadcast September 17th and 18th 2005

10. *Spooks* Season 5 Episode 3, 'The Cell', broadcast September 26th 2006

11. *Spooks* Season 5 Episodes 6 and 7, 'Hostage Takers', broadcast October 16th and 23rd 2006

12. *Spooks* Season 6 Episodes 1 and 2, 'The Virus', broadcast October 16th 2007

13. *Spooks* Season 6 Episode 4, 'The Extremist', broadcast October 30th 2007

14. WTQV, Terrorism expert says at least one person tipped off to London attacks, July 7th 2005

15. Arutz Sheva, Report: Israel Was Warned Ahead of First Blast, July 8th 2005

16. Ynet News, London, Tel Aviv blasts connected, July 11th 2005

17. Stratfor, Israel Warned United Kingdom About Possible Attacks, July 7th 2005

18. *7/7 Ripple Effect*, John Anthony Hill, 2007

19. *Spooks* Season 7 Episode 3, 'The Tip-Off', broadcast October 28th 2008

20. BBC News, 21/7 suspect's claim 'is amazing', April 11th 2007

21. Metro News, July 21 plotter collaborated with July 7 terrorists court told, March 23rd 2007

22. GhanaWeb, Parents got Ghanaian "suicide bomber" to confess, December 28th 2007

23. Cass Sunstein, Conspiracy Theories, Harvard University Law School Public Law & Legal Theory Research Paper Series, Working Paper No. 08-03, January 15th 2008

24. DEMOS, The Power of Unreason, Jamie Bartlett and Carl Lewis, August 29th 2010

25. Home Office narrative, page 19

26. 'Real' Irish Republican Army (rIRA) statement, January 28th 2003

27. op cit, The Power of Unreason

28. op cit, Sunstein, Conspiracy Theories

Conclusion

1. July 7 Inquests, 24th November 2010, morning session, page 67

2. July 7 Inquests, 1st February 2011, afternoon session, pages 77-84

3. July 7 Inquests, 6th May 2011, morning session, page 27

Select Bibliography

Ahmed, Nafeez, *The London Bombings: An Independent Inquiry*, Duckworth, 2006

Ahmed, Nafeez, *The War on Truth: 9/11, Disinformation and the Anatomy of Terrorism*, Olive Branch Press, 2005

Butterworth, Alex, *The World That Never Was: A True Story of Dreamers, Schemers, Anarchists and Secret Agents*, Vintage, 2011

Cottrell, Richard, *Gladio, NATO's Dagger at the Heart of Europe: The Pentagon-Nazi-Mafia Terror Axis*, Progressive Press, 2012

Ganser, Daniele, *NATO's Secret Armies*, Frank Cass Publishers, 2005

Griffin, David Ray, *Debunking 9/11 Debunking*, Arris Books, 2007

Home Office, *Report of the official account of the bombings in London on 7th July 2005*, The Stationery Office, 2006

Intelligence and Security Committee, *Report into the London Terrorist Attacks on 7 July 2005*, The Stationery Office, 2006

Intelligence and Security Committee, *Could 7/7 have been Prevented?* or *Review of the Intelligence on the London Terrorist Attacks on 7 July 2005*, The Stationery Office, 2009

Intelligence and Security Committee, Annual Report 2010-2011, The Stationery Office, 2011

Rimington, Stella, *At Risk*, Random House, 2004

Shenon, Philip, *The Commission: The Uncensored History of the 9/11 Investigation*, Little, Brown, 2008

Websites:

The July 7th Truth Campaign main site and inquests blog:

http://www.julyseventh.co.uk/index.html

http://77inquests.blogspot.co.uk/

The Patrick Finucane Centre:

http://www.patfinucanecentre.org/

The Corbett Report - Open Source Intelligence News:

http://www.corbettreport.com/

WideShut UK - news and analysis website:

http://wideshut.co.uk/

Resistance Radio - alternative media in a new world order

http://www.resistradio.com/

Media:

7/7: Seeds of Deconstruction, Tom Secker, 2010

7/7: Crime and Prejudice, Tom Secker, 2011

7/7: What Did They Know?, Keelan Balderson, 2011

7/7: An Historical Analysis, James Corbett, 2011

Jaguar at Luton station car park, July 7th Truth Campaign, 2010

The Last Word on CCTV, James Corbett, 2011

Index